"I think about y̶ think about marriage…"

"Because we are friends," Michal pointed out.

"Because we are friends and because I want to be Amish and because I want to follow Christ and because I want to be a farrier," retorted Milwaukee. "That is what my head is filled up with. Not a wedding ceremony."

"You are going to talk to the bishop soon, aren't you?"

"Tomorrow."

"And you are so sure you've had enough *Rumspringa*?"

"I guess."

"No more movies. No more motorbikes." Michal suddenly flashed him a grin that reminded him of her sister Tabitha. "No more fooling around with the top of my head."

He felt his face flush. "That I don't feel so sure about stopping just when I've got started."

"No?" She reached with her hand and tugged his head down.

"If you are going to be Amish soon and I am not, we had better find out how we feel about each other…before we miss our chance."

Born and raised in Canada, **Murray Pura** has lived in the USA, the UK and the Middle East. With over two dozen works of fiction and nonfiction to his credit, he has published with HarperCollins, HarperOne, Baker, Barbour, Zondervan and several other publishing houses. He works in many genres, including historical fiction, classic or literary fiction, romance and Amish fiction. Currently, Pura lives and writes at his home by the Canadian Rockies.

A ROAD CALLED LOVE

Murray Pura

Recycling programs
for this product may
not exist in your area.

ISBN-13: 978-1-335-92160-4

A Road Called Love

First published in 2014 by Helping Hands Press.
This edition published in 2021.

Copyright © 2014 by Murray Pura

This edition published by arrangement with Harlequin Books S.A.

For questions and comments about the quality of this book, please contact us
at CustomerService@Harlequin.com.

Harlequin Enterprises ULC
22 Adelaide St. West, 40th Floor
Toronto, Ontario M5H 4E3, Canada
www.Harlequin.com

Printed in U.S.A.

A ROAD CALLED LOVE

Chapter One

"Michal."

"Mmm."

"Michal!"

"What?"

"Wake up. Come on. Wake up. It's my birthday."

Michal opened her blue eyes and stared at her younger sister. "It's still dark out, Mischief. I can hardly see your face."

She watched the slender body in the white nightgown flit to the window that faced east.

"No, I can just see some silver," Mischief said. "The sun's coming up."

Michal propped herself on an elbow. "The only silver I see is from the stars. They're still out."

"Not much longer." Mischief ran back and jumped on Michal's bed. "I'm 16 finally—holy, sweet 16, can you believe it?"

Michal smiled. "It is rather hard to believe. Considering you act as if you're nine or ten." She reached out a hand. "Come here." She kissed her sister on the cheek. "Happy birthday, Mischief."

"Brush out my hair?" She gave Michal a brush and untwisted her long braid while she sat facing the window and the dawn. "I was outside already, you know."

Michal sat up and began to run her hand over the young woman's hair, looking for knots and tangles. "Really? Doing what?"

"Oh, you know, talking to Sprinkles, hunting down Kitkat. Old Brownie guarded me the whole time, don't worry." Sprinkles was a horse born the same year as Mischief, Kitkat a cat almost as old as the horse, Old Brownie a dark brown bloodhound that doted on everyone in the family and who was at least ten.

"I'm not worried. We live in Marietta, Pennsylvania, not Pittsburgh."

"I used the door, you know."

"Ah, and papa said you could?"

"Sure. He gave me the talk last week."

"The *Rumspringa* talk?"

"*Ja.*"

Their ground floor bedroom had two doors. One led directly outside.

Another opened into the hallway and kitchen and the rest of the house. Mischief had not been permitted to use the outside door until she was of age. To use it would have been considered "sneaking around" and trying to "get away with something." She would have been punished. But now she was 16 and she could use the outside door without any fear of discipline. Michal had been going in and out of it for more than two years.

"So tell me about the *Rumspringa* talk," prodded Michal as she began to use the brush on her sister's long dark hair.

"Why? You've had it."

"I want to know if anything's changed in two years."

"I don't think so. Papa said I can do whatever I like. Even leave Marietta if I want. When I am ready to be baptized and truly become Amish then it all changes. Then I am making the big commitment to God and to the people. Mama and papa hope I will do that, he said. But first I must 'get everything out of my system' and be sure that when I take my baptism vows I really mean them."

"Your hair seems thicker and darker every week. It shines like a raven's wing."

"Oh, you used to say crow's wing."

"Not since you were twelve. Have you been using egg on it or something?"

"So what if I have? Nick says it's like black gold."

Michal stopped brushing until Mischief turned her face toward her. "Really? Nick said that?" Michal asked.

Mischief narrowed her eyes. "Why is that so hard to believe?"

"I did not think St. Nick had poetry in him. Just carburetors and camshafts."

Mischief tossed her hair. "Men who ride bikes are winged warriors, he told me. So why shouldn't he have a poem or two in him?"

Michal put a hand over her mouth so that she would not laugh out loud. Mischief glared at her. "What is it?"

"Come on. Winged warriors? Did he read that in one of those motorcycle magazines that is always rolled up in his back pocket? American Rider or Hot Bike?"

Mischief tossed her hair again so that a great part of it hit Michal in the face. "What would you know about it?"

"Sometimes I see Milwaukee with one."

"Milwaukee?" Now it was Mischief's turn to suppress a laugh. "What would he know about bikes?"

"Why, you know he has one of his own."

"He has some scooter made in China. Get real, Michal."

Michal frowned. "*Get real?* He has a motorbike, Mischief, a Honda Rebel, and it is not made in China."

"Oh, 250cc, excuse me, look out, Thunder Road. Nick's Harley is a 1979 1000cc Ironhead."

"And even if it were from China, so what? China is a beautiful country." Michal gave Mischief's hair a hard yank with the brush.

"Ow!"

"You have been spending too much time among the English," Michal growled.

"So what? It's *Rumspringa* now. I can see Nick as much as I want. Papa said it is all right for me to date now."

"Yes. I'm sure he had Nick in his mind when he told you that."

"Oh, I apologize, it has to be a good Amish boy." She turned around and grabbed the brush from Michal. Then she gave her a sharp smile. "Not for me. Not when it's finally *Rumspringa*."

Mischief bounced off the bed and went to the window. It was full of golden light. "Here it comes. I am truly of age now."

"Maybe not. Didn't mother say last week you came out at seven in the evening?"

Mischief laughed. "No one counts their birthdays that way. I'm official." She continued to look through the glass and began to hum, *"You're all ribbons and curls, oooh, what a girl, eyes that sparkle and shine, you're sixteen, you're beautiful, and you're mine."* Then she turned back to face her older sister, the sharp smile still on her lips. "You have been *Rumspringa* for two years now. What about you? Are you satisfied with life among the plain people? Do you want to be Amish forever?"

Michal nodded. "Yes, I think so, yes."

"Then why haven't you taken your baptism vows?" Michal hesitated. "Well—I'm not ready yet."

"Why not? You're 18, almost 19, why haven't you made up your mind? Why won't you make the commitment?"

"I'm still praying about it."

"Oh, praying." Mischief began to brush her hair herself. "You and Milwaukee are always praying, aren't you? And not getting anywhere with each other or your Amish vows."

"Milwaukee and I are only friends, good friends."

"Really? And you've never kissed this good friend?"

"Not Milwaukee, no."

"But you've kissed Silas Stoltzfus. I caught you, remember?"

Michal flipped her hand in the air. "Don't bring that up. I was younger than you are now. It was just my foolish period."

Mischief widened her eyes. "Your foolish period? What about David and Samuel and Elijah? They were all last year. And Saul Miller was only, what, four months ago?"

"So I've been foolish a long time. That's why I'm not ready for baptism."

"You kiss them all, but you won't kiss Milwaukee? That sounds to me like you are serious about him."

"I am not."

Mischief came and knelt on Michal's bed. "Do you drink?"

"Not so much."

"Smoke?"

"Not so much."

"But you've gone to parties in Lancaster City and Philadelphia." Michal shook her head. "Really that stuff doesn't matter to me."

"What does matter?"

"Oh—family, God, our church—you."

"You mean now that you've finished sowing your wild oats it matters."

"What wild oats?"

Mischief got up and paced the room, running her hands back through thick hair that gleamed like dark water in the sunlight filling the room. "In and out through the door, two in the morning, three in the morning. Milwaukee's scooter putt-putting away. Or Saul's truck. All of you sowing your wild oats. Did you think I really was asleep all those times? Eyes closed? Head on the pillow?" She grinned. "It's my turn now."

Michal sighed. "You make such a big thing out of it. I hardly did anything. The boys hardly did anything."

"Yes, that's the trouble, isn't it? That's why you're not ready for baptism yet—you still haven't gotten it out of your system. Well, I'm getting it out of mine. Then there'll be lots of room for God and baking bread in an oven heated by wood and doing laundry with a scrub board. Yes, then I will want to be plain again, who knows? But, right now, I've been plain long enough."

She came and stood over Michal with her hands on her hips. "Speaking of God, why didn't you go anywhere?"

Michal frowned. "What do you mean?"

"I mean there's more to life than Shoofly pie and Lancaster County and William Penn Pennsylvania. Didn't God make a big, beautiful world?

"That's what the preachers always tell us, *ja?* But how many of them go out there to see it?"

"Mischief, Pennsylvania is beautiful, Marietta is beautiful, all the rolling green hills and the Susquehanna River—"

"Sure, sure, but what about Montana? What about Seattle? What about California and San Francisco and Los Angeles? Haven't you ever wanted to see those places? Look."

She got on her knees and tugged a wooden box out from under her bed. Opening the lid she brought out dozens of postcards bright with photographic images. She began to hand them up to Michal one at a time.

"The Grand Canyon—isn't that so amazing? And Carlsbad Caverns. And Glacier National Park. Here's the Painted Desert. And an arroyo carved out by water in Arizona—doesn't that look like something from the Bible?"

"You should not have photographs."

"Why not? We're both in *Rumspringa,* aren't we? Do you see me bowing down and worshipping them? What do you think of this?"

She placed a photograph of a pure white beach in Michal's hands. The water that lapped against the sand was a shimmering turquoise as clear as freshly washed glass.

"What do you think?" she asked again.

"It's very pleasant," replied Michal.

Mischief snorted. "Is that all you can say? Thank our God, sister. It's a miracle, a blessing. Don't you want to reach out and just touch the sand? Think how nice it would be to skinny dip in water like emeralds."

"Mischief!"

"Oh, sister, no men around of course." Her sharp smile returned for a moment, then quickly was replaced by a look of sheer innocence that Michal could see was not contrived. "I like the boys and I like the attention they give me. I like Nick's Ironhead. But do you know what I really want to do? I would trade all the parties and bottles of beer and cigarettes and kisses for an open road and an open sky—I want to see God's world, I want to see mountains and oceans and the huge redwoods. I want to have a palm tree fan me while tropical air blows overhead as soft as silk." Suddenly she stopped and looked worried. "What time is it?"

They both glanced at the windup clock on the small table that stood between their beds. It was five after six.

"Quickly, get dressed," said Mischief, swinging her arms at Michal as if she were shooing cattle. "Let's get outside as soon as we can."

Michal climbed out of bed. "What's the big hurry?"

"I don't want to waste a minute."

As Michal tied her hair back in a bun and put on a long blue dress with a black apron Mischief pulled on a pair of tight faded jeans and a short tee shirt she took from a corner of the closet. She left her hair loose. Then she dabbed perfume on her wrists and throat. When Michal turned from placing her prayer covering on her head Mischief was fastening her final earring. A black belt with silver studs was around her waist and a jean jacket draped over her shoulders. She used a black leather bag for her purse.

Michal could not keep the shock from her face. "What are you doing?"

"I'm 16, dear sister, and this is my *Rumspringa*. I've seen you in jeans and tees plenty of times."

"But not right here, right in the house, mother and father and your little brothers—"

"They won't see a thing. I don't have time to change in the restroom at Roy's gas station like you always do."

"What do you mean mother won't see you? Soon she'll be looking for us and asking for our help with breakfast."

"Come. Come outside."

They used the special door and stepped into grass soaked in a thick, silvery May dew. Michal wore her sturdy black Amish shoes while Mischief had put on a pair of Nike runners. Immediately Old Brownie spotted them and came trotting over, his tail wagging. Both sisters rubbed his long ears and spoke sweetly into the big, dark, sad eyes. Faintly there was the roar of a jet and Mischief straightened and looked up into the blue sky. White contrails had appeared far overhead like perfectly straight painted lines.

"You see?" she smiled. "From Philadelphia to where? Denver? Mexico? Hawaii? Japan? I want to fly, Michal."

"The Amish can fly."

"I don't mean as a passenger. I want to hold the wheel. I want to steer the plane." She glanced at her sister. "You know the English girls can drive at my age. As soon as they are 16 they can drive their own car."

"I know that."

"Imagine. The freedom. The highway in front of you like a magic carpet. I could go anywhere. With a plane and a car I could go to Paris or London or Madrid. I could go all the way to Australia and see kangaroos and crocs." She took her sister's hand. "Don't you want to do exciting things like that? Don't you want to see God's big world? You can't tell me you don't feel bottled up here like some sort of museum exhibit from the 19th century for tourists to come and gape at."

"Really, I feel fine," Michal protested.

"Then take your baptism vows and stay put. What's stopping you from becoming a fully committed Amish woman and remaining here until they plant you in the ground permanently like a crop of tobacco? Wear your prayer covering and be a draw for the tourist dollars, sister—do you know how much Pennsylvania made on the quaint Amish people last year from people driving by and flying in to photograph us? Eat our pies? Buy our handmade wooden furniture and our hand stitched quilts? Nick told me. You'd be surprised."

"I honestly don't care."

"The Amish are big business. It wouldn't pay to have us up and fade away. They need good strong Amish women to stick around and make sure there's plenty of babies."

Michal could feel herself losing her temper. "The Amish are not fading away. Our numbers are growing here in Pennsylvania and in Ohio and Indiana. Now there are even Amish communities in Missouri and Minnesota and Iowa. And not just from large families. There are more converts now."

"Good. They can take my place. Then I won't have

to feel guilty if the Amish cease to exist because I hit the open road." She put her hands in her pockets. "Face it. You're no more content here than I am."

"I am happy enough. We have a wonderful family."

Mischief nodded. "Yes, we do, a wonderful family. But it's not enough, is it?"

Michal felt the heat in her face. "Of course it's enough. More than enough."

"Then make it stick. Spring Communion is in a few weeks, isn't it? Say you want to be Amish till you die. You and Milwaukee both. Get the baptism. Then you can have an Amish wedding and people will give you grandfather clocks and butter churns for gifts."

Michal felt as if a rock had formed inside her and was sinking down, taking whatever good spirits she had woken to into a dark murk with it.

Mischief saw the look on her face and regretted she had said so much. She put her arms around Michal's neck. They were the same height with the same shining black hair and the same striking blue eyes.

"Look at us. God had given us this rare match of blue eyes and black hair. How can any man resist us? Nick says he gets completely lost in my eyes. They are so blue he forgets any sense of direction and loses his way."

"He said that?" A small smile played over Michal's lips. "Close enough. I'm only adding a bit."

"Your winged warrior."

"Yes. More than you know." Then, arms still around her sister, she said in a low voice as if the whole Amish community was listening in, "Come with me."

Michal made a face. "Come with you where?"

"Everywhere else. The world outside Marietta and

the Amish faith. The highway. The back roads. America. Come explore America with me. Find another God with me, a bigger God than the Amish God."

"From the back of a Harley?"

"Or the front. Girls can drive Harleys too."

"What about Nick?"

"Oh." She laughed quietly. "Nick is a condiment. There are spicier things to season life with. Like a Michal. Come with me and I'll ditch Nick and we can be the Rolling Thunder Sisterhood."

Michal was genuinely surprised. "Ditch your winged warrior? I thought you loved him."

Mischief grinned. "Love? Love? When did I ever say anything about love?" Then she grew serious and whispered, "You and I have been together 16 years today, everywhere together. I know all your thoughts and feelings and you know mine. You are not happy here, Michal. You are not sure becoming Amish is the right step. So come with me. You and I have never been apart. Come with me and we will discover what it is we want together. Maybe it's this place and this life. But maybe it's not." She hugged Michal. "You will never be content to take your vows until you leave and truly make your own decision to return. You must have figured that out by now. You have to get out. Like Peter and James had to walk away from their fishing nets, yes? Or Paul had to leave his home in Tarsus. Or Jesus himself had to leave Nazareth." She kissed Michal on the cheek. "Or Ruth had to leave her country and all she was familiar with and follow Naomi. You are restless, sister. You have to get away if you ever want to put down roots here someday. Get away and find out what you want and what God wants. Let me be your Naomi. And you can follow me and be my Ruth."

Michal felt a surge in her heart and her eyes gleamed briefly. "Who will be our Boaz?"

Mischief smiled and hugged her sister again. "Boaz will have to find us. God will have to send him and he will have to find us wherever we are."

There was a rumble from the road that ran past their house and it grew louder and louder. Mischief gave her sister a final kiss. "Hey, think about it. Gotta go."

Nick thundered into the yard on his black and silver Harley Ironhead.

He had a long braid of dark red hair, a red beard he kept trimmed to his jawline, and an earring. He wore dark brown leather pants and biker chaps and skullcap. Mischief's father, a tall and lean man, stepped out of the barn. She spotted him.

"Papa!" She ran over and threw her arms around him. "What is this?" he asked quietly.

"Nick is taking me into Philly for my birthday."

"But—your mother has a cake for you—we have gifts—"

Mischief bit her lower lip. "I know. I'm sorry. We can do that tomorrow. Nick and I have been planning this trip for weeks. He got time off from the garage."

Her father nodded and could not keep himself from smiling. "So this is my girl who jumps into rivers and onto the back of the stallion we keep in stud, hey? Feet first into her *Rumspringa*."

"That's her." She grinned. "I love you, papa. Have a good, good day, please." She kissed him on the cheek.

"Sure, sure, I will think back on my own *Rum-springa* when I got sick smoking a cigar. Leave those alone, hey?"

"I will."

"Here is your mother."

A tall woman with broad shoulders stood on the porch. Mischief gave her father a final tight squeeze with her arms and ran across the yard and up the steps to the porch.

"Ma!" Again the strong hug. Mischief was two inches taller. "Can't you at least stay and have breakfast with us?" her mother complained, hugging her daughter back. "It is your birthday, my little one."

"I'm sorry, ma, we have to get into Philadelphia and it's the only day Nick could get off this week. I'll be back tonight. We can have the cake tomorrow. But you can give the boys a piece each from me today, okay?"

Mischief could see her mother wanted to be cross. But she could not resist her youngest daughter's energy and enthusiasm, something Mischief had always possessed and which the mother had never been able to scold her for. "All right. Get into your *Rumspringa* and get it over with. Just don't spend as much time there as your sister."

"I won't." She gave her mother the sharp smile. "Papa said he got sick from cigars."

The mother laughed and kissed Mischief on the top of her head. "*Ja*, among other things."

"What about you?"

"Oh, I got sick on plum *Schnaps* and pizza. Really, I was crazy. But never as crazy as you. Your father is the only man who has ever seen me with my hair down and for that he had to wait until our wedding night."

Mischief smiled at the tone of disapproval that had crept into her mother's voice. "Yes, I know, ma, a woman's crowning glory is her hair. Well, mine is still my crowning glory whether all the men in the world see it or not."

"Okay, you go, that Nick will scare the horses and wake the boys."

"Oh, the boys are already up." She stepped back from her mother and waved energetically at two faces pressed against a window on the second floor. They smiled and waved back.

"Have some of my birthday cake!" she shouted up at them. "Tell me tomorrow if it's any good!"

"Hush, my girl," laughed her mother. "The neighbors will think there's a fire. Oh, one minute you are almost 30 and the next not yet 12, isn't it so?"

"I guess."

Her mother ran a hand down her daughter's cheek. "In all this do not forget your family loves you and is here for you, all right? And do not forget the love of God. Or the grace of Christ."

"I won't. Thanks, ma. See you." A final hug and kiss and she was down the steps to Nick and the Ironhead. He got a hug too. Smiling, he handed her a brown jacket like his that he'd pulled from a saddlebag. She put it on and zipped it up. Then he handed her a helmet. He himself did not wear one. Slipping it over her head she got on behind him.

Michal walked up to them. "Take care, Nick," she said.

He gave Michal a thumbs up. "Sure I will. Don't worry about your baby sister. This is her first grownup day."

"Oh, yes?" Michal raised a hand in a wave. "Go easy, Mischief. Okay?"

Mischief lifted the visor of her silver helmet and her blue eyes gleamed like sky. "No worries, big sister. I will avoid *Schnaps* and cigars for sure. See you tonight. Or tomorrow. Whichever comes first." Then she grew serious and her eyes darkened like evening. "Remember what we talked about. Think it over, okay?"

"Yes, I will. And I shall pray about it too."

"Sure, pray about it. Get God involved. Why not?" Then the blue lightened again as if the sun had come out in her eyes. "I'm 16. You can't call me Mischief anymore, you know. I'm a woman now. Next time we see each other you have to use my Christian name."

"Even if you still are a handful?"

"Even if. Bye."

"We good to go?" Nick asked her. "Yeah." She dropped her visor.

Nick walked the bike forward and then throttled up. The Harley's roar shook the air. The Ironhead rumbled down the lane to the main road.

Mischief waved her hand a final time then wrapped her arms around Nick and leaned her head against him. Her sister and parents waved in response. On the back of their jackets Michal could see an eagle with spread wings and the words LIVE TO RIDE, RIDE TO LIVE. Then the Harley was on the asphalt and speeding east into the sun, the engine changing pitch as Nick switched gears.

"Christ go with you, Tabitha Troyer," Michal whispered.

Chapter Two

Michal sat in the dark of the Hollywood & Vine movie theater in Lancaster City and held Milwaukee's hand while she ate from the bucket of popcorn that was wedged between them. It was a double feature. The first film was *The Witness*. She'd already seen the movie twice. It never failed to amaze her that Kelly McGillis didn't leave the Amish for a life with Harrison Ford. On the other hand, the blonde Amish man that liked her was not bad looking. Of course, Ford's character wasn't a Christian and Kelly's, despite her weaknesses, certainly was. So was her sister Tabitha the Kelly McGillis that fell for a man that was English and left the Amish? If so, who was Michal? The Kelly McGillis that stayed and married the Amish man and put down roots?

"The old man is just like Isaac Beachey," said Milwaukee out loud. "I swear he talks the same, walks the same, acts the same—"

"Shh!" went someone behind them.

Michal smiled and patted his hand. "Whisper.

You said the same thing the last time we watched the movie."

"Because its true!"

"Shh!"

The second film was called *The Dove* and that one she had never seen before. It was 30 or 35 years old, but a good copy with good color and sound Milwaukee pointed out, this time using a soft voice she scarcely knew he had.

"Not Blu-Ray though," Michal whispered.

"Whose house could we use that in?" he whispered back. "*Rumspringa* or not, my parents won't let me bring a TV home and neither will yours."

"Have you ever wondered how long this *Rumspringa* of ours will go on?"

He shrugged.

The film was about a young man named Robin sailing alone around the world. It had a strange effect on her as the hours slipped past and she almost got up and walked out more than once. Green waves, huge blue skies, tall palms, a white sail filled with wind that pushed the young man from country to country and continent to continent and world to world—her feelings alternated between a strong sense of being trapped in Lancaster County and never seeing the open sea or a palm tree and a sense of excitement and freedom and hope. When they walked out of the cinema into the streetlights and darkness a fine rain had fallen. She could smell the wet pavement and a thrill went through her.

They went for pizza and Coke later at Sally & Bo's 2 for 1 and sat at a black and yellow booth. She told

Milwaukee *The Dove* had upset her one moment and exhilarated her the next.

"What do you think is going on?" she asked. Milwaukee bit into his Canadian bacon.

"Please don't say anything with your mouth full," she chided as he was about to reply.

He rolled his eyes and kept chewing. When he was finished he sipped some Coke. "Can I talk now?"

She made a face.

He picked up another slice of pizza without thinking about it. "Okay, for you, the movie is a big deal, yes? So maybe you want to travel, you know, see the world of the English. It gets your blood pumping. But then you remember you will take your vows and live by the Susquehanna forever. Not so bad, but maybe not so great. This kid sails around the world and you sit on your porch shelling peas for 60 or 70 years, you know?"

Michal felt the rock sinking in her chest again as she had with her sister that morning.

Milwaukee bit into the pizza, glanced at her dark blue eyes, then kept chewing and did not speak until he had swallowed. "You can be very German, you know that?"

"What a surprise. I'm Amish."

"No, see that's what you're not, you're not Amish."

"Really? What am I then?"

"You're in-between. Here in Sally's you're almost English with your Coke and pepperoni pizza—which is getting cold."

"I'm not hungry."

"You're always hungry."

"Apparently tonight I'm otherwise."

"Another thing that's German—I've never seen you with your hair down."

"The Amish would say you're not my husband."

"Well, we're friends, right?"

"Yes."

"We agreed on that two months ago."

"Yes," she nodded. "This ponytail is all you get."

He laughed. "See? And now you're flirting like an English girl."

"I am not flirting. And how would you know what English girls do?"

"Sally's is full of them every time we come here."

Michal lifted her eyebrows. "Studying them, are we?"

He shrugged, ate pizza, swallowed. "So what does it matter to you? We're friends, not lovers."

Michal felt blood come to her face. "That is so."

"Anyway, back to the movie. It had some nice scenery and Deb Raffin was cute, but you know, my mind kept wandering back to Marietta and Esau. This farrier business is fascinating. We had a difficult mare yesterday and he showed me how to lock her leg just so and prevent the girl from kicking my head into next Sunday. The more I learn from him the more I want him to let me do everything, take over all of our people's farrier work. So I'm watching the movie and not watching the movie at the same time. And I start to think maybe I'm ready to be baptized this Communion, maybe I'm finally ready to be Amish." He pried another piece of pizza from his plate, deliberately stretching the cheese as far as he could. "But, you know, you're not, Michal, you're really not."

Michal felt her temper rising. "How can you sit

there and tell me that? How can you tell me that and—
and—" She stumbled, then suddenly burst out in German, *"Zeug Ihr Gesicht mit Pizza!"*

"I am stuffing my face with pizza because one of us is hungry."

"I am as much Amish as you are!"

"No, you're not. You're not Amish. And neither am I. This is not a DNA thing. No one is born with an Amish gene. You become Amish, I become Amish, once we take the vows and are baptized. Not before. It's the heart thing, *ja?* It's the soul thing. And judging by your restlessness I am closer to making that commitment than you are."

Michal curled her hands into fists. "Gideon!" Then she stopped, startled at the word she had just uttered.

He smiled around a mouthful of Canadian bacon and cheddar cheese. "Ah, the forbidden name."

She dropped her eyes. "I'm sorry."

"That's okay. Just make sure the next time you use it you mean it."

"If there is a next time."

He nodded. "If there is a next time."

She stood up. "I will use the restroom. Then I want to walk."

"All right. Should I get them to box up your pizza?"

"I don't care. I'll probably feed it to Old Brownie."

The restroom was empty and she stared at herself in the mirror. Her mascara was holding up and her eyeliner. But it wouldn't if she started crying. *Call me Milwaukee,* he had told her months before. *That's my nickname and it's where I was born. But if the day ever comes when you are sure—not just think—but are sure you have fallen in love with me. Then.*

And only then. Please use my Christian name. It was bad enough she had him thinking she was getting more English while he was getting more Amish. Now she had botched the whole name business as well. Where was her head tonight?

He carried the white pizza box with Sally & Bo's in yellow and black across the lid while they walked up and down the streets of Lancaster. It had begun to rain again, but it was more like a mist and drifted down over the city and the cars and the people. At first they didn't say much to each other because, Michal knew, it was obvious to Milwaukee that she didn't want to talk. After five minutes of silence between them, a silence filled by car horns and revving engines and other people's voices and laughter, she finally reached out her hand and took his. Yes, it was a funny thing, there was not supposed to be a drop of romantic blood in their friendship, yet they had held hands almost from the start and thought nothing of it. Finally she stopped at the Lancaster County Courthouse.

"Let's sit on the steps under the pillars," she said quietly. "Your jeans will get wet."

"I don't care."

"I do." He peeled off his jean jacket and laid it on the steps. "Oh, Milwaukee, don't do that."

"Sit, please."

"No, I can't."

"Come on. It's already there waiting for you."

She sat on the jacket and smiled up at him. "So you're one of the princes I read about."

"That's me." He sat beside her.

She leaned her head against his shoulder and took his hand again. "Now you'll be wet."

"I like the rain."

"This hardly counts as rain."

"It's moisture, isn't it? That's enough."

She sighed. "I don't know what's wrong with me. Mischief—excuse me, Tabitha, who is 16 today and a woman—thinks I need to get out of Lancaster County for a while."

"All on your own?"

"Oh, no, she thought we might head out together."

"What about Saint Nick?"

She shrugged in her Lee Stormrider. He reached over and put up the corduroy collar against the mist.

"Well," he said, "sisters know sisters. And you're pretty much champing at the bit."

"You really think so, do you? Just because of the way I reacted to a movie?"

"No, I have seen other things over the past few months."

She stared up into his face. Small water drops beaded on his smooth white skin. "What things?"

"I don't know. You seem distracted. At church you don't sing like you used to."

"Pardon me?"

"I mean, you are one of the best singers among our people. You're like a robin or meadowlark. A year ago you used to put everything into your hymn singing. I could pick out your voice even if I couldn't see your face.

Now—the energy isn't there. It's like you are just going through the motions."

She clutched his hand more tightly and felt a coldness in her head and chest. "Not so good."

"I'm sorry—"

"Why sorry? It's true. I know it's true."

"I'm sorry that somewhere inside you are not—complete."

Despite the ice in her body she could not keep herself from smiling. "You were always clever with the words. That is the way to put it. I'm not all there."

"I didn't mean that."

"But that is what it is. I look out the window when the pastor is preaching and I am gazing at birds or horses or trees. When we pray my mind wanders. When we sing, oh, I used to like to soar when there was the singing, *ja?* But now, I know the songs, I have heard them all a million times, I want something different, different tunes, different melodies, different words that go with different notes." She leaned into Milwaukee with a kind of fierceness. "I need to see God in different places. I need to see God with different words and different songs in different places. I need to see myself in different places. What am I going to do?"

Milwaukee said nothing for a few moments. He could see she was crying quietly. Carefully, afraid she might snap at him, he put his arm around her. To his surprise, she accepted the intimacy and drew against him more closely. He fought an overwhelming urge to kiss the top of her head, all shiny and smooth like a black and chrome motorbike beaded with rain.

The perfume coming from her hair seemed stronger and richer in the wet. He knew that if she happened to glance up at him with those incredible blue eyes framed in damp black glistening strands of hair, some stuck to the soft skin of her cheeks, he would not be able to stop himself from kissing her on her perfect mouth. Feeling a bit dizzy—dizzy with hormones his sister

Katie would tell him—he breathed in and out deeply and slowly and looked at what traffic he could see beyond the high stone sides of the courthouse steps. Then she actually reached up with her fingers and touched his lips and face. It sent waves of shock and delight through him.

"How does a 250cc handle the interstate?" she asked in a small voice. "The Rebel?" Despite the wonderful chaos going on in his head he managed a laugh. "You'd be screaming."

He risked looking at her and it was what he'd feared—she was smiling up at him with eyes that were large and blue and shimmering.

"Take me away," she said.

He wasn't sure what to say. "Now?"

"Sure, now. Tomorrow. Next week." Then she settled her head into his chest again and he was spared the mascara and eyeliner and the blue midnight of her eye color. "But you won't do it, will you? You are a good Amish boy. You will go to the bishop and the pastors in a few days and tell them you want to be baptized and join the church. They will talk with you and pray with you and ask around and find that no one has anything against you. Your baptism will be a sure thing. In three weeks they will pour the water over your head."

"It's not that easy."

"Of course it's that easy." Her voice was muffled by the heavy cotton of his black Honda tee shirt with the white wing. "For you, anyway. Haven't you attended those special classes with the bishop and ministers for the past couple of months? Haven't you learned the 18 articles of the Dordrecht Confession of Faith? Haven't they asked you not to grow your hair out and to stop drinking alcohol and going to parties?"

Milwaukee did not respond.

"So *Rumspringa* is winding down for you. Soon there will be no *Rumspringa.* You will be baptized, you will be Amish, you will become our people's farrier when Esau finally figures out he is 88 and not 18. You are ready to settle in, get married, and grow a beard. For me, it is just the opposite. I don't want to settle in. I can't settle in. You said so yourself. My heart is not in it. Even my singing is not singing anymore. You have to stay. I have to go. Didn't you remind me tonight we are friends, not lovers? So you marry Becky Miller or Sarah Stoltzfus or Dorcas Smucker. I head out on the Interstate. That's it, that's the plan, that's what God has brought to pass."

Michal was squeezing Milwaukee's hand so tightly he thought she would break his fingers. But she had nothing more to say and neither did he so the hiss of tires over wet pavement filled up the quiet between them. He held her a little more closely and she did not resist. Finally he did press his lips briefly against her hair and breathe in her perfume and she did not resist that either. Eventually he was the one to break the silence.

"Dorcas Smucker?" he asked her. "Dorcas Smucker?" he repeated. "Well—"

"Dorcas Smucker?"

Michal could keep stop herself from giggling. "Perhaps not."

"Perhaps?" He risked one more kiss to the top of her head and got away with it. "You make it sound like I only want to get baptized because I will drop dead if

I don't get married to someone as swiftly as possible. Marriage has nothing to do with it. I hardly think about marriage." He felt her shift positions beside him and added quickly, "I think about you. But I hardly ever think about marriage."

"Because we are friends."

"Because we are friends and because I want to be Amish and because I want to follow Christ and because I want to be a farrier. That is what my head is filled up with. Not a wedding ceremony. And not Dorcas Smucker."

"You are going to talk to the bishop soon, aren't you?"

"Tomorrow."

"And you are so sure you've had enough *Rumspringa?*"

"I guess."

"No more movies. No more motorbikes." She suddenly flashed him a grin that reminded him of her sister Tabitha. "No more fooling around with the top of my head."

He felt his face fill with blood. "That I don't feel so sure about stopping just when I've got started."

"No?" She reached with her hand and tugged his head down. "If you are going to be Amish soon and I am not we had better find out how we feel about each other before we miss our chance." Her lips came against his and the warmth and softness made him dizzy again. "How's that?" she asked.

"Pretty great."

"Pretty great? Not totally great?" She kissed him again and this time held it longer.

"You're right," he said. "Totally great."

She smiled. "So now I'm hungry. Where is my pizza?"

Milwaukee gave her the soggy box. "The cardboard has had it, but I'm sure the pizza will be okay."

She lifted the lid and pulled out a piece, then held the box toward him. "Do you want some?"

He shook his head. "I'm the one who's not hungry now."

"You? Since when?"

"Since you fooled around with my lips." They both laughed.

"Is that all it takes?" she asked, chewing and swallowing. "You are all it takes."

"So if I head out on the interstate, if I really do that, you would miss me?"

"Yes."

"But you still think I should go?"

"Yes."

"Why is that?"

"Because if you stayed here it wouldn't be the Michal I kissed tonight."

"Well, it will never be. I change a little every day and so do you."

"I mean it wouldn't be you at all. Just like it isn't you singing anymore or you praying anymore. I'd have lost you just because I talked you into staying here."

Michal stopped eating her third piece of pepperoni pizza. "So where am I now?"

"Here for a while. But if you stay too long, nowhere."

"Where do I need to be?"

"Out there." He waved his hand at the street. "Out there among the English."

"Where out there?"

"Anywhere. Everywhere." He kissed her forehead. "Just not here anymore."

"Never here anymore?"

He kissed her damp black hair two or three times. "Not never. Just not now. You have to go and come back and then it's you."

"You sound like my sister."

"No one ever said Tabitha was stupid. Crazy. Wild. Unpredictable. But lacking in love or passion? Lacking in loyalty? Lacking in brains?" He shook his head as he kissed her hair again.

She smiled. "Are you fooling around with the top of my head?"

"Yeah—baby."

She grinned and punched his shoulder. "Take the baby home. It's after one. Sure you don't want any pizza?"

"How can you ask a man that? My heart is too full to even consider my stomach."

"Oh, yes?" She got to her feet holding the pizza box. "Maybe you really will miss me." She bent and picked up his jean jacket and handed it to him. "I told you it would get wet."

"Everything's wet. Your lips are wet."

"And you like them that way?"

"I love them that way."

Michal gave Milwaukee the box so she could hug his arm with both of hers while they walked back to the movie theater. There was still a fair amount of traffic on the street and headlights constantly flashed over them.

Both felt there wasn't anything else to say so no

one made an effort to load the dead space with chatter. When they reached the blue Honda Rebel it glittered under the streetlamps as if it had been washed and waxed.

"Will you miss this?" she asked. "My bike? Where's it going?"

"I mean when you become Amish."

"Oh." He grinned. "I thought you meant the interstate." He hesitated. "Why should I lie to you? I'm not so spiritual that I won't miss riding."

"Lots of men and women who are spiritual still ride. Tabitha has told me about all the Christian bike clubs."

"Amish bike clubs?"

"No. Just plain old garden variety Christian bike clubs—Baptist, Methodist, Four Square, Pentecostal, Alliance, Vineyard, yes, even Mennonite—"

"All right, all right, don't make it harder than it already is." He unlocked one of his saddlebags and gave her a dark blue rain shell with the North Face logo on it. "I've only got one of these. Please put it on."

"What about you?"

"I told you. I like wet."

She pulled the jacket over her Stormrider while he packed away the pizza box. "The sleeves are too long."

"Roll them up."

"And the hood is meant for a giant."

"Pull on the drawstrings." He handed her a blue helmet and tugged one down over his own head. "Get on. Let's go." Then he smiled. "Do you want to drive?"

She was startled. "Me?"

"Sure, you."

"I only have my beginner's."

"Good enough. I'll be right behind you."

"But no, I've only handled this bike two or three times."

"And did a great job at it."

She shook her head. "Thank you, but not tonight. Another time."

"Okay."

Michal gripped the handles on each side of her seat as they rode out of the city onto the highway. The small drops of rain stung her hands like tiny pebbles. At Roy's she went into the restroom and wiped off her makeup. She pulled her Amish dress out of the pack she'd stuffed into one of Milwaukee's saddlebags and crammed her jeans and tee shirt inside instead. Then she did up her hair and put the rain shell and helmet back on.

"My wild Amish girl," teased Milwaukee when she came back out to the parking lot.

"I'm not Amish, remember?"

"You have fooled everyone."

"Yes, well, apparently even myself."

They sped into Marietta and three or four hundred yards from Michal's home Milwaukee turned off the engine and let the Honda coast. Then he walked it up the road to their lane while she walked beside him. At the turnoff she patted him on the cheek.

"I'm all right. You don't have to accompany me up to the house."

"I have done it every other night."

"But it's raining more now."

"I don't care. I'd rather have the extra five minutes with you."

At the back door that led to her room she took her pack out of its saddlebag and peeled off the North

Face jacket. Then she kissed Milwaukee quickly on the cheek. "Will you stop by tomorrow? I think mama would like you for Saturday supper."

"Yes. I'll try."

"Try? When do you ever say no to one of my mother's feasts?"

"It wouldn't be for the food."

"No?" Her eyes flashed in the rainfall. "I let you fool around with my lips and the top of my head and this is what happens?"

He pulled her into his arms. "Would you feel better if nothing happened?"

She smiled and put her fingers on his mouth. "Shh. Of course not. But perhaps we had better slow down."

"Slow down? I thought we had to speed up. In a few weeks I'll be Amish and then we'll be stuck with a horse and buggy and kissing behind barns and bushes."

"As opposed to kissing behind my parents' house or at the Lancaster County Courthouse? Anyway, you are right. We're running out of time." She stood on the toes of her boots and kissed him on the mouth with a burst of strength that knocked him backward. She laughed, putting her hand over her mouth. "I don't think you are ready for me yet. You are right. I need to get on the interstate. And you need to stay here and pack away more oats."

"You talk as if I should eat like a horse."

"Exactly like a horse."

Michal kissed him briefly on the mouth and then opened the door to her room. She did not expect to see Tabitha in her bed though it would have been a pleasant surprise. They could have talked about their day and their men.

Her head whirled as she dropped it back on the pillow. What had she been thinking? Why had she let Milwaukee kiss her so much? Why had she kissed him so much? She lay on her right side and then on her left. She had been a little reckless. They were friends, they were friends, they were only friends.

I kissed him because I wanted to kiss him. I let him kiss me because I wanted him to kiss me. Yes, he is a friend. But I love it when he is close to me and tender to me. I feel safe. I don't feel so confused anymore.

She forced herself to stay awake, expecting her sister to arrive. At four she gave up and slept and immediately began to dream. The images were draped in white and peaceful, but later she could not remember a thing she had seen. Before she knew it a hand was shaking her shoulder roughly. She opened her eyes to a room flooded with sunlight and her mother's white face.

"Oh, mama," she said, squinting and sitting up, "I'm sorry. I meant to help you with the breakfast—"

"Never mind that," her mother said in a harsh voice. "Your father has gone to see the sheriff and I need you up now to take care of the boys."

A sharp feeling cut through Michal's body. "What? Papa has gone to the sheriff? What is it? What's wrong?"

Her mother shook her head. "Nick's parents drove to our house a half hour ago and asked if he was here. They are worried sick."

Michal's head was whirling from lack of sleep and her mother's news. "Where is he? What did Tabitha say?"

Her mother's eyes were large and dark. She pointed at Tabitha's empty bed, neatly made up just as it had been the day before. "Your sister did not come home. Neither of them came home. None of their friends know where they are. No one knows a thing." Then her mother put her hand over her mouth and her face broke up as she began to cry. "It's as if Tabitha and her boyfriend have vanished from the face of the earth."

Chapter Three

Later, when he thought back, Milwaukee would wonder why the bishop and ministers had said nothing to him about Tabitha. By ten in the morning when they met with him they would have known, but they did not speak a word concerning the missing girl, even though they must have realized there was a close friendship between Tabitha's older sister and himself. But no, they had asked him about his *Rumspringa* habits of the past two years, if he could give up movies and motorbikes, if he was ready to follow Christ as a true believer and be baptized into the Amish faith and settle down in Marietta.

"Esau tells us you are good with the horses and the hooves and the horseshoes, so?" said Bishop Eby.

"I love the work," Milwaukee replied.

"Of course Esau may never retire. Then what will you do for a job?" Milwaukee was surprised by the question. "I—I'm not sure. I suppose I would help my father with the dairy herd like my two older brothers. It's just that I was hoping to do something—a little different—"

The bishop and pastors had smiled. "We only pull the good leg, eh, Master Bachman," the bishop said. "When we spoke with Esau about all this he admitted he wanted to slow down and spend more time with his grandchildren."

"Slow down?" Milwaukee raised his eyebrows. "He said that?"

"*Ja,* it is surprising. He may even mean it. We think you are all right on that score. But you, the bike, can you put it aside and come back to the horse and buggy?"

Milwaukee shrugged. "I have enjoyed the bike as most Amish have enjoyed the plowshare. But it matters more to me to be among you, to live and die among you, as one of you, not live a life as an outsider."

"Yes?" challenged one of the pastors, Dorcas Smucker's father. "Yes," Milwaukee responded with some strength.

The bishop ran his stubby fingers through a long gray beard and nodded.

It was Esau who wound up telling him about Tabitha when Milwaukee showed up at his house just before noon once the meeting with the leadership had concluded. He always had lunch with Esau and his wife and after they ate he and Esau usually headed out to the stables. This time the older man paused under a shade tree, took off his black hat, and wiped his forehead with a red bandana.

"It is warm for May."

"It is," Milwaukee agreed.

"The flies will drive the horses crazy." He put his hat back on and looked at the dozen or so mares and geldings in his pasture. "Tabitha Troyer began her *Rumspringa* yesterday."

"Yes, I know."

"So she never came home."

Milwaukee was surprised. "Not at all? What about Nick Ferley?"

"No. He did not return home either."

"Nick and Tabitha—they did not call? The Troyers have heard nothing from Tabitha's English friends?"

Esau took off his hat again as if the news was too solemn to permit him to wear it. "There is no word." He looked at Milwaukee. "I think you should go to the Troyer home."

Milwaukee felt the same way, but realistically what could he do except say words that might lighten their hearts for few seconds? "I don't think I can make much of a difference. What they need is Tabitha back. Someone needs to go out and look for her. The police need to go out and look for her."

Esau nodded, still gazing at the horses. "There is work in the stables to do. But the Troyers need God's people now while she is missing. It will not be so important once she has returned to them." He put his hat back on his head. "Speaking into the Troyers' hearts is also holy work for a farrier. Did you walk?"

"Yes."

"Come. We'll hitch my gelding to the buggy."

It took only ten minutes to reach the Troyer house. As they pulled into the drive the sheriff's car was just coming down the lane. He gave them a nod and turned onto the main road. Mr. Troyer was still standing in the yard.

"God be with you, Simon," said Esau. "We have

heard about Tabitha and wish to pray with you and your wife."

"Come into the house, both of you. There is coffee. Rebecca is with a few of the women in the back. We won't bother them."

He looked very tired as he turned to walk up the steps to the porch, his legs moving slowly and his hand resting on the railing for support. Halfway up he looked back at Milwaukee. "Perhaps you should talk with Michal. You are friends. Of course there is coffee here at the table for you. But if you would spend a few minutes with her."

"Of course, Mr. Troyer. Is she in the house?"

Michal's father jerked his head in the direction of the barn.

She was rubbing down Sprinkles with a brush, slowly and rhythmically. Old Brownie was at her feet and Kitkat was curled up next to the bloodhound's chest. The horse stood quietly, now and then swinging its head back and biting at a fly that had made its way through the barn door. Michal was wearing a dark blue dress with a black apron and a white prayer *Kapp*. She kept her back to Milwaukee even though he knew she had heard his footsteps on the boards and straw. He removed his broad-brimmed black hat and held it in his hands. A shaft of sunlight, full of spinning bits of dust, covered Michal's arms and the small spots on the horse's back.

"Tabitha did not run away," she said in a quiet voice that nevertheless made Sprinkles prick up her ears. "People that run do not wait to say goodbye. She could have slipped out at three in the morning. Nick could have met her a quarter mile down the road. No one would have heard a thing. But she let us see her, him, the bike. She kissed all of us, waved to the boys, spent time with Sprinkles. Now I see what she was doing. Not running. But going. Truly going and not coming back."

Milwaukee stayed where he was. "Have you heard from her at all?"

"Not us. But Sheriff Bueller has. For him she is 16, it is a *Rumspringa* thing. Unless a law is broken she is an adult and making her own decisions. But to be sure there was nothing of abduction in her disappearance, the sheriff put out a notice. Police in Virginia pulled them over."

"Virginia?"

"They were almost in the Carolinas. The sheriff said they took the 95 south from Philly. State police told him the two were fine and she was obviously happy to be with Nick and on the road. There was no sign of duress or that she was being forced to remain in Nick's company against her will. Really, there was no reason at all for the state troopers to detain them. They weren't even speeding and they were riding in compliance with Virginia motorcycle laws. But Tabitha agreed to talk with Sheriff Bueller so they patched her through."

Michal found some mud on one of Sprinkles' legs and picked up an oval currycomb in the straw. She began to rub at the gray dirt to loosen it. Milwaukee waited.

"So?" Michal spoke up again. "She tells Bueller it would have been much too difficult to have told us what she planned to do. There would have been tears, perhaps a fight with mother and father. She wanted to leave in peace and love and that was how she did leave.

Yes, she knew it would be hard on us once we realized she was gone, and she was half-expecting the police to pull them over before they vanished into the Great Smoky Mountains, but she felt that was still better than a big scene at the house with the boys watching all the anger and pain."

She put down the currycomb and picked up the brush once more. Dust raced about furiously in the sunlight as she applied it vigorously to the horse's leg.

"St. Nick had left a note for his parents, hoping to spare them some of the shock, but they never found it until an hour ago. So not so bad a boy, hm? The sheriff told me I was to look under Tabitha's pillow. Do you see that paperback on the stool near the door?"

Milwaukee picked the book up. It was well thumbed. The cover showed an old man with a dog sitting on a grassy knoll. The title was *Travels with Charley, In Search of America.* He flipped through the first few pages. At the front was an inscription written in flawless handwriting: *Meet me and God in Arizona. Seriously. Love, Tabitha.*

Michal finally glanced back at him. "You are looking very plain today."

"Yes. It is an 'almost Amish' day."

"How did your talk with Bishop Eby go?"

"It went well."

"So. At least your world is right-side up."

"I'm sorry."

"Oh!" burst Michal. "Don't be sorry! Why should you be sorry that your head is screwed on right?" She dropped down in the straw, tears cutting across her face. He stepped toward her, but she quickly put up her hand. "No, no, stay where you are, last night was enough, more than enough. I let things go too far. We have no future together. What is the point? You are Amish, I am not. You belong here, I don't. But where shall I go?" She sank her head into her hands. "She makes it sound so easy. Arizona might as well be on the moon."

"It's not so far, Michal—"

She snapped her head up and glared at him through her swollen eyes and tears. "So I will also vanish down the highway on the back of someone's Harley-Davidson motorcycle? And then what? Mother and father have no more daughters. They worry themselves sick and before I return they are dead and buried from grief. How can I go now? How can I head out into this big, beautiful world of yours and find this me, myself and I who is missing or find this God I have lost sight of? Impossible. Truly, it would kill them. I am stuck here." She put her head down again. "But do not get your hopes up. Not for you to marry and kiss goodnight. I would not wish that on my best friend and you are my best friend, Milwaukee. I would make you miserable— half of me here, half of me there, a bit of me gone east, another bit gone north. I'm the girl who's all over the map. No, I do not inflict myself on you any further. Get baptized and find a good Amish woman, really, a good one, hardworking, pretty, committed to God, head over heels in love with you, okay? Find her and build a life on the Susquehanna. I'll stay in this house and be the Amish *Jungfer,* the spinster, take care of my parents, read postcards from Tabitha who will be in Paris or Barcelona or Rome. Maybe the pieces shall come together for me that way and God bestow his blessing. Who knows? But you go, go now, yes, go."

Milwaukee was stunned by the turn of events that had completely altered his relationship with Michal from the night before. "I—don't know what to tell you. I wish we could pick up where we left off last night."

"Well, we can't!" she almost shouted. "I am fond of you, Michal."

But she did not respond or raise her head.

"I will pray for you," he murmured, not knowing what else to say. "Good. Pray all you want. Surely God will listen to you where he will not listen to me. Fast, pray, sing hymns. But just go now. Go, go." Milwaukee placed the paperback back on the stool.

Her head came up, the tears still running from her eyes. "Did you see what she did with the cover?"

Milwaukee, who felt like his chest was full of lead, glanced at the book. "No."

"The title. She crossed out the C in Charley."

He looked more closely and realized the cover said *Travels with Harley, In Search of America.* She saw his smile and laughed a little. "Cute?"

He nodded. "Sure, cute." But inside himself it was still gray and heavy and dark. She saw that too, she knew what it was that came bleakly out of his eyes, but there was nothing she could do about it. Life was what it was that afternoon and she could not mould it into the shape she wished.

Ah, but I have hurt you badly. I am sorry, so sorry, to pass on the pain, but I am filled to the brim and it just spurts out of me. Goodbye, my once upon a time friend.

Milwaukee left the barn, placed his hat on his head, and started down the lane. He had not gone a hundred feet before the door to the house opened and Michal's father leaned out.

"Master Bachman. Come and have that coffee now."

"Oh, *danke,* but I must get on."

Mr. Troyer beckoned with his hand. "Please, I have a favor to ask of you, a very big favor. Come. Come."

He waited in the doorway until Milwaukee reached him. "And my daughter is how?"

"Not so good, Mr. Troyer. I'm afraid I was not able to help her much."

"You don't know. With Michal, you think it is a no, a day or two later and she is telling you it was always yes, that you misinterpreted her."

Esau nodded as Milwaukee took off his hat and sat at the kitchen table. Mr. Troyer stood over him.

"So. Coffee? Cold buttermilk? Lemonade?"

"You know, Mr. Troyer, I think a glass of buttermilk."

He set a glass by Milwaukee's hand and then brought a ceramic pitcher from the icebox and poured. Milwaukee drank half of it off in one swallow. Mr. Troyer filled his glass a second time.

"Gute?" he asked Milwaukee, pleased at the young man's thirst.

"Sehr gute. Danke schoen."

Mr. Troyer sat down. "Such a day to wake up to. This is why we must always surround ourselves with prayer. Only God knows what is coming along the fence line so it is best to remain close by his side."

Esau murmured *amen.*

Michal's father tapped a finger on the tabletop. "So what does the sheriff tell me, young man? Did my daughter explain?"

"Yes."

"But she did not tell you this other because she had already gone off to the barn. Daniel Bueller looks me in the eye and tells me not to think of going and getting Tabitha and bringing her back here. She is an adult he says a hundred times. I bring her back to Marietta against her will and it is abduction. Kidnapping. The law will arrest me. A father tries to rescue his youngest daughter, but this is a crime. How does that sit with you?"

Milwaukee said nothing.

Mr. Troyer continued to tap his finger. "What does he think? I will mount a posse as if I live my life in the middle of a John Wayne western? I, who have no car, no truck, will catch up to her? I, who own no weapons, will put a gun to young Nicholas' head and order him back to Pennsylvania? I understand the only way in which I can influence my daughter and her boyfriend is to reason with them. *Come, let us reason together, saith the Lord.* Only this holy reasoning and prayer can turn the two of them around. The prayer can be done from anywhere. I do not need to leave Marietta to pray for my youngest daughter. But the reasoning—how shall this be accomplished? There is no telephone, we have no idea if she will write, and even if she writes, how do we write back to someone who is in Pennsylvania one day and North Carolina the next? What do you think?" He looked at Milwaukee.

Milwaukee was holding his empty glass. "I don't know, sir."

"Even while the sheriff is warning me about what I cannot do I am thinking and praying about what is possible. How can I talk to her? How can I reason with her?" He looked at Milwaukee more closely. "So?"

"I don't know, Mr. Troyer."

"I cannot. It is simple. I cannot. In her present state of mind she will not reason with me." The finger tap. "But her sister she will listen to anytime." He glanced across the room at nothing and nodded. "Michal can reason with Tabitha." He stared at Esau and then at Milwaukee. Raising his hands he moved them together slowly and deliberately until the fingers were interlaced with one another. "How to bring them together?"

The grandfather clock struck four in the afternoon. Mr. Troyer waited until the final gong was finished, running his hand over his mouth and dark beard. Then he got up, brought glasses for Esau and himself along with the pitcher of cool buttermilk, and poured enough for all three to have a good drink. Then he sat down, sipped at his glass, and leaned back in his chair.

"But," he began again, "there will of course need to be more prayer to God Almighty, more discussion amongst the people. My wife I must speak with, and Bishop Eby, and Pastor Smucker, and the others in leadership.

"Your parents must be consulted, Master Bachman, and yourself naturally, as well as the one you are apprenticed to here, Esau. And Michal, I will hear what my eldest has to say, yes, much talk, much prayer, nothing is well that is done hastily." He seemed to drift off, staring past Esau and Milwaukee and through the wall on the other side of the kitchen. Then suddenly he leaned forward and grasped Milwaukee's arm, his dark eyes only inches from the young man's face, fingers digging into skin and bone with a desperate strength.

"But this, this," he said with an intensity that almost frightened Milwaukee, "it comes to this. For the love of Christ, I ask you not to take your vows this month, not to be baptized, to forego joining the Amish faith. I know it is too much, far too much for you to consider, but it is a father who asks, yes, begs, for this same love of Christ, that you take that motorbike of yours and go out on the highways and back roads of America, for as long as you must, until you find my daughter. And I ask you to take Michal, my Michal, on what I know can only be a very hard and long road, with you."

Milwaukee was stunned. "I'm sorry, Mr. Troyer. Am I hearing you right? You cannot be serious, can you?"

Mr. Troyer locked his eyes on Milwaukee's, his fingers still gripping the young man's arm. "There are very few things I have been more serious about. I plead with you—go, take your motorcycle, and find Tabitha."

Chapter Four

"Are you going for a walk, Michal?"

"Yes, mama, a long prayer walk. I need to clear my head."

"So long as you remember the bishop and the pastors are here to speak with us at four."

"Ja, ja."

The day was bright. Michal walked quickly down the drive and across the road, opening a gate into a hayfield. A small beaten path skirted the field and headed toward the river. Michal took it. Her pace remained brisk. As she made her way through the green grass that was as high as her chest she whispered prayers and hoped God would provide her with answers she could clearly hear and clearly see.

Sometimes you speak to us in ways that are not obvious, Lord, you know that yourself, and no doubt you have your reasons for doing so. But here we have such a strange set of circumstances it would be helpful if you did not add to them. Sometimes we are to ask for signs, sometimes not. Well, I must ask you for a sign. It is one thing for me to up and travel across America.

I don't even know if I want to be Amish. But is it fair to ask it of Milwaukee? He is ready to commit himself, to settle down, to marry. His Rumspringa *is over. Why should he be pushed into spending months on the road when his heart is here? Surely this is not just.*

The Susquehanna was swollen with the rains of April and May and moving with strength through the green hills. Michal opened another gate and took a path that followed the riverbank for miles. Most of the time she could see the water, but other times the trees that had burst into leaf blocked her view. Robins and blackbirds streamed from branch to branch, calling back and forth. As always, the river and the life that thrived on its edges combined to lift her out of the gloom she was struggling with, but still there were no easy answers.

Of course, when is it that you make things easy? It would be enough to ask you what we should do about my father's request, yes, and now my mother's plea. But I treated Milwaukee so badly that afternoon in the barn how on earth can we travel together? I have not spoken with him since.

Really, there is nothing to say. I told him to get out of my life and he has done what I asked, gentleman that he is. I do not feel inclined to hunt him down and apologize. There are no words I'm aware of that can make up for my rudeness. And if I were he, I would not wish to spend a year or half a year on a motorbike with me, myself, and I.

Now and then, at any time of the year, even winter, Michal might run into deer if she took the path she was on or any of the others that wound through the trees and brush at the top of the bank or along its sides.

Suddenly, as she prayed, she came upon two spotted fawns without their mother. They froze and stared at her. She stopped walking immediately and spoke softly to them. Their wet black noses twitched and their large dark eyes studied her intensely. Then, lifting their hooves high and stepping carefully, they slowly turned and moved down the bank into a thick cluster of trees with fresh yellow-green leaves.

I wish I could just live in the forest like the deer. Mother says make peace with Milwaukee. I am too ashamed to make peace. I am too ashamed to go to his house. And even if I did apologize, so I still don't believe it would be a good idea for us to go together on this search for a needle in a haystack. It would not work, you yourself know it would not work, Lord. He is almost Amish. I am almost not Amish. We both need to move on. Don't you agree?

She came through a thick screen of brush and there was Milwaukee. He was seated on a boulder 30 or 40 feet straight down the bank from the trail and hurling stones as hard as he could. Now and then she saw that he was rewarded by a far-off splash as his throws connected with the Susquehanna.

Lord, do you find this funny? Was it a slow day?

For a moment she thought about carrying on and going quietly by without saying anything. He wouldn't even know she'd been there and gone. But she realized that would be cheating—whatever game God was playing, she had to go along with the rules. Milwaukee should not be there. The two of them had never gone to the riverbank together, it was not one of their spots. Other young people, both Amish in *Rumspringa* and non-Amish, came to the river to neck in the bushes and smoke cigarettes or drink beer.

But this was not something she and Milwaukee had done. Yes, and others came to walk and pray as she was doing, but again this was not something the two of them had done. She had no idea if Milwaukee had ever come to the river before today. But he was here now. And it was no accident.

Having made up her mind not to try and slip past and instead to see where this chance meeting led—a meeting she knew was not chance at all, but had God's fingerprints all over it—on impulse she decided to throw a few stones of her own. Bending down and picking up four or five, she stood up, braced her legs, twisted her arm back, and threw the first one with all her might. It did not reach the river. She tried again, biting her lip and trying to summon every ounce of strength into her right arm. This time she saw the splash and so did Milwaukee. He had not been throwing anything for a few minutes and she sensed his confusion as he sat with his back toward her in his Levi's denim jacket and faded jeans.

He must think it is a fish jumping—bass or walleye or perch or even rainbow trout or catfish or northern pike.

She took three stones in her hand this time and flung them all at once, hoping at least two would make it. To her surprise, she did better than that—all three stones reached the river and all three raised big white splashes. She had no doubt this was God again. It made no sense otherwise. Milwaukee sat staring straight ahead a few more moments then he slowly twisted his neck and looked behind him.

Michal was sure she would see a frown. After all, she had practically picked him up and hurled him from the barn. Standing there in her navy blue dress, black apron, and white prayer *Kapp* she timidly put up her hand in a small wave. Their eyes met. His were brown and warm. She felt a quiver go through her and was more than a little shocked. What was this? What were her head and body doing to her? Milwaukee was just a friend, and an estranged friend at that, thanks to her.

He smiled his big, full, beautiful smile and some of his light brown hair was in his eyes along with the sunlight. The quiver went through her again. For a moment she didn't know what to say, what she was feeling was so unexpected. Why should his hair or eyes or hair matter to her or affect her? A few days ago she'd wanted to pitch him on his head. But the worst—or the best, she thought later—was yet to come. She heard him speak her name for the first time in almost a week.

"Michal."

She froze like the fawns had frozen.

"You always had the arm to go with your looks."

She felt the blood come to her face, starting at the throat and working its way up over her nose and cheeks and forehead to her hairline.

"Uh—Milwaukee—hi," she finally got out. "Did someone tell you I was here?"

"No, no."

"Because I didn't say a word to a soul. I didn't even know I'd wind up here myself. Esau pretty much ordered me to take the day off. Go pray, he said. Go think. Go listen. Then you will know what you should do. So I wandered this way and at first I was going to go back to the house and get a fishing pole, but then I realized I really didn't want to see anyone, not my brothers or mother or father, there was no one I wanted to speak with, so I came straight here without fetching my pole. But I was wrong, you know."

Michal continued to feel upended by the surge of strong emotions seeing Milwaukee had unleashed. "You were wrong?"

"Yeah. 'Cause I definitely like seeing you." Now something started up in her chest.

"Do you have any idea how beautiful you are standing there all Amish like that? With the sun pouring over you? Black apron, black hair, blue eyes. My good, good, stunningly good-looking friend. Man, I've missed you. I'm sorry we quarreled."

Michal's head was reeling from his lavish compliments. "You're sorry?"

"I was going to come by and apologize. But the whole week has been crazy with that idea of your father's going the rounds. Some people are saying, hey, it's *Rumspringa,* if Tabitha Troyer wants to go to Mars or Pluto, let her go, it's time to stop living her life for her. But others are saying, look, this is dangerous, it's not as if Tabitha is 20 or 21, she is only 16 and she is out on the streets and highways of America with a boy who has no connections to the Amish faith. So who knows? But your father and I have met a couple of times on our own."

Michal finally managed to get her focus back enough to make her way down the slope to the boulder where Milwaukee was sitting. He moved over and she sat beside him, her hands in her lap, looking at him as if she were seeing him for the first time.

"Did you know that?" Milwaukee asked.

Michal had no idea what he was talking about. "No, I didn't."

"Once we met by chance at the post office and went off a ways and chatted—though I suppose it wasn't by chance, was it? Do you think anything is really by chance, Michal?"

Why am I still light-headed? This is crazy. "No," she replied.

"And the other time he dropped in and spoke with my parents and my brothers and myself. Everybody has their opinion about your father's request, Michal, and everybody has their own ideas about what I should or shouldn't do, or what you should or shouldn't do for that matter. Of course, I have been working all this through, praying all this through. My parents think I should help your father, by the way, so do my brothers. Hey, since you're here and I don't have to get up the nerve to go to your house—" the fascinating smile— "I wanted to tell you, well, I noticed how well you sang on Sunday."

Michal was startled. "I sang well?"

"Not the same as the old days, but you weren't half-hearted, you know? You sang as if you were reaching out for something, reaching out for God."

"Oh." She smiled. "It must be my anguish."

Milwaukee's face grew somber and he nodded. "You miss your sister. You are worried about her. You wonder how your parents are going to hold up."

Again she looked at him as if she were seeing him for the first time. "Yes, all those things."

"I don't know what to say to you. Your father thinks you can talk Tabitha into returning home. I think Tabitha is so strong-willed she won't listen, at least, not right away. But if we did go on the road the chances of finding them anytime soon—unless God intervenes—are pretty slim. So that would mean there was plenty of time for the highway to get inside of her head and, who knows? She might be ready to come back to Lancaster County by August or September if you put things the right way."

Michal put a hand on Milwaukee's arm as if the incident in the barn had never occurred. "You don't need to feel you must go on this journey or my family will fall apart. We'll make out all right. Lots of other Amish families have faced worse *Rumspringa* experiences than this—jail time, teen pregnancies, drug overdoses, driving under the influence, car wrecks. Tabitha is smarter than that."

"But she's far away, Michal. Anything could happen to the two of them and you wouldn't know for days or weeks if they needed your help. I think the people who support your father's request are the ones who can truly put themselves in his shoes. If it was their daughter, they would pray for God to send someone who could help them. Those who say his idea is foolishness, well, it's not their daughter, the emotional connection isn't there, they don't get it. I feel a lot of, I don't know, sympathy, empathy, what's the word I want?"

He looked at her for help. Then he shook his head and began to laugh. "What?" she asked, smiling at his laughter. "What is it?"

"No Amish girl should look like you look, Michal. You are so distracting I swear it's a sin."

The heat was in her face again. "Why do you say that? I am dressed as plainly as I can dress."

"Yes. Which only serves to highlight your incredible eyes and skin and three AM hair by contrast."

"My three AM hair?"

Milwaukee leaned back and closed his eyes, still

laughing in stops and starts. "The whole thing is crazy. I swore I would never talk with you again after our *spuckte,* our spat. I really felt low. Avoided you at church. I suggested to your father he get one of my brothers to go on this—this rescue mission. Mark rode a BMW during his *Rumspringa,* yes, a big one too, 750, it should be Mark I told him, not me, all because I didn't want you and I to be stuck together for six or seven months. So your father says to me finally, *My Michal is suddenly an ugly duck to you?*"

Michal burst out with her own sharp laugh and grasped Milwaukee's arm again. "He did not."

"He did. Anyway, it's all crazy, how could Mark be Amish and ride a bike? But I'm trying to work up all these feelings against you, you see, no more Michal, no more Michal, and then you drop out of the sky here today and I can't stop talking to you, blah, blah, blah, on and on, like I've had all these thoughts in my head and no one to share them with until you come along. It's been pent up in me and now I'm some sort of gusher. I am supposed to be cross and look at me—I'm so happy to see you. Even if you were your father's ugly duck I would still be babbling away. But—" He sat up and opened his eyes and looked at her. "You are very easy on a man's eyes."

Oh, I am going to burn up if he keeps talking this way and looking at me like that.

"Well, Milwaukee, well," she stumbled. "I—it is— not just you who feels this is all very—strange—our meeting like this. I did not think—we should travel together either, I had convinced myself we were—in-compatible. For a moment I thought I should just sneak past you here, but I think—I really think—God had something to do with this."

"Oh? God Almighty? You truly think you and I are that important?"

"Are you teasing me?"

"I never tease blue-eyed girls."

She smiled. "No? Well, I do think this chance encounter by the river was—planned in advance—by someone—else."

"If that's so, what are we to make of it? We are sitting here together after we both swore we would never sit together again—what does it mean?"

Michal looked down at her hands. A ladybug was slowly making its way along her thumb. "I guess I'm not sure."

"Well, can you tell me what you think of your father's idea now?"

"Now?"

"Yes. Right now. Not what you thought last night or at breakfast this morning."

Michal's lips curved upward again, but she kept her eyes on the ladybug. "I suppose—because it matters so much to mother and father—I would go—if the church is behind it—I would go—"

"With who? With who would you go?"

The ladybug flew, its small red wings whirring. Michal looked up at Milwaukee. "With you. I would go with you."

He did not reply. Neither of them looked away. Eventually Michal reached for his hand and held it.

Milwaukee cleared his throat. "I—I told your father I would honor you—that I would not cross the line— that I would honor you and your family—"

She smiled and leaned her head against his shoulder. "Of course you would."

"That—somehow I would not let him down—that I would find your sister—I don't know how I can make a promise like that—but he is in so much pain—your father—your mother—"

"We."

"What?"

"We. How can we make a promise like that? You and I."

She sat up and faced him, holding both of his hands now. He gave a small smile. The light brown hair was in his eyes again. Her emotions had settled inside her head and chest, but not by much. She reached over and gently brushed the hair aside. It made her fingers tingle. She had no idea what her touch did to him, but his smile widened.

"All right," he finally responded. "We."

She had never seen the brown in his eyes look so deep and dark. "But," he went on, "just because we want to help your family that doesn't mean the bishop and the leadership will agree with the plan."

"It does not matter," Michal said.

"Of course it matters. Your mother and father have to live here for the rest of their lives."

"And the Marietta Amish will let them, my dear. It is not my parents who are taking a Honda Rebel down the freeway. It is you and I. And we are *Rumspringa*. We are not members of the church. The bishop breaks nothing in the rulebook by letting us go. Until we are baptized we remain *Rumspringa,* the ones who 'run around'. So we go and run around, and they let us go out and run around, just as we have been running around for the past two years."

"Well, that is another thing, Michal."

She could not help smiling as she watched him grow older and more serious in front of her eyes.

He misunderstood her smile. "I'm not kidding. Taking a 250cc bike onto the big asphalt is no joke. Every semi that roars past us will make it feel like we've been hit by a twister. If we get a double trailer it'll be our own personal hurricane."

"So we take the back roads."

"I don't know the back roads," he protested.

"We get a map." She was still smiling at his grownup intensity and at the situation God had maneuvered them both into. "I'll navigate, you drive. Pilot and co-pilot. Deal?"

"But we don't even know where we're going. We don't even know where Tabitha and Nick are. They could be on the interstate and we're puttering away on the cart and donkey route and we miss them."

"Well." She thought about that. "God will have to navigate too. You said yourself he would need to intervene if we were going to find Tabitha on a million miles of open road. God knows what we have to work with. So he has to work with us with what we've got."

"And what have we got?"

"Five loaves and two fishes. If he wants us to have more than that he will have to multiply them."

"You make it sound so easy."

Michal shrugged. "He's done it before." She put out her hand. "Deal?"

Milwaukee laughed. "You are so crazy. The leadership have not even given their consent yet."

She kept her hand extended. "They will. I told you. We are *Rumspringa*."

He shook his head. Then he gripped her small hand. "Deal."

"Now hug me. We are never someplace like this where only the deer can see us. I'm not sure why we didn't come to the river together."

Milwaukee folded her into his arms, feeling more alive with her close to him than he had all week. "It's because we did not care much about hugging or kissing each other."

"Perhaps the road will change that," she murmured.

"Perhaps."

"You might make an Amish woman of me yet. Anything can happen on the open road." She put her head on his chest. "Isn't it marvelous what God has done for us today?"

Milwaukee held her more tightly. Inside his head everything was turning around and around.

"I can't believe this," he said.

Chapter Five

The Shenandoah River was twisting and turning far
below them as they made their way through the Blue
Ridge Mountains of Virginia. It was the first time she
had ever seen a waterway that deserved the description
"serpentine". She felt that if the loops of the river drew
together much more tightly they would be snipped off
and form their own pools or ponds and the Shenandoah cease to exist.

"Oxbow lakes!" Milwaukee had shouted as they
raced along. "What?"

"When the loops get so tight they break away from
the main stream they form oxbow lakes. That's what
they're called."

She leaned forward and placed her gloved hands on
his shoulders so that she could talk into his ear. "How
did you know that's what I was thinking?"

"I know all."

"You know all?"

"Well. God knows all. But I know what he chooses
to tell me."

The green, blue, and gray of the mountains were

a relief after a day spent in and around Washington, DC. The traffic, exhaust, and heat had been so bad they'd given up, parked at a motel, rented two separate rooms, then gone walking to see the monuments. Milwaukee had loved the cavernous depths of the Lincoln Memorial and been touched when he read the words of the assassinated President's Second Inaugural Address. There was so much about forgiveness he wondered aloud why Miss Beachey had not taught them the speech, and recited lines of it in front of Michal and others who stood nearby with their bottles of water and digital cameras.

With malice toward none; with charity for all; with firmness in the right, as God gives us to see the right, let us strive on to finish the work we are in; to bind up the nation's wounds; to care for him who shall have borne the battle, and for his widow, and his orphan—to do all which may achieve and cherish a just, and a lasting peace, among ourselves, and with all nations.

Michal had been most moved by the mirrored black wall that listed the American dead of the Vietnam War. She had lingered by the sculpture of women nurses holding a wounded soldier while one of them looked skyward for the helicopter. From the sculpture she watched as people took rubbings of names, or placed flowers, or just squatted down and stared at a particular part of the wall. She and Milwaukee had both seen two older women, once mothers and now, she hoped to God, grandmothers, break down and weep in front of the names etched in stone for 1968. She had leaned her face into Milwaukee's arm and denim jacket and wept herself.

"Ah, that there is always war and always pain that can't be healed because of it."

Milwaukee asked if she would pray with him at the White House. Standing at the black iron fence and looking at the fountain and the wide green front lawn they whispered prayers for the President and their country in Pennsylvania Dutch. Around them people were taking photographs and one small group held signs and protested the war in Afghanistan. Beyond them they saw a man and a boy kneeling and making the Sign of the Cross.

When they returned to the motel they ate some of the food both their families had stuffed into the Honda's saddlebags, said goodnight, and opened the doors to their separate rooms. They had agreed to get up at four and leave the city before gridlock occurred, but when they started on their way at 4:30 AM after a prayer and a coffee there were already more cars and trucks than either of them liked. Finally they got out of the city on Interstate 95, but the speed and volume of traffic was not much of an improvement from the streets of the capital and twice Michal thought they would be sucked under the tires of heavy rigs. Finally they made their escape onto a secondary roadway Michal had found on the map and entered an entirely different world.

It was one of old trees bending over tea brown creeks, of pink and white cherry blossoms scattering through the air in the short and sudden bursts of showers, one petal pasting itself to the arm of Michal's jean jacket. There were miles of gray split rail fences and pastures and horses. Time and time again small bronze plaques popped up by bridges and streams and fields as the road twisted south and west. When they stopped for lunch at a turnout near a wooden bridge and laid their jackets out in the sun to dry Michal had a chance to read two of the plaques that were only a few hundred feet apart. One said that Union and Confederate cavalry had clashed at this stream on May 14th, 1862 and the Union troopers put to flight with the cost of several dozen lives on both sides. The other said a platoon of Federal infantry had fought a pitched battle with two platoons of Confederate soldiers on April 27th, 1864 and that there were graves marked by stones further back in the trees.

"This is beautiful old-fashioned countryside," Milwaukee said as he dangled his bare feet in the swift silver and green water.

"And yet men have died in war right here," Michal told him with a plaintive look on her face.

"Is that what the plaques said?"

"Yes. Now I wonder if all of the ones I've noticed talk about the war to save the Union."

"If all the signs looked the same they probably did."

"But these were not even the big battles like Gettysburg or Shiloh. Just little fights. Who could remember all of them? Who was taking notes?"

Milwaukee trailed his fingers in the stream. "I suppose the officers were. And the men whose friends were shot. And the people living on the farms nearby."

Michal stared at twigs rushing past between the banks. "It seems to me we always commemorate the wars, but never commemorate the times of peace. Why are there no plaques saying Bill and Mary Bishop watered their livestock here for 63 years, were married for 77, raised five children, 12 grandchildren, and 29 great grandchildren, died in their beds a year apart and are buried under an oak tree on the land they cleared?"

Milwaukee tossed several small stones into the creek. "I suppose because there was no tragedy. No sudden death. If Bill had drowned here watering his thoroughbreds or Mary had been swept away in a flash flood coming back from Lynchburg then there might be plaques up. But no one commemorates the normal, Michal, no one remembers the routine, do they? Even we have a hard time remembering the days and weeks where nothing out of the way happened."

Dark caught them still in the Blue Ridge Mountains so they parked at a large turnout where a camper had also settled in for the night, locked and chained the bike, took out their sleeping bags, climbed a slope through a belt of trees, and opened the bags at a flat stretch of grass, crawling in with their clothes still on. They were above the treetops and could see lights shining all along the Shenandoah Valley while over their heads the stars put on their own show.

"Oh, it's beautiful," said Michal. "But am I going to freeze to death up here?"

"I hope not, " Milwaukee replied. "But it isn't July yet either. Weren't you wearing a yellow bandana under your helmet today?"

"Yes."

"So put it back on. Your head will be the one part of your body that gets cold if you don't."

"Okay." He heard her rustling around. "And—what about bears? Are there bears up here?"

"I don't know. These are mountains. I guess so."

"You guess so?" Milwaukee heard irritation creep into her voice. "You drag me up a mountainside in the black of night and you guess there might be bears?"

"Hey—what happened to my winged warrior?"

"That's Nick."

"Well, you're mine. And we're out on the open road now. Just you, me, and God. You're not going to fall apart on Day Four are you? Michal Deborah Troyer? Deborah was a fighter, remember?"

Michal was quiet for several minutes and Milwaukee wasn't sure if she was silent out of anger and thinking up a retort or whether she was mulling things through. He decided she had fallen asleep when suddenly she spoke up.

"Deborah the Winged Warrior and Savior of Her People needs a bit of help tonight. So why are you lying so far away?"

"I promised your father—"

"Will you stop that? I know you are not going to take advantage of your winged warrior. How about your promise to me?"

Milwaukee frowned in the dark. "Which promise is that?"

"To protect and defend me. Suppose a bear wanders along and wants a bite of my arm?"

"Michal, this is not Alaska or Montana—"

"Never mind where it is or isn't. I need you closer to me. Not too close. Just close enough."

"What is close enough?" Milwaukee asked her.

"I need to be able to hold your hand. If a bear attacks me I can handle it if I know you're there. Once it starts to hurt I'll squeeze your hand more tightly and then I'll be okay."

Milwaukee began to laugh quietly, putting his head into his sleeping bag while he did so, but she heard him anyway.

"What's so funny?" she snapped. "Get over here."

"But I'm warm."

"Stay in your bag and wriggle over. I don't care how you get here—just get here."

Milwaukee squirmed and used his knees and elbows to slither and slide toward her. Once he rolled completely over and got dirt in his mouth. He began to cough and spit.

"Is that you?" she asked suddenly.

"No," he growled irritably. "It's the Killer Bear of Shenandoah Valley."

"Ha ha," she said.

"Okay. I'm here."

He reached out and touched her. She screamed.

"Michal!" he said in a harsh whisper. "Stop! It was my hand! My hand still connected to my body!"

There was quiet again. Then he heard giggling.

"Oh, oh, crazy me," she laughed softly. "The people in the camper are probably calling the state police on their cell phone right now."

"You have got to calm down, Michal. We're in Virginia. Not the trackless wilderness of the American West."

"Not yet anyway. Okay, you're close enough. Can I have your hand again?"

"Are you sure you're not going to try another scream?"

"Just don't touch my face. So where is this hand of yours?"

"Here." His night vision had improved and he laid it on her stomach.

She latched onto his hand with both of hers. "Good. Good. Well, I'm ready to sleep now. How about you?"

"I was."

"Did I scream away your sleepy feeling?"

"Something like that."

"I'm perfectly relaxed myself. Look at how gorgeous the stars are. It's as if they're only a hundred feet away."

"Mmm."

"Don't be cross. God is watching over us. Do you mind if I pray out loud?"

"Pray away."

She spoke in High German, thanked God they were safe, and requested the same protection for Tabitha and Nick. Then she began to pray for their parents and the Amish community in Marietta, spending a few moments on each person. After five minutes she began to slow down and suddenly stopped. Milwaukee thought she had decided to pray silently. Then he heard her deep regular breathing and knew she had fallen asleep. Despite that, her hold on his hand was as strong as ever. He wondered if he would be able to get to sleep with his right arm stretched out like that.

Lying on his back and watching the stars his mind wandered back to the people Michal had been praying for and the day of their departure. The talk with the leadership that final morning had surprised him. He expected more discussion and warnings about a young man and woman traveling alone together. Instead they were focused on not bringing Tabitha back prematurely.

"We have *Rumspringa* for a good reason," the bishop

had told him and Michal as they sat together in the Troyer kitchen. "In the past, too many young people were being baptized and then breaking the *Ordnung* over and over again, doing things they should have gotten out of their systems long before. So, all right, we decided we needed to keep young men and women back from something so serious as their commitment to Jesus Christ and the Amish faith until they truly felt ready. That is why we permit the "running around" time. The young people who do *Rumspringa* are far more faithful in keeping their baptismal vows."

"It is not that we don't wish young Tabitha back safely within the fold," Pastor Smucker spoke up. "But if you find her, God willing, and bring her back here against her will, God forbid, not only will you have Sheriff Bueller breathing down your neck, her return will not be of any benefit to the church or her family or herself. She will not wish to take the vows nor will she be ready to take them, do you see? Better she get this all out of her head, this open road and seeing America business, and then come back to us and say, *Yes, now I am ready to follow Jesus, now I am ready to be Amish.*"

"We only wish to talk with her and persuade her to reconsider this road trip," Michal responded, hands folded in her lap. "I am her sister. I would never try to bring her back by force."

"Gute, gute," smiled Pastor Beachey. "We try to keep both the laws of man and the laws of God. But here is something else I want you to think about. It may be if you were to go out on the roadways and tracks of America looking for your little sister God might have something in store for you yourself, Michal Troyer."

"What do you mean, pastor?"

"Well, as I have prayed about this matter, some thoughts have come to mind: *Suppose God wishes to show the older sister something? Suppose God has a plan to touch Michal Troyer's heart?* After all, you have not yet taken your vows, hm? And you have not indicated any desire to do so. No doubt you are working things through with the Lord. Good, good. But this—open road—may be as much about yourself as it is about your sister. You both have concerns to clear up with the Lord and it may be this is how he intends to help you do it. Open road, open heart—I don't know. But I wonder if this is your journey, Michal Deborah, not simply your sister's?"

The bishop grunted. "Pastor Beachey makes a good point. We assume it is all about Tabitha. It may be all about you." Milwaukee sensed that Michal was not only squirming in her seat as the bishop fixed his gaze on her, but squirming inside. "Or you, young man." The bishop transferred his gaze to Milwaukee.

He was startled. "Myself? But I was ready to take the vows this month."

The bishop nodded and hooked his thumbs in his suspender straps. "You think you are ready. We think you are ready. But it may be that God says, *No, wait, not just yet, there are two or three things I must show Master Bachman, and I need all of America to do it.* Who knows? It may be so."

The two pastors said *amen* in quiet voices.

No further words were spoken. Milwaukee listened to the ticking of the grandfather clock in the hall. Michal glanced around the table at the three bearded men.

"Is that it?" she asked.

Bishop Eby smiled. "I think so."

"It sounds like you are giving us permission to take the motorbike and head down the highway."

"You do not need permission. You are *Rumspringa*. Do as you wish. Go and run around."

The two pastors laughed.

"But—" Michal hesitated. "I would like your blessing as well."

"Thank you. Of course. Perhaps I did not make myself clear." The bishop leaned forward, his large hands clasped together on the tabletop. "We believe God has a plan in this, yes, even in your sister's disappearance. You and young Master Bachman are part of that plan. You could not do it if you were not *Rumspringa*. Taking a motorcycle across the country? It would not be permitted. But, here, look, you are not yet baptized, not yet Amish. You are free to go. So much of *Rumspringa* is foolishness, and crazy, childish games. But you have an opportunity to do something with your *Rumspringa* that is more than just wildness or indulgence or—experimentation—*ja*?

"Here you have a chance to save a soul, to alter a life. If anyone is in Christ, he is a new creature, there is a new world. And not just one life, not just Tabitha's life. Your life, Michal, Nick's life, Master Bachman's life—yes, many lives can be made new. Who knows what God is up to? But something like this does not fall into place due to human effort."

The bishop and pastors stood up.

"Of course you have our blessing, children. Go with God. Please, let us pray for the two of you."

Their heads bowed, Milwaukee and Michal received 20 minutes of prayer. The rest of the morning and afternoon passed quickly—the loading of the saddlebags, money from his family and the Troyers and even the Amish community, changing into blue jeans and jean jackets at their homes.

"No need to wait until the washroom at Roy's garage," Bishop Eby had teased Michal, who had reddened like a rose. "I do not plow in my Sunday best. You do not ride in a cotton dress, no matter how good and plain."

As they had straddled the bike with dozens of people standing about and wishing them well Milwaukee had heard Mrs. Troyer speaking softly to her daughter.

"Every day, once the boys are in school, I will walk the mile to that telephone hut the church has. I will wait there 15 minutes to see if you will call."

"But mama," Michal had protested, "I know I shall not be able to call you each and every day."

"No, but some days it will be possible, others not. So I will wait and see and spend my time in prayer for you and Tabitha and Milwaukee and Nicholas Ferley. God has a plan, yes, there is always a plan even if we do not recognize it or see clearly how it is working out. So when you can call I will be the one to pick up the phone."

"What time, mama?"

"Nine o'clock each morning. I will sit in that hut between nine o'clock and nine-fifteen each morning. Even if it takes you a year to find your way home again."

She had kissed Michal and Michal had thrown her arms around her mother.

Milwaukee's father had taken his hand. "You are much loved, my boy. Every day there will be prayer and every night."

"Thank you, papa."

"Come back to us."

Then Mr. Troyer stood before him. "I did not ask a small thing, may God forgive me, and what you are doing is not a small thing. My wife and I will always be grateful. No matter what occurs or does not occur."

"I want to do this, Mr. Troyer. I want to try."

Mr. Troyer nodded. "I see that. In Christ we live and move and have our being. May it be as God intends. Thank you." Surprising Milwaukee, Mr. Troyer had wrapped his long arms around him and kissed him on the cheek, his beard scraping Milwaukee's face. Then he had given Milwaukee a small black leather book. "It is the Bible in German. Luther's translation. The print is small, but you have a young man's eyes. I have had the book since I was 15. So may the reading of it bless you."

"Oh, no, sir, I can't—"

Mr. Troyer had continued to press it into Milwaukee's hand. "So may the reading of it bless you."

They had rumbled along the road and past the Amish farms where some farmers had begun to take their first cut of hay. Several waved to Milwaukee and Michal as they motored slowly by. At the turnoff that led to the highway out of Marietta a buggy was drawn up by the side of the road. Bishop Eby was standing beside his horse and waiting for them. Milwaukee stopped, but did not switch the engine off. The bishop smiled and put a hand on each of their shoulders.

"So you go, and you go with God," he said. "No day will pass by without prayers for the two of you and those you seek. In the Lord's good time may you find them. In the Lord's good time may you find what is in your own hearts as well. Just remember." Here he leaned in toward them and dropped his voice. "It is not our world out there. Yes, God is active in all parts of it, I believe that, but it is not a place where what we value is cherished. There is much hate, children, there is much violence. I have heard of the beauty of mountains and deserts and seas, such beauty that overwhelms a man. But the danger, Milwaukee, the danger is also great.

"Watch. Pray. Be wise. Again and again, turn to God. If you have desperate hours or days of fear, turn to him who turns the earth."

There was no moon as Milwaukee lay on the slope in the Blue Ridge Mountains and the sky seemed to grow darker and darker and the stars thicker and brighter until the gleaming flow of the Milky Way was obvious. Michal's grip had not loosened as time passed. Milwaukee wanted to lie on his side, but could only do so by turning carefully and facing her. Michal's skin was pale in the starlight. Looking at her he thought again that she was the most beautiful woman he had ever seen, on a movie screen or off. He began to get drowsy as he gazed at her quiet features and thought there were a lot worse ways for a man to fall asleep in a strange place.

Thank you, my Lord, for this gift. I hope you have others just as pleasant in store. I'm sure there will be more than enough of the other kind.

Chapter Six

"Hey, wake up, sleepy head!"

"What?" Milwaukee shook his head and squinted up into a blaze of sunlight. Michal was grinning and standing over him with her yellow paisley bandana covering her hair.

"Come on, rise and shine, my brown-eyed Amish boy! It's Day Five!"

"Who's counting?"

"I am. I'm keeping a journal too, just like John Steinbeck. Come on. I need something hot to eat."

"What time is it?"

"Almost seven. And I need to get to a phone too."

At the bike Michal spread open a map and they estimated that Roanoke was closest to where they had camped. Milwaukee traced the maze of roadways with his finger. "We don't have to get on the Interstate 81. We can stay on the Blue Ridge Parkway and waltz right in."

They sped through the green mountains to Roanoke, parked at a diner and had a breakfast of pancakes and sausages and scrambled eggs, then Milwaukee stretched his legs while Michal used a pay phone.

"Ma?"

"Michal, is it you? Thanks be to God."

"What's the matter? Is anything wrong?"

"Nothing is wrong. But it has been three days since the last time you called."

"I'm sorry, mama. We have been in the mountains. The Blue Ridge Mountains. I had no opportunity to use a telephone."

"How are the mountains, my dear?"

"Beautiful, beautiful. Have you had any word from Tabitha?"

"No. No word."

When Michal finished her call she found Milwaukee standing by the Honda with the map open on the seat.

"How is everyone?" he asked, glancing up.

"They are fine. Everyone Amish in Marietta say hello and maybe a few who aren't Amish."

"What about Nick and your sister?"

"They haven't heard a thing. Neither have Nick's parents, the Ferleys."

"Well then I guess I'm not sure which way to go."

"Show me."

She bent her head next to his to look more closely at the lines on the map. Milwaukee became acutely conscious of the scent of her hair that was only inches from his face. She had washed it using a shampoo she'd purchased from a store across the street. He could see her hair was still damp under the yellow bandana. Michal glanced at him.

"What?" she asked. "Nothing."

"Well, it's something. Did I grow another head?"

"Just your hair—it's nothing."

"My hair is nothing?" Her full smile, as close to him as her hair, agitated him and he looked back at the map.

"We'll be in North Carolina soon. I can cross over at Danville. Then I'd like to head for Durham and Raleigh. There's something I want to see."

"Milwaukee."

He looked back at Michal. Her blue eyes gleamed as they caught the morning sun. A finger touched his mouth.

"It's okay to like me. We made up at the Susquehanna, remember?"

The dizziness came over him that he had not felt since their movie date in Lancaster City. "Yes, I remember."

"Well, you seem so—distracted—and restless."

"It's got nothing to do with you, really, I know we're friends."

She nodded and made a little face. "You're just not sure what kind of friends?"

"No, it's just—" Milwaukee's mind raced, looking for the right thing to say. What he felt did have a lot to do with whether they could go back to the intimacy of that movie date or whether that was a closed door. But he had no intention of bringing it up and did not want a kiss from her in sympathy. "I'm not sure—what to do—or where to go—"

She stared into his eyes a moment and then straightened up. "Well, wherever we go, I need a shower tonight and we both need a laundromat."

"Right." Milwaukee continued to study the map without seeing anything, aware that she was still staring and trying to figure out his mood. Finally a number caught his eye. "The 86 is a secondary highway I can pick up at the state line. It'll take us right into Durham."

"Okay," she said, not breaking off her stare.

"Okay," he responded, folding up the map and avoiding her eyes. "Let's do it."

She put her hands on her hips. "Is there something you want to tell me?"

"No." He put on his helmet. "We're supposed to be finding your sister, remember? Let's not waste any more time."

"Who's wasting time? The trip is supposed to be about us too—remember?"

A half hour into North Carolina an east wind blew a late spring storm in off the Atlantic. Cold rain, ice pellets, and sleet pelted them as they rode past dark green fields and rolling forests. Milwaukee pulled over so they could put on rain ponchos, but by then they were both soaked through. They carried on, passing gray wooden shacks and huts and small white houses.

Once they came into Durham, the storm still blasting, Milwaukee followed signs to Duke University and motored slowly from one end of the campus to the other.

"Isn't the chapel cool?" he asked Michal.

"It's like pictures of old Gothic churches in Europe," she replied. "The students all look as if their heads are glued to cell phones."

"Well, I wish we had one. Then we wouldn't always have to hunt down pay phones. They are getting scarcer and scarcer."

"No cheap cars on this campus."

"Not many."

"Will you walk one of the quads with me?" he asked.

"And a quad is what? You say quad and I think of one of those four wheelers the English herd livestock with in Pennsylvania."

"No, it's one of those grassy lawns with buildings on all four sides.

Let's do this one with the clock tower. I think they call it the Crowell Quad."

"Okay."

"You don't mind the rain?"

"What rain?"

He glanced back at her as they came to a stop. Rain and wet covered her face. Long strands of black hair were plastered to her skin just like the night they sat on the courthouse steps in Lancaster. Her smile was full, her teeth as white as the sleet that had covered their shoulders on Highway 86. Feelings rushed through Milwaukee in a gust. He looked away quickly and turned off the engine.

Students were hurrying past, most without rain jackets, many texting or talking on their cell phones as they walked and ran. Milwaukee and Michal made their way around the quad, their runners sinking into lush grass and water, looking at the high tower and stone buildings. She took his hand.

"I haven't had a hold of one of these since I fell asleep and asked you to chase away the bears."

"Sorry my fingers are so cold."

"Warmer than mine. So what's this about, Milwaukee Bachman?"

"Duke? I don't know. I read about it somewhere. The New South. Equal education and equal opportunity for the great-grandchildren of former slaves and former slave owners. Makes me wonder why the Amish only go as far as eighth grade. Why can't we go to college? Why can't we take Masters degrees or doctorates? What's the sin in becoming a physician or an attorney or a PhD? Or even a minister who can read the Bible in Hebrew and Greek the way it was written, find out what other Christians believe, not just the Amish and Mennonites, read books, discuss, argue, learn to listen to another point of view, change, grow—you know?"

She smiled and squeezed his hand. "I'm the almost not Amish. You're the almost Amish. At least you were last week."

Milwaukee shrugged in his poncho as the silver rain fell. "I just don't know why the Amish deny their children higher education. How come we can only have 19th century rural occupations? Grain farming, dairy, blacksmithing?"

"Farrier."

"Yeah, okay, but I want to know who decided it had to be this way? God?"

"I suppose the leadership would tell you that is what God has ordained for the Amish. It may be something different for the Baptists or the Episcopalians. But God has told the Amish to be the plain people. That's the package. Take it and be baptized. Or leave it—and walk away."

"I want to find another school. It's not far from Durham."

"Which one is that?" Michal asked.

"The University of North Carolina at Chapel Hill."

"Okay, Wyatt."

He looked at her. "What?"

"Wyatt in Easy Rider."

"I'm not Peter Fonda's Wyatt, " he protested. "Well, you're sure not Dennis Hopper's Billy."

They got back on the Honda and she leaned forward to speak into his ear as he switched on the engine. "Why can't we have biker names?"

Her head was very close to his. "I—uh—okay, but what for?" he managed to get out.

"Just for fun. Can't we have fun?"

"Sure—okay—I guess—"

She punched his shoulder. "There you go acting all weird again. You and I need to have a talk."

"Now?"

"No, not now. Take us to Chapel Hill. And think of a biker name that suits me."

"How about Almost Not Amish Biker Girl?" Milwaukee suggested. "Ha. Too long."

They pulled into Durham traffic. "*Biker Madchen* in German."

"Good. But not good enough."

"*Biker Kuken* for Biker Chick," he tried again. "Oh, my mother would love that," laughed Michal. "So yes?"

"So no."

"I'll have to think about it."

"Don't take too long," she said. "I already have yours picked out."

"Really? What is it?"

She leaned forward and spoke into his ear again. "Chrome."

"Chrome? Why Chrome?"

"Because you shine," she told him, "I shine," he repeated.

"You do shine."

"That's the Duke Medical Center," he said to change the subject.

"It's huge. Look at all the lights."

"Yeah."

"And what's with all the helicopters?" she asked, craning her neck to stare up at the roof of the massive building. "They make it look like a military base."

"And that's something else. Wouldn't it be cool to learn to fly a chopper? Save lives? But no, good Amish boys can't do that either."

"Or good Amish girls."

They rode south and west a few miles to Chapel Hill in the ongoing rain and again puttered through different parts of the University of North Carolina campus, stopping under another high clock tower near the university stadium.

"Do you have a thing for these things?" she asked.

"What things? Universities?"

"Clock towers."

He laughed. "Just keeping track of time. Each of us has only so much time."

"That's a pretty serious thing to say on a road trip."

He sat on the bike, its engine idling, and watched the minute hand move. "This is more than a road trip, Michal."

She shuddered and he glanced back at her. "Are you all right?" he asked.

"Sure, I'm okay, it's just—"

Without thinking he reached out and touched her hand and cheek. "You're freezing. You're shivering." He yanked up the side of her poncho and pushed the sleeve of her jean jacket back. Her arm was wet and chill and covered in bumps. "Why didn't you say something?"

"Why, I didn't—I mean, it hasn't been that bad—it was nice to see you excited about Duke and Chapel Hill, I really didn't want to interrupt the process—"

"The process?" he throttled up the Honda. "I've got to get you to a warm room and hot shower."

"Milwaukee."

"What?"

"Don't be angry. I liked seeing you—intense—"

He gave her a crooked smile, not sure what to make of what she'd just said. "Yeah?"

"Yeah."

"So now you're about to see me intense about getting you in out of the storm."

"Please find trees." She put a hand on his shoulder. "The trees in North Carolina are incredible. Please find a motel tucked away among the trees."

Their eyes met a moment. "I will," he said.

Racing down a small highway he saw a place off the road that consisted of rustic cabins that looked clean, solid, and well maintained. A small forest was all around them. He pulled in and got her into a deluxe suite and took a shoebox for himself.

"What are you doing?" she demanded. "We don't have money to throw away like this."

"Throw away? I'm trying to keep you alive. Besides you're the Queen of the Highway."

"Don't talk nonsense!" she flared. "I am not the queen of anything."

"Having food, shelter, and clothing we shall be content. So be content. Besides, they gave me a discount."

Her nose had reddened in her anger. "A discount, *ja?* And why should the English offer you a discount?"

"Just a crazy reason. Bess Miller painted that Jesus fish on the Honda's tank last year, right? And inside the fish she painted a motorcycle."

"So?"

"So they give discounts to Christian bikers—25% because the owner became a Christian through a biker club that was part of a Pentecostal church."

Still wanting to argue, Michal changed tactics. "And you call that a crazy reason?"

"Never had it happen before. The Amish don't look twice at the fish. I'm sure most would like to scrape it off with a razor blade because they consider it a graven image. Are you ready to get in out of the rain now?"

She was not ready, Milwaukee could see. There was some final word she obviously needed to get in. She crossed her arms over her chest as water ran from the hood protecting her head. "And what kind of deluxe suite have you put me into? Something to do with Harleys and outlaw bikers with great beards and even greater bellies?"

He grinned. "It's the honeymoon suite." Her mouth opened in surprise, but she had nothing to say. He began to walk the Honda to his own small cabin. "They have a laundry room and a café at the far end. Meet you for supper in an hour?"

She did not respond. "Yes?" he asked again.

"Ja, ja," she finally replied, coming back from whatever thoughts had transfixed her.

They let their laundry run while they ate. Both wore dry denim and ate as if they hadn't had a meal in days. Michal had placed a different bandana over her wet hair and others in the café glanced over at her more than once.

"You know you are drawing attention to yourself?" smiled Milwaukee. "Not very Amish of you."

"What? Why?" She looked down at her clothes. "It's just indigo denim and it's even baggy. Well, sort of."

"It's not the shirt or jeans. It's what you put on your head."

Her eyes went upward as if she could somehow see the bandana. "What's wrong with it?"

"It's bright."

"So?"

"Looks good on you." She grew quiet. "Oh."

"And it's the American flag."

"That's an okay thing, isn't it? I mean, this is America—or did we take the turnoff into Mexico by mistake?"

"We Amish don't fly the flag."

Michal frowned and Milwaukee marveled again at how good she could look whether she frowned or grew angry or even flew into a rage.

I have got it bad. This is not good. The road is too long to have it this bad.

"We Amish?" she snapped. "You said yourself no one's Amish until they're baptized."

"You're right."

"I'm in *Rumspringa*. I can fly the flag if I want. Even if it's from my head." She played with her grilled chicken, poking at it with a fork. Then she looked back up at Milwaukee and her blue eyes were the indigo of her denim and made him jump inside. "Besides, I've never agreed with that stand. They say the flag always means war and the military. No, it doesn't. Not to me. Maybe we don't have to fly it from every house, but—" Then she stopped and thought about what she'd just said. "We *could* fly it from every house though, couldn't we? What would be wrong with that?"

He shrugged and looked down. "Just not used to seeing you in a do rag. Or wrapped up in the flag. But I like it."

"You do like it?"

"I just said I did."

"Because one moment it seems to me we're friends, and everything is good, like right now, and then I do something or say something—I don't know what—and you shut me right out and I don't understand how I've hurt or upset you. Could you explain that to me, please?"

Milwaukee wiped his mouth with a paper napkin. "Don't want my stuff to shrink or wrinkle. I'd better check the dryer."

She reached across the table and seized his wrist. "Oh, no, you don't, Milwaukee Bachman. I've been checking my watch and the dryer still has 22 minutes to go. Now we've been on the road almost a week and there are going to be a lot more weeks after this one. I'm not going to spend them trying to get inside your head and figure out what's wrong with me. Is it my nose? My hair? You don't like my Amish accent anymore? I speak my mind too much? What is it?"

"Nothing—nothing—"

"It's something, Milwaukee Bachman, and you're my friend and Christian brother, you could at least be honest with me." Their eyes met. "Please," she said.

Milwaukee sighed loudly and leaned back in his

chair, closing his eyes and rubbing his forehead with his fingers. "How do I put this into words?"

Michal felt ice drop from somewhere inside her right into her stomach. Nevertheless, she wanted it out of Milwaukee and prodded him. "Try. You are the one who is clever with words."

"Not about you, I'm not." He sat forward and put his hands on the table. "Okay, look, there's nothing wrong with you. You're better than a movie, better than any woman I've seen on a film poster. Sometimes your eyes are blue steel, other times they're sky, then they're river or sea or storm and it's all—spectacular."

Michal's voice was soft. "Those don't sound like good reasons to be irritated with me."

"I'm not irritated with you, I'm—I'm irritated with myself. Michal, I like you too much. We've got thousand of miles to go and I like you too much. I want every day to be that rainy night in Lancaster. I'd never get tired of it—your touch, your kisses, never."

She had taken her hand from his wrist, but now she grasped his hand in hers. "We can have Lancaster again, Milwaukee."

He shook his head. "Not on this road trip. I made a promise to your father. I am not going to dishonor your family or mine."

"Oh, for heaven's sakes, are we back to that again?" She tightened her grip on his hand. "You treat me like a sister and a friend and—most of the time if you're not in one of your *I'm confused about Michal moods*—a very special woman too. So let's build on that."

"Build?" Milwaukee looked at her and laughed. "Build? I already have a tower as high as heaven when it comes to you. Michal Deborah Troyer is the most beautiful woman I've ever seen in my life. I lose sleep thinking about you." He put her hand to his lips and then gently put it down again. "Something as simple as that—you have no idea what it does to me. You smile, I pick up the scent of your hair, your head gets close to mine, your eyes shine like sapphire, and I'm gone. You're a lightning storm in me, yes, don't smile, it's like thunder and lightning going through my head and my heart. What am I supposed to do with that?"

She played with his fingers as they stared at each other. For a moment she wondered if people at other tables could hear their conversation and then didn't care—they were using Pennsylvania Dutch that she doubted any of them knew.

"I have feelings for you too, Milwaukee Bachman," she said. "And they can be pretty strong, yeah—" She smiled. "Twister strong."

She could see by his face that her words pleased him, so that was something, she thought.

"That makes me feel great," he admitted. "It really does. But all the more reason to—to "chill out" as the English say—*Beruhige dich*—and just slow everything down—well, except the bike."

But she didn't laugh at his little joke. "So what does that mean? Can we not hold hands any longer? You haven't kissed me since the courthouse in Lancaster— do we not kiss until we reach San Francisco or Seattle? Do we never make eyes at each other? What are we? Casual acquaintances? Brother and sister? Ships that pass in the night? Tell me what it is right now that is between us, Milwaukee Bachman."

He shrugged. Neither of them had let go of the other's hand. "We are waiting," he said.

"Waiting?" Michal felt like she wanted to jump through the ceiling in exasperation. "Waiting for what?"

"Waiting for God."

"What is it that God has to do?"

"Make it clear." He squeezed her hand, let go, and got to his feet. "You are still the best friend I've ever had."

Michal's eyes widened. "Oh. I am? Terrific. Just what I wanted to hear. Great. Thanks. *Vunderbar.*"

"No, really, I—"

She waved her hand at him. "Go check on your dryer. Time is up. Everything is wrinkling and shrinking. Hurry."

Looking miserable, he left the café. Aware that there had been a fight of some kind, people were still glancing her way, but not, she knew, because of the do rag. She tried to eat more of her chicken, but gave up and asked the waitress to box it for her. Milwaukee's plate was empty—he had finished his food before the confrontation.

"Smart man," she whispered. *Kluger Mann.*

She went and sat in her honeymoon suite and folded the laundry he had dropped off while she remained alone at the café. When she had tried to pay the bill and leave the restaurant she found it had been taken care of.

Smart man, kind man, but not her man. She obviously scared him to death.

Michal went and stood in front of the floor length mirror that was in the shape of a heart. Removing her do rag she began to brush out her hair, then stopped and examined herself critically. What was it about her that got him worked up so much? Her nose was too small, her mouth too wide, her eyes too gray and far apart, her hair too black and too wavy. At almost six feet she was too tall as well. What was the big deal? Why couldn't he just like her in a normal boyfriendy way and tease her and kiss her now and then? But no, *nein*. It was *Alles oder nicht* for him. All or nothing.

She blew out a lungful of air as noisily as she could and shook her head.

"The rest of the trip," she said out loud to her image in the mirror, "is going to be a disaster."

Chapter Seven

The next day was cloudy and cool. Michal pulled her hands up into the sleeves of her jean jacket and crossed her arms as she walked across the parking lot, stars and stripes do rag on her head. She caught a reflection of herself in the glass as she opened the door to the café.

Oh, mama, I am a whole lifetime away from Marietta, Pennsylvania.

Milwaukee was seated at a table drinking his coffee and staring into space. She sat down and was determined to be cheerful even though she felt muddy and rainswept inside. Smiling, she picked up a menu.

"Hi," she greeted him.

He eyed her cautiously. "Good morning, Michal."

"Did you order?"

"Not yet. I was waiting for you."

"Why, thank you. What looks good?"

"I was thinking waffles and strawberries with whipped cream. Real whipped cream."

She raised her eyebrows. "Trying to fatten me up for the kill?"

He looked down at his coffee and smiled a small, awkward smile. "I'd never try and ruin a good thing."

The words caught her by surprise. She hadn't expected him to start the day off with a compliment. Well, if he liked her that much why couldn't he loosen up a bit so they could enjoy the adventure God had set up for them?

She thought so much she never responded and then the waitress was asking her if she wanted coffee and if they were ready to order. They both asked for waffles with strawberries and whipped cream.

Michal sipped the steaming black coffee the waitress had poured. "Do you have my father's Bible on you?"

Milwaukee tapped the chest pocket of his denim jacket. "Would you read us something from it, please?" she asked.

Milwaukee tugged it free and flipped its pages. "Don't know what part."

"Oh, let us do the time honored thing and allow it to open where it wills."

He set it down on the tabletop. Some pages fell to the left, others to the right.

"Where are we?" Michal wanted to know. "Judges."

"Judges, okay."

Milwaukee began to read about the tribe of Dan looking for a place to settle and sending out spies. Michal noticed people were glancing their way again that morning as he read out loud to her in German. *I suppose,* she thought, *they cannot figure us out.* She sipped from her coffee. *Well, we can't figure ourselves out either.*

Milwaukee had stopped. "What is it?" Michal asked.

"The next verses seem—strange, *seltsam*."

"Well, what are they?"

He looked down at the Bible and shook his head. "Crazy, crazy, *verruckt*."

"Oh, you can drive me *verruckt,* Milwaukee Bachman. Read the verses out loud. Please."

"Ja, ja."

Then they said to the priest, "Please inquire of God—will our journey be successful or not?" And the priest answered them, "Go in peace. Your journey has God's approval."

"No!" Michal laughed. "Show me!"

Milwaukee pushed the Bible over to her. "Judges 18 verses five and six. And your father did not underline them as he does in other places so there is no reason the Bible should have opened there on its own."

Michal was reading the verses. "What do you mean *no reason*?"

"I mean no human reason."

Michal looked up from her father's Bible. "But this is wonderful. Don't you think it is wonderful?"

"Sure, sure, but it's still strange."

"Why? It's God talking to us through his Word. Didn't he promise to do that? Doesn't he do that all the time?"

"Sure, but—it still surprises me when it happens and then I wonder if I myself made the Bible open there, you know, on purpose."

"Did you?"

Milwaukee made a face. "I've never read those verses before in my life. I don't even like Judges."

Michal laughed again. "It's so refreshing when God gives you a kiss on the cheek."

Milwaukee smiled. "Or a manly clap on the back."

The waffles came, Milwaukee gave thanks for the verses and for the food, and they began to eat with far more energy than either of them had had when they entered the café. Milwaukee drenched his waffles in maple syrup, Michal was content to smear the whipped cream over her pieces and take them into her mouth like that.

"Where will we head today?" she asked after she had swallowed a large portion.

"I don't know," he answered.

"A university maybe?" she teased.

"I've had enough of those to frustrate me at being Amish for a while, thanks. No, I'm wondering about Tabitha and Nick. Did they go west to Tennessee and the Great Smoky Mountains? South to Myrtle Beach or Savannah?"

"Are those far away?"

"No."

"Then they're probably not in either of those places anymore, are they?"

"Unless they decided to stick around for a week or two. Do you ever think about what you'd say to your sister if we ever caught up with them?"

He gave her one of his intense, serious looks, his eyes dark.

Michal nodded and scooped up a forkful of strawberries and whipped cream. "Of course, I think about it. But God is sure going to have to put some words in my mouth when the time comes. I have no idea what she'll listen to and what she won't. She could be in any mood."

"Do you think she'll ever phone home or send a letter or—?"

"What time is it?" Michal jumped out of her seat with whipped cream still on one side of her mouth. "It's five after nine. I've got to use the pay phone outside."

"Do you need quarters?"

But she had already run out the door. People glanced his way. He used his fork to poke a strawberry into his mouth. *No, we are not having another fight, but think what you like, it makes no difference to me.*

Michal was back in a few minutes. She leaned on the table with both hands, her eyes gleaming. "They are in Florida."

"What?" Milwaukee put down his fork. "How do you know that?"

"Mama told me they got three postcards yesterday afternoon, all at once. One from a place called Sarasota, another from Orlando, a third from—Key Largo? *Ja,* Key Largo."

"But when were they mailed? And from where?"

"My mother is so smart. She had them in the pocket of her dress because she was sure I would ask her questions. One was mailed ten days ago, another a week ago, the third five days from today. But they were all Florida postmarks."

"Okay." He got to his feet and drained his coffee cup. "Finish your breakfast and we'll make a run for it. I'll gas up and after that we can pack our clothes in the saddlebags. We should try the interstate again."

"Are you sure the interstate's a good idea?"

"We can go straight as a ruler into Florida. There's no faster or more direct route."

But the 95 was no kinder to them than it had been at the beginning of their road trip. The Honda did not have the speed or size and vehicles constantly ignored the 250cc bike or crowded it. Milwaukee grit his teeth and complained he needed a touring bike, 1000 or 1200cc, but even a 750 would make a difference. Michal prayed while he muttered. In the middle of one prayer a large motorhome swayed into their lane and sideswiped them. Milwaukee fought for control as they skidded onto the asphalt shoulder and then laid the bike down, afraid they might flip. Sparks flew and metal shrieked. Michal felt her blue jeans and denim jacket ripping and tearing as she fell free and went sliding across the pavement. Then she was lying still and staring up at the gray North Carolina clouds with grass under her hands.

Milwaukee's worried face was suddenly right above hers, helmet off. "Are you hurt? Are you hurt?"

"I don't feel anything."

"You're bleeding. I'll get the med kit from the saddlebags. What about your head? How's your head?"

"It got banged around a bit. I feel okay."

But he was gone. She kept staring at the clouds. Then she heard a roar that got louder and louder. She knew it was the engine of a large motorcycle. It suddenly stopped. A voice boomed out.

"Hey, you kids okay? Whoever was at the wheel of the motorhome didn't even see you when they changed lanes."

A rough bearded face with a skull and crossbones

do rag took the place of the gray sky. He wore two ear-rings and there was a scar down one cheek.

She laughed. "You look like a pirate of the Carib-bean."

"Well, missy, I ain't Johnny Depp, sorry to disap-point." He turned his head. "What have you got there, buddy? I'll clean up her elbow and shoulder. You take care of the leg. Make sure you get all the fabric and grit out of the wound. Got alcohol in that bag?"

She heard Milwaukee's strained voice. "There's a big tube of Polysporin. And an antibacterial spray."

"We'll use both. You lay the bike down on pur-pose?"

"I didn't want to flip."

"Quick thinking." He looked back at her. She breathed in a strong scent of tobacco and leather. "Now honey, can you move your arms, your legs?" he asked her.

She moved all of them at the same time.

"Someone may have called for an emergency ve-hicle. Y'all don't need it. You're right as good God's rain. Just a bit of a slide after all." He turned his head to talk to Milwaukee again. "Gimme one of them water bottles and a towel."

"Yes, sir."

"No one's called me sir since I was a Navy Seal so don't start it up again. Where you kids from?"

"Pennsylvania."

"Yeah? What are you doing on the interstate in that scooter?"

"That's all we've got."

He grunted. "Y'all better stick to the secondarys after this."

Milwaukee's voice sounded apologetic. "We were trying to make time."

The pirate head disappeared, but she could still hear his voice. "Why? You in a race? Use plenty of water. Slop it on."

For the rough man she took him to be his hands were surprisingly gentle and careful. He folded back the edges of her jean jacket and she twisted her head and watched as he brought out a folding knife and cut away the torn denim. Then he cleaned her wound with water and dried it, used the antibacterial spray, finishing up by placing thick wads of gauze on her elbow and upper arm and taping them securely. She could feel Milwaukee awkwardly cleaning her knee and leg and trying to get the gauze in place after the spray.

"I can sit up," she said.

"Okay, missy, but take it slow."

She felt a bit dizzy, but stayed upright. The bearded man cautiously removed her helmet and checked the top and back of her head with his fingers.

"No blood. At least on the outside. Hurt anywhere I'm touching?"

"The only places that are sore are where you two bandaged me."

"Good helmet. Took a few whacks for you. But mostly what we got here is road burn. Now how about your boyfriend?"

Michal was going to say, *He's not my boyfriend,* but decided to let it go. She saw that Milwaukee's right shoulder was torn open and bleeding.

"I'm fine," Milwaukee told the big man, who was at least a foot taller and 50 pounds heavier, none of it fat.

"You ain't fine," the man grunted. "Let's clean 'er up."

On the back of the man's leather jacket was a winged skull with a large patch over it that said HELLS AN-GELS. Underneath the skull was another patch that said LOUISIANA. It startled Michal and she felt a twinge of fear. Hells Angels were outlaw bikers that committed crimes and dealt drugs—why had he bothered stopping to help them?

"Okay, let's see if your scooter'll run."

Milwaukee waited, thinking the man was going to try starting it.

When the man realized this he folded his thick arms across an even thicker chest and shook his head. "Not me, Ace. Don't touch such bikes. You go ahead."

Milwaukee picked up the bike, rolled it onto the wide shoulder of the Interstate as traffic zipped past, then straddled the Honda Rebel and switched on the engine. It coughed once and snarled to life. The man made a face.

"What a surprise." He went to his black and chrome Harley. "Fayetteville's only a little ways ahead. We'll get off there and put you on the 87 down to Cape Fear where you can pick up the 17. That's a decent secondary that'll take you all the way to Orlando if you want. Where you headed?"

"Orlando's one of the stops," Milwaukee. "So that'll work?"

"Yes, sir."

"Knock that off, Ace. Keep your helmets. I guess you're under 21 so you'll have to wear 'em there too." He patted the back seat of his Harley. "I believe your girl'd best ride the Fat Boy until we get you to the secondary. You agree?"

Milwaukee looked glum. "Actually, yeah. It'd be safer."

"You okay with that, missy?"

Michal wasn't, but didn't know how to say no to someone who had just given them so much help. "I'm okay with that."

"Climb on. You two have extra gear? Another pair of jeans? Jackets?" Milwaukee nodded.

"We'll pull into a gas station at Fayette and you can change over." He straddled his Harley and started the engine. It swiftly drowned out Milwaukee's Honda. "Name's Skid by the way."

"I'm Michal. My—boyfriend—is Milwaukee."

"Milwaukee's not bad for a biker name, not great, but not bad—drop Michal, it doesn't work. I'll call you Roadburn for today. Let's go. Stick close—Milwaukee. By the way, kid, your scooter looks a heck of a lot better with half its paint scraped off."

They waited for a break in traffic and then moved back into the stream of cars and trucks. Michal rigidly held the sides of her seat as they thundered along the 95, refusing to put her arms around Skid even if she went flying off the bike. As they rode the gray cloud cover peeled back to blue sky and sunshine. At Fayetteville they turned off the interstate and stopped at a gas station where her and Milwaukee could get changed. Then they sped down the 87 toward the Atlantic. At a small town called Tar Heel they pulled off at JC Chicken Ribs 'n' BBQ and Skid treated them to a lunch despite their protests.

"What y'all gonna do in Orlando?" Skid asked as he dug into his ribs. "The Disney thing?"

"Well, we're hoping to meet up with friends," Michal told him.

"Yeah? They biking it too?"

"They're on—an Ironhead."

Skid stopped eating to look at her. "No kidding?"

"A 1979 Ironhead."

"Well, Roadburn, you have trouble locating them just ask around at the bike shops in 'Lando. No rider's gonna forget he saw a 79 Ironhead."

A little over an hour later they were bypassing the city of Wilmington and heading south on the 17, Michal still resolutely clutching the sides of her seat. At a town called Calabash they turned into a motel that was attached to a restaurant with a blue and red neon fish.

"End of the line, boys and girls," he grinned, "and time for Poppa Bear to get outta your hair and head on down the line. I gotta make Savannah, Georgia in time for supper. Now this here," he waved a hand to encompass the town, "this is your Carolinas fishing village thing. Like seafood? Hope so because if they see you ain't local and won't buy a plate of their famous Calabash-style fried fish they'll tie scrap iron to your feet and sink you in Tubbs Inlet, I'm not kiddin', they're real killers and fishmongers. I'd tell you to press on, but prices start to soar the closer you get to old Myrtle and she's only a little ways further on. You'll have a better night of it if you stop here."

"We could keep going," Milwaukee insisted.

Skid shook his head. "Rest up. Change your dressings. Have a good bath and soak 'em clean. You'll get through South Carolina tomorrow morning and be in Georgia for lunch. If you can extinguish that fire in your tails just a bit you'd love Sava, I know you'd love it, and stick for the rest of the day."

Michal was off the Harley and standing beside Milwaukee. "Thank you, Skid. You helped us out of a real jam."

"No problem, Roadburn."

"It means a great deal to me—to us. God bless you."

Skid stared at her and then burst into deep and rough laughter. "I can't remember the last time anyone said that to me. I thought God and me lived on different continents."

"Well, I'll say it again, Skid—God bless you. We'll be praying for you."

"Whoa, Roadburn, this is taking me way out of my comfort zone. Next you'll be saying Jesus loves me or something like that. No, wait—" He laughed and threw up his hand. "I see you're just about to open your sweet mouth and do just that. I gotta go. You two ever make it as far as the Louisiana Purchase look me up at New Orleans Harley. Maybe we can work something out and get you a real hog." He revved his engine and looked at Milwaukee. "Take care of Roadburn, mister. She's a keeper. Don't let the man in the moon steal her from you."

He called back over his shoulder as he eased back onto the 17, "And get some new gloves. The ones you guys got on now make it look like you did 25 miles on your hands."

Skid roared into traffic and was gone. Milwaukee looked down at his gloves and then at Michal's. Most of the leather on the heels of the palms was gone, he realized, on his and hers, black streaks they'd left on the pavement of Interstate 95.

"Some day God served up, hey?" he said.

They were both still watching Skid's HELLS AN-GELS back recede to the south of them.

"Our Samaritan," she said. "I suppose if I'd tagged him with that he would have keeled over."

"He almost did keel over. Something tells me God is not a big topic of conversation at Hells Angels clubs."

"Maybe not so much. At least not out loud."

"So—are you ready for some Calabash fish—Roadburn?" She smiled at him. "Is that going to stick?"

"It's pretty cute. I think so."

"May I have a warm bath first? Then the meal?"

"Okay with me. But I can smell the salt sea and it's like a lure to this farm boy. I'll take a walk down to the docks and look at the fishing boats while you're washing up."

Michal almost shrieked. "Oh, you will not! The bath and food can wait. I've never seen a fishing boat in my life. Take me to the sea, my brown-eyed Amish boy, take me to the sea—before the man in the moon does it instead."

She wanted to link her arm through his, but hesitated. "May I? Or is that moving too fast for you?"

He gave her a sheepish grin. "Moving too fast? Not today, Roadburn." Milwaukee reached out a gloved hand and touched her face. "I could have lost you, couldn't I? But thank God I didn't. Yes, thank the God of second and third chances."

Chapter Eight

At four the next morning the sting of her cuts and abrasions woke Michal. She dressed and went down to the docks in time to see the fishing vessels head out under the glittering stars. Then she sat on the pier in her denim jacket, jeans, and star spangled do rag, prayed, thought, and watched the sun come up. At six an on-shore breeze blew over her and warmed her to the point she decided to stay by the water another hour. The sky was a vibrant mix of bronze and blue when Milwaukee walked down to her on the gray wooden planks.

"Hey," he said. "Hey," she replied.

He sat down on the dock beside her. *"Guten Morgen."*

"Guten Morgen."

"How are you feeling?"

"Bumps and bruises. I'll be all right. You?"

"You have the big scrapes, not me. I just have the shoulder." He watched two seagulls land near them and bob in the water. "Listen. I've been thinking. We ought to throttle up on some things and throttle down on others."

Michal looked at him, perplexed. "Pardon me?"

"I mean, yesterday, you could have been, you could have been—" He hesitated, gazing out over the sea. Michal waited. He tried again. "If we were just in a normal Amish relationship I'd ask you to ride home with me in the buggy after a Sunday evening song service. But my buggy is a motorbike and the Amish song services are getting farther and farther away. I don't know. It's pretty confusing. There aren't too many guidelines to follow."

"And there are my father's commandments and expectations. You take those pretty seriously for a boy on *Rumspringa*."

"Yeah." Then he looked at her, the sunrise turning his brown eyes into a kind of gold that fascinated Michal. "I'm really unsure about whether to go left or right with you. But I know I don't want to lose you. I guess that's the part I want to throttle up. Maybe not zero to 60, but more than—more than a brother and sister in Christ."

"Oh." Michal smiled and hugged her knees to her chest. "And what does that look like for today?"

"I'm not sure, but holding hands again is good. A hug. A kiss now and then."

"So that puts us at, what? Thirty miles an hour?" They both laughed.

Milwaukee shrugged with one shoulder. "I think your father and mother would say it was all right for you to—wrap your arms around my chest when we're on the bike—for safety."

Michal felt a lightness moving about rapidly inside her. "Oh, yes, I'm sure papa would agree to anything that kept me safe."

"But your sister is the thing we must throttle down," he suddenly said, changing directions. "You know? If we caught up with them today or tomorrow—what if we walked into the diner for breakfast and there they were eating Calabash fish and fries—would they really listen to you, would your sister up and go back to Marietta after only a few weeks on the road? I don't think so. I'm not ready to go back to Marietta yet and I was supposed to be baptized by now. You yourself, do you wish to turn around?"

Michal shook her head. Although she missed her father and mother and the boys the thought of returning so soon did not appeal to her.

"So why do we think catching up to them so quickly will make a difference? Is God's timing our timing? Two or three months from now Tabitha may be ready to listen to you, but not today. So no more breakneck stunts on the interstate. We follow them as best we can, we stay close enough to run into them one day when the time is ripe, we phone your mother and ask where the postcards are from. But the rest of the time we think about two things, okay?"

Michal tilted her head and rested it on her knees, watching him get more and more intense and loving every moment of it. "And the two things are?"

"First, you and me. Even the bishop and the leadership talked about it. You and me."

"Good idea. And the second thing?"

"God, Christianity, the Amish, church, the whole thing about heaven and Jesus Christ and our souls— all of this, it is every part of it wrapped up into one package. Do we go Amish, do we go Mennonite, are we maybe Baptists inside or Lutherans or—or what are we? Do we go back to the Susquehanna six months from now and take our vows? Do we settle in New Orleans and I get a job at a bike shop like Skid? Is it maybe your sister who goes back to Lancaster County and Nick converts, but we are the ones who remain outside because we discover that is what is in us, we decide that is what God wants?" He looked back at the sea. It shimmered like hammered gold. "So this is also a big thing. Just like you and I are a big thing. Michal and Milwaukee are on the road to find the way to their hearts. And Michal and Milwaukee are on the road to find the way to God. *Straight is the gate and narrow is the way that leads to life and few find it.* We must give God time enough to work things through with us."

"Hey." Michal leaned forward and cupped Milwaukee's face in her hands. His skin and hair glowed in the early sun. "The road was always about Tabitha. But it was always about more than Tabitha. The road is love, my good friend, and God is love." She lightly kissed both his eyes. "Now let's eat some fish for breakfast and then let me wrap my arms around you on the highway so that I am safer than I was yesterday."

At first, as they rode down through South Carolina, she felt nervous about sitting behind him again on the small Honda and grasped the handles on either side of her seat so tightly her hands began to ache. When they stopped for gas in Charleston, Milwaukee did not even mention it. She went off by herself for a few minutes to look at some of the magnificent ante-bellum Southern homes and to pray to God.

So who is afraid of taking the relationship a step further now, Father? Am I not the one dragging my feet? Am I not the one holding back? We joke about this arms around his chest thing, but the truth is I would feel safer and more secure. It is also true it would add a degree of intimacy to our friendship I may not be ready for.

They carried on and still Michal kept her arms rigidly at her sides. But at a town by the highway called Coosawhatchie, leaning into a curve, she finally placed both arms across his chest and held tight. Once they came out of the curve she decided she did not want to take her hands away from his solidness and strength, that she really did feel safe when she was closer to him, and she leaned her helmeted head briefly against his back and squeezed.

"How is that, Chrome?" she asked.

"I feel like a million bucks. How about you?"

"I feel strapped in and secure. I'm not going anywhere."

"That's good, Roadburn. Because I don't want you going anywhere." They motored for hours up and down streets in Savannah, Georgia, marveling at the thick Spanish moss draping from large, crooked-limbed oak trees. Then they found a house with a bed and breakfast, surrounded by the same oak trees and moss, which looked like it had been built in the 1800s—it turned out to be 1769—and it was there they settled in for the next three days. After that they made their way further south through Woodbine and Kingsland, crossing St. Marys inlet into Florida and setting up camp at Neptune Beach for almost a week and sleeping under the stars.

"The sand is so white!" Michal exclaimed. "And the sky and sea are both turquoise!"

"A good place to bathe our wounds," Milwaukee smiled, "and let the saltwater work its cure."

"Look at how many different kinds of palm trees there are. God has finally brought me to my tropical beach. All the Amish should see such heavenly wonders."

"Well, some might call such beaches a temptation."

"A temptation to what? A temptation to worship God?"

"Is that how the color of the water makes you feel?"

"Yes, yes, yes. So will you come swimming with me?" she asked. "I have my one piece. You did pack trunks, didn't you?"

"*Ja,* I have those. You're not afraid of sharks?"

"Oh, they will no more have killer sharks here than they had killer bears in the Blue Ridge Mountains."

The seawater and sun did seem to shrink their scabs until by the end of their week at Neptune Beach hers were hardly larger than a dollar bill and his no bigger across than a fifty-cent piece. Michal cut the torn sleeves off the denim jackets they'd worn during the accident in North Carolina so they could have something comfortable in the Florida heat and humidity. Then she cut off the ripped jeans at the thigh so they had cutoffs as well. They did not bike in the cutoffs or sleeveless jackets, nevertheless by the time they made it into Orlando on highway 17 their legs, arms, and faces were like brown sugar.

"Now this is something," Milwaukee said, hugging her. "Blue eyes in a dark brown face with black hair that's going blonde."

She slapped him on his bare arm in the jean jacket

she'd cut and trimmed. "So sure when does black hair like mine turn blonde?"

"No, I'm not kidding. It must be the minerals in the saltwater combined with the heat, but you are getting streaks of silver. Look."

He pulled some of her long dark hair out in front of her eyes. The streaks were obvious and Michal was surprised because she had not noticed them before. Some were silver, some copper, some almost gold, three or four strands even a gleam of blue. She ran the hair through her fingers and laughed.

"So everything is changing. We have palm trees and tropical weather and water the color of gemstones and now we are changing too." She smoothed Milwaukee's hair back out of his eyes. "I am not the only one getting lighter. I cannot call you a brown haired Amish boy anymore. And what else is not the same?"

He kissed her on the top of head. "The churches are changing us too, I think."

Every Sunday, whether they had been in Virginia or the Carolinas or Georgia or Florida, they had attended a different church, their best denim clean as a laundromat could make it. The experience had overwhelmed them. They were used to long services in High German and Pennsylvania Dutch, sermons that could run anywhere from two to three hours in length, and slow hymns in German that praised God, but also focused on suffering for Christ and martyrdom. Everyone was in their Sunday best at an Amish time of worship, yet everyone still dressed plainly and simply, and they met in houses or barns. Now they saw pastors in colorful robes of white and gold or black and crimson who preached no more than 20 minutes or half an hour, people carrying large golden or brass crosses to the front of the sanctuaries Michal and Milwaukee sat in with the others, robed choirs singing at the top of their lungs, plates being passed for tithes and offerings.

Where the Amish used nothing but the human voice to praise God, the churches they visited played pianos and organs, flutes, trumpets, drums, electric guitars, almost any musical instrument to help them lift their voices to heaven. Some hymns were as slow as their German ones, it was true, and some hymns were originally written in German, Michal noticed, but others moved along at a blistering pace she found she could scarcely keep up with, especially if they were modern praise songs that sounded like rock tunes off the radio. The church that had bewildered and delighted her and Milwaukee the most had been a Baptist church in Savannah where the congregation had been almost entirely African-American and the music and worship beyond anything either of them had known or imagined. People clapped and jumped up and down and danced in the aisles and shouted while the pastor preached. Afterward they were invited to share in a Sunday meal with the church and that evening a time of prayer and laying on of hands. Once they made it back to their B and B Michal had asked Milwaukee to go with her to the Savannah beaches and sit among the tall grasses of the sand dunes.

A wind was up and brought waves crashing to shore. Even though it was night they could see surfers struggling to get on their boards and ride in to the sand. Michal took Milwaukee's arm in both of hers and leaned her head against his shoulder.

She spoke quietly, trying to understand herself.

"The black singing takes me out of what the English call a 'comfort zone'. But still it stirs things in me our Amish music does not always touch."

"Different things are bound to do that."

"So you think what I'm feeling is only superficial?"

"No, no, how could I say that?" protested Milwaukee. "How do I know what God is going to use in your life? It's just that something that is new usually has an impact on us. I cannot get that hymn we sang last week in that Methodist church out of my head. That "once was lost, now am found" one. The words are good and the melody is even better. You know, if it stays with me, I will consider that it has more to do with the Spirit of God than the fact it is new to me and that I find it beautiful."

She hugged his arm as a strong gust blew over them and flung her hair up and over her face. "That is what I mean. Some of these experiences are going to last. How can I say in a year's time, *Oh, I will only sing Amish hymns now until I die?* So I can never let these other songs bless me again? And it is not just the music, Milwaukee. It is the praying, the preaching, *ja,* even some of the ceremonies I like very much. And tonight when the pastor's wife put a hand on my shoulder and prayed for me, I did sense that God was there, that God was listening."

"Okay, well, we should just let God keep working on us like the sun and water, like the road, and see what we come up with at the end. Let's see what lasts."

Michal snuggled into him. "Yes, that's good, okay, that is the thing, to take more time at this and see what remains with us when the road is done."

"So and when are you going to sit up front and steer?" he asked. "Oh, not yet."

"But some time?"

"Sure, *ja,* sometime. Soon."

Michal came to realize, as the miles streaked past under their tires, that it was more than weather or landscape or churches that were changing her and changing him. The dolphins at Sea World in Orlando, and the orca, leaping and falling and smashing water into diamonds, they too got into her blood and soul. Hundreds of pink flamingos stepping carefully over emerald grasses also found a way in, as did blazing white pelicans, and vibrant parrots with plumage like a rainbow after the rain. Even the jagged toothed alligator, whose gleaming eye told her she was not looking at a half-submerged log, but a living and lethal creature, found a home in her head.

And when Milwaukee surprised her with tickets to her first ballet, Swan Lake performed at an outdoor stage in Orlando, the smooth and nimble dancers flitted in and out of her imagination for months. In fact, as Michal eventually discovered, they never left.

In all the places they stopped they always found time to visit the local bike shops and ask staff if anyone had seen an Ironhead 79, but they never had any success— until the afternoon they pulled into a Harley dealership between St. Pete's and Sarasota, on Florida's gulf coast, where every Harley bike and biker that stopped in were photographed, no exceptions. At first glance, the huge display of pictures in the window held no one that Michal or Milwaukee recognized. But then Milwaukee swore the bike in one 5 by 7 was Nick's Ironhead and they examined the riders more carefully. Michal suddenly put a hand to her mouth.

"She's cut her hair, I can't believe it, she's never cut her hair, neither have I, neither has any Amish woman in Marietta." Michal shook her head, unbelieving. "And she always loved her black hair. Now it's purple. As short as someone in the Marines and purple."

Nick had also changed his looks. He sported a braided ponytail that was platinum blonde, two huge silver earrings, and his face was clean-shaven, lean, and deeply tanned by the sun. Both of them smiled into the camera from the back of the bike. They were no longer wearing leather except on their legs. For tops they had only black leather vests with open necks.

"Did they make all the changes to fool us?" asked Michal.

Milwaukee glanced at her sharply. "How would they even know we're following them?"

"Because the Ferleys know what we're doing. They'd have told others. And eventually some of those others would have called Nick on his cell."

A few days later, as they camped by a beach in Sarasota that Milwaukee swore consisted solely of fine white sugar, Michal's mother read her a postcard from Tabitha over the telephone that ended with the lines, *If sis really wants to catch up to me she has to ditch the Honda, and maybe her Joe Amish boyfriend too, get on a Harley, and put on some speed. The Grand Canyon is still a possibility for a meeting place. And so is Big Sur in California. I might have something to say to her by then.*

Milwaukee was surprised and a little hurt by Tabitha's message. Still, he had no intention of doing anything other than staying on her and Nick's track. "Where was the card from?"

"Mama said it had a picture of Elvis on it and was from Tupelo in Mississippi. Then there was another from Graceland in Memphis and that card was all about Elvis too."

"I didn't know Elvis was a big deal to Tabitha."

"Neither did I."

"So do you want to head out tomorrow morning?"

"I don't know. I like it here."

"Mississippi's not that far really," Milwaukee said. "I was looking at points west the other day. You head into Tallahassee and then on through the Florida panhandle to Pensacola. Then you're through a little strip of Alabama in no more than an hour and suddenly it's Biloxi, Mississippi. Even New Orleans is close by once you hit Biloxi."

"I have family in Mississippi," she suddenly told him.

Milwaukee stared at her as they sat together by the water. "Amish family all the way down here? I didn't know that."

"Well, they're not Amish now, I mean, he's not Amish. Uncle Samson is my father's brother. He never took the vows, was never baptized. So he was never a member of the Amish church and never shunned. I haven't met him. He's kind of offbeat. Another rough and ready biker type like Skid. But papa says he has a heart of gold so who knows? Maybe he'll help us just like Skid did. Father wrote him—Uncle Samson will be expecting us."

"Whereabouts in Mississippi is he?"

"I have it written down in my journal. Um—it has a

weird kind of name like Naez or Natchez—something like that."

"I guess we'll find it. We've found everything else. Even the things we weren't looking for."

"Yeah." She bit her lip. "You know what? I feel like my sister has done more than just hit the road and do *Rumspringa*. I guess it shouldn't upset me, but the thing about her cutting her hair off, it's just such a violation of the Amish way it makes me feel dirty. And then she writes such rude words and calls you 'Joe Amish'. It doesn't sit well with me."

"I can handle it."

"I can't. I feel like just riding off and not watching her back anymore. Let her live out her rebellion and let you and I carry on with our journey toward God."

"You don't mean that."

"Sure I mean it."

"You always felt that staying close to Tabitha was a big part of the journey God wanted you and I to take."

Michal sighed. "It's a different spirit than I've seen in her before. I don't like it. This is crazy, but I need you to pray over me in High German, yes, pray over me in the Amish way. The praying will cleanse me from the grime. God has showed us astonishing things among his people and in his world since we left Lancaster County. But there are still good things, strong things in the faith we left behind, aren't there, Milwaukee?"

"Yes. Yes, there are."

"So pray over me, my brother. And then could we sing, just softly while kids are building sandcastles all around us, could we sing *Das Loblied* together, yes?"

"Sure."

Milwaukee prayed in German while Michal bowed her head. Waves came against the sand, children squealed and ran back and forth with red plastic buckets and yellow plastic shovels, turrets and towers and walls rose, gulls wheeled and swooped and called out harshly to one another. Then quietly Milwaukee began to sing the slow and gentle hymn of the Amish people and after the first line Michal lifted her head, eyes glistening, and joined him.

O Gott Vater, vir loben dich
Oh God our Father, we love you

Und deine Gute priesen
And praise your goodness

Die du O Herr gnaidiglich
Which oh Lord so graciously

Un uns nie hast bevelsen
On us newly you have shown

Und hast uns here zusammen gefircht
And did lead us here together

Uns zu vemanned durch dein Wort
To admonish us with your Word

Gib uns genade zu deisen
Give us grace to accomplish this

When they were done they sat and watched the sea and the shining of the sun over its rolling surface. Finally, Michal took Milwaukee's hand and brought it to her lips.

"Okay," she said, "I am ready to follow my sister again and to pray God's love into her life. I'm ready to meet odd, offbeat Uncle Samson. I'm open to the open road. So take me to the Mississippi, brother. Take me to the big river and carry me across it in your arms."

Milwaukee smiled at the color of the blue in her eyes, a color as luminous as the morning sea and as vivid as a morning sky.

"Done," he promised.

Chapter Nine

They picked up secondary highway 84 at a place called Laurel in Mississippi. Michal would remember Laurel forever because a man pointed out a copperhead snake with its light and dark brown camouflage pattern at a gas station where they stopped, her and Milwaukee attended a warm and uplifting worship service at a Southern Baptist church in nearby Hebron, and on a short walk after the church's Sunday potluck she stood and stared at a tall magnolia tree that seemed to sparkle with fragrant white blossoms. The 84 took them to the Mississippi River, but not across. Natchez was there, an old Southern town surrounded by plantations that had thrived prior to the War Between the States. Natchez had been a busy site for loading cotton on ships and exporting it to Europe. The brochures Michal and Milwaukee picked up said it had been the economic capital of the Old South.

No one answered when she called the number her father had given her for Uncle Samson so Milwaukee took her on a tour of several of the plantation homes and properties. The hallways and rooms of the houses were cavernous and magnificent, decked out in period furniture and china and carpets, the grounds always green and well manicured and spacious. But when Michal stepped into the slaves' quarters on one plantation it seemed to her she could feel the loss of freedom of the persons who had once lived there and had a panic attack that made her feel she was trapped and enslaved herself. She was not in the building one minute before she fled, half-running across the grass and taking in deep breaths of the warm, humid air.

"What is it?" Milwaukee asked, quickly following her out.

"People were worked to death here," she groaned, standing under a tall oak heavy with Spanish moss. "They were not free to come and go. Slaveowners made them stay here all their lives. No liberty, no independence. It's as if they were caged."

"I know. I'm sorry."

"The Amish did not keep slaves. Never did our people do this."

"But we did own people in other ways."

Michal looked at Milwaukee in shock, her blues darkening. "No. In what ways?"

"There were immigrants from Europe who wished to come to America, but they did not have the money to pay for passage on a ship. So the Amish paid for these people to come. But then these Europeans had to work for a certain number of years for the Amish family or community that had bought their ticket, *ja?* So usually these people had skills in stonework or carpentry or the breeding of livestock. They were called redemptioners.

They were not free to go and do as they pleased

until the cost of their passage had been paid off in full by their labor."

Michal had paled as Milwaukee spoke.

"They were not whipped or treated poorly," Milwaukee protested as he saw the color leave her face. "They ate at the same table, slept in a bed in the same house."

"But they were trapped, weren't they?" she responded.

"I don't know if they would have called it being trapped."

"They could not come and go as the Amish came and went, could they?"

Milwaukee looked away from her eyes. "No."

"For how many years?"

"Five, six—I don't know how many years."

"How is it you are aware of these things?" she suddenly asked. "I have—been borrowing all kinds of books from the library in Lancaster City."

Michal sat down on the grass and leaned against the trunk of the tree. "Every day something new," she mumbled. "Some of it good, some not, all of it an opening of the eyes."

Milwaukee had his hands in the pockets of his jeans. "What would you expect? It cost hundreds of dollars to sail from Europe to America. That was a lot of money then, like thousands now. The Amish have always been sound businessmen. Did you think they could just distribute free tickets to whoever wanted them?"

Michal had become very quiet. She hugged her knees to her chest and stared up at Milwaukee. "Not to whoever. Just the names God brought their way. Just the people God brought into their lives."

"And what would you do about the cost of the tickets?"

"Is there something wrong with the tickets being a gift to the immigrants?" She held Milwaukee with her dark-eyed gaze. "Redemption is God's gift to us, isn't it? If love and forgiveness are God's gifts to us what is the big deal about the price of a few tickets?" Then, turning her head to the side, she rested it on her knees and looked away from Milwaukee to the former cotton fields of the plantation. "But no. We make prisoners of them in an Amish community and work them to the bone. So we praise God with the labor of others' hands."

Milwaukee did not say anything for what seemed like five minutes to her, but which she knew couldn't have been more than one or two. Finally he squatted down beside her.

"Hey."

She kept her head averted. "Hey."

"How about if I take you away from Simon Legree and the plantation?"

"Who is Simon Legree?"

"A slavedriver in a novel called *Uncle Tom's Cabin.*"

"Oh, you and your books."

"He was a real villain. The kind of hard-hearted slaveowner you're talking about. The book was banned in the South and caused an uproar in the North against southern slavery. When the author, a woman named Harriet Beecher Stowe, was eventually introduced to Abraham Lincoln, he said, 'So you're the little woman who wrote the book that started this great war.' Slavery infuriated her so she wrote the story and infuriated everyone else too. Sound like your kind of woman?"

"I don't know. Maybe."

"So long as you remember that not every family that owned slaves beat them to death," Milwaukee admonished her.

"Taking away another person's freedom is bad enough," she murmured.

"And not every Southerner believed in it. The famous Confederate army commander Robert E. Lee would not keep slaves."

"But he fought to keep a country that believed in it alive."

"It's more complicated than that."

"I don't think it's complicated at all. People do terrible things to each other. Isn't that human nature? Isn't the Bible right about that?"

"Yes. But can't a real faith in Jesus change the human heart?" He touched her on the shoulder. "I want to show you a horse named Twilight's Last Gleaming."

"You don't know such a horse."

"I do. I saw him and his sign when were puttering around Natchez. Come on, Harriet."

It was a slow tour of Natchez's historic downtown with Twilight's Last Gleaming taking his own sweet time in the swampy Mississippi heat. Michal had ridden in carriages, wagons, and buggies her entire life, but never at such a leisurely pace and never past so many beautiful flowering trees and shrubs.

"What's that—Poppa?" she asked their large and cheerful driver. "I said my name's Fat Poppa Daddy, girl."

Michal glanced at Milwaukee. He shrugged.

She tried again. "Um—Fat Poppa Daddy—that purple tree we just went past—"

"That's the Redbud. But the soils hereabouts grows it purple 'stead of the red, mm-hmm."

"And the one in front of that house with the white iron gate?"

"That? Dogwood? Common as fleas. A late bloomer, real late bloomer this house, don't know why. And them pink flowers, 'fore you asks, them's azaleas, okay?"

But Michal wasn't finished. "What about that yellow climber on the high wall there?"

The driver laughed like thunder. "Y'all don't give up, do ya, pretty sally? Carolina Jasmine."

"What a lovely name. You could name a child after that flower."

"Female child, mm-hmm."

"Petunias, I know those, and more azaleas. Fat Poppa Daddy, this is such a sleepy, wonderful town."

He grunted. "Sure, yes, sleepy today and most days. I swear Gleaming spends half his walks dozing and just lettin' his hooves do the thinkin'. But then Ol' Heavens Gate up and goes roarin' out or up and comes roarin' back and all the pigeons are looking for the west side of the 'Sippi."

Michal leaned forward and put her hand on Poppa Daddy's shoulder. "Pardon me? What's Heavens Gate?"

"What'd you call me?"

"Oh." She laughed and made the driver smile a smile, Milwaukee thought, as wide as the big river itself. "Fat Poppa Daddy—what's that y'all are talking at?"

"Ha!" Poppa Daddy almost shouted, making Gleaming twitch one long mule-like ear. Daddy twisted around and looked back at Michal. "We make you a Southern mama yet." He looked at Milwaukee. "Hey?"

Milwaukee nodded. "Sure."

"Marry this girl, my man. You could cross the country a thousand times and never find somethin' sweet, never somethin' sweet, she's the long river, my man, the long one you want."

Michal grinned and punched Milwaukee's shoulder. "Hear that? Don't miss out."

He smiled. "Believe me, I don't intend to."

"No?"

"Biker club," Poppa Daddy interrupted, as Gleaming clip-clopped left down a different street. "But not the outlaw kind, not them's Angels. But big Harleys, lots of black and chrome, lots o' heat and racket, sure. Now it's Ol' Heavens Gate himself lives just there—" he pointed "—just here with the magnolias and Redbuds and azaleas."

Michal and Milwaukee gazed at the trim white house with its pillared porch and black iron fence.

"There's a cross there among his azalea bushes," said Milwaukee. "Oh, the Christian man, oh, the gospel man, that's Troy Samson, the glory hallelujah man."

"What kind of biker club is Heavens Gate?" asked Michal.

"Glory hallelujah kind like him. All over the state, all over the South."

"Troy Samson?" repeated Michal.

"Him. Mister Holy Ghost Man. Good man, you hear me, awful goodish man, but the reverend kind, you know, not that you could tell just by lookin' at him, but you hear him pray or preach, you know sure then. Heard him once at a biker rally at the church catfish fry there, good talker, but him's Mister Holy Ghost Man, no one else is touchin' his wings, no sir." He twisted around again and looked back at them, grinning. "Biker name's Ghost. In this world, but not part of this world, he says."

"Is he home?" Michal asked. "Runs a store during the day."

"What kind of store?"

"Leather. Books. Bike stuff. Holy Ghost stuff."

"It must be him," whispered Michal.

Milwaukee gave her a puzzled looked, strong lines creasing his tanned face. "Who must be him?"

"Think about it. You move out of Lancaster County. You want to change some things. Especially your Amish name. So my uncle Samson Troyer becomes Troy Samson."

"You think?"

"I'm so almost positive, *ja.*"

Milwaukee had to smile at the way teenaged slang mixed with her Amish whenever she spoke English. "But how could you know for sure without going right up to him and asking?"

"He's my father's brother. It will be in the eyes, the way he walks, an expression in the face. I'll know."

The long, slow route through Old Natchez continued on past the town hall, courthouse, and library. Finally they made it back to their starting point and Poppa Daddy curbed the horse and carriage. Then he coaxed Michal to give Twilight's Last Gleaming a couple of large carrots.

"Say thanks you, horse," Daddy encouraged Gleaming. "Come on, sally pretty gives you roots, sweet orange roots, you say your thanks yous, boy."

Gleaming bobbed his head and stamped his front

hoof twice. Michal laughed and rubbed him between his eyes. The horse nuzzled her.

"You know horses," Daddy said.

"Been around them all my life, Fat Poppa Daddy."

"That so?"

She gave him a 20 dollar bill.

"What's that for?" he asked, taking it. "You already paid at the start. You one of them rich Yankee tippers?"

"No." She got back into the carriage. "We're going around again."

"You are?" Daddy asked.

"We are?" Milwaukee echoed the driver.

"And then I'll thank you to drop us off where Ghost lives."

"Ghost? Him?" Daddy was surprised. "Why you want to do that?"

"He's my uncle." She caught Milwaukee's eye. "Pretty sure."

"Uncle? How's that?"

"My father's kid brother."

"You say that? No fooling?"

"No fooling, Daddy."

He let her get away with the shortened form of his name. "Back in the day, he told me he was from the Far East."

"Well, we're far east, all right."

"Mm-hmm."

"What about our Honda we've got parked here?" Milwaukee asked. "We can walk back and get it later. If Uncle Samson is a Harley man he won't want to set eyes on it anyway."

A few others joined them for the tour and seats got

scarce. Daddy invited Michal to sit up with him and take the reins.

"Not that you'll have so much to do," he emphasized. "Gleaming does it in his sleep like I says."

"It's sweet of you." she kissed him quickly on the cheek.

Here comes that Big Wide Mississippi Smile, thought Milwaukee, and he was right. It did not bother him. He found he liked watching the effect a bright, blue-eyed Michal had on others, especially a Michal that was coming out of her shell. Men looked at her twice in cafés and gas stations. That didn't bother him either. He had caught himself doing the same thing on more than one occasion so how could he blame them? They'd only been on the road two months, but she seemed two years older of loveliness to Milwaukee.

You're no girl anymore, girl. You're a woman. The most incredible and beautiful woman.

The azaleas, Redbuds, and dogwoods drifted past once more, along with the iron fences, gates, porches, pillars and, now and then, an American flag hanging quietly from its pole. Then they reached Troy Samson's house a second time and Daddy spoke softly to Twilight's Last Gleaming. The horse came to a stop and stood still as cars passed by. Michal and Milwaukee jumped down. Daddy extended a hand from his seat and both of them shook it.

"You say hey when next you see me," he told them. "You gonna stick hereabouts a while?"

"A little while," Michal replied. "A week? Two?"

"Like to."

"Well, I can't imagine Ghost not treating you right. Come see me and I'll gets the two of you plates of hushpuppies and Mississippi coffee that'll put a holy kink in your hair."

Michal smiled. "Is that so?"

"Mm-hmm." He spoke to Gleaming and the horse began to move forward again. "You be God blessed. You be Holy Ghosted, my beauty girl."

Michal crossed the street and opened the black iron gate into Troy Samson's yard.

"Hey." Milwaukee hung back. "What are you going to do? Sit down in his living room?"

"No. Just on his porch."

"What if it's not him?"

"It's him."

"What if it's not?"

"He makes a new friend. Or two. And so do we." Her blue eyes shimmered in the Mississippi light and heat. "But it's him, Milwaukee. Don't you feel it? Don't you?"

Milwaukee didn't feel a thing except drowsiness from air so thick he was certain he could cut it like Jell-O, stack it on a tray, and serve it up with a tall glass of lemonade on ice. But he didn't tell her that.

"Yeah," he said.

She dropped herself into a white wicker chair on the porch.

Milwaukee felt uncomfortable about being at a stranger's house to begin with and restlessly walked about the yard, looking at the trees and flower bushes. He wandered around to the back and found a large double car garage. Peering through a dusty window he could see several motorcycles and pieces of engines and tires leaning against the walls. At the back door of the house was a red brick patio and an oil drum cut

in half and resting on an iron stand. It was full of bri-
quets and covered with a grill. As he headed back to
Michal he heard the clatter of big bikes coming down
the street. One after another they appeared at the corner, turned, and pulled up in front of the house.

The Harleys gleamed with chrome and the colors
of silver, blue, red, and black. Most of the male riders
had beards, some had long hair that stuck out from underneath their helmets, women and men all wore black
leather jackets and chaps even in the heat. Behind mirrored sunglasses, Milwaukee could see that their eyes
were on him and Michal. She stood up from the wicker
chair on the porch as one tall man unwrapped himself
from his black Harley and opened the front gate. To
Milwaukee he looked ten feet tall.

The man took off his glasses. "Help you?" he asked.

As soon as Michal saw his eyes and face clearly she
smiled and said, "Uncle Samson, I have come a long
way to see you."

The man hesitated, staring at her in her star spangled do rag, then nodded his head. "I've heard about
you. My brother wrote me a letter a little whiles back.
You sure don't look like much of an Amish girl."

"Well, you don't look like much of an Amish man."

He grinned. "You come at a good time. It's the night
for our barbeque and prayer meeting. You and your
boyfriend in?"

"We're in."

He laughed and put his glasses back on. "Don't
know what you're in for, girl. Get the pig, boys, and
stick her on the spit." He looked around at Milwaukee.
"Tonight's the night we grill the fatted calf in your
honor. Amen, bro?"

Milwaukee, hands in the pockets of his jeans, watched bikers twice his size and weight peel themselves off the backs of their Harleys.

"Amen," he replied, an uncertain smile on his face.

Chapter Ten

The pig was barbequed whole, head still on, which did not bother Michal, she was a farm girl after all. The men and women, despite their black leather and mirrored glasses and girth, couldn't have been friendlier, sipping their Dr. Peppers and Pepsis and munching from bowls of various kinds of potato chips—Michal counted eight different barbeque flavors. The bikers' talk about God and Jesus seemed intense to her, but when they went inside to the living room and air conditioning she found out why. Most of them came from a background of hard drugs, alcoholism, gang warfare, and crime that they spoke about freely as they asked for prayer.

"Jesus pulled me out from under a wreck," said one of the men, who went by the name Vapor. "I know most of y'all don't know me too well yet, but I'm not throwing out a story or a cliché. I wouldn't be sitting here in Ghost's house today, but for him leading me to the Lord. I went cold turkey on just about everything, but Jesus was pretty cool on letting me hang on to my bike." Everyone laughed. "But now and then temptations come sliding on back like a water moc sliming its way through a cypress swamp. Especially cocaine. So I'd appreciate prayer, the sooner and the more of it the better."

"Let's do that," spoke up Michal's uncle who, as Daddy had told her, went by the biker name Ghost. "Y'all that want to gather 'round Vapor, feel free. If you have it in your mind to pray out loud, go ahead and we'll pray right along with you. You okay with the brothers and sisters putting hands on your back or shoulders or chest?"

Vapor nodded. "If it helps 'em pray to God for me, I'm all for it."

Practically everyone except Michal and Milwaukee got off their couch or chair and joined the circle around Vapor. Most of them prayed out loud, their hands covering the upper part of his body. Others murmured "amen" or "the blood of Christ" or "yes, Lord" while men and women asked in strong voices for Vapor's healing and for his protection against the work of Satan. Michal found herself staring at the backs of their leather jackets where there was the image of an extremely rugged and weathered looking cross in black roughly wound about with silver barbed wire. Underneath the cross, also in a distressed silver, was John 10:9—*I am the gate. Those who come in through me will be saved.* Over the cross was the name HEAVENS GATE and below it NATCHEZ, MS. A few of the crosses were silver with black barbed wire and others had three long silver spikes strewn at the foot of the cross.

If I am out of that Pennsylvania comfort zone of mine again it does not mean that what is happening

in my uncle's house is not true or not real or not of
God. I am pretty certain it means I have been used to
the Amish faith for so long every other way of pray-
ing or blessing others seems strange and off balance.

Michal was familiar with people breaking down at
Amish services so it did not seem unusual for her to
see Vapor cry in another man's arms or women praying together and weeping. People called out at Amish
worship gatherings as well, not during the hymn singing, but during the long sermons if they fell under con-
viction, so none of the cries in the room disturbed her
either. What she was not used to were persons chal-
lenging Satan or claiming the blood of Christ or talking
about how the Holy Spirit gave them power to over-
come addictions to drinking or drugs or violence.
Yet, even though her and Milwaukee kept exchanging
glances as the evening wore on, she could not deny
the utter commitment the bikers had to Jesus as Savior and Lord nor the healing effect the hours of prayer
and worship had on those who were asking for help.

Her uncle played one song over and over again on
his guitar while persons prayed and others often joined
him when it came to the chorus. By the time the prayer
gathering had come to an end around ten o'clock Michal felt she knew the song by heart and was singing
it with as much strength as she could, inviting God to
reign in her, to reign in all their hearts. She sensed Milwaukee's eyes on her as she worshiped, but she did not
turn to look at him, preferring to get caught up in the
sort of meaningful vision of God she had not experienced in years. Even when she knew it was only Milwaukee and her uncle left in the room she remained
with her eyes closed and continued to sing the song

softly. Eventually she stopped and saw that Ghost had his head bowed over his silent guitar while Milwaukee was lying down on one of the couches with his arm over his eyes.

A minute or so after her singing had stopped Milwaukee sat up.

"I have to say," he told her quietly, for Ghost was still sitting with his head bent, "I wasn't sure I'd ever hear you sing like that again. And certainly not at your uncle's house in Mississippi."

"I felt—free—"

"Well—your freedom freed me."

"What do you mean?" she asked.

"It's just that watching you get caught up in worship again, listening to your voice move like air from an open window around the room, it turned some things over in me. " His eyes were the dark brown she had learned to associate with his most thoughtful and intense moods. "I'm glad we're on the road together, Michal. Grateful it isn't over or that we haven't turned back."

Things began to flicker once again in Michal. She had no idea what words she could use to respond to Milwaukee or if she should even attempt to describe feelings she had for him that never disappeared and were always ready, it seemed, to burst into light and heat. It was when he spoke in a certain way or his eyes carried a particular color and depth and rested on her in a manner that was extremely focused that everything she felt for him came back to life. Her time of worship had not only drawn her closer to Christ, but also, for some reason, closer to him, yet she could not think of any way to express this, so she sat looking back at Milwaukee and unable to part her lips and speak.

"You two an item?"

Ghost was staring at Michal and Milwaukee. Michal found her voice. "Well—we don't know."

"You need more time yet. You need more of the road." He put his guitar into its case. "I know about that. Believe me, I know all about that." He was sitting on the floor and leaned back against a chair, putting his hands behind his head. "We prayed for everyone else. Your turn now, Michal, Milwaukee. But to get to you we gotta start with me. You don't know who I am or how I got to this place and I'm the only one who's going to be praying over you tonight." He looked at Michal. "They tell you why I left Marietta?"

Michal leaned forward on her chair. "My father only said you had never been baptized and therefore you had never been shunned."

Ghost nodded, his hands still behind his head. "I can't blame Simon for not telling you more than that. I could ream off a million things about why I split 20 years ago. I wanted to serve in the Marines. Wanted to see the world outside my door. Wanted to ride a Harley every day for the rest of my life. But it's none of those things. The road always boils down to love in the end. If the love stops, the road stops. I left Marietta for love." He stared straight at Michal. "We both fell for Becky—your mom. Both of us worshiped the ground she walked on. But I loved my brother more than I loved her. And in the end, I left, I left for good, so that your father and your mother could become husband and wife."

Michal felt a shock run through her body. "What?"

"Sounds like Hollywood, doesn't it? But Simon wasn't about to back down when it came to Rebecca, the beauty of Lancaster County, and Rebecca couldn't make up her mind between the two of us, so I made up my mind for her, and for him. I loved them both. So I took to the road. And let them have the love they needed to have together."

Michal struggled to find the words she was looking for to respond to her uncle. "You didn't—marry—you didn't fall in love again?"

Ghost shook his head. "After Rebecca?" He glanced over at Milwaukee. "She looked a lot then like Michal looks now. How about it, Kee? Who stacks up to Michal? If you can't have her, who do you know, who have you met, that's just as beautiful and just as full of the love of God?"

Michal could see that Ghost had caught Milwaukee off guard. His face paled as he thought of the various answers he could give to her uncle. Then she saw in his eyes that he had decided to tell the truth. "There's no one, Ghost. No one like her. If I lost her, like you lost her mother, I'd have to batch it forever—just like you're doing."

Michal began to tremble all over both at Ghost's words and at Milwaukee's. Even when she clenched her hands together as tightly as she could it would not stop. *What is the matter with me? What is going on? I feel as if I could just throw myself on the floor and weep.*

"It's a lot to take in," Ghost said, "but there's something else you need to know. Your sister was here a few weeks ago. Her and Nick stayed over a couple of days."

Michal looked at him in surprise. "But—how did she know where to find you?"

"She had a bunch of addresses of different people she'd lifted from a book your father kept in his dresser. I'm not the only one from Marietta who was never baptized."

"How is she?"

"Good. Hair was wild—longer on one side of her head and orange—shorter on the other side and black."

"What?"

"Those are the Harley colors. Makes me think of Hallowe'en. We did some work on Nick's Ironhead and they headed out for Tupelo. I had a couple of chats with Tabi—that's what she wanted me to call her." He sat up straight and took his hands from behind his head. "Look, your sister is loving the road, but it's not gonna last forever. She misses Penn, misses Marietta, misses everything Amish. I'm not kidding you. Where are we at now? July? She'll be back home by the time the pumpkins are ripe and next spring she'll be baptized. Tabi will stick until the day she dies and they'll be burying her in her wedding dress."

"You can't be serious, uncle. If that is so then why all the fuss? Why the dramatic exit? Why was she in such a frenzy to see America if she loves the Amish way so much?"

"You ever wonder why she bothered to keep in touch?" Ghost asked. "Why the postcards home when she could have just as easily dropped off the map?"

Michal stared at him and said nothing. She had her trembling under control, but every now and then a tremor shot through her body.

Ghost took off the black do rag with a silver cross he'd been wearing all evening. His hair was cut short and the color of coal like her father's. He had one silver earring in his right ear and it was also a cross.

"Most Amish kids never learn the story of Hansel and Gretel," he said. "But I think you probably picked it up anyway, am I right?"

Michal nodded.

"Tabi's postcards were the breadcrumbs. She wanted to find her way back home again. She never wanted to lose touch with Marietta. And she never wanted Marietta to lose touch with her." He stood up and came over to Michal and picked up a chair, flipping it around so that the back of the chair faced her and he could lean against it with his chest. "Tabi wanted you to follow her, Michal. She wanted you out on the road a lot more than she wanted to be out on the road for herself."

"Pardon me?"

Ghost rubbed his hand over his mouth. "I doubt your sister would ever have made the effort to talk Nick into a road trip if it hadn't been for you. I think the whole thing would have just remained wishful thinking. But she saw that you were falling apart—losing faith in yourself, in the Amish, and in God. She convinced herself the only way to bring you back to your senses was to get you out of Marietta and make you look at the world away from the Amish prayers and hymns, away from anything to do with the Amish life. Then she was sure you'd realize what was most important, what was most valuable, that where your treasure was your heart would be also." Ghost gently unclasped Michal's hands and held them in his, the Troyer blue eyes in his face fixing themselves on the Troyer blue eyes in hers. "Michal, I told you the road was about love or it stopped being a road to anywhere or anything that mattered. Tabitha took to the road so that you would take to the road. This trip you're on has nothing to do with her. This is your journey, not hers. The only reason she headed out at all was because she loved you.

"All the risks she's taking on America's highways are because she loves you. And all the risks you're taking are because you love her."

Michal looked at him in disbelief and then began to shake again, more violently than before. He held her against his chest as she began to cry.

"I need to go to her," Michal groaned.

"No. She doesn't want you to go to her. She doesn't want to travel beside you. Not yet. Not until you find what you need to find on your own. Then you can meet up. But not before."

"What—what am I supposed to find?"

"What you lost."

"I don't know—how to do that."

"It's already happening." Milwaukee was kneeling beside her and rubbing a hand over her shoulders. "Tonight. On the sand dunes at Savannah. In the churches we visited in Florida and the Carolinas. You're making your way home."

"I don't—feel like I'm anywhere yet."

"We need more time."

"How much time?" Michal asked, her voice quavering.

"The kind of road we're talking about doesn't have a clock like other ones do," Ghost said softly. "All you can do is follow your sister wherever she goes. You're the one who will know the day your heart and soul come together. And I have a hunch Tabitha will know too. Because God will tell you both at the same time.

See, this is a spiritual thing, Michal. The asphalt and bikes and skies and palm trees are just scratching the surface. You gotta go deeper to the real road. The God road. When he gets you where you need to be it's like seven tall fountains will burst upward in your soul. Until then you keep going and you don't stop. Not on the pavement. Not in the spirit. You understand?"

Michal quivered. "I don't know—I don't know."

Ghost held her more tightly as she continued to tremble. "It's all right. You're with family. Blood family and spirit family. You're going to get strong. You're going to finish the journey. And you're going to find the Lord's way while you're making your own way. It will all tie together so tight you'll never unravel it again."

"I feel frightened now. Everything's reversed. I don't know my role. Don't know what I'm supposed to do."

"Each day you'll understand a little bit more. Each day you'll get a little bit farther." Ghost rested one of his large hands on her head and blessed her. Then he said, "Don't hold back, Michal. It's not a road of fear. It's a road called love."

Chapter Eleven

Day 76

I am sitting out in Ghost's backyard while Milwaukee
and him work on a bike in the garage. They are always working on a bike in the garage. I haven't seen
anything come out of all their work yet and there's
been more than two weeks of it. But they are happy
doing it, they get closer to each other every day, and
when I hear Ghost pick up his guitar—he doesn't call
it a guitar, he says it's a Martin, which is supposed
to make it different or something—and they start to
sing a song about Jesus together, I don't care if I ever
see anything mechanical come out of that shop. The
music is enough.

 I've figured out that there's no such thing as a quiet
night in Mississippi. Everything is singing or humming or chirping or calling. Katydids, bullfrogs, night
birds—for all I know the alligators have a tune too, and
the possums, and the water moccasins. The peaceful
Pennsylvania dark where you might hear an owl hoot
or a fox bark is unknown here. When you sit out after

nightfall in Mississippi you had better come prepared to listen to a symphony.

My first night here was such a shock. Everything my uncle had to tell me took me by surprise. Even after I thought it was all over with my shaking and uncle had gone to bed Milwaukee had to hold me while we were sitting and talking on the couch. You'd think I had some sort of illness. Milwaukee joked about it and said he was glad I had the shivers because then he got to hold me close for a long time. I'm glad it made him happy, but I was a mess for the next couple of days as I tried to sort out everything I'd been told. Not just what Ghost had said about falling in love with my mother or about Tabitha going on the road to force me to go on the road. What Milwaukee had said played around in my head a long time too—and we've never spoken about it. What does he mean when he says if he couldn't have me he'd be a bachelor the rest of his life like Ghost? Can he really feel that strongly about the two of us? If he does, well, when is he going to show it?

But now it's 16 or 17 days later and a lot has settled down in my head and heart. God has a purpose for me being on the highways and byways—he used my sister's love to get me here and he used my love for my sister to get me here. I don't think it's just about me though. Despite what Ghost and Tabitha think, God has something for them in store too, and for Milwaukee as well. It's all tied in together. But I have no idea how it's going to "play out", as the English say. In a few more days we'll be back on the map and heading for Louisiana and Texas—what will God have up his sleeve there? I don't know. I just follow my sister and follow the road and somewhere in there I am follow-ing the Lord too.

It will be August before we leave Natchez and say-ing goodbye to Ghost is going to be awfully hard. I'll probably shake and cry all over again. It just seems so sad to me—why couldn't he have fallen in love with someone else after he decided to give my mother to his brother? There are a lot of beautiful women in the world, I don't care how Ghost and Milwaukee go on about how mama looks or I look. Couldn't he have asked one of them to marry him? And what if it doesn't work out between Milwaukee and me? Is Milwaukee going to come and live with Ghost and help run the biker church and the leather shop, two bachelors rid-ing Harleys and reading the Bible and moaning about their lost loves over bottles of Dr. Pepper? It sounds crazy. But I have no idea what is going to happen by the time this road trip is over. Only God knows and he only tells me things a little bit at a time.

Michal volunteered to run the leather and gift shop in Natchez for three or four days while Ghost and Mil-waukee were out doing what they called "field testing". She didn't mind. Once Daddy found out where she was he found an excuse to bring Gleaming by every day. He always brought cold bottles of Dr. Pepper for both of them and they drank while they sat on the wooden bench in front of the shop that was called, predictably, Heaven's Gate.

"How you like living with that Holy Ghost Man?" Daddy asked her one afternoon while they sipped their Dr. Peppers.

"Oh, he's sweet," Michal smiled. "No shouting or

thundering. He can be very quiet when he's inside his house."

"No fooling?"

"Wouldn't know he was alive. Daddy, do you know something about his house?"

"What's that?"

"Everything in it is made in the USA. Just like his shop here."

"No one can buy like that anymore. Not without paying a million bucks for a shirt."

She shook her head. "He goes to yard sales and second hand stores and he finds stuff made by General Electric and Westinghouse and RCA, you know, toasters from the 50s, fridges and freezers from the 60s, TVs from the 70s. I don't know how he does it, but he gets the parts he needs to keep them running."

Daddy drained his Dr. Pepper. "What about clothes?"

"Same thing. Made in USA jeans from thrift stores and the Salvation Army. Shirts. Jackets. And what he can't find he makes or has someone else make." Michal swung her hand with the Dr. Pepper toward the store window. "What do you think's in there, Daddy? Leather jackets made in the States or made by Ghost. I'm not kidding, he has a big sewing machine in his basement. Same with leather chaps and gloves or anything—if it's not made here or he can't make it, he won't sell it."

Daddy frowned. "Who in America gonna make underwear for you these days?"

"Oh, that," she laughed, "that's the best part. He has these biker mommas in their 60s and 70s, tough as steel, but hearts big as the Mississippi, and he pays them to make socks and underwear as well as shirts and jeans or other items he can't get or doesn't have time to make himself. Sells them through the store. He pays the ladies well too."

"How's about the microwave? Or the computer?"

"His computer is all USA, Daddy, he pieced it together himself. As far as a microwave goes he doesn't want one. He says it just puts radiation in your food and in your blood. Regular oven or toaster oven made in the 50 states is fine for him."

"Oh, he's got the bases, all the bases." Daddy looked at her closely. "Now what are you doing next, sally pretty? How long before you are the road girl?"

She patted his back. "Not till next week. So we still have a lot of days to visit with each other."

"And what are you gonna do out there you can't do here?"

"Well, Daddy, I started this trip looking for my little sister. She's out there biking with her boyfriend."

"Find her?"

"Oh, we know where she is. But it turns out it's not her I have to find. The road is something I have to do, Daddy, something I have to do for me. I need to see rivers like the Mississippi and the Red and the Rio Grande, I need to meet people like you and Ghost and this friend of Ghost's named Vapor and listen to what you all have to say. The boy I'm riding with, I have to find out what we mean to each other. And God's in amongst all of that too—that's the most important piece to the puzzle."

Daddy raised his thick gray eyebrows. "The way you talk I'd have thought God's already a for sure thing."

"I know about God. Yes, I must be honest and say

I know God as much as any person is able to. Jesus Christ is God's face and eyes and heart—I can see that, I can feel that, I know who he is. But somewhere along the way my eyesight blurred, Daddy. I stopped seeing as clearly and I lost sight of what I believed and who I was. Now I'm trying to get it all back."

"And a long trip is gonna fix all this?"

"When I meet people like you and Ghost, yes."

"I ain't much of much."

Michal took his hand. "Don't ever say that, Daddy. You're made in the image of God and he loves you. You're something special."

He stared at her. A group of people came along the sidewalk and walked into the store. The bell on the door jangled. Daddy stood up, letting go of her hand.

"I got to get back on my route. And you got customers."

"Are you coming back tomorrow, Daddy?"

"Does the sun shine on Mississippi?"

The talks with Daddy went on daily and so did the phone conversations with her mother. At first she had been afraid to say she was staying at Uncle Samson's and just said they were in Mississippi and not that far from Vicksburg. The morning Michal finally told her mother they were staying over in Natchez at the home of father's brother there was a catch in her mother's voice and a quick change of subject. The awkwardness went on day after day. Several times Michal was tempted to confront her mother about what had happened 20 years before, but never had the courage to ask the question. At night, lying in bed and listening to the air conditioner turn on and off, she wondered if Uncle Samson had been her mother's first choice and father second, a choice that had been taken away when Samson made his own decision and up and left her in his brother's arms. Had she regretted she'd spent so much time trying to make up her mind when, in her heart, she had already decided on Samson, but couldn't bring herself to say the words and break father's heart?

This kind of thinking always led her to dwell on her relationship with Milwaukee. One moment the two of them were holding hands, the next they weren't, one minute hugging, the next not, one day a kiss, then no more kisses for a week—what was going on? Was it her fault in some way? Was she failing to encourage him to approach her? Turning these thoughts over in her head in the middle of the night, the air conditioner humming loudly, flipping onto her back and then onto her stomach, it often took her hours to get to sleep. Especially if her sister came to mind—and her sister always came to mind.

It bothered her that Tabitha was racing around Texas on the back of Nick Ferley's Ironhead because she felt she had to somehow sacrifice herself for her older sister and try to save her soul. All along Michal had thought Tabi had a crush on Nick and wanted to see America for herself. Now she knew this was not the case. Ghost made it sound like Tabi was only a matter of weeks from getting Nick to steer a course east for Pennsylvania. So what if something happened to her kid sister while she was tearing up and down the highways clinging to Nick's back? And what if Nick was pressuring her into sex and drugs and heavy drinking? Whose door would it be laid at if Tabi wound up pregnant and addicted to cocaine?

I wasn't that bad off. Tabi didn't need to do some-

thing like this. Over time I would have sorted it out. An-
other year or two and I would have been right as rain.

But as Michal lay awake in the Mississippi nights
she knew that she had been in terrible shape spiritually
and emotionally and that another year or two probably
wouldn't have changed a thing—except that she might
have up and left early one morning on a train, plane,
or Greyhound. Two months on the highway—the heat,
the sea, the new faces, Skid, Ghost, Daddy, Christians
praying and singing and clapping their hands—it had
all begun to work its way deep inside of her. She was
not the same person in July and August that she had
been in May. Lifetimes seemed to have been crammed
into the weeks she'd been on the road. And Milwaukee
had been right—she sang that night at the prayer meeting in Ghost's house in a way she hadn't in years. God
had been close enough to touch. No, her sister had done
the right thing—she, Michal Deborah Troyer, was the
one who needed the open road and open skies more
than Tabitha did. She'd just never faced up to it. And
the only reason she had done something about it was
because Tabi had forced her hand by fleeing south on
a 79 Harley.

"Would you ever go back to Lancaster County?"
she asked Ghost over red beans and rice one swampy
evening on the back patio, Ghost grinned and poured
more hot sauce on his plate. "What brought that out
of nowhere?"

"Oh, it's not coming out of nowhere, uncle. I spend
half my nights thinking about everything and everyone that affects me."

Ghost chewed and swallowed before replying. "It
wouldn't be your mother that'd keep me away. And

much as I love my bike I guess I could park that and find myself a good horse." Milwaukee stared at him with surprised eyes that expressed doubt and Ghost protested, "Seriously, Kee, I could. Really. I've done so much riding I've about had five lives." He looked back at Michal. "I'd kind of like the wood stoves and ice boxes again. I'd kind of like living completely off the grid."

"What would you work at?" she asked.

"Blacksmithing. And if I couldn't do that—farrier."

Milwaukee exchanged a glance with Michal while Ghost's head was down.

Ghost drank off some Coke from a tall glass that tinkled with seven or eight ice cubes. "But it won't happen. I'm where the Lord wants me."

"How do you know that for sure?" Michal pressed him.

"For sure? Those are big words." He wiped his mouth with a paper napkin. "If I go back to Marietta and take the vows and promise to live the *Gelassenheit,* the obedience, the surrender, well, who's gonna help Vapor? Who's gonna give the bikers and addicts and gang members a new start? Who's gonna give them Jesus? You think the suit and tie preachers are gonna go into bars and strip joints to pluck souls out of hell? That's not what they're good at. But it's what I do, Michal. I look for the fallen angels." He finished his Coke. Then he got up and began clearing dishes. "I can't save those lives if I'm with the Amish in Marietta. It's not what the Stoltzfuses and Millers and Beacheys are called to, it's not how they serve the Lord. Do you think I could be content to pound an anvil and eat Shoofly pie and sing *Das Loblied* while Vapor's begging for prayer or dying of an overdose in a gutter in New Orleans? Can't happen, Michal, it can never happen. This is where I belong. Not at a barn raising or a Sunday night hymn sing."

"But—some belong at the barn raising."

Ghost and Michal looked at each other and both slowly smiled. "Yeah," he admitted. "Some do."

There was a wall of bamboo Ghost had nurtured at one side of the back yard that Michal went to when she was free. Once she made her way behind it the growth was so thick no one could tell if she was there. Ghost had set up a table and chair for her and she liked to write in her journal in the glowing green light the sun cast over everything behind the bamboo. She was hard at her writing after the store had closed on a Wednesday when she heard a person's feet moving in the grass beyond the wall. Hesitating, she waited to see if whoever it was would walk into the enclosure or leave her alone. Then the sound stopped and nothing else happened.

Michal finally lost her patience, wanting to continue with her writing, but not willing to go ahead if she had to set down her pen and talk with someone. "Hellooo? Who is it?"

"I—didn't want to interrupt." Milwaukee's voice.

"Well, you have, so you might as well come in."

Her annoyance vanished instantly once Milwaukee stepped behind the tall bamboo. He was in a JESUS ROCK CAFÉ tee without sleeves that Ghost had lent him and it was covered in grease and oil, as were a pair of jeans he had on. But it wasn't the grease and oil that caught Michal's attention. It was Milwaukee.

He was surprised by her stare. "What is it?"

"Oh." Michal flushed behind her tan. "Nothing."

But it was something. He had been so busy in the garage with Ghost they'd hardly seen each other except at meals or prayer meetings or the Bikers' Church that met on Sunday mornings. His appearance had completely changed from the image she kept in her head. His skin was as dark as a spadeful of Pennsylvania dirt, his hair as bright as sunlight with the do rag of the Mississippi state flag off his head, his eyes a flashing amber, like a lion, and there was more muscle on his arms and on his shoulders than there had been when they'd rolled into Natchez three weeks before. The whole effect of him standing there, a yellow and green halo from sun and bamboo shimmering over his strong and slender body, made all the old feelings start up in her heart and chest and head again. Then he smiled and she said softly to herself, *Oh, my golden one.*

"Are you okay?" Milwaukee asked, suddenly looking concerned.

Michal smiled and passed a hand over her face. "Sure—I'm just—a little warm—"

"Well, can I take you out of the heat a moment and show you something?"

"What's that?"

"There's something in the garage I'd like you to see."

"You're going to let me into the garage?"

His smile returned, shining in his deeply tanned face. "One time offer. Ladies with blue eyes and sort of black hair only. Between now and sunset."

Michal got to her feet. "Sort of black hair?"

Her do rag was off, just as his was, and her hair was

loose over her shoulders and back. She saw him glance at it and then look quickly away.

"It's like black diamonds," he said as he led the way out from the bamboo enclosure, "and every diamond has a dozen different colors of its own."

She caught up and walked beside him. "Are you going poet on me?"

"I can't think of any other way to describe it. And I've been thinking about it a lot."

"A lot?" she teased him. "Are you flirting with me the way the English boys flirt with their girls?"

A small smile slipped over his lips. "I'm a long way past flirting, Michal Deborah Troyer. You've been riding in my buggy almost every day for over two months."

Her eyebrows arched upward. "That sounds serious. What exactly does a long way past flirting mean? A kiss behind the barn? A walk in the bushes along the Susquehanna River? Sharing the same ice cream cone?"

He glanced at her with his amber eyes. "I'll tell you in a minute. But first, there's this. Come here."

They were at the side door to the garage. Nearby was a small motorbike hidden under an orange tarp— Milwaukee's Honda that had been parked there since their arrival and covered up by Ghost almost immediately. Milwaukee pulled his Mississippi do rag out of a jean pocket and wrapped it over her eyes.

"Hey!" she laughed. "What's this?"

"It has to all hit you at once," he explained. "What has to all hit me at once?"

He didn't answer, but she heard him opening the door. Then he took her hand firmly in his and led her inside. The garage was air conditioned so the change from the heat and humidity of the back yard was sharp.

Milwaukee took her forward a few steps and then stood still.

"Okay?" Milwaukee's voice.

"Are you asking me if it's okay?" asked Michal. "It's okay, Kee." Ghost's voice.

"Okay," Milwaukee responded.

Michal began to laugh at all the "okays" until the do rag was off her eyes and she could see clearly—then she put her hands to her mouth.

"Oh, my goodness. It's beautiful. It's beautiful." Then she looked from Milwaukee to Ghost. "What is it?"

Both their jaws dropped open.

"What do you mean, 'what is it'?" growled Ghost. "It's a Harley!"

Michal's face reddened under her tan. "I know it's a Harley. I'm not that Amish. But there's so much black and chrome—it looks better than any Harley I've ever seen. What kind is it? Whose is it?"

Her reply pleased Ghost and his expression went from scowl to smile in the blink of an eye. "That's my girl. To your first question: it's an FLSTF Fat Boy, 2007, lovingly restored and customized by Ghost and Kee incorporated, Harley mechanics and beautifiers. We've added chrome, especially to the wheels, jazzed up the engine, I made the saddlebags out of naked, drum-dyed leather in my basement—this baby is ready to shoot the rapids. 'Cause when a person crosses the Mississippi east to west they're heading into huge country—Texas, New Mex, Zona, Vada, Cali, the Pacific Ocean, the Rockies of Colorado and Montana and

Wyoming—no fooling around, it's the big time, the big road, and you gotta be ready—prayed up, gassed up, backed up."

Ghost's speech confused Michal.

"What are you talking about?" she asked. "Whose bike is this?"

Ghost smiled. "Yours, lady be good. Yours and Kee's. My wedding present."

Michal felt the blood leave her face. "What?"

"You think I'd send my niece into the Mojave Desert on a bike made in China?"

"Japan," Milwaukee corrected.

Ghost grunted. "No one from my family crosses the Father of Waters on a scooter. They go on a Harley or not at all. You got some combat riding ahead of you. You need a hot piece of American steel to do it right. The bike's my gift and my pleasure."

Michal recovered enough to put her arms around Ghost and kiss him on the cheek twice. "Thank you, thank you, uncle. But it's too much, it's really too much."

"It's a small thing in the scheme of God's universe, Michal, but I hope it'll help you get through to the other side."

"What other side?"

"The other side of whatever it is you gotta find and put back in yourself." He patted her on the back. "Now you and Kee need to talk. After that we'll head up to Biscuits and Blues for a bite."

He left the garage, closing the door tightly behind him. Michal walked around the bike and ran her hand over the leather seat and gleaming handlebars. She felt Milwaukee's eyes on her and finally looked up. A shaft of sun from a skylight had found him and he shone like gold. As their eyes stayed connected she felt an energy she had never experienced in him before. The image of a lion walking through tall grasses in jungle heat fixed itself in her imagination. His eyes gleamed and pulled her in and she found she was at a loss for words even though she had plenty of questions.

"Wedding?" she finally managed to get out. Milwaukee smiled slowly. "Ghost's joke."

"Oh—it's a joke?"

He remained standing in the Mississippi light. "There's something you don't understand. And I understand so little it's as if I don't know anything about it either. But I'll try and explain. We're up and down and all over the map when it comes to our friendship— is it two buddies sharing Coke and burgers at a fast food hangout? Or is it a boyfriend and girlfriend eating popcorn from a bucket in a movie theater? Or is it a man and a woman thinking about spending a lifetime together?"

"You tell me."

"I've tried to tell you before. One look from you can turn me inside out. The scent of your hair, your hand on my shoulder, the briefest of kisses can send me around the moon and Jupiter. You don't think it's true because I don't follow through on it. The day I follow through on it I'll take you in my arms so hard you won't be able to breathe. You'll feel hot and cold at the same time. I'm not kidding, I'll burn you up. You have no idea what I'm holding back and how hard it is to do it. The most crazy beautiful woman is a few feet away from me and I'm this massive dam pushing back a wall of water that could tear up trees and shift mountains."

He began to walk toward her like the lion in her mind. Everything inside her was screaming for him to hold her. He did. Then his hand smoothed back the shining dark hair from her face.

"I'm going to do this once, right now, right here. The next time I do it will be the moment I ask you to marry me. Okay?"

Michal had no idea what was coming, but being locked in his strong tanned arms was almost enough. "Okay."

He put his mouth on hers with more strength than any boy had put into a kiss on her lips. She collapsed in his arms and put all she had in the kiss back. He never stopped. His feelings poured from his mouth like air into every part of her body. Her heart hammered and her head swirled and she had no sense that her legs were holding her up. He held her more and more closely and took what breath was left right out of her body. Still the kiss went on until she felt she was going to drop.

Then his lips were at her ear and he whispered, "The next time means I love you so bad I can't exist without you. The next time means I want you to be my wife forever. The next time I don't stop, I don't ever stop. Okay?"

She leaned her head into his chest and listened to the strong beating of his heart while she tried to catch her breath.

"Okay," she said.

Chapter Twelve

Saturday was the ride to raise money for children with Down syndrome, the elderly with dementia and Alzheimer's, as well as the adults and teens who struggled with ADHD. Michal had never experienced anything like it. She wrapped her arms around her lion's chest and rode through the streets of Natchez while dozens of bikers from Heavens Gate rode in front, in back, and all around them. The roar was enormous and it exhilarated her. Then they took to Highway 61 and went south to Baton Rouge. It felt so different to be riding a big powerful bike rather than the Honda that she laughed out loud from the sheer joy of it. In Baton Rouge they were joined by other Heavens Gate bikers until there were more than 300 of them making the streets and buildings and windows shake. At the end of the ride they put on a huge barbeque in a park. They raised more than seventy thousand dollars, not just from the barbeque, but from the people and businesses who had sponsored the ride.

Before the Natchez chapter headed back north Ghost called everyone together for a short gospel message and an altar call. Michal was astonished to see that Fat Poppa Daddy had joined the ride before it left Natchez and went up with others at Ghost's invitation. The crowd was so great she could not get to him afterward, but later, as they headed up Highway 61, Milwaukee brought his Fat Boy alongside the bike Daddy was hitching a ride on. Daddy saw Michal, grinned his Mississippi grin, and reached out with his hand. She took it, smiling back, and they held on for several long seconds before the bikes had to pull apart.

Sunday she saw him again at the Biker's Church that met at a restaurant outside of Natchez. The parking lot was full of motorcycles when her and Milwaukee and Ghost pulled up. Inside, a biker pastor from New Orleans named Bubba Win had already opened with prayer and a rock band was leading the crowd in a time of energetic worship. She spotted Daddy at a table near the front, lifting his hands and clapping and singing as if he were in a black Baptist church and had been doing it all his life. This time the two of them got to talk afterward and no matter what he said, whether it was about God's love and forgiveness, the new spirit he had in him, or what she meant to him, he always ended up with tears in his eyes.

"God's beautiful, he's beautiful," he cried. She hugged him. "You're beautiful, Daddy."

Monday was the day of departure. Ghost gave them his Hog Breakfast of bacon, sausage, ham, white gravy and biscuits, hash browns, scrambled eggs with salsa, and pancakes. Michal ate until she thought she'd die and finally threw up her hands: "No more. I cry uncle."

Outside on the street a dozen bikers had assembled to say goodbye and escort Michal and Milwaukee across the big river for the first time. Ghost had a few final surprises: a cell phone loaded with prepaid long distance minutes, and a set of leathers he'd made himself in his basement—biker chaps to go over their jeans, vests to go under their jackets, and what Ghost called his Brando jackets with braided lines, 2.0mm thickness, and gunmetal zippers and hardware. They had, of course, the Heavens Gate backs—Michal's cross was silver, Milwaukee's black. He topped their kit off with leather covered half-helmets.

"Ohh, you are looking good, looking good," he smiled once they had put everything on. "One more thing." He handed them each a pair of mirrored sunglasses. "You are part of the club. So now reflect your Father's glory."

"Amen," responded Milwaukee and Michal at the same time and looked at each other in surprise. The bikers laughed.

"Now you're getting it," grinned Ghost. He held out his arms. "Come here, you two."

He prayed over them in his Mississippi biker slang a few minutes and then startled Michal—and everyone else—by breaking into High German and blessing them like an Amish bishop. Eyes closed, she found Milwaukee's hand. The prayer made her feel braver and more hopeful about the weeks that lay ahead on the other side of the river.

"Amen," Ghost suddenly said and hugged them both. "*Geh mit Gott.* Go with God."

The bikes started up and began to head down the street. At the corner stood Daddy with Twilight's Last Gleaming and the carriage. He raised his hand as Michal and Milwaukee slowed to make the turn. She raised her hand to him in response.

"We have to come back," Michal said into Milwaukee's ear. "We will."

They went across the bridge and across the broad gray Mississippi River into Louisiana, bikes on all sides of them. Then, as Highway 65 opened up in front of Michal and Milwaukee, the others began to peel off and turn back. The last to leave was Ghost on his sapphire Fat Bob with its twin headlights. He made the sign of the cross over them and was gone.

"Hey, Roadburn."

"Hey, Chrome."

"Shall I open her up?"

Michal hugged him tightly across his stomach and chest. "Yes."

"Hi, mama."

"Oh, it's good to hear from you, Michal. How are you? Are you still in—Natchez?"

"No, ma, we're in Louisiana now. We're camping at a place called Natchitoches. It's another old town like Natchez and it's very beautiful and peaceful."

"A postcard came from Tabitha when she was at a Kentwood in Louisiana. But all the others are from Texas."

"What's in Kentwood?" Michal wanted to know.

"Oh," her mother sighed noisily, "another one of her singers was born there—is it this Britney Spears? She says their family has a big house in the town she wanted to look at. And they ate at a diner that was just across the state line in Mississippi that the Spears girl spent a lot of time at, it was near a place called Osyka, the walls have signed posters of her, and news clippings about her visits."

"It surprises me that Tabi is interested in such things."

"Nothing surprises me about your sister anymore. Tomorrow I will get a postcard and she will tell your father and I she is on the moon."

"Well, at least she is writing."

"Yes, yes, thanks be to God. Do you think you will be able to meet up with her and have that talk soon, dear? It is getting on to September in a few weeks."

"Mama, you know this has to be a talk she wants to have otherwise it will be a waste of time."

"But—"

"Ma, really," Michal argued, "she will just get on the bike and tell Nick to drive away."

"Then what will you do?" Michal could hear hurt and a tinge of anger in her mother's voice. "Just drive in circles around Texas and Louisiana?"

"One day she will write a date and a place in a postcard," Michal explained without raising her voice. "Then we will know she is ready to meet with me."

"So suppose you run into her and Nicholas by accident?"

"It won't be an accident. She will believe, as I will, that it was meant to be."

"And you think she would talk if God arranged such a meeting?"

"Yes, mama, she would."

When Michal wondered out loud to Milwaukee about the possibility of such a meeting he looked up from wiping down the Harley. "If it's not about her rebelling, but all about getting you out on the road, when do you think Tabi will tell us exactly where she is going to be on a certain day?"

Michal shrugged and put her hand on his shoulder. "When she decides I have spent enough time away from home."

"What day is this?"

"Day 89. I need a hug."

He straightened and put his arms around her. Then, as always when he hugged her now, he kissed the top of her head. Today she wasn't wearing a do rag so he pressed his lips against her freshly washed hair.

"Are you fooling around with the top of my head?" she teased. "You bet. I like it."

"Do you? Well, at least it's clean."

"I like it clean. I like it wet. Reminds me of that night in Lancaster. But I'll take it anyway it comes."

"Oh, yes? Dirt, dust, oil, exhaust?"

"Sure. They just add flavor."

She laughed. "You're crazy."

"Yeah. Crazy love." He tilted her face toward his and kissed her slowly on the lips.

"I thought no more kisses until the big one," she murmured.

"Are you kidding? I never said that. When the big one comes the big one comes. You'll know it. Until then, it's the nickel and dime stuff."

"Okay, well, I'm glad we cleared that up."

"I like the nickel and dime stuff," he said and kissed her again. "So do I."

They spent ten days motoring around Louisiana completely on their own. Their relationship had taken a turn toward the romantic in the garage in Natchez,

Mississippi, like spring becoming summer, and now everything was different. Every day the hesitancy that had been a mark of their friendship eroded in the sunlight and grace of the Louisiana highways and bayous. She asked him to brush out her long dark hair and he did it gladly and gently. He washed her feet and towel dried her hair. When she came to him and asked to be held he stopped whatever he was doing and took her into his arms. Soon she only needed to tell him with her eyes and he understood. The strength of his body and his caress always calmed her and drove away whatever fears had found their way into her head and heart. He prayed with her more frequently, often in High German, read her father's small black Bible to her, sang hymns and Christian songs together with her, old ones and new ones both.

And always now there were the kisses, sometime short and kind, but often long and deep. Again and again he told her how beautiful she was, how the blue of her eyes astonished him, how the darkening color of her skin was an enchantment, how he literally thanked God for the wonder of her face and the softness of her lips. He bought her things, little things, earrings of silver that matched the long bright streaks the Southern sun had put in her hair, a necklace of gold that caught the bronze highlights, a brooch set with a small turquoise stone that matched the gleam of several long strands and reminded her of the waters of the Florida gulf. Often he came up behind her quietly, putting his arms about her, and brought her back into his chest and more of the kisses he seemed incapable of bringing to an end, pressing his lips to her smooth black hair, her shoulders, her neck.

Milwaukee showered her with so much affection and devotion and sweetness that, after days and days of it, Michal realized she was starting to believe she *was* beautiful, and dazzling, and irresistible, sensations that were new and startling to her. She had always felt Tabitha was attractive, but not her, that other Amish beauties were entrancing, but not her, that men worshiped the ground lovely Marietta girls walked on, but no one even noticed if she passed by. Suddenly Milwaukee had her believing she was one of the most remarkable women in America—a perfect beauty, compassionate, steeped in God, sparkling with life and humor and good will, a person of many gifts who sang like an angel from heaven. When he came to her with a tiny bottle of essence of magnolia one evening and insisted he dab it on her himself, lightly touching her wrists and throat and behind her ears in a careful and kind way she could not protest against, he told her he was anointing her with the precious nard of the South, the perfume that embodied her spirit and her heart and all her loveliness.

"I am setting you apart for God tonight," he said, kissing her gently on the neck where he had just placed a drop of the fragrance. "The old ways are gone. A new woman has come."

The richness of his words continued to surprise her. "Do you really mean the things you say to me? Or are you just trying to be nice?"

"Both." He lifted her chin. "Look at my eyes. What color are they?"

"In this light," she told him, as the sun set in a coppery mix, "your eyes are gold."

"And that's how I feel about you. Gold is how I feel about you."

Michal was unable to think of anything to say in reply. His praises and compliments washed over her in glistening waves that cleansed her and soothed her like the turquoise waters she had swam and bathed in at Sarasota and Neptune Beach.

It never stopped. One day of love from Milwaukee followed another day of even greater love and even greater praise and poetry.

"I can't resist you, you know," he whispered one night as they lay in their sleeping bags side by side. "Ever since I opened up one of the sluice gates in that dam of mine back in Mississippi the feelings just keep coming and coming. I hope I'm not irritating you."

"Irritating me?" Michal turned toward him in the dark. "Is that what you think?"

"Well, I don't really know what to think. Isn't it over the top? Don't I bore you? Am I a pest? I just want you to understand I can't help myself—you're impossible to resist."

Her hand found his face. She ran her fingers over his skin. "Milwaukee Bachman, of all the things God is using to transform me from a person who thought they were an ugly duckling, physically and spiritually, into a swan, you are at the top of the list—above my sister, the highways, the Harley, the seas, the palm trees, everything. Do you have any idea how you make me feel? I'm not only a princess in a story who glows from head to toe, I feel like the kind of believer who sees God in everything all the time just because of how you pray for me and how you read God's word to me and how you—caress me, as if I were some sort of bright blue flower a person found tucked away in the dark corner of a bayou. Christ is using you to bring me back to life, Milwaukee. Much more of this and I'll either die and go to heaven—or start using your Christian name."

She felt him smile in the dark.

"That would be cool, Michal. But that wasn't my intention, you know. I haven't even thought about the name thing, to tell you the truth. I only wanted to love you. I never expected anything in return except your willingness to let me go ahead and do that."

Michal leaned over and kissed him in the black of the night that surrounded them. The bullfrogs and katydids filled up their ears with their raucous music. She put a lot of energy into the kiss.

"Hey, Roadburn, that was great," he laughed softly, "but a little intense don't you think?"

"Kissing is just another way of talking, Chrome," she told him quietly. "And so what are you saying to me?"

"That when you love someone don't be surprised when the day comes that all that love comes back to you and gives you more than you ever dreamed or imagined."

Chapter Thirteen

On either side of them, as they thundered south on Interstate 55 toward New Orleans, vast swamps began to appear. They were thick with forests of green trees that were interlaced by lanes of open water. Now and then Michal spotted small houses perched on the swamp waters. Once she saw three men holding fishing poles weaving through the swamp in a small boat. Not far from the city a large lake opened up on her right and an even larger one on her left. She knew from studying the map and showing it to Milwaukee that it was Lake Maurepas on the right and Lake Pontchartrain on the left. Short rows of houses attached to docks rested quietly on the edges of the waters.

She leaned her head over Milwaukee's right shoulder. "Don't these people worry about alligators?"

He shrugged. "I guess they get used to them."

"And what about Hurricane Katrina? Why wouldn't these houses have been washed away?"

"Maybe they've been rebuilt."

"They don't look rebuilt. They look old."

The I-55 turned into the I-10. Milwaukee wasn't sure

where to turn off and finally took the last exit before a long bridge. Then he followed signs to the Convention Center and French Quarter. Both of them expected to see damaged buildings and streets that had not been repaired since the vicious hurricane of 2005. Instead they were both surprised to see tall, thick-trunked palm trees erect and sturdy in the afternoon breeze, all around the Convention Center and marching down avenues and lanes nearby. The buildings were just as solid and clean and firmly rooted as the palms.

Leaving their bike in a parking lot, and locking their leather jackets and chaps in their steel and leather saddlebags, they walked into a French Quarter vibrant with music and people and the sharp scent of spicy cooked meat.

Holding hands, Michal and Milwaukee wandered among the shops and tables and stalls near the Mississippi waterfront, looking at everything from necklaces and rings to jackets and paintings and bottles of hot sauce. A waiter managed to coax them into his restaurant and they sat down at an open air table to a basket of fresh bread and butter followed by plates of fried chicken that rested by heaps of red beans and rice. A woman sang in a soft jazzy voice into a mike accompanied by a keyboard player and a man with an electric bass. People streamed past, some lingering to listen to the singer, others to glance at a copy of the menu that was on display, the waiter that had pulled Michal and Milwaukee into the restaurant hovering over the potential customers. Halfway through her meal Michal leaned back in her chair and closed her eyes.

"I'm full," she smiled, "and it's so warm out I feel like having a nap."

"Aren't you going to finish your food?" asked Milwaukee who was pouring hot sauce over his rice and beans.

"I'm stuffed. Didn't you see the size of the chicken they gave us?"

"A *demi-poulet*. He said it means half a chicken."

"There's so much French around here."

Milwaukee nodded, his eyes on his plate as he chewed.

"The brochure I picked up says they have parishes instead of counties and have kept a lot of the French names and customs. From when this whole area was owned by France. And when you see the word Acadia that's because the British threw thousands of French-speaking people out of Nova Scotia and New Brunswick in Canada. Eventually some of them settled here."

"Why Acadia?" asked Milwaukee.

Michal opened one eye. "The brochure's in my purse."

"Can't you remember?"

"Of course I can remember. I'm just too lazy to think right now."

"I don't feel like rifling through your purse."

Michal waved a fly off her face. "Oh, you can be as annoying as a bluebottle—the region these people were forced out of was called Acadia. It included parts of Canada and America—I think they said it went as far south as Philadelphia."

"No way." Milwaukee looked up from his plate.

"Swallow first, please."

Milwaukee rolled his eyes, swallowed a mouthful of chicken and beans, and even wiped his lips with a paper napkin. "Am I cleared to speak now, *mein Fuhrer*?"

"There's no need to be sarcastic."

"For all we know there could be connections between the Amish and the Acadians."

"Ha."

"Well, you said Philadelphia."

"You and your crazy ideas. Go to university and write a paper on it and become famous."

"Maybe I will." Milwaukee turned his attention back to his plate and poured more hot sauce on everything he could see. "I saw the word Cajun in the menu for some of the dishes."

"That was in the brochure too. I think they said it was slang for the Acadians who settled in Louisiana, a sort of nasty label for them. Now it's a good word."

A gust from the riverfront scattered their napkins and was strong enough to knock over their peppershaker as well. Milwaukee left his chair to pick up the napkins and, as Michal righted the shaker, the cell phone in her black leather purse began to play the tune to The Star Spangled Banner. She dug and brought it out before it had reached "the twilight's last gleaming".

She looked at the call display.

"It's Ghost," she said to Milwaukee as he returned to their table with the napkins. Then she pressed a green key and said, "Hello, uncle."

"How are you today, my blue-eyed girl?" Ghost asked her.

"I'm very good, uncle. So is Milwaukee. We're eating at an open air table in the French Quarter in New Orleans."

"You in New Orleans? Remember to look up The Rev."

"We'll get a hold of Bubba Win today or tomorrow, for sure."

"How's the weather?" Ghost asked.

"Warm, warm, and warm," she answered.

"Yeah? Now listen, your sister called. They're in Arizona. I gave her your cell number."

"Did she ask for it?"

"She didn't even know you had a cell. Now she does. I think she'll call or text. Have you done any texting?"

"No. I only use the phone to call my mother."

"Do you know how texting works?"

"I don't."

"Just go into the menu, okay?" Ghost explained. "You'll see an icon for messaging, an envelope. Click on that. You can create and send a message from there or go into your inbox and read one. Actually, if you get a text, you'll be able to open it and read it without going into the menu if you do it right away."

Michal laughed. "It sounds strange. And confusing."

"It isn't. You'll get onto it after a few tries. You're smart. How's the bike?"

"Runs like the Mississippi."

"Yeah? Praise God. Given it a name?"

"Not yet."

"Okay. We're praying for you. Don't forget to get a plateful of catfish and hushpuppies. Let me know when you hear from Tabitha. Bye."

"Bye. God bless you."

Milwaukee looked at her as she pressed a red key to end the call. "What's up?"

"Ghost gave Tabi our number," she told him, laying the cell on the table.

"Yeah? She called him?"

She nodded. "He said back in Natchez that Tabi calls from time to time ever since their visit."

"You think she'll actually call you?"

"I really don't know."

"You want me to ask the waiter to box up your stuff? Like to do some more walking?"

She smiled. "Now that I'm wide awake again, yes."

At first they went up and down the streets, avoiding Bourbon as Ghost had advised them, but making their way along most of the others, looking at the old world architecture and fancy ironwork of the balcony railings.

Iberville Street took them to the stone and pillars of the US Customs House and following Decatur Street they came upon the statue of Joan of Arc and the red brick and white pillars of the US Mint. Eventually they made it to Basin Street with its great spreading trees and ancient houses and the "stone huts on asphalt", as Michal called them, of what her brochure said was St. Louis Cemetery Number One.

"Do you want to go inside?" Milwaukee asked.

"What?" Michal responded in a startled voice. "Walk around among the dead?"

"Well, it's not as if they're there anymore. You've been in the Amish cemetery at Marietta plenty of times."

"Yes, and we have flowers and trees and grass. Take me somewhere romantic, Milwaukee Bachman, somewhere romantic and natural."

"Romantic?" Milwaukee stared at her. "Is that the mood you're in?"

"Somewhat. Though the present location is diminishing my ardor rapidly."

He grabbed her hand. "Quick. There's a park. Let's run."

"Why? Is the park going to disappear?"

"No, but your ardor might."

She laughed and ran beside him. "Do you always take me so seriously?"

"When it comes to ardor, sure."

He made her go harder than she had ever run in her life so that by the time he stopped under a huge tree and she leaned against the trunk they were both panting and couldn't even talk or laugh properly. But his eyes said it all and she tugged him toward her.

"Like me, brown-eyed Amish boy?" she asked.

He smiled, still catching his breath. "Who wouldn't, blue-eyed Amish girl?"

She glanced around them quickly. No one was nearby, most of the people were on the far side of the park. She put her hands on both sides of his face and kissed him on the mouth as hard as she could and for far longer than she had planned. Then she fell back against the trunk of the tree.

"How was that?" she asked him.

"I guess I've lost my breath again."

She gave him a sharp smile that reminded him of her sister Tabitha. "Oh, yes? Do you think you can handle another?"

"As long as that man standing behind you doesn't object."

Michal sprang away from the tree and looked behind her, face reddening. There was a black statue of a man in a suit holding a trumpet down by his side. "Oh!" she cried and turned back to him, punching him on both shoulders again and again while he laughed and backed away from her, his hands up to defend himself.

"Hey," he protested, "I never said he was alive."

"You! You don't deserve another kiss!"

"Not even a short one?"

"Not even a short one!"

Suddenly he seized her and hugged her in such a way that he pinned her arms to her sides. She struggled to get free, but he would not let her go. Finally she stopped wrestling with him and stood still. Their eyes came together.

"You're my prisoner," he told her.

"So it would seem," she responded quietly, her eyes remaining on his. "What are your intentions?"

"To get my second kiss. And maybe a third or fourth."

"Really?"

He touched his lips to her cheek. "Hey, you taste like salt."

"I think it's called sweat."

"I thought girls and women didn't sweat."

"No, they glow. But which am I, Milwaukee Bachman? Girl or woman?"

"That's an easy question in The Big Easy."

"Is it?"

He put his lips to the black hair that was hanging loose well past her shoulders and far down her back to her waist. "Too easy. Besides being—easily—the most beautiful woman in New Orleans, you are also the most beautiful woman in the world. With an emphasis on woman. And an equal emphasis on beautiful."

Her lips parted softly. The sun was caught up in his

brown and blonde hair and made it a golden mane that was the same color as his sunlit eyes.

"Come here, my man," she whispered. "Come here."

They kissed again and this time neither of them were inclined to break it off so the kiss kept on and on until Milwaukee felt he was in a completely different head space, one that was infinitely better and far more full of life than wherever he had been a few minutes before. He felt her hands running over his back and decided he could do this forever and never eat again or take a drink, just kiss her and hold her and love her.

Suddenly a strange sound broke upon them—it was a buzzing combined with a short tune neither of them could recognize. Then it stopped.

"What was that?' asked Michal, still in Milwaukee's arms.

"It came from your purse," Milwaukee told her, afraid to say he thought it was her cell because he knew that would end their romantic interlude.

"My purse? You mean it's the phone?"

"I guess. Unless your lip gloss buzzes."

She didn't laugh. Pulling herself away she bent down and picked up her purse. Bringing out the electric blue cell she looked at the call display.

"It says I have a message. From Nick Ferley."

"It's Tabitha."

"What do I do?"

He stood beside her. "Just look at your display. See? It says open. So if you click on it you'll be able to read the message."

Michal did as he said. Words appeared on the screen.

Do you hate me?

Michal put a hand to her mouth. "Oh. Why would she say that?"

"Ask her."

"How?"

"Click on reply. Then use the keys like you would a typewriter or a computer keyboard to write your message."

Michal looked at him with her eyes narrowed. "Milwaukee Bachman, I've never used a computer or a typewriter in my life. How do you know so much?"

"I had a cell once."

"Since when?"

"I was 17—look, just hold the phone in both your hands and use your thumbs like this to push down the keys. Spell out your message as if you were printing."

He typed, Tabi, I don't hate you.

"Wait, wait!" squealed Michal grabbing the phone from him. "What are you doing?"

"You don't hate her, do you?"

"No, but—"

"So all I did was get you started. Finish the message. Hurry, before she thinks you're not there and puts her phone away."

Michal fumbled with the phone, dropping it as she tried to type with her thumbs. "I can't do this."

"Of course you can. Just hold the cell firmly. It's not a feather."

"I know it's not a feather. Don't shout at me. This is hard enough."

"Michal, I'm not shouting at you."

"This is going to take forever to tell her anything."

"Keep your sentences short."

I love you. Where are you?

"Now what do I do with my sentences?" she asked, staring at the screen.

"Send them. See how it says send? Just click on that."

"And that will make it go?"

"Faster than a jet. Faster than a heartbeat."

"Never mind heartbeats." She clicked on send. "Is that all?"

"It will tell you in a moment that your text has been sent."

Michal saw words appear on the screen: Your message has been sent to Nick Ferley.

"Show off," she said, but he saw a small upward curve come to her lips. "What happens next?"

"If she's still there she'll write back."

Suddenly the phone buzzed in her hand and she almost dropped it.

Then the tune they could not recognize played for a few moments. "What's this?" she asked, staring at the cell.

"Same as before. You've got a text. Click on open and you can read it."

I love you too. It's been soooo long, hasn't it? R u OK?

"She's spelling weird."

"Just using shortcuts. Everyone does it when they text or send emails."

Michal banged at the keys with her thumbs, made mistakes, asked how to clear them, and sent her new text.

Yes, I'm great, except I worry about you. Where are you now?

In a few moments Tabitha responded: We're near Yuma. Haven't been to the Canyon yet. Where r u?

New Orleans.

Still with Joe Amish?

Yes. He's great. You should see how he looks.

Tabitha texted, Really?
Michal typed, His hair is all gold and his arms and face are all tanned. He rides the Harley like a pro.

What Harley?

Ghost had one Milwaukee helped him repair.

How does Joe Amish treat u?

Stop calling him that. I never had so much attention from any man.

Ever.
Tabitha's reply was quick. OK, that's great, I guess. I'd have to see it to believe it. R u going to hang out with Bubba Win while u r in NO?

Yes, we'll spend some time with him.

He's very cool. So tell me—how is it with u and God and all things Amish?

Michal hesitated a moment before answering. I'm thinking things through. God feels a lot closer especially since our time with Ghost.

That's great.

So does that mean we can all go home now?

Tabitha texted, U can go home anytime u want, sis. Michal responded, I'm not heading back without you.

And I'm not heading back until I know you're in one piece again.

I'm doing okay, I am.

It's too soon. Stay on my tail.

Michal moved her thumbs swiftly. When are we going to meet?

Don't know.

You said the Grand Canyon.

Tabitha messaged, Maybe not the Canyon. Nick is seeing a lot of friends. Maybe California.

Maybe California? I haven't seen you in three months. Is this a game to you, Tabi?

It's no game, sis, believe me. Gotta go. Love u. Text me whenever u want.

Michal quickly got in, Can't I phone? Can't we talk?

Not yet. Bye.

Michal slumped on the grass and leaned back against the tree trunk. "How was that?" Milwaukee asked.

"It was good to talk—if you call this texting thing talk." Milwaukee put his hands in the pockets of his jeans. "But?" Michal ran a hand through her hair and looked up at him.

"Something's wrong. She's not talking right. A lot of what she says is okay, but there's something else going on. And whatever it is, it's not good."

Chapter Fourteen

"How do you feel about this Milwaukee boy?"

"Milwaukee? Oh—he's great."

"Are you in love with him, Michal?"

"In love? I—I don't know. But my feelings for him get stronger every day."

"How does he feel about you?"

"Well—if actions speak words, Pastor Bubba—I guess you could say he's—crazy about me—I'm sorry, that sounds so immodest and proud—"

Bubba grunted. "But it's the truth. Anyone spends five minutes around you two can see he's all filled up with Michal Troyer. Not a bad thing considering who you are."

Michal frowned. "What does that mean?"

"It means you're a child of God, a real one. So's he, for that matter. All God lean, no fat. Even caught up in you he's still caught up in Jesus. That's obvious."

"How can he be both?"

Bubba grinned, the smile changing his face, Michal thought, from the grim look of a linebacker in the football games she'd seen, to one of sunshine, blue skies, and acres of open space. "Hey, baby girl, a man can't love God and love his woman at the same time the human race would come to an end."

Michal smiled too, lowering her eyes and feeling a blush moving across her cheeks. She felt one of his large hands come to rest on her head where her long hair was bound up under a do rag of the Heaven's Gate barbed wire cross in silver and black. He was blessing her, his rich, deep voice rolling out of his chest and throat.

"Lord, here we have Michal Deborah Troyer, in love with you, and falling in love bit by bit with the man you've brought onto the road with her, to protect and defend and bless her. Guide her steps, steer her like they steer their bike, open up her eyes and soul like you open up the road and the vistas and people of America to her and her man. Take her farther with you than she's ever been before. Take her farther into your love than she's ever been before. Take her farther into human love than she's ever been before. Bless her long journey and may it always be in you, for you, and toward you that she rides."

Michal lifted her head once he removed his hand. "No amen, Pastor Bubba?"

"Not yet. Got another prayer to do when we've finished talking about your sister."

"Tabitha? I don't know what else to tell you."

They were sitting on a corner of the flat roof of a small warehouse Bubba used for services and to feed and shelter the homeless and destitute. New Orleans was spread out around them from a three-storey height including many areas Bubba had pointed out to her where the trees had come down and the streets and homes been underwater. A warm breeze blew over them as they sat in the chairs and at the table Bubba always kept on the roof.

Bubba ran a hand over his bald head and Michal could see he was also running words through his mind and trying to decide what to say to her.

Finally he shrugged, half to God and half to himself, it seemed to her, and leaned back in his chair, fixing her with his deep-eyed gaze.

"Okay, baby girl, this is probably going to shock you, but your sister has called me every day since we met, that's right, every day since way back in July when they come through after Ghost fixed Nick's Ironhead."

Michal felt her mouth open. "Every day? What? Why?"

"I don't know. Not sure. You're the first topic of every conversation. Before I met you it was about how she thought you'd lost God and God had lost you. Wanted me to pray for you every time I bent the knee and bowed the head. Then when she found out we'd met in Natchez it was questions about whether you were changing, getting closer to God, getting closer to the real heart of you, the God heart. Just called this morning, you know. So I told her, yeah, Michal's a God woman, for sure, reads the Word, helps me feed the street people, makes the kids that don't laugh laugh big and hearty, prays with folk, tells them about the love of Jesus, brings them to him."

"What does she say?"

"She's desperate to hear it, eats it up when I tell her how you're getting along with Jesus, it seems to calm her, please her."

"Well, Ghost made it clear she started this whole

road trip as a means of getting me out on the road too. It was supposed to be a way of shaking me up and helping me see what mattered, see God, see my soul, wild stuff like that."

Bubba grunted. "Not so wild, Michal, you know that. Ain't it done those things?"

"Yes, yes it has, pastor—sorry."

He nodded, looking at her steadily. "The next topic is always your man. She calls him Joe Amish. Seems worried he's going to hold you back, stunt your spiritual growth—"

"But, pastor, he's done just the opposite—"

Bubba held up a hand. "I tell her, you've been here what now, four days? I tell her, look, the dude is good for you, dotes on you, the way his hair is growing out no one would know him for an Amish kid from Penn—except for his accent, he doesn't talk like one, doesn't act like one. She seems to be afraid he's hardcore Amish and wants to turn you into one too. I say, hey, Tabi, seems to me he's helping Michal unpin her wings, helping her fly, and I tell her no man loves his woman with his eyes the way I seen Milwaukee love Michal Troyer with his."

Michal felt the heat spring to her face. Somehow she was able to ask Bubba, "What happens—when you tell her all that?"

"She listens. But I don't think she's ready to believe it. Keeps telling me he was about to be baptized Amish when she took off and you followed, dragging him with you. I guess she doubts his sincerity, thinks he's acting in a certain way, pretending to be a free road biker right now, but later on he'll turn you into a proper Amish woman whether you like it or not."

Michal almost jumped to her feet. "Oh, Bubba, I'm not an eight year old, I'm not going to let a man mould and shape me like a lump of playdough regardless of what it is I want to be or what it is I believe."

Bubba put his hand up again. "Anyone who spends time with you can see that strength in your heart. But Tabi won't see it until the two of you meet up again and spend time together. And she's not ready to do that yet."

"Why not?"

"Keeps saying it's not time. I don't know what she's waiting for. She knows your faith is growing mile after mile." He laced his hands together and rested them on the table and stared at her. "Funny thing is, just like Ghost, I get the feeling she's had enough of the road, wants to go home, see mom and dad, cook supper on a wood stove, ride in a carriage instead of on the back of a Harley."

Michal turned this over, only half believing it, just as she had only half believed it in Natchez, Mississippi. "It makes no sense, pastor. She's all worried about Milwaukee making me more Amish than Jakob Ammann, but she gives you and uncle the strongest impression she herself wants to be Amish until she dies."

"That's right."

"It's crazy."

"Yeah."

Michal sat still, not knowing what else to say or think. Bubba cleared his throat. "Something else."

What next? But she raised her eyes from her hands to his face.

He tugged a black and orange business card from the pocket of his jeans. Then he flipped it toward her across the table.

"You know this guy by any chance?"

Michal picked up the card. The Harley-Davidson symbol was on it and, orange on black, the name Skid Wilson. Underneath it said, Sales and Service, New Orleans Harley-Davidson.

"Skid," she said. "He got us out of a jam in the Carolinas. We had an accident."

Bubba smiled. "So what he told me was legit. Nick needed a tune-up after putting on some miles since the work Ghost had done on his bike. So he went to the dealership on Airline Drive. It's only a few blocks from here. When Skid heard their story, or whatever part of their story they told him, he said he'd met Tabi's sister in North Carolina."

"He sure did."

"All right, all right." Bubba thought to himself for a few moments. "Clears up some stuff."

"What stuff?"

"Well, he came to me and talked a bit after Tabi and Nick took off for Texas."

Michal almost laughed in disbelief. "A Hells Angel comes to a preacher to talk things over?"

"Hey." Bubba fixed her with a look. "Heavens Gate and the Angels have done rides for cancer and for war amps together."

"Are you serious?"

"Oh, yeah, I'm serious. The Angels have even let us pray before we started our rides together. Hey, once they pretty much ordered us to pray."

Michal was incredulous. "The angels from hell wanted you to pray?" Bubba's voice became quiet. "Even angels from hell need the love of Almighty

God." Then he took her hand in one of his. "Didn't God send one of them to help you out in North Carolina?"

Michal made a sheepish face. "Yes, pastor, yes, he did."

"So—were you planning on dropping in on Skid?"

"We were. We owe him, Bubba. Neither of us have forgotten that."

"Good. I told him I was pretty sure we'd see you and Milwaukee in New Orleans."

A gust of children's laughter found its way to the roof. Bubba got up and looked over the edge. Michal joined him. Below them Milwaukee was playing a game of frozen tag with six or seven boys and girls who often spent the night in the warehouse. He was in his blue jeans and sleeveless denim jacket, darting back and forth across a strip of asphalt. Bubba watched Michal as she watched Milwaukee. It was impossible to miss the light that came into her eyes and the smile that spread across her face and changed everything about her looks, taking her from dark and anxious and unbelieving to a face that had strong measures of light, peace, and faith.

Thank you, Lord, he said to himself.

"Okay, so, well, what did Skid have to say to you?" she suddenly asked.

"Hmm?" Bubba had been daydreaming about Michal and Milwaukee. "You said there was something else and then you gave me Skid's business card."

He nodded. "Yeah. There's something else. And I want to do more praying onto you. But you got to see Skid first. And you got to hear what he has to say."

"About what?"

"Your sister. And her boyfriend."

A chill went like an ice snake up her spine. "Is it bad?"

"Just go talk to him. You got your own worries about Tabitha, don't you? So maybe Skid's got some insight. Maybe it'll help."

"When should I go?"

"Now. Right now. Just get back in time to help me and the team serve up the evening meal. Got 154 mouths to feed, remember."

Michal began to head to the trap door and the staircase down from the roof. "What was his address again?"

"It's on Skid's card."

"How do we get there?"

"You still got that street map, yeah? Use that. It ain't far. Part of Airline Highway. That way." He pointed out over the streets and houses. "Busy road. In Jefferson Parish like us here."

September New Orleans heat and humidity drenched them as they fought traffic and inched closer and closer to the Harley dealership. It so happened that when they finally rumbled into the parking lot Skid was standing outside and talking with a person in a suit they assumed was a customer. Skid was in clean jeans and a black long sleeve shirt with his hair combed back and neatly braided. Even his beard had been brushed and braided in two places. He turned to stare as Milwaukee rolled the 2007 Fat Boy right up to him and practically nudged Skid's polished black boots with the front tire. The stare became a glare as Milwaukee revved the engine and drowned out Skid's conversation with the suit. Then, as Michal dug him in the ribs and whispered, "That's enough, Amish boy," Milwaukee cut the engine. Skid's eyes were still piercing when Milwaukee took off his mirrored sunglasses and leather-covered half-helmet.

"Help you?" Skid asked with a generous amount of ice. "Looking for Skid," said Milwaukee.

"You found him. Fact, you almost drove over him."

"What? The suit here?" asked Milwaukee with a laugh.

"Mr. Simpson? No." Skid almost snarled and drew himself up so that he looked 20 feet tall again just as he had in North Carolina. "I'm Skid."

Milwaukee continued to play his game even though he could feel Michal's eyes burning through his back. "You're Skid? I expected someone taller."

Skid's eyes hardened into a kind of black obsidian, a shiny black rock Milwaukee recalled pocketing in Virginia.

"I guess I'm about as tall as I need to be, sir," Skid growled. "Can I help you find a pair of boots with a four inch heel to help you out of your inferiority complex?"

"Skid!" said the suit in a shocked voice. "Think customer service!"

"Yes, sir," Skid grunted as if in pain.

Milwaukee wanted to keep going, but Michal spoiled things. She removed her sunglasses and then her helmet. He couldn't see her, but he knew she must have done it by the way Skid and the suit suddenly looked past him, their eyes widening simultaneously. Once Skid spent another moment with those sky blue eyes Milwaukee knew he'd remember who she was and where he'd seen her before. So he played out the rest of his charade quickly.

"Mister Skid," he said, pulling off his glove and extending his hand, "I'm so pleased to meet you. We hear you offer great advice about obtaining a true Calabash fish fry. Which highway do we get on from here to get to that big plate of fish and greens?"

Skid finally pulled his eyes away from Michal and looked at Milwaukee again. Milwaukee watched the wheels turning. Then Skid glanced at Michal once more and back at him. His face broke open like an earthquake into a big toothy smile. His hand crushed Milwaukee's and then he pulled him in and cracked his back with a hug.

"Hey, Milwaukee and Roadburn! Hey, boss!" He turned briefly to the suit. "I met these kids in Carolina. Months ago. Only then they were scutting along on a bike from Beijing. Now look at them. They growed up."

The boss smiled and shook Milwaukee's hand. "Welcome to New Orleans. And congratulations on the '07 Fat Boy. Where'd you pick that up?"

"Mississippi, sir," Milwaukee grunted from within Skid's embrace. "It's been customized," the boss said.

"A biker named Ghost."

The boss stared. "Ghost? Troy Samson? Natchez? Heavens Gate?"

"Yes, sir. All of those things."

"Wow. You don't just have a Harley, son. You have a Boeing F-35 Joint Strike Fighter on rocket fuel."

"Hey, look at this beauty!" Skid dropped Milwaukee so that his feet touched the ground again and caught Michal up in his arms. "You get better looking every day."

Michal laughed. "Thank you, Skid. You do wonders for a girl's self-esteem."

"Hey, customer service."

Milwaukee turned to look at the long hug Skid gave Michal. It was like watching Ghost scoop her up when they were in Mississippi except it was a little more ardent. He didn't mind. After all, he and Michal were a package, but they weren't special delivery. Not yet.

Michal caught his gaze and smiled. "What is it?"

"Your hair," Milwaukee said.

It was hanging loose and black and shining down her back.

"Oh," she said. "Well, I had to think of some way of putting an end to your prank on Skid. Honestly, Milwaukee, you'd have gone on until you had poor Skid twisted up one side and down the other."

"So you took off glasses, helmet, do rag, and—hairpins?"

She shrugged with one shoulder. "I had to do something to get Skid to notice me and remember who I was. How else could I put a stop to your second childhood?"

Skid roared with a laugh like three Harleys starting up. "Hey, give her credit, Milwaukee, it sure worked."

Milwaukee kept smiling at her and felt a rise of warmth and light within his chest. The smile was different and deeper and stronger than anything Michal had seen before. She did not understand it, but she felt it. She could not pull her eyes away as he stood there in the parking lot of the New Orleans Harley dealership with his thick and curly sunny blonde hair and smiled at her with everything that was in him, never once breaking eye contact.

"Yeah," he finally said.

Chapter Fifteen

Skid's boss gave him an hour and he jumped on his bike. Michal and Milwaukee followed him five or six minutes through traffic until he pulled into a restaurant and ordered them all shrimp jambalaya and Pepsi. He listened to their stories and joked with them as they ate and drank. Then he pushed his chair back and worked at his teeth with a wooden toothpick.

"You've both changed a lot," he said. "But you've been on the road, what? Three months?"

"Longer than that now, Skid," Michal replied, holding Milwaukee's hand under the table, happy to be with the biker who had come to their aid in North Carolina, but also anxious to hear what he had to say about Tabitha and Nick.

"Well, before you were white as trouts' bellies, now you're dark as road rubber. Your baby fat is gone and Milwaukee's put on some weight where he needed it. And the slang!" He laughed, poking around his mouth with the toothpick. "Your accent was stronger before and your English way too English for a biker. Now you sound semi-South and all-American."

Michal was worried. "Do I sound really bad?"

"Nah. You sound really good. And look even better."

She smiled. "Thanks, Skid."

Skid glanced at Milwaukee. "You don't mind if I talk up your woman?"

"No." And Milwaukee didn't. "You give me good ideas about what to say to her next."

"Yeah?" He grinned, rolling the toothpick back and forth on his tongue. "Well, I ain't no poet, but I know a good thing when I see it."

He pushed his chair back and his mood suddenly changed. His face went granite. Digging in the pocket of his jeans he pulled out a few quarters and loaded them into the small jukebox that sat on the table in their booth.

"Y'all don't mind some Led Zeppelin?" he asked, not waiting for their answer. "Y'all don't mind Black Dog?"

Neither Michal nor Milwaukee had any idea what he was talking about. The music began to blare out of the speakers, just enough for them and not so much it would upset the people at the other booths. Skid leaned forward and, without thinking about it, Milwaukee and Michal did the same.

"I'm a motorhead," Skid told them, but his voice was low. Michal could barely pick out his words above the loud rock music. "Give me a bike to work on, make it strong to ride, give me some gas and asphalt, and I'm a happy man. A beer or two and my day's done. Some Angels need more. A lot more. I don't have to spell it out for you." Skid took the toothpick out of his mouth, looked at it, and snapped it in half between two of his fingers.

Then he locked their eyes with his. "I helped that Nick kid out and tuned the Ironhead that Ghost had worked on. He brought it into the shop and hung around while I played with it. I didn't mind. Didn't take me more than an hour and a half. At first we're just talking bike while I went at it. Then he asks me how to score."

"Score?" Michal stared at him. "You mean drugs or—?"

"I mean drugs. Not for personal use. He wanted to distribute."

"What did you do?" asked Michal.

"I told you—I'm a motorhead. Said he'd have to talk with somebody else. So I guess he did. Blacktop—he runs our Angels group here—Blacktop let me know the kid made connections for some pickups in Denver and Yuma and Santa Barbara. He got some stuff here too."

"What stuff?" Milwaukee wanted to know.

"Heroin. Bindles of heroin already packaged for sale. I guess that's how he's paying for the road trip. But he's gonna get it in bulk too. I think the idea is to sell some to dealers up north and make a bundle."

"How much of a bundle?" asked Milwaukee. "Millions."

Michal's head was swirling. "What about my sister? What does my sister have to do with this?"

"Only saw her the once. After I'd wheeled his bike outside and he'd paid the bill. They were arguing in a corner of the parking lot. I didn't hear much. Just this: She was yelling that he'd promised to stop dealing if they did the road trip together and he asked her how she thought they were paying for food and gas and motels with hot showers. Then she was arguing about why he had to get so much of the heroin—yeah, she used the word out loud, she was pretty heated up, looked good and scary with her blood red hair. Nick grabbed her by the shoulders and told her to shut up. She slapped him and he slapped her back. Then he hit her with his fist and she went to her knees."

Michal thought she was going to faint. She felt Milwaukee's arm go around her shoulders and Skid took both her hands in his.

"Look at me," Skid said to her. "Skid, I feel sick," she groaned.

"Look at me." She did. "Everyone's got codes. Even the Angels got codes. You don't do that to your woman. If you slugged your babe at an Angels rally a half dozen guys would haul out their switchblades and wanna carve on you. An argument is one thing, none of my business, but hittin' your sister like that was something else. I came at him from across the lot. Before I get there she's looking up at him with blood by the ring in her lip—yeah, her lower lip is pierced in three places with rings—and she says, 'You promised you wouldn't take drugs back for Ryan, you know he dishes them out to kids in Grades Five and Six', and Nick kind of laughs and tells her, 'Hey, I break promises like I break the laws of America, you know that, now shut up and back off or I'll lay a beating on you'. Then I get there and pick him off the ground so that his boots are hanging and I tell him about the code. I tell him there are Angels everywhere and all it takes is a phone call from me and they'll find him and, if the girl is bruised, discipline him. Then I tell him another part of the code—no one deals drugs to schoolchildren, no one makes a living at it, no one stays alive long enough to turn a profit—I made myself as plain as I could. I'm no Sunday School teacher and this ain't First Baptist Church of New Orleans, I told him. Then I dropped him and got your sister to her feet. Had a clean bandana I wiped her mouth with. Asked if she wanted to stay with me or someone else she knew. She told me she might wanna stay with ol' Bubba Win, the Baptist preacher. Then she changed her mind, apologized to Nick, hugged and kissed him, and they took off on the Ironhead together. That's the last I saw of her in Orleans. I went to Bubba. We've done rides together. But she never went back to him. I think they lit out of the city as soon as Nick got the brown he wanted."

Michal closed her eyes. "This started out as a rescue mission for Tabitha. Then it turned into a rescue mission for me. Now it's back to saving my little sister. I feel like we need to head right out and find her and get her away from him."

"And if she won't go with you?" asked Skid.

Michal opened her eyes and Skid thought they were the hard color of a blued revolver. "I'll take her."

"Do you know where she is?"

"The other day she was in Yuma. We can start there."

"That's a long way from here. Pretty much in Cali. What if Nick moves on?"

"I can't just sit here, Skid."

He squeezed her hands and released them. "Didn't think you were. Feeding and taking care of the homeless ain't sitting."

"So who takes care of my sister while I take care of other people's sisters?"

Skid nodded. "I'm not a praying man, but before you do anything go back to Rev Bubba, get it straight in your head, then do what you have to do." He took a card out of his pocket and gave it to her. It was white, not like the orange and black business card Bubba had given her. All it had printed on it was his name, Skid Wilson, and a phone number. "That's my special cell. And I mean special cell. Hardly anyone gets it. It's my trouble shooting line. I don't expect it to go off unless the person calling is a friend who's in way over their head. If that happens, I don't care where you are, call me. I'm serious. I would take it as a personal insult if I heard you got into a mess and didn't ring me up. Very personal." He looked at Milwaukee. "Get it?"

Milwaukee nodded. "Got it."

"Time to head back and sell Harleys for Simpson. And you two need to have a pow wow with Bubba." He got up. "I hate to be the bearer of bad tidings. Come here, Roadburn." She slowly stood up and he swept her into his arms. He smelled like tobacco and gasoline, just as he had that day in North Carolina. "It's gonna turn out. You hear me? It's gonna turn out."

Milwaukee tried to take Michal's hand when they got off the bike at Bubba's warehouse, but she pulled away.

"What's wrong?" he asked, hurt.

"I just don't want anyone to touch me."

"So suddenly I'm 'anyone'?"

"I need to be alone."

"But Bubba expects us to help with the cooking."

"I need to be alone in my head."

"Michal," he almost pleaded, "I want to help you."

"Do you?" she snapped in a cold voice. "Then leave me to myself and my prayers."

The parking lot began to fill with cars and bikes

as people came in to help Bubba out with the evening meal. Some were Heavens Gate, some Missionary Baptist, some Southern Baptist, some from non-denominational groups and house churches. Michal stalked past them all. Milwaukee followed slowly, putting on a smile and waving to persons they'd worked with on other nights and mornings. Many of the homeless were already inside seated at the long tables, talking, waiting, the children darting up and down the aisles. Bubba asked Michal to help cook up the catfish and got Milwaukee involved in mixing the batter for fried ice cream. While everyone was digging into their fried fish and hushpuppies and greens, Milwaukee was coating balls of frozen ice cream with the batter he'd helped put together. Momma Thunder from Heavens Gate dropped the balls into hot oil and fried them, placing three to a plate for people to come up, take back to their seats, and eat. It wasn't until the dishes and pots were washed and dried, the tables and benches put away, and the sleeping mats brought out that Bubba finally asked Michal and Milwaukee to join him on the roof.

Michal sat as far away from Milwaukee as she could possibly get.

Milwaukee saw Bubba's eyes flick from him to Michal, but at first the pastor said nothing about it. He only asked how Michal was doing since she'd spoken with Skid.

Michal sat like stone in her chair. "How am I supposed to feel? Some—monster—is beating up my sister and buying drugs to sell to dealers in Pennsylvania, dealers that are going to try and get 11 and 12 year olds hooked. It's a mess. Suddenly it's not much of a road trip anymore."

"What are you going to do?"

"I want—I want Milwaukee to take me to Arizona. I'm going to find Tabi and get her away from Nick. If Milwaukee won't take me I'll buy a ticket on a Greyhound."

"Why wouldn't Milwaukee take you?" Michal stared at Bubba. "I don't know."

He pressed her. "Did he say he wouldn't take you?"

"No."

"Then what's the deal?"

Michal would not look at Milwaukee. "I'm not sure."

Bubba kept his dark gaze on her. "Nick hit your sister."

"Yes. And heaven knows what he has done to her since."

"Do you think Milwaukee's responsible for that?"

Michal began to tremble just as she had done in Natchez. "Well, he—he's—" She didn't finish her sentence.

"He's a man?" asked Bubba. "Just like Nick's a man? So he's part of the same gang? He'll do the same things Nick does?"

"I don't know."

"Sure you know. Take a deep breath and look at him."

"No."

"He's brought you all the way here from Pennsylvania. Look at him." Bubba's commanding tone forced Michal to turn her head.

"Now tell him he's just like the other men, the ones who hit and hurt and abuse," Bubba said.

"I can't."

"Why not? He's tried to hit you, hasn't he? He's threatened to throw you off the bike, hasn't he? He's warned you he'll lay a licking on you every day you've been on the road—right?"

Michal was holding Milwaukee's gaze, her blue eyes filling, but she didn't respond to Bubba's prodding.

"Go ahead," ordered Bubba. "Get it off your chest. Tell him he's the same as Nick. Tell him he's the same as the dealers who pop heroin in little kid's veins. He is, isn't he?"

"No, no, he's not, he's—" Michal dropped her head onto her chest and the tears broke over her face. "Nick is beating her. He's beating my little sister."

Bubba nodded at Milwaukee who went to Michal quickly and knelt, gently gathering her head into his chest. She put an arm around his neck.

"I'm sorry, I'm sorry," she sobbed. "I don't know what I'm supposed to do or how I'm supposed to feel. I don't know what to say to anyone. I don't know how to talk anymore."

Bubba got out of his chair and knelt with Milwaukee, placing a large hand on each of their heads. "Then let's talk to the Lord. Hey, Jesus, you know what's going on. You know about Tabi and you know about Nick.

"Maybe things are worse, but maybe they're not. Maybe Nick is looking over his shoulder for Hells Angels sent by Skid. I sure would be if I were him. So maybe he's cool. But, Lord, Michal isn't cool. She's hurting inside, she's all ripped up, and she doesn't know where to turn. It's all confusion inside her head. But, Lord, you promised to keep us in perfect peace if our minds are stayed on you. So bring your child here back to that place of perfect peace.

"Calm everything down. Fill her mind, Lord, be her everything again. Help her to know who her friends are and not to push them away. It's a tough time, Jesus. Open the road for her again. Show her where to go and what to do. Protect her sister. Change Nick's heart. Bless her soul. And give Milwaukee the strength to be there for her and to defend her. In your good strong name. Amen."

He had no sooner pronounced the amen, the sun setting and the roof the colors of red and brass, than a buzzing and short tune came from Michal's bag. Using one hand to get the tears out of her eyes she used the other to find the cell phone.

"It's a text," she said. "A text always comes with the buzz and a few notes."

She read the message out loud. Hey, sis, where r u? We're on the road to Denver.

Michal thumbed her response. Why Denver? I thought you were in Yuma?

Nick has friends to see in Colorado. And I want to see the Rockies. Are you okay?

Of course I'm okay. Why wouldn't I be okay? Skid said you two had had a fight.

A reply to Michal's text did not come for several minutes. Finally Tabitha messaged, Sorry. Nick has pulled over for the night. It's a cute little motel. Oh, we're fine, sis, really. I hope Skid didn't exaggerate. He started to act like some father in control of everything

when he saw me and Nick blowing off some steam—
that's a weird English expression, isn't it? It was no
big deal. Nick and I sorted everything out. Don't you
and Joe Amish ever fight? Or is it always Disneyland?
     Michal replied, I don't know if you'd call them fights.

Well, Nick and I have been cool since New Orleans.
Really. Very cool. You have nothing to worry about.
How's your prayer life?

Could be better.

U still hanging out with Bubba?

Yes, we served about 150 people tonight.

     Tabitha asked, Catfish?
     Michal replied, Catfish and hushpuppies and fried
ice cream.

Fried ice cream? Are u kidding? Who did that?

Milwaukee.

No way. Maybe he's a better dude than I thought.

Yes, maybe.

How did he keep the ice cream from melting?

He coated it in a thick batter. Then you only fry it for
a minute and it's perfect.

OK, he has to make that for me sometime.

    Michal texted, California?
    Tabitha responded, That could work. We're heading there after Denver. I'll let u know.

How long will you be in Denver?

A few days. OK, I have to help bring the gear in. C u. Love u.

Tabi, God bless you, Christ be with you.

    There were no more texts in reply.
    Michal sagged in her seat. Bubba and Milwaukee were still kneeling on either side of her.
    "Pastor?" she asked, eyes closed.
    "What is it, child?"
    "Is Denver far away?"
    "It's a long haul."
    "What route would you take from here to there?"
    She opened her eyes as Bubba got up and sat back in his chair.
    Milwaukee remained at her side and, without noticing she was doing it until later, she ran a hand through his hair and slowly played with his curls, lifting them up and then letting them fall through her fingers. But her eyes were on Bubba Win.
    "Get on the I-10 again and head west," he told her. "When you hit Houston get on the Interstate 45 North. That'll take you past Dallas to Denton and by then it's the I-35 all the way to Oklahoma City and Wichita, Kansas. You with me?"

"I'm with you," Michal replied, her hand absently running through Milwaukee's hair.

"Get on the 135 North out of Wichita. You won't be on it long. At Salina—you're still in Kansas—hang a left and stay on the Interstate 70 all the way to Denver. If you need to head west out of Denver for California stay on the I-70 until you hit the I-15 near Bryce Canyon in Utah. Then stick with the I-15 South. You'll run down through Vegas to San Bernardino and San Diego. If you need to hit LA or the coast just get on your old friend the Interstate 10."

"What if we need to get to this place called Santa Barbara?"

"Not a problem, child. Y'all get on the old Number One and follow it north up the California coast. You'll find it." Then he smiled his big smile. "The mountains are gonna blow you away. And then the Pacific gonna do the same. Your eyes and the Pacific, you know, they're twins."

"Will you put that in writing, Bubba?"

"What? That your eyes are blue as the ocean?" Michal smiled. "The directions."

"I will." He got to his feet. "Let's do breakfast with the people before you head out in the morning."

"Yes, sir."

Bubba took the trap door down from the roof. Michal and Milwaukee were alone and it was night, the stars opening up the sky with drops of silver.

"Hey," Milwaukee said to Michal softly. She smiled down at him. "Hey."

"You fooling with the top of my head?"

She laughed and then burst into tears. "I don't deserve you. How can you put up with my mood swings?

I dump everything on you. You should leave me, no, I mean it, leave me, let me sort out this Troyer mess on my own, why did my father drag you into it? It's no concern of yours and who knows when I'll turn into Godzilla again, *nein, nein,* go, go, really, just go."

"Don't you ever get any new lines?"

"What?" She blinked at him through her tears.

"You need a new scriptwriter. Haven't we seen this scene already in the first part of the movie? Go, go, you said to me in the barn." He waved his hand, imitating the way she'd acted the afternoon they realized Tabitha had vanished down the highway. "Go, go. And I was stupid enough to listen to you that time. Not this time. I have a better scriptwriter than you."

He lifted his hand to her damp face. "We started together. We finish together. Whatever that finish looks like. Okay? As God is our witness?"

He shook her head. "I'm no good for you. I'm no good for anyone."

"Let me be the judge of what's good for me and what isn't."

"Really, Milwaukee, I can't promise you anything, I can't guarantee I won't turn on you again some morning, that I won't climb on my broomstick and fly nasty circles around your head."

He laughed. "Actually, you've done that already. Hey, you do it every morning, every afternoon, every time I see that lovely face you hide behind. Except you use white wings, not a broomstick—*Engel.*" He had used the German word for angel. "And the circles aren't nasty. They're pure gold. Make me dizzy, it's true. But I like the kind of dizzy you make me."

She shook her head again and could not keep herself

from smiling and laughing while the tears still came. "Oh, you're crazy, a crazy boy, what is a poor Amish girl to do with you?"

"Fall in love with him. Nothing less will do." He put fingers to her mouth. "Shh. No words. Nothing yet. Just think about it. Pray about it. Now, are we heading out in the morning? Together? Till the finish? As God is our witness?"

"Milwaukee—"

"As God is our witness?"

She gazed at him and her feelings for him were roaring up inside again like a wildfire. The tears stopped. "Yes."

He got to one knee and took her head in his hands. "Okay, now this is it. We are going to find your sister. We are going to take her home. She's going to be safe. Do you hear me?"

"*Ja,* I hear you."

"But do you believe me?"

"*Ja. Ich glaube, Sie.*"

"Okay, now that that's all settled—" He brought her mouth to his and kissed her softly under the starlight of New Orleans. When it was over she looked at him and felt a calm inside that was like a windless Gulf morning. He stood up and held out his hand. She took it and got up.

"Did that kiss mean anything special?" she asked. "It was gentle as—as light."

"Of course it meant something special." He smiled. "Kisses are just another way of talking. Didn't you know?"

She put her arms around his neck. "So translate for me."

"There's no word for it in English."

"German then."

"Nothing there either. Sorry."

"So how does this Amish-not-Amish girl know what you're talking about?"

"Listen closely and I'll tell you again."

His lips came onto hers. A weakness went through her and she clung to his back.

Oh, she thought to herself, *I am going to die in this man's arms long before I reach Denver.*

Chapter Sixteen

Day 111

We are in Salina, Kansas. From here we go west on the Interstate 70 to Denver. It was sunny when we left Wichita at 7 this morning, but now the horizon south and east is turning purple and black. I guess there will be a thunderstorm as the day heats up—it is already almost 80 even though it's the middle of September. Milwaukee and I think we can beat the storm and will be heading out as soon he's back from cashing travelers checks at the bank. Salina is a nice place and we had a good breakfast at one of the cafés. Not quite up to one of Ghost's Hog Specials, but we don't need one of his breakfasts unless we plan to go without food for the rest of the week.

We flew through wheat fields all morning. It's not like home where harvesting is done by horse and cart. Here the big green and yellow combines reap, thresh and winnow the crops. They seem to be working extra hard with the storm threatening.

Milwaukee pushed it all the way from New Orleans

to Houston and then from Houston to Oklahoma City. I had to be the one to tell him I couldn't handle any more days of 12 hours in the saddle. Of course he is determined to catch up to Tabitha in Denver for my sake as well as hers. But I don't want another skid and scrape like North Carolina. I can't help my sister if I'm in a body cast or laid up in some hospital in Oklahoma or Kansas. So back to eight hour rides and I pray if they are in Denver first they will hang around for a couple of days. Then again, it's not as if we'll know where they are and it's not as if they're going to tell us where they are, especially if Nick is dealing or Tabi is determined to keep on avoiding me.

Our plan kind of unravels in Denver if we don't miraculously spot them.

Even though Milwaukee was on a kind of race he was determined to see the Alfred P. Murrah building in Oklahoma City—I mean the memorial park where the building once stood before it was blown up by Timothy McVeigh. The reflecting pool was beautiful, but the Field of Empty Chairs, each one representing a person killed in the blast, brought everything home to me and I got very emotional. Especially when I saw the smaller chairs for the 19 children and noticed three unborn children were listed with their mothers' names on their mothers' chairs. It was too much. I thought of the school shooting at Nickel Mines and the poor little dead Amish girls and that just intensified the pain and my tears. Milwaukee had his arm around me for two hours. The only thing that gave me any sort of comfort was a statue across the street where a Catholic church stands—it is called Jesus Wept and has Jesus turning away from the blast site in grief, his hand over his face. Jesus, who wept over Lazarus and Jerusalem, and whose heart broke for the widow of Nain who had lost her only son. How can I not feel close to a God who has a human heart and a human face in addition to all the divine power that upholds the universe?

But Denver has its own sorrows because of the shooting at Columbine High School in Littleton. The library where most of the students were shot is no longer there, Milwaukee tells me, but a new one was built and dedicated to their memory. Oklahoma City is enough to think of all of it, he says, and that is why he will not stop at Columbine. It is also why he did not take us to Virginia Tech where there are 32 three hundred pound stones for each of the students and professors killed in a shooting there in 2007.

"Why do you want to remember these things?" I asked him after I had cried myself dry.

"Do you think their mothers or fathers or friends ever forget?" he asked me. "Do you think there is ever a day that goes by when they don't remember the people they loved and lost? Do you think God himself forgets?"

"No," I told him.

"So why should we?"

I am grateful for the chance I still have of saving my sister from something that could take her young life away from her. I am grateful for the roads of America that take me to her as swiftly as possible. I am grateful for the man God has placed in my life to carry me safely down those roads.

I don't know what I would do without him. Often I think I am just on the verge of using his Christian name and declaring my love for him, but then something in-

*side holds me back. Honestly, I don't understand what
is wrong with me. I am long past feeling only the affection one has for a close friend. So many times when he
holds me and kisses me I wish it would go on forever.
God must wonder at my hesitancy. Most women don't
have a man half as fine as he has given me in Milwaukee Bachman and yet I refuse to commit myself. I need
my head and heart examined. What will it take to push
me over the line and call him by his name?*

"Hey, Roadburn, you ready?"

Milwaukee came out of the bank tugging on his
leather gloves.

Michal was sitting on the bike and using the long
seat as a writing surface. She smiled, putting away her
pen and journal. "Hey, Chrome, I am." She pulled her
helmet on over her head and the star spangled do rag.

"So let's *schnell* and beat the storm. They warned
me inside that there could be funnel clouds around
Salina soon."

"How far did the map say it was to Denver again?"

Milwaukee straddled the Harley that they had finally decided to name The Big Easy after New Orleans.
"About 400 miles. We'll be there this afternoon. God
willing. Has your sister answered any of your texts
this morning?"

"No."

"So we haven't heard from her for what now?"

"Two days."

Milwaukee twisted around and looked back at her.
"Are you okay?" Michal put on her mirrored sunglasses. "Pretty okay."

"What's the Bible verse for the day?"

"Psalm 72 verse three: *The mountains shall speak peace to the people.*"

"Amen. You will be seeing plenty of mountains today, Michal. Denver's the gateway to the Rockies, they say."

"Will you pray for us?" she asked.

"I will."

She took off her helmet again while Milwaukee bent his head and prayed slowly in High German. Then he turned the key in the ignition and the Harley's rumbling filled the parking lot.

"Let's go with God!" he shouted. "You ready for the day, Roadburn?"

"I am, Chrome."

"No matter what comes our way?"

"No matter."

"So hug me like you mean it and we'll head out."

She wrapped her arms around him and squeezed as hard as she could. "Whoa!" he laughed. "You been bench pressing or something?"

"What?"

"Never mind. Your strength is cute."

"That's all? Just cute?" She put everything she had into a second hug. "Okay, hardcore cute."

They made their way to the interchange north and west of the city and turned left toward Colorado. She thought that a half hour of riding would leave the angry cloud cover behind. But the storm system seemed to follow them and got darker by the minute. The wind began to pick up. As they zipped past a community called Russell strange cloud formations began to form in the south, long and cylindrical and winding down toward the ground. She tapped Milwaukee on the shoulder and pointed. He nodded. Soon they were near Hays in western Kansas and, if anything, Michal thought the sky looked worse. Milwaukee pulled off the highway for gas. Wind was blowing dust and paper in circles around the pumps.

"This used to be Fort Hays," he told her as he topped off the tank. "It was an important army fort during the Indian Wars. The Seventh Cavalry was posted here for a while, that was Custer's regiment. And the Tenth Cavalry, the African-American regiment, the buffalo soldiers."

She had no idea what he was talking about. "You are a walking book. But it needs illustrations."

"Later. Let's pay for the gas and use the washrooms and get out of here before it starts to rain."

Inside the station the woman at the till warned them about the approaching storm. "Could be a lot more than rain or thunder. Everybody's seeing funnel clouds."

"Yes, we saw some," Michal told her, "but they were far away." The woman picked up on her accent. "Where you two from?"

"Pennsylvania."

"You get tornadoes there?"

"Yes, we had a bad one in 2009. It was only an EF1, but it still caused a lot of damage."

"Well, an EF1 is plenty enough for anybody. You keep an eye out. One of them snaky clouds could touch down anytime. Where you heading?"

"Denver."

"Still a long ways to go," the woman said, unsmiling. "You watch out. Sure you can't wait it out here? We got a good coffee shop. Fresh sandwiches every day."

Milwaukee thanked her. "We'll keep our eyes wide

open, ma'am. But we have an important appointment in Denver we can't miss."

"Well, I warned you," the woman grumbled. "Just make sure your appointment in Denver doesn't turn into an appointment with The Man Upstairs."

As they straddled their bike Michal put a gloved hand on Milwaukee's arm. Both of them had their leather jackets and chaps on. The wind whistled over their heads and through the power lines, but the leather kept them warm.

"What do you think?" she asked.

"We've got to move on," Milwaukee insisted. "Nick can get from Yuma to Denver in good time. We don't have a minute to spare. They could be there and gone if we miss a beat."

"If they're even there in the first place. Tabi still isn't texting. They could be anywhere."

"Yeah, and Nick could be getting her to tell us Denver when he's really heading for Santa Barbara, just to throw us off and keep us at a distance."

"Or the mountains might be messing up reception," Michal suggested.

Milwaukee nodded. "Could be anything. But you want to know what I really think? They are in Denver, Nick has some dealing to do, and he won't let her text because he's afraid we might push it and catch up to them there if we knew."

They continued west on the I-70, the airstream mixed with escalating winds shrieking in their ears. Traffic was not as heavy as it usually was on an interstate, but there were still cars and trucks, though few semis.

"Where are the big rigs?" Michal asked, putting her

head against his. "Too much wind. Too much threat from the storm."

"And here we are."

"Here we are. The Penn State Two."

"More like the Lancaster Loonies," she said. "Ha. Ha."

Not far out of Hays Michal began to hear a shrill wailing sound and finally identified it as a siren.

"Do you hear that?" she shouted. "Yeah! Just like home!"

Lightning was flashing south of them to their left and they could both feel the increased force of the wind. Suddenly, right in front of one of the strikes of forked lightning, a huge black funnel cloud touched down and began churning across the fields toward the highway.

"Milwaukee!" she yelled. "I see it! We can outrun it!"

"They go 60 miles an hour!"

"And we're doing over 80! We can beat it! More dangerous to lie flat in the ditch and have it go right over us! Toss us around like straw and snap our necks, sure!"

Michal could feel the bike vibrate and the whine of the engine increase. Milwaukee bent lower over the handlebars. She tightened her arms over his stomach and chest and bent with him, keeping her head turned to the left so she could watch the tornado.

At first it was moving to cut across the interstate just ahead of them. As she prayed, it began to sheer back toward Hays and she gave Milwaukee a short, sharp squeeze in relief. Immediately she felt guilty because her prayers were doing nothing to keep the tens of thousands of people living in Hays safe. So she whispered, *Let it come our way, Lord, we can handle it much better than a city.* A minute later the tornado changed direction again and headed directly at them.

"It's coming right at us!" Michal shouted.

Milwaukee glanced to the left. "By the time it reaches where we've been we'll be long gone!"

But the tornado did not appear to diminish in size or distance. As Michal watched, it grew larger and larger and seemed to be following them west along the highway.

"We're not shaking it, Milwaukee!"

He glanced to his left again. "Hang on! Were going to do an Elvis!"

"What are you talking about?"

"Elvis Presley rode his Harleys hard! Hundred, hundred and ten miles an hour!"

"How do you know?"

"Read it in a book!"

The Big Easy picked up speed as the tornado roared down on the interstate. Michal was certain the dark swirling cloud would hit them head on. She saw fence posts flying upward and long strands of barbed wire flailing the air like whips. But bit by bit their Harley pulled ahead. The tornado did not change direction again and surged across the highway behind them. Michal counted to sixty-seven, stopping when the spinning wind struck the asphalt and swept over it to the wheat fields on the other side, using a speed limit sign for a marker.

"Thank God!" she shouted into Milwaukee's ear. "We were at least a minute ahead of it!"

"There's another!"

A second funnel cloud had touched down and was throwing up dirt and debris several miles ahead. It moved away and toward Hays, but then, just as the other had done, turned back and aimed for the highway.

Milwaukee slowed in hopes of having it pass over the lanes well in advance of them. However, when he slowed, it appeared to slow, and when he sped up, it did so too. Finally he gunned it and tried to outrace it just as he had the first tornado. Michal prayed and held her breath without knowing it. As the snake cloud loomed over them and the wind seemed to be trying to throw the Harley into the air she felt her mouth go instantly dry and the hairs on the back of her neck lift.

Oh Gott, she prayed, *bewahre uns. Oh God, save us.*

The Big Easy hurled itself along the blacktop as if the wind were directly behind it and thrusting the bike forward. Michal leaned over Milwaukee's shoulder to read the speedometer. It said 120. There were no more numbers after that.

"Oh, boy," Michal muttered, having the ridiculous thought as the wind tore at her helmet and jacket that the expression was the same in English as it was in German.

No vehicles were coming toward them, but ahead four or five cars and pickups were racing west just as they were. However, as hard as Milwaukee was pushing the Harley, the trucks and cars were pushing harder and going faster. Soon the bike was isolated on the highway with the whirling funnel screaming down upon it. Michal expected to be plucked off the seat, her arms torn away from Milwaukee's chest, and her body sent spinning into space. The shrieking in her ears grew louder and louder.

Then, for a moment, and the briefest of moments at that, the spiraling column of black wind seemed to hesitate as it ripped up a crop of wheat and tossed a red combine to the heavens. The bike took the gift and howled past. The tornado suddenly redoubled its speed and bore down on the asphalt lanes like an enraged and insulted demon. Using the combine as a marker, which the wind had flung down by the interstate in a display of foul temper, Michal stared behind them and counted, one—two—three-four. At thirty-six the tornado blasted across the roadway and plowed into a massive field of corn, chopping the tall stalks to the ground and cutting a wide path right through the plants as if, Michal imagined, someone unseen was wielding a giant scythe. She put her head on Milwaukee's back and breathed out. There were no more funnel clouds ahead. Moisture returned to her mouth.

Suddenly they hit a wall of rain so ferocious the Harley wobbled and Milwaukee lost control. Michal was sure they were headed for the ditch.

Then the bike righted itself, firmed up against the pavement, Milwaukee cut the speed to 80, and they split the rain showers like a dart. In minutes they were both soaked through, but were moving steadily through the curtain of silver and gray water.

Five minutes later, the rain slamming into their heads and backs like fists, thunder banging and lightning bursting on their eyes and cracking the sky, Milwaukee slowed the Harley. Michal saw they were turning off into a lane that took them to an old gas station where two RVs were already parked to wait out the storm. The station was boarded up and abandoned. Milwaukee motored the bike around to the back and parked under an overhang. Then he cut the engine, climbed off, and tried the back door. It was nailed shut. Without hurrying, rain bouncing off his helmet and jacket, he opened a saddlebag, took out a short crowbar, and pried the door open. Then he extended a hand to Michal.

"But you broke in!" she protested, without moving from the seat of the bike.

He made a face. "Broke into what? A gas station that was shut down in 1975?"

"Still."

"Michal, there's tornadoes all around us. God forbid, but people may have been killed already. It's an emergency situation. Do you think the state troopers are going to arrest us because we saved our lives by hiding out in a derelict gas station?"

Pouting, she got off the Harley. "Derelict!" she snorted as she walked past him and into the station. "You and your English dictionary."

It was cool inside. A counter was still in place, and several shelves and metal racks, but there were no chairs or stools and all the tables had been unbolted from the floor and removed. Broken glass littered parts of the floor and Michal could smell mice. But Milwaukee had gone back for clothing and ran into the station with the shirts and jeans, hunching over in the downpour to protect them, so they had a chance to get warm and dry.

There was one washroom with no toilet and a stained sink and they changed in there, first Michal and then Milwaukee. She was delighted that the mirror over the sink was intact and only needed to be wiped clear of dust and grime.

They hung up their wet jeans and tees as well as their jackets and chaps. Milwaukee went into the garage through a small door and came back with old tires, stacking them to make two seats and wiping them down with a bandana from his pocket. Then he placed candy bars and bottles of water on the counter in front of the seats.

"I suppose you'll tell me they were in some ancient machine in the garage and are a million years old, but still taste great," Michal said.

Milwaukee sat on one set of tires and unscrewed the cap from his water bottle. "Nope. They've been in the saddlebags since Houston."

She smiled and sat next to him. "I guess they'll be okay then." Tearing the wrapper on her bar she looked at him while he drank. "You're crazy, you know."

"You always say that."

"Well, so who else but a crazy man would try to outrun two twisters?"

"We beat them didn't we?"

"Not by much."

Milwaukee bit into his Milky Way bar and chewed. Mouth full of chocolate and caramel and nougat he asked her, "What would you have done?"

"Swallowed first."

He ignored her. "It was the only option that left us in control."

"We were in control?"

"As long as we were on the bike we had a little bit of it, yes. More than lying in a ditch while the bike sailed to the moon—or sailing to the moon with it."

"I thank God we made it through."

"I do too."

She finished her Three Musketeers, drank from her bottled water, screwed the cap back on, and sat facing ahead for a few moments. Finally she turned to Milwaukee. The sharp smile of the Troyer sisters played over her lips.

"I found I liked the thrill," she said.

He stopped drinking and looked at her in surprise. *"Ja?"*

She nodded, still smiling in the special way she shared with Tabitha. He laughed. "So did I. What a pair. What will God do with us?"

Michal started getting out of her seat. "I think—" she began, stepping over to him, but the buzzing of her cell phone interrupted her. The bag was on the counter and she yanked the phone from it.

Hey, sis, sorry I've been out of touch. We've been so busy here in Denver, just going like nuts. Hardly had time to eat and sleep. Where are u? Still in New Orleans with Bubba Win?

"They're in Denver," she told Milwaukee. "I'm going to tell her we're only hours away."

"Go ahead. Let's see what they say."

Michal moved her thumbs rapidly. We are only a few hours out of Denver. Where can I meet up with you so we can finally have a good sister-to-sister chat?

The response took several minutes. R u kidding me? I thought u were hundreds of miles away.

No. I'm in Kansas. Not far from the Colorado border. There's a bad storm, but as soon as it's over we'll be on our way again. Where can I meet you?

Almost five minutes went by. Michal sat back down with the cell phone in her hands, waiting. Neither her nor Milwaukee spoke. Then the cell buzzed and played the short tune.

Reception is bad.

There were no more messages. Ten minutes went by and Milwaukee got up and stood behind Michal, gently rubbing her shoulders.

"Do you think reception is bad?" she asked him.

"I think Nick is bad." He kept rubbing her shoulders. "I know you're scared. Here's what we're going to do. The heavy rain won't last forever. As soon as it lightens up we'll get back on the road. I'm sure the weather will improve as we head west."

"Why—why can't we call the police now?" Michal asked in a weak voice.

"We could. But if Tabitha tells them the same thing she told the Virginia state troopers, that she's happy to be with Nick, they won't be able to do a thing. If we tell them he could be carrying drugs, and he isn't, they won't be able to arrest him. Then he'll take it out on Tabitha because he'll suspect we tipped off the police. If he does have drugs, if he has heroin, they'll both be charged. Your sister will go to prison."

Michal trembled and Milwaukee rubbed her shoulders more vigorously.

"So we try and find them all on our own," she said. "How are we going to do that if they don't want to be found?"

"I doubt Nick will let her text again. Not for a while anyway. If he does, it'll just be so he can find out where we are. We'll be flying blind for a while, Michal. All we can do is head west and hope for the best."

"Hope for the best? Is that it?"

Milwaukee softly kissed the top of her head where the American do rag was still firmly in place.

"Hope for the best. Pray for a miracle."

Chapter Seventeen

The rain eventually dwindled to a gray silence. Milwaukee and Michal quickly packed up and turned west onto the I-70. Within an hour they were out from under the cloud cover and the sun sparkled on The Big Easy's chrome. As time streamed past they began to ride into a golden sunset and catch their first glimpses of tall blue and white peaks. Then it was dark and they came into a Denver lit by thousands of squares of windows and round headlights. Milwaukee took them straight to the west end, just a few blocks before the interstate broke away from the city and made a line for Utah.

They rented two rooms at a motel. Milwaukee, suddenly drained of energy after their run from the twisters and the long ride to Denver, lay down on his bed—as he told Michal in the morning—and never got up until jerking awake at 5:30 AM.

Michal had a shower after they stopped at the motel and then waited for him in a small café where they'd planned to have a snack. She finally gave up, bought a wrap and orange juice, and sat on their bike in the parking lot. She looked west at the skyline while she ate. A moon gleamed off the mountain peaks and a fresh coat of high September snow. The sight seemed to fill every nook and cranny inside her. She didn't even have words to praise God for what glowed and glistened in her eyes. The whiter the moon shone the whiter the snow shone in response. Now and then a star cut through all the shining with a sharp and intense luminosity all its own.

Although part of her was worried terribly for her sister, another part could scarcely contain her excitement at taking in the Rocky Mountains for the first time. She wrote in her journal while she sat on the Harley: *No words for it, just feelings turning over inside I don't think have turned over for a long, long time, not since childhood, if even then.*

Milwaukee knocked on her door at quarter to six the next morning. "Hey," he said.

"Hey," came a muffled response that sounded like it had emerged from under a pillow.

"I've got a coffee and a Danish for you. We need to get going."

"What time is it?'

"Almost six."

"Can't I sleep another hour?"

"No."

"Why not?"

Milwaukee knocked on the door again. "Did your sister text you during the night?'

There was a minute of silence. "Nothing," Michal finally told him.

"Did you plug it in and charge it overnight?"

"Ja, ja."

"So I want to get up the freeway to a turnout. Keep

an eye on the traffic that goes by. In case they're still here. Maybe they'll head out sometime over the next hour."

"Do you think they're in Denver right now?"

"No. But we need to do something."

Michal had slept deeply, her head full of mountains and stars.

Standing beside Milwaukee in the dawn coolness, sipping her coffee and gazing at the mountains under the light of an early sun, she experienced the same surge of power and wonder as she had the night before. Once again the awe was intermingled with fear for Tabitha, yet the beauty and majesty of the Rockies was not diminished. As they rode into them the feeling of strength they gave her continued to increase. She began to murmur a psalm to herself.

Ich hebe meine Augen auf zu den Bergen.

She leaned forward and spoke into Milwaukee's ear. "I lift my eyes to the mountains—where does my help come from?"

Milwaukee twisted his head toward her. "My help comes from the Lord, maker of heaven and earth."

"So will good things happen today?" she asked.

"Why not? Good things happen as often as bad things. People just don't notice them unless they are as big as mountains."

They rolled through foothills that were still green with summer, but now and then Michal saw spots of bright yellow from trees that a magazine in her room had said were aspen. The trees gave way to grass and the grass gave way to rocky slopes bare of everything except a few scraggly bushes. Soon the massive peaks surrounded them with gray and white, sometimes blocking the light, sometimes letting it through, until the sun was high enough to streak all the slopes with color. There was a turnoff for viewing the peaks and taking photographs full of cars and RVs and Milwaukee turned into it. They sat on the bike and watched everyone rushing past while Milwaukee handed Michal chunks of beef jerky.

"This is breakfast?" she wanted to know.

"Well, there is cold water in your BPA free water bottle. I filled it from a container of spring water this morning."

"I'm teasing. Jerky and cold water suits the mountains as far as I am concerned."

"Really?" Milwaukee changed his position on the bike so that he was sitting and facing her. "You are turning into a mountain woman, are you?"

"I don't know." She smiled. "Aren't you supposed to be keeping an eye out for a 1979 Ironhead?"

"This is more interesting."

"You could at least be looking at the Rocky Mountains."

"I prefer the view I have."

Michal laughed. "So who is watching the traffic?"

"You can handle that, can't you?"

"Suppose I would rather watch you?" she asked.

Milwaukee made a face. "Why would you want to do that? I'm just me. The same as I was yesterday."

"I liked the man from yesterday."

Milwaukee kept glancing at the traffic. "You can be most annoying. I thought of gazing at you first."

She took his hand. "We'd better watch for the bike together. Look, here comes a bunch."

Five riders zipped past on what Milwaukee said were Honda Gold Wings, each of them a brilliant fiery red.

"Why, they are very beautiful," said Michal.

"Try and convince Ghost of that."

They continued to eat jerky and watch for motorcycles. Every two or three minutes bikes snarled by and each time Michal could not stop herself from getting her hopes up. But each time it was a disappointment. No Ironheads and, even if Nick had switched bikes, no one that looked like Tabitha or Nick.

"Would you recognize your sister with helmet and leather on?" Milwaukee asked her.

"Of course," Michal responded. "How?"

"Her posture. The way she held her head. Just the whole feeling. Her spirit."

Milwaukee continued to scan traffic. "You sound pretty confident."

"She's tried to fool me before with costumes and wigs. It never works."

Milwaukee lifted the arm with his wristwatch. "Five more minutes."

"Then what?"

"Utah." He looked at her jacket. "Did your leathers finally dry out?"

"They did."

"Ghost gave us some mink oil to treat them with after they'd taken a lot of rain or snow. Remind me to do that that tonight."

"And where will we be tonight?"

"God knows. Ask him."

"I do."

He smiled and turned the key in the ignition. "Saint Troyer."

She wrinkled her nose in a way Milwaukee had never seen before. "No saint. Just one girl worried about another girl."

"Hey." His brown eyes were deep before he placed his mirrored glasses on. "We're going to find her. And she's going to be all right. Nick may have a mean streak, but he's no monster."

His eyes and words warmed her. "I pray you're right."

"You ready for some big vertical?"

"I am."

"Then let's do God's masterpiece." He revved the engine. "One of them anyway."

Michal's warmth increased by several degrees. Milwaukee could have meant places like the Grand Canyon or Niagara Falls or the Pacific Ocean when he hinted at God's other masterpieces. But somehow she sensed he meant her. As their Harley roared back onto the I-70 she gratefully wrapped her arms around him and for a few minutes leaned her head against the curve of his back.

Lord, be with us this day, the day you have made. Take us where we're meant to be even if we aren't aware it's you who is directing our steps.

Most of the day was rugged peaks topped by snow and frost and pinned a September sky almost as blue, Milwaukee told her, as her eyes. She asked if it wasn't a very proud thing to say a person's eyes outdid God's creation. He told her she was God's creation. She had no answer to that so continued to hug him tightly and luxuriate in his closeness, his devotion, and the brilliance of the mountains. Always a concern for Tabitha was caught up in this feeling of bliss, but she also felt, as Milwaukee had said, that they would find her and Nick would not harm her. She also believed God had his hand on her sister's life and everything would come together, eventually, in a way that blessed and made sense and honored Jesus Christ.

They finally crossed the state border into Utah, rolling down out of the big peaks into land that was still green, but which bore, to Michal's mind, a hint of desert, even though she had never in her life seen desert. They stayed at a motel, bathed instead of showering, ate a good meal at a restaurant where they were waited upon by a teenaged girl named Skye, then found a place to watch the famous Green River pass. After that, Milwaukee spent an hour in her room, rubbing down their jackets and chaps with paste from a small plastic tub of mink oil while they glanced at different programs on the TV set. Finally Michal clicked the set off.

"Why are the shows so violent?" she asked out loud. "Why is it always about murder, murder, murder, as if killing someone were fascinating or interesting?"

"Sometimes people speak peace," Milwaukee murmured, working on her jacket, "but it's a rough society, it's a rough age."

She sat on the edge of the bed next to him. "Do you ever want to be back in Marietta?"

He did not look up. "I think your jacket took more water than mine."

"Well—I was covering your back, wasn't I?"

He glanced up and smiled. "You're right. You were."

"Answer my question."

"Sometimes yes, sometimes no. There are things I miss and things I don't ever want to go back to."

"Like what?" she challenged him.

He spread mink oil on the back of her jacket, over the silver cross and black barbed wire and Bible verse from the gospel of John. "I miss the fall. The colors. The harvest. It would be turning now. I miss Esau and the horses and the smell of hay and straw. The quiet. I miss the quiet. And buggies coming down the road instead of cars and trucks."

"What do you miss that's spiritual?"

"All that I've told you *is* spiritual."

"You know what I mean. Amish churchy things."

"Well—I do like long sermons if they go somewhere. The English sermons are too short—what can you say that really gets into your soul in 15 or 20 minutes?"

"Just sermons? That is all you miss?"

"Some of the hymns. But, to tell the truth, I'd rather have guitars and instruments than only voice all the time. Really, Michal, every time I think I could go back and be baptized something pops into my head—no more Ghost on his Martin acoustic, no more piano, not ever, no more saxophone or drums or violins—and I think: 'What? Why?' The Amish are not holier because they have no acoustic guitars or electric keyboards."

"It's a different path in Christ, Milwaukee, that's all. Not a holier-than-thou thing."

He glanced up from her jacket. "So? What about you? What do you miss besides your family?"

"Besides my family? Why—I miss the homemade food, the jams, the pies, the church dinners, the talking and laughing, the community, I miss all that the most."

"That's everything."

"No, not everything. I myself don't want to listen to one or two or three hour sermons anymore. No more *a capella* singing—I want the guitars just like you do. And no more prayer caps, please, I'd rather have a do rag. Sure, the horses, I miss the horses and the wagons and the clip-clop of the hooves. But I'd rather have a bike like the one we have now."

"Truly?"

"Yes, I like traveling like this. If we found Tabitha tomorrow morning and papa came to get her on the train I'd say, *Papa, I love you, but we will not be home for Christmas.*"

"No."

Her face grew defiant with strong sharp lines around her mouth and at the corners of her eyes. "I would so positively say that."

"And then when it came time to settle down, where would that be?" asked Milwaukee, holding up her jacket and examining it for spots he'd missed.

"I haven't seen enough of America to answer that. But if I had to do it tomorrow I would go back to New Orleans or Natchez. Or somewhere in-between."

"Baton Rouge?"

"Maybe. If I wanted a city as big as Pennsylvania."

"Here. Hold out your arm." Milwaukee put her jacket on her. "Would you find the sweetness there?"

"Sweetness?"

"What the TV shows cannot give you. Or the traffic or the freeways. The sweetness of a people always praying and always blessing." Unconsciously, Michal tugged the heavy black jacket around her.

"That is such a way of putting it."

Milwaukee watched the different movements in her face as she thought about what he'd said. The blue in her eyes turned, bit by bit, into a deep twilight. Her lips parted as she concentrated. He shook his head to clear it of his fascination with her. It didn't work.

"You know," he said, "I could do this all day and all night."

She came out of her reverie and looked at his face as if noticing him for the first time. "Do what?"

"Star gaze."

"What do you mean? We're inside."

"Stars sometimes come indoors."

She finally caught his meaning and smiled the Troyer sharp smile. "But." Milwaukee stood up. "I'm beat and tomorrow's another big day."

She pouted. "Too beat to kiss a star?"

"You bet, too beat. Kissing you in the mood I'm in is a three hour job. I need my sleep."

She was about to say something else when he took mink oil and dabbed it on her forehead, the tip of her nose, both cheeks, and her chin. Startled, she did not know how to respond. He bent and kissed her lightly on her open mouth. Then he opened the door to leave, picking up his jacket and chaps as he did so.

"Now you are waterproof," he told her. "Just smear it around a bit."

She jumped up and grabbed several Kleenex from a pink box on a table. "Oh, you are a crazy boy again. I'm going to get zits."

"As if that would make any difference."

"Of course it makes a difference. Who wants to see a zit on a woman? Who wants to kiss it?"

"Please, please, don't tempt me to prove otherwise or I'll be here until midnight."

Michal was staring into a mirror and frantically wiping at the thick paste. "Sure, sure."

"I looked up a topographical map on the internet while we were in the restaurant. You'd gone to the washroom. Tomorrow is all desert. And the day after that. And the day after that. Are you ready for it?"

Michal went into her bathroom and Milwaukee heard the tap running. "Of course I'm up to it," came her voice. "Why wouldn't I be up to it? We're already in the desert anyway."

"Well, you've never been in this kind of desert before."

"I was never in mountains before. Or under palm trees. Or close to cypress swamps. Neither were you. We made out just fine, didn't we?"

"The desert has rattlesnakes. And scorpions. And Gila monsters. Black widows that are 17 times more poisonous than most rattlers. There are tarantulas too."

Michal poked her head out of the washroom while she toweled her face. "Are you trying to scare me, Amish boy from the Susquehanna?"

"I don't know. Are you scared?"

"Not at all."

She marched out of the washroom and picked up the small Bible her father had given Milwaukee from the bedside table. Flipping to a page she'd marked with a sales slip, she began to read in German, *"Trostet mein Volk—"*

Milwaukee interrupted, reciting in English: *"Comfort ye, my people, saith your God. Speak ye comfortably to Jerusalem, and cry unto her, that her warfare is accomplished, that her iniquity is pardoned: for she hath received of the Lord's hand double for all her sins. The voice of him that crieth in the wilderness, Prepare ye the way of the Lord, make straight in the desert a highway for our God. Every valley shall be exalted, and every mountain and hill shall be made low: and the crooked shall be made straight, and the rough places plain. And the glory of the Lord shall be revealed, and all flesh shall see it together. For the mouth of the Lord hath spoken it.* Isaiah chapter 40, verses one through five. Amen."

Michal was staring at him and now, he noticed, the blue in her eyes was more like the deep lavender of June lilacs in Marietta.

"Amen," she said. "Did Mrs. Beachy require you to memorize that?"

"No. It is a chapter I have always liked since I was a boy. Because of the stuff about eagles later on, I think."

"So you have the whole thing in your head?"

"For many years. Yes."

"I think it is meant for us, for this next part of the road trip—*make straight in the desert a highway for our God.* Do you agree?"

He shrugged, still standing in the open doorway. "Sure. Why not?"

"I think our luck, as the English put it, will change. I think a great blessing is about to fall upon us."

"Well, I don't want to argue with the Lord about what he wishes to do, Michal, but I believe our luck, if you like to call it that, has been pretty good so far, and that our blessings have been even greater."

"Oh, do you?"

"I do. So if he's going to turn up the volume, I'm all for it. I may not be able to handle it, but I like the idea."

Michal made a pretend frown. "What can't my big brown-eyed Amish boy handle?" She came to him and put her arms around his waist. "Tell me."

"The door's open, Michal."

"So?"

"You still have the Bible in your hand."

"The Lord doesn't mind."

Milwaukee laughed and leaned against the doorframe. "I can see it.

The clock will strike twelve and here I'll be in this doorway."

"You can run."

Suddenly Michal saw his eyes darken as he dropped everything he was carrying in a heap. He put one hand under her chin. "I told you. I'm tired. Certainly too tired to run."

They kissed for several minutes. Then she whispered in his ear, "Take me into the desert. Take me to my sister and take me to my God. And please be sure to tell me, night after night, how much I mean to you. Under the stars and with the sands and rocks all around us, tell me again and again how much you love me and how forever a love can be that is rooted in the undying love of an undying God."

Chapter Eighteen

Michal sat up in her motel bed with a jolt. Her mind spinning, she looked at the red numerals of the digital clock by her bed—4:30 AM. She sank her head into her hands and tried to pray, but the strident voices from the dream keep breaking into her thoughts.

You cannot keep playing games with Milwaukee like this, Michal. It is not right. Tell him you love him or leave him alone.

I am not playing games with him, mother.

Of course you are. Hugging him, kissing him, telling him how much you care for him. But you never commit yourself.

I am not sure.

How sure do you need to be?

It's not so easy, mama. It's very confusing.

Oh, you are not confused at all. You're just afraid to give him your heart.

Shouldn't I be?

There are some things you will never feel and never know until you are committed to those you care about. It is true for your faith in God and it is true for your faith in a man who could become your husband.

I can't take that final step. I always pull back. You don't understand how difficult it is for me.

You think I don't understand? I lost the man I loved because I played the very game you are playing now.

What are you talking about?

I married your father, I married Simon. But it was his brother I loved. It was Samson who made my heart skip a beat. I thought I was being clever when I played them off against one another. No, I would never commit to either, I would never commit to Samson, I thought I had all the time in the world. Until the day Samson up and left and I lost him forever.

So you do not love papa at all?

Of course I love him. He is a good man and I grew to appreciate the person he is. But it was never like a fire in my heart.

Oh, mama—

You will lose him, Michal. You will lose Milwaukee if you do not make that commitment.

He's not going to leave me out in the desert and ride away. He is not that kind of person.

Others could take him from you.

What others? He has ever mentioned another woman. He never even looks at other women.

I am not talking about women. I am talking about the men Nick is associating with. The drug lords he is playing games with. If Milwaukee takes Tabitha away from Nick they will hunt him down.

Mama, you are frightening me.

They will hunt Milwaukee down and take Tabitha back—she knows too much.

Mama—

They will kill him, Michal.

She threw back the covers and went quickly to the washroom where she ran the tap and kept splashing cold water over her face. Without using a towel to dry off she walked back and sat on the edge of the bed. She was wearing a 3XL tee shirt Milwaukee had bought for her in New Orleans: I Love The Big Easy. A large red heart took the place of the word love. Drops of water falling from her cheeks, she stared at the wall and a cheap print of the Green River flowing between its banks.

I don't know what to do, Lord. I'm scared.

She got dressed and brushed her teeth. Then she stepped outside her room. It was after five now, but still dark with only a hint of gray light from the coming dawn. Stars were overhead, far away and white. To the west, large desert buttes and hills rose up and dominated the horizon, black and huge against the gray in the sky. She did not feel the sense of adventure she had the day before. Instead she was sick with dread.

We are going into a strange land, Lord. It terrifies me. Will you not talk? Will you not comfort me? What is going to happen to us?

She stood for a long time and then finally went and sat on the bike. Slowly the sky peeled away to blue and yellow as the sun rose behind her. The buttes brightened and did not look so fierce. A quiet voice inside her head asked: *Do you trust me?*

She hesitated, unsure of everything—Milwaukee, Tabitha, the future, the danger. Then she said out loud, "Yes, Lord, I trust you."

Commit your way to me.

"I do."

Commit all your way to me.

"What do you mean? I'm not holding anything back."

But now there was only silence. Michal got up off the bike and began to pace, constantly running her hands back through her long hair, as the sunrise washed over everything like a golden sea, bringing Utah to life. At first she pretended to herself and to God that she did not know what he was talking about. Then one thought kept pressing in on her, one face, and she knew the time had come to stop playing games with a child of God who meant the world to her. Still, she felt no peace, but only anxiety.

Milwaukee came out of his room at 6:30, hair still wet from a shower.

It glittered in the vivid sunlight.

"Hey," he smiled. "You look like you're ready to go."

"I'm ready, all right." But she did not smile back. "I could use a hug, Milwaukee."

"Hugging you is never a problem for me." He gently put his arms around her. "How's that?"

"More."

"More?"

"Hold me more tightly. Please."

She closed her eyes and rested her head on his chest, listening to his heart as his strength surrounded her, protected her, calmed her. The pressure of his arms on her back and shoulders felt wonderful. The long hug made the morning a gift again.

"Hey," he said, looking down at her. "Hey," she answered, opening her eyes.

"Are you up for some coffee and a breakfast?"

"I am now."

They ate quietly and she was finally able to smile at him as they sipped their black coffees and poured maple syrup over their waffles.

"Did your sister text?" he asked her. She shook her head.

"I'm going to do a U-turn and go back a few miles to a place called Moab. It'll cost us a few hours. But I think it's important."

"Why Moab?"

"They say it's a place God made special."

Light from the window had found its way to his eyes and they were liquid gold.

"Okay," she said.

When they hit the I-70 again, wrapped in their leathers, the road felt good, the air grew warmer and warmer. They turned south on secondary highway 191 and soon desert was all around. The red sand beauty of Moab astounded both of them and Milwaukee often stopped just so they could look at the buttes and towers and pinnacles and arches. He recited Isaiah 40 in German at Looking Glass Rock: *They that wait upon the Lord shall renew their strength, they shall mount up with wings as eagles.* She read Psalm 139 out loud from her father's small Bible at the rounded tower of Church Rock: *If I take the wings of the morning and dwell in the uttermost parts of the sea, even there shall thy hand lead me, and thy right hand shall hold me.* They prayed often—for each other, for Tabitha and Nick, for their families and the Amish back in Marietta. Then Milwaukee turned the bike around and they made their way back to the I-70 and thundered west under a sky that came closer than it ever had, he admitted, to her eyes, but still it fell short.

A quiver went through her as he romanced her in the way he always did with his words. She refused to shut the sensation down or cut it short. Yet it continued to seem vain to her to say her beauty was greater than the beauty of God's sky.

"How can you say God has fallen short?" she demanded.

"Not God. The sky's color. He has put his best work into you."

"Oh, you are crazy. What is the difference?"

"Your eyes shimmer in a way the sky cannot."

"Milwaukee, we are surrounded by all this and you say I am more?"

"Of course you are more. You are always more. You have beauty, you have a voice, your eyes dance, your lips are redder than the sandstone—of course you are much more than rock and sand and sky. No matter how incredible they are you outshine them all—you are a living soul, Michal."

As always, she came to the point where she did not know how to respond to his argument and said nothing else. But this day she savored the words and turned them over and over in her mind and heart and would not set them aside. A glow worked its way through her as rich as the desert sun that gleamed over the landscape. She luxuriated in it. *He loves me,* she said to herself again and again, *he loves me.* And she let herself believe it.

Near the junction with Interstate 15 they sat on their Harley at a turnout and gazed at the vast panorama of butter yellow buttes and cliffs and caramel-colored bluffs that stretched from east to west and north to south.

Milwaukee said, "How come everyone talks about the Grand Canyon in Arizona or the beaches in California and Florida, but no one says anything about southwestern Utah?"

"It's amazing," Michal agreed. "Don't you think I've finally met my match?"

She waited for his usual argument in response, but for a long time he said nothing, staring out over an immense desert that dominated their world. Expecting more superlatives about her beauty, she found herself feeling disappointed when they did not come. He did not speak for something like seven or eight minutes. She finally kissed him lightly on the cheek.

"Are you still on this planet?"

Milwaukee kept staring at the bright sands and plateaus. "I was thinking about our last morning in New Orleans."

She was surprised. She couldn't remember anything about it except saying goodbye to Bubba Win and his people.

He turned and looked at her. "You led the worship singing." Images came swiftly to her mind. "Oh, that."

"Oh, nothing. You were incredible. Imagine if I could get a helicopter to drop you on that tabletop mountain over there. And then you began to sing. What a glory. What a wonder." He smiled, the sunlight in his eyes and hair. "It's so easy to love you. The big easy."

She tried to find some words to reply to him with, but her tongue and mind would not work together. He was looking out over this awesome desert beauty and all he could think of was her standing in it and singing songs to God. It was too much for her to take in.

Milwaukee turned the Harley back on, the sound echoing from the high sand cliffs. "You helped those people find their way to Jesus. You made a bigger difference than the food we served that morning. You make a bigger difference than anything else in my life except God himself."

Michal remained speechless. Her insides in a tumult, a roar going through her head that was louder than the bike's engine, she put her arms around Milwaukee as he took the I-15 south.

"What's the plan?" she finally managed to get out.

"California. By way of Nevada."

"Where are we spending the night?"

But he did not answer her and she did not ask again. The Big Easy hummed through the brown and yellow land, clipped a corner of northwestern Arizona that gusted with wind, then came to Mesquite, Nevada, where Milwaukee took them off the highway and along a track that headed past sand dunes and far out into the desert. Moving slowly and carefully, he kept them going for more than an hour until they were buried among hills and dunes and rocks and green bushes she knew were called Joshua trees.

Then he parked the bike under a cliff and brought out their mats and sleeping bags.

"This is your Hotel Los Angelos," Milwaukee announced. "And you are the angel."

Michal stood with her arms crossed over her stomach, hands pulled up into her sleeves. "Are you kidding me? I thought you were bringing us out here to see something you read about."

Milwaukee dug two submarine sandwiches out of a saddlebag and held them up. "Supper."

She laughed. "When did you get those?"

"Last night in Green River after you were in bed. I've had the ice pack on them all day. There's a couple of slices of apple pie too. And your favorite drink— Lime Crush."

"No! How long have you had this planned?"

"I don't know. Maybe as far back as Marietta?"

"You have not."

Milwaukee laid the subs and drinks and pie out on a

flat toffee-colored rock. "Remember that Eagles' song I played for you once? *Peaceful, Easy Feeling?*"

"I don't."

"There's a line, *I want to sleep with you in the desert tonight, with a billion stars all around.* So I've been thinking about doing just that for what is it now? Four months?" He sat down at the rock and grinned. "This is the night. I recommend holding my hand too once we're in our bags."

She smiled at his enthusiasm. "Why? Are there bears out here?"

"Snakes."

She rolled her eyes and groaned. "Oh, yes, of course, snakes, just what I need to be reminded of."

"No harm will befall you if you hold my hand when you turn in." He opened the wrappers on the subs and paused. "Now let me ask a blessing."

After he had prayed in English, a first, they ate and drank. Then they sat facing a purple and red sunset. Strips of cloud turned into streaks of fire. They hardly spoke. Michal leaned against him and took one of his hands in both of hers. A couple of shooting stars got them excited before the air began to cool and she decided to crawl into her bag. He sat beside her for a while as the sky turned a velvet black. As his billion stars started coming out the black turned into a blazing white.

"Hey, what do you think?" he teased her. "Would you rather be in a motel with a shower and a roof?"

"As if you don't know the answer to that."

Milwaukee laid flat on his back, hands behind his head, mesmerized by the spots of brightness. "They're not all white, you know. I looked through a university telescope once, a big one. Some stars are red, some gold, some blue. Depends on how old they are and how hot they're burning."

"I didn't know that."

"It was an amazing experience. I saw this cloud moving through space, a thin long white thing, twisting and turning as if it had a mind of its own. There was no sound, of course, it was millions of miles away, but that just made its movement more eerie and mystical. You know? The professor saw my awe, took a glance for himself, and told me it was a nebula, an interstellar cloud of dust and gases. Amazing."

"When did all this happen?"

"Just after I started *Rumspringa*. It was at Penn State Erie, Behrend College, The Mehalso Observatory. A tour for prospective high school students. I could have looked through that telescope all night. God is amazing, the forces he sets in motion out there—" He tapped his head and heart. "And here and here."

The feelings for Milwaukee that Michal had not blunted, but which she had permitted to linger and move around inside her and latch onto the other feelings she had experienced for him over the past four months, had not diminished with nightfall and the day's end. Listening to him talk, watching him lying nearby on the sand, gazing at the desert sky of a million lights, she sensed that everything seemed to be converging inside her like a storm surge that overwhelmed all her fears and protests. She recalled her mother's words in the dream and realized she did not want to lose Milwaukee to anyone. Yet she continued to hold herself in check.

Lord, I'm afraid to say it. I'm afraid to tell him. Once I do it changes everything, everything.

"If you were put in prison for being a Christian," Milwaukee spoke up, still stargazing, "if you were in China or an Islamic Republic or something, and they permitted you to have, say, a couple of different books of the Bible with you in your cell, which would you choose?"

"My goodness, where is your head taking you tonight?"

"It's too easy to say the Gospel of John and the Psalms, almost anyone would want a gospel and the Psalms, so you have to come up with two other books—the jailers are half-decent and they give you those outright—but you have to say which gospel."

Michal sat up in her sleeping bag and wrapped her arms around her knees. "So am I supposed to go first?"

Milwaukee remained on his back. "If you've already made up your mind."

"Oh, I'm not that fast. There are 66 different books. And I find decisions hard."

"Okay, I'll go. Gospel? Luke. I love the stories in Luke and they tell me it's the most beautiful Greek in the New Testament. Instead of translating the Bible by committee or by a single man, they should get four different translators to do the four different gospels, and then you'd get the feeling for the different way each writer spoke. So with Luke I also take the good doctor's other book, Acts, more great Greek and more great stories.

"And why can't I learn Greek and read the Bible the way it was really written?"

"Who says you can't?"

"You know who says I can't."

"Well, you would have to learn Hebrew too."

"Fine with me. But the Bible Jesus and the apostles used was in Greek too, I mean the whole Hebrew part, they used a Greek translation they call the Septuagint, the LXX."

Michal laughed softly. "My boy of the books."

Milwaukee sat up and faced her. His skin was white in the starlight. "Seriously, Jesus had a Greek Bible, the old part, before there was a New Testament written about him and the first Christians. Have you ever heard Greek? Big, long ominous words, perfect for talking about heaven and hell and God and Saviors."

Michal smiled and laid her head on her knees, watching him. "What about your other choice?"

"Oh, Isaiah, I have to have Isaiah and my eagles. It has so many prophecies about the Messiah, about Jesus, Bishop Eby told me it was like another gospel anyway, 'The Fifth Gospel' he calls it."

"Does he?"

"No more of the Troyer stalling. What are your choices?"

"What Troyer stalling?"

"You always ask questions when you want to slow things down."

"Do I?"

"See?"

Michal lifted her head from her knees and rolled her eyes. "Oh, all right, Mister Psychoanalyst. I choose the Gospel of John."

"Why?" asked Milwaukee.

"Who says I have to say why?"

"Come on—why?"

"I like—I like the images of light and darkness—it's a more midnight gospel, a mystical gospel—" Her voice trailed off as she thought about it.

Then she said quickly, "And before you get on my back, I want Revelations for its colors of heaven and I want Job for its story of suffering and redemption. There."

Milwaukee stared at her. "The Apocalypse? With all its bloodshed and darkness and judgment?"

"And all its Christ and light and wonder, yes."

"You're an odd duck for an Amish-not-Amish."

"No odder than an Almost-Amish like you."

Milwaukee grinned and laid back down in the sand, hands under his head again, eyes returning to the thick white color of the Milky Way. *"Canst thou bind the sweet influences of Pleiades, or loose the bands of Orion? Canst thou bring forth Mazzaroth in his season? Or canst thou guide Arcturus with his sons?"*

"Hey," responded Michal, "that's my book."

"His book. That you borrowed. Sweet dreamer."

"Is this another nickname for me?"

"Sure. I have one for every day of the year. My thoughts about you are infinite and inexhaustible."

"How can anyone's thoughts about another person be infinite and inexhaustible?"

"Because your faith in Christ makes you immortal, Michal. And me too. So I'll always be around."

Michal smiled in the dark and once again felt everything in her rising to the point of rushing out and through her mouth into the night, bidden or unbidden. "Always?"

He turned his head from the stars to look at her. "Always. Even though it says we don't marry in heaven, that we're like the angels, I'll find a way to charm you there too. A loophole. Believe me."

She kept her eyes on his. "I believe you."

"Is that okay?" he asked.

"Yes, it's okay." Then she closed her eyes, fought down her fear, opened her eyes again, and let her heart and soul spring out of her throat into the desert night. "I love you, Gideon."

Chapter Nineteen

The buzz and the tune woke Michal up. She lifted her head from Milwaukee's chest, where she had placed it before falling asleep, and struggled with the zipper of her sleeping bag. The sky was still spotted with stars, but she noticed a bright orange line in the east. Her arms free, she pulled the cell phone from her leather purse and read the text message.

Hey, sorry Nick and I have been so quiet. We're in Vegas. Where r u?

Michal moved her thumbs rapidly. We were in Utah. Now we're just over the border and camping in Nevada.

The response arrived quickly. Really? Where?

I think Mesquite.

Help me out here. Are you really in Mesquite?

Well, it's the closest place. We're about an hour into

the desert. Help me out here. How long do you think it will take u to show up in Sin City? Mesquite's less than 80 miles from Vegas.

Michal texted, I don't know. Milwaukee's still asleep. Two or three hours?

Tabitha replied, Meet me.

Where?

But there were no more messages. Michal waited five or six minutes, then texted her sister again. Still there was no answer. She leaned over and shook Milwaukee's shoulder.

"Hey," she said, "I've been talking to Tabi."

Milwaukee opened his eyes and blinked several times. Then he stared at her. "What did she say?"

"She said they're in Vegas and that she wanted to meet up with us."

"Seriously? Where in Vegas?"

"She didn't tell me. And now she's not talking."

"Can I see?" Milwaukee reached out his hand for the cell phone and she gave it to him. He read the texts. "That's funny."

"What's funny?"

"How she keeps saying 'help me out here'. That's an expression the English use." He put the phone back in her hand. "She's never said that before, has she?"

Michal shook her head. "No."

"So what do you think?"

"I don't know. It's almost as if she was texting me without Nick looking over her shoulder. Then she stopped because he showed up."

"Yeah. And she used that 'help me out here' because she does want help. But if Nick looks at the texts she's sent before she can delete them he won't get too suspicious." Milwaukee unzipped his bag and stood up in his jeans and tee shirt. "Let's go."

Michal had also slept in her clothes and got to her feet. "But we don't know where to find her."

"Unless Nick's trying to throw us off, we know she's in Vegas."

"Do you think this is a Nick thing?"

Milwaukee pulled on his leather jacket that he'd been using as a pillow. "No, I don't. I think she's calling for help. Pack up and we'll get out of here and back on the I-15."

They were ready in less than ten minutes and Michal got on the bike behind him as they prepared to ride out of the desert to the highway. Before he turned the key she placed a hand on his shoulder. He looked back.

"You okay?" he asked.

"I just wanted to say a couple of things before we head out. Thanks for caring about my sister so much. And thanks for caring about me so much."

He smiled. "You made me a new man last night, Michal. Taking care of the Troyer sisters is the least I can do."

She smiled. "You were doing it long before I told you I loved you."

"So now I want to do it even more."

The sun was up and sheeting the desert in a copper light. His eyes turned from brown to gold to bronze. She put a hand to his face and kissed him on the lips.

"Hey, I like that," he said. "What a way to start the day."

"*This is the day the Lord has made*, Gideon," she replied, quoting Psalm 118.

"*We will rejoice and be glad in it.* Easy to do when someone like you kisses someone like me."

"You always make it sound like I am so much and you are so little. The truth is, you are a big deal, Gideon Milwaukee."

"Oh, yeah? To who?"

"To God. To me."

"Well." He started the engine. The powerful sound filled the desert. "I don't think much else matters then."

She leaned toward him so he could hear her. "Can we pray?"

"I'm going to be moving pretty slowly. We can pray as I get the bike back to Mesquite."

"I'm worried about Nick."

"What do you mean?"

"That he won't let us take Tabi."

"If your sister wants to come with us and he tries to stop her all we have to do is get a police officer's attention."

The Harley was rolling through the desert terrain, past hills and brush and dunes.

Michal could not shake the dream about her mother from the day before. "What if Nick has help?"

"Help?"

"I mean the sort of people he's been dealing drugs with?"

Milwaukee shook his head as he carefully steered the bike past rocks and sharp dips in the sand. "They're not going to be hanging off his neck in a place like Las

Vegas. They won't be anywhere near him. Don't worry. Nick isn't going to want any trouble. If it's Tabitha's wish to come with us then that is what is going to happen."

His words gave Michal the sense that everything was going to turn out all right despite the lingering bad feeling the dream had given her. Still, she knew she would feel much better if they gave the whole thing to God once again. With a hand on his back and the other on her leg she continued to hold her head close to his and pray in a mixture of German and English.

Though a lifetime had taught her that High German was the language of serious prayer, the road had taught her that any language linked to a prayer from the heart was enough. So she found herself beginning in German, then switching to English, then going back to German as she spoke to God. When she paused to think and listen Milwaukee waited a minute or two and then jumped in, praying out loud in English from beginning to end. When he was done Michal closed with a prayer in German. The moment they reached the highway at the southern end of Mesquite the Harley howled as Milwaukee throttled up. She hugged him with a burst of love and strength and they sped the 77 miles to Las Vegas in just over an hour.

As she prayed silently and thought of her sister the land began to flatten out so that the desert stretched like a tabletop from west to east. Even with the wind of the ride the sun's heat began to penetrate her leather jacket and she knew once they stopped she would have to peel it off and lock it in one of the saddlebags. Traffic grew congested as they neared Las Vegas and never let up once they were inside the city. It seemed to Michal there were four lanes going in one direction, four lanes going in the opposite direction, and the cars and trucks were as thick going as they were coming.

Milwaukee roamed up and down Las Vegas Boulevard on the Harley as they scanned the hundreds of people on the sidewalks and looked for Nick or Tabitha. Every time a motorcycle showed up in the perpetual traffic flow they practically jumped, swinging their heads, expecting to see the 79 Ironhead. Michal found it difficult to concentrate on the people and not be pulled away by the tremendous size and over-the-top architecture of the hotels and casinos. The Luxor with its Sphinx and pyramid and obelisk fascinated her. So did New York-New York with its imitation skyscrapers and Statue of Liberty. The fantasy castles of Excalibur, the huge body of water at Mandalay Bay, the Eiffel Tower and hot air balloon of Paris, all this and the many reflecting pools and fountains and tall palm trees combined to make her fight to keep her focus on faces and bodies.

"There is so much water," she said, leaning close to Milwaukee's ear, "and so many palm trees and so much imagination."

"The water and palms are okay," Milwaukee replied, "but the rest is all fake. You know, like an illusion or a mirage. The real pyramids and Eiffel Tower and Statue of Liberty are all somewhere else."

"The people don't seem to mind."

"Our race likes to be dazzled and tricked. We love magic, don't we? What isn't real seems to be more important to us than what is real."

After an hour patrolling the busy boulevard Milwaukee and Michal parked and locked the bike and left their leathers in the saddlebags that they also locked. They went into several of the lobbies of the hotels, asked if Tabitha Troyer or Nick Ferley were registered as guests, entered a dozen different casinos and walked among blacknesses interspersed with pools of golden lamplight, saw men in tuxedos with silver Rolexes and women in long black dresses whose throats glistened with diamonds. Once they couldn't find their way out of a casino because the exit was not clearly marked. Michal had a brief and unpleasant sense of being trapped in a dark cavernous space for weeks or years while people around her, in drops of fiery light, laughed, stacked columns of colored chips, spun shiny roulette wheels, or placed cards slowly down on green baize tabletops. When they finally made their way back out to the blue sky and sunshine she took a deep breath and sighed, "Thank our good God for air and light."

"A casino is a long way from an Amish barn raising," Milwaukee agreed. "I miss that now and then."

"What do people do in Las Vegas if they do not want to be part of all this?"

"I don't know. But if we found a phone book and looked up all the churches in Vegas I'll bet you there would be dozens."

"You'll bet me?" Michal lifted her eyebrows. He smiled. "Just a figure of speech."

"Well, you are probably right. Wherever there is vice in America there are churches nearby trying to change everything. That is a good thing."

"Many of the people here wouldn't even think of Vegas as a center of vice anymore. They wouldn't like to hear you use that word. We are here to relax, they would tell you. It's not a sin to relax and play, they would insist."

"How do you know they would say all that?" demanded Michal.

He shrugged. "They say it in Lancaster and Philly. It seems as if everyone's been to Las Vegas at least once or twice."

"No one has ever talked to me about Las Vegas. What do you tell them when they make all their excuses?"

"It's not even like excuses. They're pretty bold and defiant about it. You know—I dare you tell me it's wrong to hang out in Vegas. It's not just gambling, Michal. There are big concerts and shows, all the stars come here. Boxers have some of their most important matches, UFC have fights here all the time. There are beauty pageants."

"That is what you tell them?"

He brushed several strands of hair out of her eyes. "No. I tell them I would rather see the great Redwood trees in California. They are real, they are substantial, they touch the face of heaven."

"Truly? It is important to you to see those enormous trees?"

"Yes." He put his arm around her. "But for now we must finish this.

We are playing the needle in the haystack game. You and I could be going in the front door of a casino and they could be going out the back door. They might be eating in a restaurant a mile from here."

"Or they could be gone."

"Or they could be gone. So let me buy you lunch at a place that allows us to keep watching the roads and sidewalks. Whatever Nick was doing here he's going to show up on Las Vegas Boulevard eventually. And probably more than once or twice. If they're still around we'll spot them. That is my prayer."

"So the bishop and pastors said something like that." She put her arm around his waist and they began to walk. "We will see them when we are meant to see them so long as we keep looking. Meanwhile, God is working on you and I."

"That part is obvious and very easy to spot."

She leaned her head against his shoulder. "Yes, for all Las Vegas and all the world. You know, Gideon, strangely, I am not so worried for Tabi as I was yesterday or a few days ago. There is a stillness inside. It must be God. But what does it mean? That she is all right? That we are going to meet up with her soon? That the danger has passed?"

"I think we will find out and it will not be such a long time from now.

Let's get off our feet and eat something and see what shows up."

They had chicken and guacamole wraps and bottled water with wedges of fresh lime and sat on a plaza that looked out over the boulevard. They spent an hour there. Nothing happened. The faces they scrutinized in the crowds were never the faces they wanted to see. Once Michal thought she was going to drowse in the warm sun, but Milwaukee began to talk about taking the highway to Los Angeles and she listened to his voice and became more alert. Then they started walking again.

In time the sun dipped into the desert and lights blazed around them as hotels flipped their switches and fountains turned to red and gold, pools glittered green and blue, the Sphinx and Eiffel Tower and Statue of Liberty shone as if they were on fire, and thousands of windows made it seem as if night had not even fallen. Exhausted from walking all day, Michal and Milwaukee found another outdoor table and bit into burritos as headlights and smiling people flashed past them. Now and then bikes rattled by, but it was never Tabitha and Nick. Where did all the men and women come from? Michal wondered. She hardly ever saw the same person twice.

"Should we stay overnight somewhere?" she asked Milwaukee.

"I don't see the point," Milwaukee replied. "If they're not here, they're not here."

"You sounded more confident a few hours ago."

Milwaukee was bending a plastic straw into all sorts of shapes with his fingers. "Sometimes our prayers are answered in ways that we can see as clear as day. Other times it's not so easy. Maybe we need to get on the road so I can get the razzle dazzle of Vegas out of my system."

"Are you sure you're okay to ride?"

"The desert air will shake this place loose. Come on. God has something to show us somewhere else."

They stood up at the same time and looked toward the boulevard and its blur of lights at the same moment. They both caught a glimpse of a man in a white tee shirt steering a Harley through a backup of traffic. The Harley was an Ironhead. The man had no hair and neither did the woman on the seat behind him who did not have her arms around the man. They were down at

her sides. Then the man sped up and weaved the Harley
through the vehicles ahead of them. They were gone.

Michal grabbed Milwaukee's hand. "It was her."

"I thought so too. But are you sure? She looked
pretty hard without any hair."

"It was her. It was my sister."

They ran several blocks to the Harley, dodging bodies, then jumped on and headed onto the boulevard.
Milwaukee darted in and out of traffic and horns began
to blare, but he kept going. Finally they were free of
most of the congestion and following the signs south
to Los Angeles and San Diego. Milwaukee pushed the
bike, trying to catch up with the Ironhead, while Michal held onto him and prayed quickly and silently.
Then they spotted the tail light of a motorcycle.

"Is that them?" asked Michal.

"It is. That woman's head is as bare as the moon."

"What are you going to do?"

"Follow him until he stops at gas station or something and gets off his Harley. Then zoom up."

"You'd better drop back so Nick doesn't notice you."

"Would he even recognize us?"

But even as Milwaukee spoke the words, they could
see the man and woman glance back at them. The man
seemed to snarl. Then his motorcycle leaped forward
with a roar and vanished into the blackness ahead.

"Gideon—" Michal began.

"Hang on as tight as you ever have," Milwaukee
told her. "This is it."

Their bike screamed and shot into the desert night.

Chapter Twenty

At first it was easy for Michal to keep her eyes on Nick and Tabitha and the Ironhead. It was right in front of them and Milwaukee was only about 100 yards back. Then as Nick darted in front of semis and other vehicles the game became more difficult and she often lost sight of them for minutes at a time. But Milwaukee always caught up to the Ironhead again despite the tricks Nick tried. Her arms around him, Michal sensed a strength and fierce determination in Milwaukee that was a lot more than she was used to. It was as if a different part of him had been unleashed. As much as she wanted him to rescue her sister she felt a stab of worry over how far he might go to make sure he kept his promise not only to her, but to her father and mother.

"What are you going to do?" she asked as they raced under the stars and over the blacktop.

"He'll pull over eventually," Milwaukee replied, twisting his head toward her. "For gas if for no other reason. That's when we'll settle this thing for good."

"How are you going to settle it if he won't give Tabitha up?"

"He'll give her up. I guarantee it." The bike surged forward as he put on a burst of speed. "We'll be in California in another ten minutes. Then it's the Mojave Desert. Nick won't fool around with that. He'll gas up in a place called Primm."

But when Primm appeared with its own Vegas-style bright lights and casinos and restaurants it was Milwaukee whose bike began to cough, not Nick's, and with a shout of desperation Milwaukee was forced to slow and turn into an all-night filling station. He stopped the Harley by a pump and jumped off, watching in frustration as Nick put on as much speed as he could and the Ironhead literally shrieked ahead into the black desert. For a moment Michal thought Milwaukee was going to start running after the bike. When he turned to face her there were tears in his eyes, something she had never seen before.

"We should have gassed up in Vegas," he groaned. "We should have gassed up in Mesquite. I'm sorry. I'm sorry."

"It's okay," she said, putting a hand on his arm. "All we could think of today was finding them. You can't remember everything. We'll fill our tank and catch up."

"He'll be gone, long gone into the mountains and the Mojave."

"God has helped us this far, Gideon. He will help us tonight too."

Milwaukee hung his head. "Okay, yes, okay." Then he said something in German that sounded to her like *Lord, we need the big wagonload of help, nothing small.* He glanced at the pump. "We have to pay inside first. I'll be right back—" A siren wailed and cut him off as a squad car of the Nevada highway patrol ripped out of the restaurant parking lot next to them and took off down the I-15 toward the California border.

"An accident," Michal said.

Milwaukee watched the patrol car, all lights flashing, vanish into the night. "Maybe."

Suddenly he ran into the station and Michal saw him give the clerk several bills. Then he raced back out, put 30 dollars in The Big Easy, and jumped on.

"Stay here," he told her. "I'll be right back."

"What do you mean stay here? I'm not—" Michal began in surprise. "I need your seat for your sister. Go into the restaurant and order a coffee. Pray. Give me fifteen minutes."

"What? What are you going to do?"

"Those police weren't chasing coyotes."

He roared out of the station and onto the highway. Hardly able to grasp what he was doing and what he'd just said, Michal stood at the pump and stared at the cars rushing past toward California or toward Las Vegas. Then she went and sat on the edge of a large circle of concrete that protected the trunk of a tall palm tree. She knotted her hands together and kept her eyes on the traffic coming from the direction of the state border. Prayed in German and English. And waited.

Fifteen minutes came and went. Twenty. Twenty-five. She could not sit still any longer. Standing up she wandered about the lot. A beautiful hotel stood back of the restaurant and gas station, surrounded by palms and high bushes. Its windows glittered like gems. *What a nice place that would be to sleep at tonight. But we never spend the money on such hotels.* Hands in her pockets she drifted toward the highway again. Half an hour. Thirty-five minutes. *Oh, Gideon, where are you? This is killing me.*

At the moment her watch indicated the passage of thirty-nine minutes and she felt like hitting her head against a wall she heard the unmistakable growl of a Harley. The Big Easy rumbled off the interstate and up to her followed by the patrol car. Tabitha leaped off from behind Milwaukee and ran to her, tears streaking her face, laughing, her arms open for her sister's embrace. Michal hugged her with all the strength God and the road had given her, kissing Tabitha on the cheek and on her bare head over and over again.

"Oh, I love you," Michal cried, feeling the wet on her own cheeks. "How I've missed you. How I've prayed for you."

"I'm sorry, I'm sorry, I'm sorry," Tabitha sobbed, kissing her sister back.

Then they began to speak to each other rapidly in Pennsylvania Dutch. The two highway patrol officers, one of whom was a woman, stood outside their car, watching the reunion unfold. Milwaukee turned to them.

"I told you they were sisters."

The woman officer smiled. "Not just sisters. Close sisters."

The male officer grunted. "Still like to see the older sister's ID."

"Can we give them a minute?" Milwaukee asked.

"Not a problem."

Milwaukee walked slowly up to Michal and Tabitha as they hung off each other and talked without stopping, their eyeliner black trails on their skin.

"Hey," he said.

Michal looked at him, smiling through her tears. "What is it?"

"I told the police I was taking Tabitha back to her sister. Tabitha told them she wanted to ride with me. They just had to be sure I wasn't going to be another Nick Ferley and take off at high speed for Vegas with her hanging off my back."

"What did they do with Nick?" Michal wanted to know.

"Gave him a three hundred dollar ticket for speeding and kicked him out of Nevada," Milwaukee told her.

Michal made a face. "He'll never pay it."

"Then he'll get picked up the moment he sets another foot in the 'All for Our Country' state."

"So Nick's out of our lives for now?"

"For now. Anyway, the police need to see your ID. To be sure you really are Michal Troyer."

"Oh." With one arm still around Tabitha's waist she dug into her purse and pulled out her wallet. She handed it to Milwaukee who pulled out the Pennsylvania ID card with her photograph on it and gave it to the police. The woman officer shook her head.

"Why are some people so photogenic? Ought to be a law."

Her partner studied the ID closely. "I thought the Amish didn't believe in photographs."

"They don't," Milwaukee explained. "But some of the leadership recognize the importance of ID or a passport for those who are going to spend time away from the community."

"And where is that community?" the patrolman wanted to know. "Marietta, sir," Milwaukee answered.

"Marietta, Pennsylvania. Right on the Susquehanna River."

The patrolman handed the ID back to Milwaukee. "Tell Michal to take better care of her kid sister. No more Hells Angel boyfriends."

"Yes, sir. We won't let her out of our sight."

"Good idea."

Milwaukee put out his hand. "Thank you. Thank you both."

The patrolman hesitated. Then he nodded and shook Milwaukee's hand and got back into the squad car. The woman officer smiled, gave Milwaukee's hand a shake, and slid in behind the wheel of the car. They drove onto the highway and headed west for the border again.

"I have a lot to say," Tabitha told them.

"I know." Michal hugged her again. "Let's get you a meal at the restaurant here."

"Wait a minute." Tabitha turned to Milwaukee. "You're not even family. But you've been on the road all these months and brought my sister to me. I've never even been nice to you. So thank you for all you've done. And forgive me."

Milwaukee smiled. "Believe me, being on the road with Michal and looking for you has been my pleasure. It has been the great adventure of my life. I am just glad you are with us now and that you are okay."

She put her arms around him and buried her head in his shoulder. He was surprised that her arms were as strong as Michal's. He gently and brotherly kissed the top of her bare head.

"God bless you," he said.

At first Tabitha told them she was not hungry. But Michal talked her into a wrap and then, watching Milwaukee eat a half order of ribs, asked for the same. Digging into the ribs, sipping a Coke, licking her fingers, the smile Michal loved came back and, now and then, the laugh.

"It was many things that put me on the road with Nick," she explained over the meal. "Yes, I wanted to see things that were different from anything I knew in Lancaster County. Yes, I was worried about you, Michal. I hoped they would send you after me to talk me into coming back so you would see God's big old world—and spot God again too."

Michal reached across the table where she sat facing her sister and squeezed Tabitha's hand. "I am very grateful for what you did for me. I am not the same person you left behind in Marietta. I feel so alive on this journey. So close to Jesus."

Tabitha brushed a hand against her eye. "Thank God. But there was, you know, another reason I went on the freeways. To get Nick out of Pennsylvania. He was starting to push drugs. I thought if I got him on the road and away from the drugs he'd see there were better things to do with his life. I knew he loved me and that he'd do the trip just to be with me. So that was my hope. That I and the road would mean more to him than money and narcotics."

"Do you love him?" Michal asked with a worried look.

"No. No, I don't. But I care about him. And I was upset that—that—" Tabitha fought for the right words. "Ryan had told him there was lots of money getting drugs into the hands of fifth and sixth graders. Nobody had really cornered the market on those ages, Ryan said, everybody was pushing to junior and senior high and college kids, it was a great opportunity for Nick. Can you imagine? So I wanted him away for the sake of those schoolchildren too, not just because I wanted Nick to become a different person."

"Did it work at all?" Milwaukee asked. "I mean, did the road trip ever get his mind off dealing?"

Tabitha shrugged and looked out the window. "Who knows? For a while maybe. We would talk about God together, about whether or not we had souls, about heaven and hell, good and evil, everything. I thought he'd dropped all thought about going back to Philly and Lancaster and dealing. Then he started making all sorts of calls from his cell while we were in Florida. He left me in motel rooms and went to pick up things we needed, he said. Once we got into Louisiana I realized he was being a kind of courier and ferrying drugs from one community to another. Finally I guess they trusted him enough to give him what he wanted— enough heroin to take back up north to make a fortune, a fortune he'd split with them. When I figured this all out I didn't know what to do. Should I contact local police? Should I contact the FBI?"

She stopped eating and stared at her sister and Milwaukee.

"He watched me like a hawk whenever I had that cell phone in my hand. Read over every text I sent you. Always wanted to know where you were, how close you were getting. Then he started to become suspicious, paranoid. Wouldn't let me talk to you at all. Those last messages I got out, telling you we were in Vegas, he never knew about them and I erased the bunch before he could find out. But, like I said, he got more and more paranoid. Almost like he knew what I'd done anyway.

So he kept the cell in his jeans from then on and just made calls on it to the people he said were his business associates."

Milwaukee put down his glass of water. "Did you ever meet any of them?"

"No. Just one man. Just one."

"Is that all?"

"Yeah." She pushed herself back from the table. "I'm full. They can box the rest."

"Okay," said Michal. "Are you feeling all right?"

"No. Talking about all of it makes me sick. And tired."

"For sure." Milwaukee got up. "I'll take care of the bill and get them to take care of our leftovers."

"Do you want to use the washroom before we head out?" Michal asked Tabitha.

"Yeah. Where are we going?"

Milwaukee gestured at the parking lot with his thumb. "Meet me at the bike and we'll discuss it. See you two in a minute."

When Michal and Tabitha left the restaurant the bike was not where they had left it. Looking around Michal spotted it in front of the hotel with the bushes and palm trees and the shining windows. Milwaukee was standing and waiting.

"Hey," said Michal as she and her sister came up to him. "What's going on? Trying to lose us?"

He laughed. "I'm going to lose you all right. Here." He tossed her a card. "Seventh floor. View of the sunrise over the desert. Get lost."

Michal took the card, astonished. "What are you doing? We can't afford this."

"Of course we can. You haven't had a shower in

days, the Troyer sisters are back together again, everyone needs a long, safe sleep. You don't think your parents or the bishop would approve if I told them all that Tabi has been through?"

Michal hesitated, glancing at the card in her hand. "Still."

"Where will you be?" Tabitha asked Milwaukee, her face looking like the face of a woman of 22 or 23 and not a girl of 16. "Will you be close?"

"I will. I asked for a suite with separate rooms and doors. I'll follow you in. But then I'll be on my own. Just a shout away."

Tabitha put a hand on his arm. "Thanks."

"You'll be okay. Your sister has arms like Arnold Schwarzenegger after four months on the road."

"Oh, sure." Michal grinned and punched his shoulder and saw Tabitha smile out of the corner of her eye. "You're the one who looks like they've been pushing weights."

Milwaukee struck a dramatic bodybuilder's pose. "I push American steel down the highways of this country for a living."

Tabitha laughed. "*Ja,* you have the accent nailed at least."

"Well, okay, if it's paid for, it's paid for," said Michal. "I really do need that shower. Let's go up."

"And I need your cell. May I?" Milwaukee held out his hand. "Who do you need to call?"

"Ghost."

"What? Why?"

"To tell him we have Tabitha with us safe and sound for one thing.

"For another, to tell him I need to meet up with someone from Heavens Gate in Primm or Vegas."

"Why someone from Heavens Gate?"

They entered the lobby and pressed the button for the elevator. Michal found the cell phone in her purse and gave it to him. The bell chimed, the elevator door opened, and the three of them got in. Milwaukee pushed number seven.

"I don't know if any of us will wake up in time to see it," said Milwaukee as the elevator began to move with a hum, "but the woman at the front desk said the September dawns have been spectacular."

Ignoring his chit-chat, Michal persisted with her questions. "Why do you need to meet with someone from Heavens Gate? For prayer?"

"Good idea. I had something else in mind. But we can do that too."

"What is this something else you have in mind?"

The elevator chimed again, the doors slid open, and they stepped out, Milwaukee punching the speed dial for Ghost's number and scanning the doors for their suite at the same time. "Here it is," he announced a little ways down the carpeted hall. "You have the key card, Michal. Your hot shower awaits."

She leaned her back against the door. "It can wait a little bit longer.

"You're up to something, Gideon Milwaukee Bachman. What is it?"

"When you think about it, you can't put three riders on a Harley. The highway patrol will pull us over. Probably be our friends from tonight too. Not a good thing."

"So? What is your solution to that?"

Milwaukee smiled what Tabitha knew her grandfather would call "a big cheese-eating smile". Although she felt ready to drop, and fear of Nick and the men he worked with scraped in the pit of her stomach, Tabitha could not keep herself from being amused at the give and take between her sister and Milwaukee. He was no Joe Amish—Milwaukee was far too interesting and good-looking for her to call him that anymore.

"You are my solution," Milwaukee told Michal, putting the phone to his ear.

Michal threw up her hands in exasperation. "Oh, I will never get my shower. What on earth are you talking about?"

"You have a beginner's. You can push your own Harley now instead of hanging onto me. Not that I didn't like it."

Michal's eyes widened. "Are you so crazy? I can't do that."

"If you can't do that then we aren't ever going to get out of here.

Unless you want to plop your sister on a Greyhound or Amtrak or an American Airlines flight."

Michal's blue eyes blazed. "I just found my sister. I am not going to *plop* her on a bus or a plane. I am myself going to make sure she gets home safely and in one piece. How can you suggest dumping her on a Greyhound or on Amtrak, Gideon? Seriously, how can you talk like that?"

"Then we are in agreement." Milwaukee, still smiling, turned slightly away to speak into the cell. "Ghost? Hey, it's Kee. We're great. We've even got Tabi with us now. Really. She's fine, just fine, cute as ever even without a shred of hair on her head. Looks like Demi Moore in *GI Jane*. No kidding. So thank God she is with us now, tell the others who've been praying. Yeah. Yeah. Listen, before we get into that, I need to ask you a favor."

"Gideon!" Michal hissed. "Don't you dare!"

"Are any of your Heavens Gate people in Vegas or Mesquite? We need to borrow a bike because there's three of us now. Yes, a bike, an American-made Harley. No problem?"

"Gideon!" Michal was standing in front of him and glaring, the tip of her nose reddening under her tan. "No!"

"Michal's going to ride it. With Tabi. She's got her beginner's. She's a big girl, she can handle a Sportster at the very least. Here. She wants to tell you herself how enthusiastic she is about this. About the strength God has given her to get Tabi out of harm's way by running her own hog from Nevada to Pennsylvania."

He put the phone in Michal's hand. Her eyes lightning flashes, she took it. Greeted Ghost. Tried to get out of it and couldn't. Said she trusted God. Said she knew he would give her the grace and strength she needed. Told him she loved him. Clicked off and slumped to the floor.

"He told me some guy named Shot would be here by noon," she said out loud, staring at the wall, her fury evaporated. "He called him up and was talking to him on another phone at the same time he was talking to me."

Milwaukee squatted beside her. "Great. You're going to be terrific."

"Sure, sure, terrific."

"It was either that or the Greyhound."

"Forget your Greyhound. You know it can't be the Greyhound."

"Then it has to be you."

"Yes, me, oh, boy." She looked at him. "You're crazy. Why am I in love with you?"

He grinned. "Probably because of that."

"You think?" She closed her eyes and put her head against his shoulder. "What have you and God got me into?"

"Something wonderful. Riding your own Harley. Wow."

Despite herself, a smile flitted over Michal's lips. "*Wow*. You and your English expressions."

He put his arm around her. "Love you, baby blue eyes."

Her eyes still closed, her smiled broadened. "Love you, brown-eyed Amish boy."

"Hey." Tabitha had to put her hand against the wall to stay standing, she was so tired. "If this drama is over, can I get inside the room? I'd like to hit the washroom and have a hot, soapy, sudsy bath. You two can stay out here in the hall all night, if you like."

"Okay, mom," said Michal. "Thanks for your permission." She opened her eyes and flipped the key card to Tabitha. "Take as much time as you like. I'm interested in staying up to watch that spectacular September dawn with a biker dude I know."

Chapter Twenty-One

Michal saw the sun rise over the desert country around Primm, but not with Milwaukee. Tabitha pulled the covers off her at dawn and yanked aside the drapes so that oranges and yellows and reds poured into their room.

Michal wanted to keep sleeping. Tabitha tugged her up by the arm and dragged her to the seventh floor window. The land was as bright as a flame. They held hands and sat on the broad windowsill as if they were back at the house in Marietta.

They both wore long tee shirts. Michal had her I Love The Big Easy one on and Tabitha had a white one with a map of Mississippi and the state flag. Natchez was marked on the map with a large red star. Underneath the map and flag were the words, in cursive, *God Bless Mississippi.* The dark tan of Tabitha's head and arms contrasted pleasantly with the white of the shirt. Despite all Tabitha had been through, Michal thanked God she could still see her sister's beauty and a shining in the perfect blue eyes. A silver cross that hung from her ear caught the rush of desert light as Tabitha turned toward Michal, her eyes shimmering.

"It's so beautiful," she said in a quiet voice. "God is so beautiful. You and Milwaukee are so beautiful. I'm sorry."

Michal gathered Tabitha in and held her. "How can you be sorry? You wanted to help Nick. You wanted to help me. You wanted to bless. There is nothing wrong with any of that."

"I thought I could save everyone. Who do I think I am? Only Jesus can do that. Not me."

Michal stroked Tabitha's head and felt the soft fuzz growing back over the bare skin. "You did not try to be Jesus. You tried to be *like* Jesus. There's a difference, you know. The people who say they *are* Jesus want to be followed and worshipped and obeyed without question. They always wind up harming others. Those who want to be *like* Jesus are not the same. They want others to get closer to the real Jesus, to pray to him, worship him, obey him. They are disciples. Not demigods." She kissed her sister's head. "You're the disciple kind. The good kind who point to Jesus instead of pointing to themselves."

"But I put everyone in danger." The tears were flowing down Tabitha's cheeks.

"So there's danger on the road. There's danger back in Marietta too. People get killed on the highways in Lancaster County. Horses kick and break open heads. Amish men fall off barn roofs."

"What I tried to do made no difference. Nick is still Nick, only worse."

Michal put her hands on either side of her sister's face and pried it gently from her chest, smiling into her wet eyes. "How can you say that? Look at me. Am I the droopy Sad Sally you left behind in Pennsylvania in May? And Milwaukee—what does he look like to you? Joe Amish?"

Tabitha laughed softly. "If that's Joe Amish then all men should be Joe Amish. He looks like some golden lion in a man's body."

"So you see what the road has done for him? Your road?"

"God's road."

Michal nodded. "Amen to that."

"But I still worry. About what Nick will do. About what the drug dealers will do."

"You didn't see anything. You don't know anything. They are going to leave you alone, Tabi. You won't see Nick in Lancaster County again."

"How can we know for sure?"

"It's God's road. You said so yourself. Let him give us the map. Let him handle it."

They went back to the queen bed and fell asleep again, the sun roaring around the room and brightening the skin on their faces and arms. It was Milwaukee who finally woke them up, knocking on the door between the different rooms of the suite. When Michal mumbled a response into her pillow he asked if he could come through and get out the door. He wanted to go down to the restaurant for coffee and *Pfannkuchen*. She pulled the covers over her head and Tabitha's and he was through and out the door of the room in a few seconds. Then Michal thought about the pancakes and shook her sister awake.

"Tabi!"

"Mmm."

"Get up. It's time to get up."

"Mmm. No."

Michal leaned close to Tabitha's ear. *"Pfannkuchen. Pfannkuchen mit Ahornsirup."*

Tabitha opened an eye. *"Vas?"*

"Ja. Pfannkuchen mit Ahornsirup und Erdbeeren."

Tabitha opened both her eyes. They were a rich dawn blue like her sister's. "Maple syrup and strawberries. Yes?"

"Gideon has gone down to order his. He is probably already devouring them."

Tabitha shot up and threw back the covers. "Yikes. We had better hurry or they will use up all the batter on him. For us they will have only potatoes. *Kartoffelpuffer.*"

"But you like potato pancakes."

Tabitha was pulling on her jeans. "Not for breakfast I don't. Hurry up. I'm not waiting for you."

There was batter enough for everyone, Michal and Tabitha were happy to find out, because the breakfast menu was served all day. The sisters sat together and ate with Milwaukee on the other side of the booth. As they talked back and forth Michal realized Milwaukee had been up and showered and shaved while they had their second sleep, his hair and skin gleaming like copper in the light streaming through the windows. Again she thought of a male lion with full tawny mane striding through the tall grasses of Africa with the slow, powerful, almost insolent cat movement. Again she felt that, no matter what happened when it came to Nick and his gang, God would use Milwaukee to protect them and everything would ultimately turn out all right.

At ten to twelve, five minutes after they had finished eating, two Harleys pulled up in front of the hotel, one ridden by a round man, the other ridden by a round woman with Jesus tattoos on her bare arms. Milwaukee walked over from the restaurant to see if it was the man Ghost had called up. It was him—Shot Scott and the woman, his wife, was Shoulder. He tried to shake their hands, but they pulled him into their bellies and hugged him like he was a child. Milwaukee waved the sisters over and they both got the same treatment.

"It's not right," protested Michal when they presented her with the chili pepper red Sportster that Shoulder had motored in on. "This is your Harley."

Shoulder snorted. "It's God's Harley, darlin'. When you and Jesus are done with it just bring it back to me in East Vegas. No hurries, darlin'. I haven't ridden behind my man in years. Lookin' forward to it actually."

Michal got on the Sportster and moved it slowly about the parking lot, its engine purring. Then with Shoulder on behind and Shot on his Harley beside her, they went up and down the streets of Primm, finishing with a ten minute ride east toward Vegas, stopping at the town of Jean, and racing back at 75 miles an hour. Shot patted Michal on the shoulder when they got off their bikes in the parking lot.

"She's coming fine," he said to Milwaukee and Tabitha. "Tall girl, strong arms, strong legs, she's coming fine. Give her some more road hours and she'll be near perfect."

"Where you headin' today?" asked Shoulder. "I don't know," answered Milwaukee.

"California," Tabitha spoke up. "I want to see California."

Milwaukee was surprised. "Are you sure? Nick's probably still there."

Strong lines appeared around Tabitha's eyes and mouth. "I don't care where Nick is. I need—I want to get to California. Once we do that we can head to Pennsylvania."

Michal stared at her sister, trying to understand what lay behind the sudden burst of determination that bordered on anger. Not just her, but all the others also hesitated a moment while they took in Tabitha's little flare up. Then Shot hauled a large map out of one of his saddlebags and spread it over the seat of his bike.

"Well, if California is your call from the Lord no one should get in your way," he announced. "But if you want to avoid the route you were using last night, and give Michal here a chance to grow used to the saddle, why not take a secondary highway like the 95? Lookie here."

They all gathered around Shot's map, a grim, dark-eyed look remaining on Tabitha's young face as she watched Shot's stubby finger trace a line south.

"There's an unpaved road going east from Primm to the 95. It's not bad. We've been on it, say, Shoulder Bessy?"

His wife nodded. "A good ride, but you can't do speed on it."

"No," Shot grunted. "Good Lord didn't cause men to make that track for speed. Now you can go ahead ten or fifteen minutes into California and pick up the 164. That'll shoot you east to the 95 pretty good and you won't lose the time and distance you would if you went back to Vegas to make the connection. Take the 95 down to Needles and then do a quick jig on the I-40 and hook up with the 95 again all the way to Blythe. Then take the I-10 west for Palm Springs and San Bernardino and LA." He looked up at Tabitha. "You like heat?"

Tabitha smiled, changing the appearance of her face completely. "I do."

"Then this trip'll give you plenty of it. Don't be in a rush. Take your time. Let the Holy Spirit do the talking." He folded up the map and put it back in the black leather saddlebag with its silver studs. Then he sat on his bike's seat facing them. "You get into the Big Maria Mountains close to Blythe you'll see a small white and red Spanish-looking building just off the highway, the Big Maria Mission. Stop off and see if Father Raphael is in. We call him Father 'cause he used to be a priest. Now he's pastor of the church there and has a beautiful Mexican wife and about 112 kids." Shot stopped to laugh, the sound erupting from his belly and exploding out through his throat and mouth. "He's got a different take on how he does things on account of his background. There's more ceremony in his services. Not in a bad way. It's close to the heart of Jesus. Time it for a Sunday and you'll see what I mean. Say, Shoulder Bessy?"

She nodded. "God's truth. We gonna pray for these young ones before we turn 'em loose?"

"Sure are."

He got up from his bike and grasped Tabitha's hand in one of his and took Milwaukee's in the other. They all linked hands.

"Why don't you start us out, momma?" Shot asked.

"All right."

Shoulder prayed a good five minutes, Shot prayed

another five or six. Then it was quiet. Finally Milwaukee realized neither of the Troyer sisters were going to say anything out loud and he closed the blessing off with a short prayer and an *amen*. There were hugs all around. Then the three Harleys boomed at the same time and Shot and Shoulder headed east for Vegas, her arms wrapped happily around his robust girth, and Milwaukee rode side-by-side with Michal and Tabitha, the black Harley and the red Harley zooming west and over the border into California.

At first Michal had to fight down waves of fear. Tabitha sensed that and leaned close to her, placing her arms around her sister. "You're doing great," she said. The love helped calm her.

Milwaukee stayed just off her left shoulder, smiling and giving her the thumbs up. That too made a difference. Then as the miles passed the bike's power and the rhythm of the road worked its way into her bones and blood and head and heart. Soon Michal felt a burst of exhilaration that it was her who was steering the Harley, her controlling its movement, her pushing it down the highway and through the desert. The enormous strength of the sky and landscape she was blazing through made her want to shout with a fierce joy as sun and wind burned her face.

She grinned over at Milwaukee. "I feel wonderful!"

"What?" he yelled back.

"Wonderful! Wonderful! *Wunderbar!* Riding is a gift of God!" He laughed. "I hear you!"

They got onto the 164 just before the interstate headed up into a mountain pass, changed directions, skirted the Mojave National Preserve, and rode east through rough, flat desert back into Nevada to the 95 where they turned right. Not pushing it, Milwaukee watching Michal like a father hawk, they re-entered California and made it to Needles in under an hour where they stopped and gassed up. Milwaukee hovered over the two sisters.

"You guys okay?" he asked several times. "You doing okay, Michal? You feeling up to it, Tabi?"

Michal smiled at his concern. "Yes, papa. The bike rides well and I feel like I am definitely in control. You don't have to worry."

"You sure?"

"I'm sure. It doesn't hurt to have such a handsome escort on a black and chrome Fat Boy tucked in beside us either. Does it, sis?"

"I love it," Tabitha grinned.

They actually got a blush and a few moments of awkwardness out of Milwaukee with their words. Then he popped on his half helmet and led the way back onto the highway. Their day had started late and the sun was low in the sky when they reached Vidal Junction and decided to camp out in the desert away from a scattering of RVs that clung to a restaurant and gas station. When Milwaukee filled up his tank and Michal's the clerk at the till told him he could camp out anywhere, there were hundreds of acres at his disposal for no cost.

"You can go miles into the desert if you have a mind to boondock it," the man said. "There's a few rattlers around, but they shouldn't bother you any."

Michal rolled her eyes. "Thank you. Snakes. That's great."

The man looked at her. "You don't like snakes? They're beautiful. Part of God's creation. Don't trouble them and they won't trouble you."

"Well, I'll keep that in mind."

"Have any decent pup tents for two?" Milwaukee asked the clerk. "I do," he replied.

"Any desert-colored ones?"

"Got some army surplus desert cam."

Milwaukee spotted them on a shelf behind the clerk. "Hand me down one, please."

"Is that for you?" Michal wanted to know.

"No," Milwaukee told her. "It's for you. And Tabi. To keep the snakes out of your hair."

"I don't mind snakes," said Tabitha. "I saw a water moccasin in a cypress swamp that was awesome."

"Hey." The clerk looked at her closely for the first time. "Tell me about that."

"Oh," laughed Michal. "The whole world is crazy except for me."

They went miles out so they couldn't see the service station anymore and put up the tent just as the sun disappeared. Milwaukee had bought some sandwiches and bottled water from the clerk and they ate and drank around a small, slow fire Tabitha started with a Zippo lighter and a pile of dry mesquite branches. The smell of the burning wood was strong and pleasant, thought Michal, and smiled to see her sister gathering more dead branches which she added bit by bit to the fire, careful not to get pricked by the long thorns that stabbed outward from some of them.

"So now you're the girl scout," Michal teased her.

"Well, Nick and I slept outside a lot. But I liked it more than he did and I usually did all the work."

"A good Amish woman."

Milwaukee stretched out on his back, hands behind his head, a posture Michal was getting used to. "*Ah, gute*. The stars are coming out. The greatest show on earth."

Tabitha looked upward and nodded. "I feel the same way. Nick just crawled into his sleeping bag and crashed. I stayed awake and watched everything."

A buzzing sound made Michal reach for the small leather bag she used for a purse. The others watched while she read the display of the cell phone, the white light gleaming on her face.

"What is that English phrase?" she asked. "Is it *speak of the devil*?" She handed the phone to Tabitha.

"I love you," Tabitha read out loud. *"I'm sorry for my screw ups. Tell me where you are and we'll get together again. I really need you."*

Milwaukee sat up. "Is he for real?"

Tabitha made a face. "He doesn't need me." She lifted a chain that was around her neck and a key glinted in the bright orange of the mesquite fire. "He needs his stash of heroin."

Michal frowned, anxiety rushing through her like cold air. "What do you mean?"

The phone buzzed and played its short tune again.

"I know you're there, T," she read to them. *"Come on, let's talk. Where are you anyway? Nevada? California? Heading home to Penn?"* Tabitha looked at her sister. "Can I turn this off?"

Michal shrugged. "I mostly had it on in case you called or texted. Go ahead. We don't need it tonight."

Tabitha clicked the red key. "I know where the stuff is and he doesn't. That's what this is all about. We were headed there when you caught up with us the other night."

"So he knows where it is now," Michal said.

"No. Only that it's in California. I told him I'd give him directions."

"Why not just tell him?"

Tabitha stared at her sister, the dark-eyed look back on her face. "Because I was afraid he'd kill me and dump my body in the desert if he didn't need me for the information."

Michal couldn't believe what she was hearing. "No! Nick is not that kind of person."

"You don't know him anymore, sis. He's not the same guy." Tabitha drew up her knees and wrapped her arms around them. "I wanted to live. And I didn't want him to get his hands on the stash. So I said I'd guide him to the location."

Milwaukee put his hands over the fire, keeping his eyes on Tabitha. "How come you know where it is and he doesn't?"

"A few weeks ago one of Nick's partners took me for a ride on a Greyhound. He didn't want Nick along. Said we'd be back in a couple of days. Nick said okay. I was scared out of my mind. The partner, Tommy, he bought us one-way tickets to Sacramento by way of LA. The bus route was down the I-10. But we got off in Palm Springs and took a taxi to one of those self-storage places. It was a solid one: high fences, lots of cameras, dogs, 24 hour security, the staff had guns. So Tommy rented a small unit and put a bunch of luggage in there and gave me the only key. *Listen,* he says, *don't tell your boyfriend where it is or I'll slit your throat.* I told him I wouldn't. Then he says, *It's worth six million on the street. You don't tell him anything. He wants to take it up to schoolchildren in Pennsylvania. That's never going to happen. I'm DEA, understand?* I didn't

know what to say except tell him I'd do whatever he
wanted. We got on a Greyhound and headed back east
a few hours later. While we were waiting for the bus he
bought me a meal, but he never spoke much after that.
The only thing I really remember is him saying he'd
brought me on it in case something happened to him."

Milwaukee and Michal were quiet. Finally Michal
asked, "Where is he?"

"He's dead." Tabitha paused. "He was supposed to
meet up with Nick the other day and Nick found him
dead with two shots to the back of the neck."

Michal put her fist to her mouth.

Tabitha was gazing into the fire. "That's what Nick
said anyway." Milwaukee was about to speak, hesitated, then made up his mind.

"Why would Nick let him stash that much heroin?
Why would he let Tommy take off with you?"

"Because Tommy was one of the leaders of the gang
Nick's been dealing with. Whatever Tommy said went.
Nick was scared to death of those guys. Still is. But
they bought his story about Tommy being executed by
a rival gang. As far as they know Nick has the heroin in
a safe place. At the right time he'll ride up north with
it and they'll split the profits with him."

White and orange from the fire ran over Milwaukee's face. "This Tommy had to have backup for an
operation like this. We have to get in touch with the
DEA."

Tabitha shook her head. "A couple of days before
he was killed Tommy took me aside when Nick was
using the washroom. He said he had been in the gang
for more than three years and that he was very deep
cover. Told me he was worried a DEA agent had been

flipped. That's the word he used. Bought, you know? That his op had been compromised. I know it sounds crazy, but he said he decided to pull me into it because he believed he could trust a Christian kid from an Amish church. That I'd do the right thing if anything happened to him. He wasn't sure which names to give me. There weren't that many who knew who he was and what he was doing. He told me he needed to make a few calls and then he'd know who he could rely on and who I could rely on. But he got shot before he could get back to me."

Michal felt sick. Her head and insides were churning. She put her face in her hands and groaned, *"Gott helfe uns."*

Milwaukee's eyes were large as he took it all in. "It doesn't make sense. It doesn't add up. This is too big an operation. Why would he trust a little girl like you?"

A tinge of anger came into Tabitha's voice. "He thought I was 21 or 22—and he said I was tough as nails." Then she picked up a handful of sand and shook it slowly and rhythmically. "I think he was dirty. At least for a while. I don't know if he really was DEA or if he'd gone rogue, you know, like in the movies. Something wasn't right. Maybe he was going to take off with the heroin and sell it and keep the money for himself. Maybe he was the one who got flipped. But at the end he just didn't want it to get into the bodies of ten or twelve year old schoolkids. So God knows what was in his heart. God will judge him rightly." She looked at her sister. "Won't he?"

At first Michal did not respond. She was scarcely listening. Her mind was swirling with so many fears.

"Won't he, Michal?"

Michal finally heard her and their eyes met across the fire. "He will, Tabi."

Milwaukee added more of the mesquite Tabitha had scrounged to the fire. "I guess you have a plan, Tabi."

She continued to shake the sand. "I need to get to Palm Springs and get the heroin out of that storage unit and destroy it."

Milwaukee half-smiled at her. "You weren't really going to take Nick to it, were you?"

"Never."

"He could have pulled the key from your neck."

"So? What good would it have done him? He had no idea what it opened. No idea where the lock was. LA? Beverly Hills? Sacramento? Needle in a haystack."

Milwaukee studied her. "He would have beaten you."

"Once he realized I had taken him to the wrong storage unit he would have. That's why I sent those *help me out here* texts. That's why I prayed you'd find us in Vegas before Nick pulled out."

"You took a big chance."

"I couldn't think of anything else. I was not going to let him push drugs to those poor kids in Pennsylvania. I was not going to let him deal that poison to anyone, not anyone. Even—even if he killed me."

The heat from the mesquite fire grew intense. Milwaukee stood up and walked back from the flames. His eyes remained on Tabitha.

"I don't think I ever knew you," he said. "I don't believe I had any idea what was inside you, what God had put within you. No, I had no idea." He walked over to her, reached down for her free hand, and pulled her gently to her feet. "You're no girl, Tabitha Troyer.

You're a woman. And not an ordinary woman. *Einer rechtschaffenen Frau*—a righteous woman. A woman after God's own heart. I though there was only the one of them in the Troyer household. I was wrong." He took her in his arms and hugged her tightly. "I will do whatever I can, whatever I must, to help. You say we can't trust anyone. We can trust each other. We can trust God. That is enough." He looked down at her face. "So much beauty under one roof. So much strength. How did your father and mother pull this off?"

Tabitha swiped at her eyes with the back of her hand, still clutching sand in the other. "No one has ever said such things to me. Thank you."

Milwaukee stretched his hand to Michal. She got to her feet and came to him, not bothering to clear her eyes, but letting the tears run down her face. Milwaukee pulled both the sisters against his chest.

"God will help us. We will do this thing. All right?"

Milwaukee prayed in High German, his voice rising and failing, almost shouting one minute, quiet as a floating feather the next. Then he said amen, kissed them both on the head, and lay back down by the fire, staring up at the constellations once more. The two sisters remained standing, holding onto one another, putting their fingers to the other's tears.

"I love you," Michal said to Tabitha.

"I love you," Tabitha replied. She glanced toward Milwaukee. "And it is so easy to love him."

"Yes," Michal smiled. "I feel the same way."

Milwaukee spoke up, hands behind his head. "But not so easy to love the snakes. You two had better get inside your tent. I think the diamondbacks are on the move and looking for a warm spot to curl up in."

Chapter Twenty-Two

They were on the road early, the two bikes keeping pace with each other, Milwaukee smiling over at Michal and Tabitha as the sun warmed them and the air cooled them and the desert spread out on their left and their right, behind them and before them. Vidal was only a few miles south of Vidal Junction and they stopped there for a quick breakfast. Michal checked her watch, counted the time difference, and phoned her mother in Marietta.

"Hey, ma, how are you?"

"*Gute, gute,* I have not heard from you for a few days. Is everything all right?"

"More than all right."

"Yes? Have you heard from your sister?"

"Ma, I have a surprise for you."

"What is that?"

Michal handed the cell phone to Tabitha. "Hi. Mother—it's—it's me—it's—"

"Tabitha! Oh, *Lobet den Herrn*! Oh, Tabitha, my baby."

Tabitha looked at Michal. "She's crying."

"*Ja,* so are you."

Tabitha smiled, her eyes glittering. "And so are you."

After the call they moved on to the Big Maria Mountains and the Big Maria Mission. The mission was easy to spot, sitting by itself in the desert, white as a snowflake, its tiled roof red as blood, the peaks purple and amber behind it. Parking their bikes among a few cars they walked into the church.

It was at least an hour before the service began. The sanctuary had simple wooden pews, white walls, and a pulpit carved from mesquite. A large cross, also of mesquite, hung from the wall at the front. Several people were sitting and praying. Light from tall windows made the room blaze in all its whiteness. They sat together in a pew and listened to the quiet.

"Did you ever get to any churches?" Michal asked her sister in a soft whisper.

"Only in Ghost's living room," Tabitha whispered back. "And then at Bubba Win's. That was it. Nick wasn't interested so he made sure we were always on the highway on Sunday mornings."

"I'm sorry. Gideon and I have seen so much that is good and holy. We have watched God do so many things in so many different ways among his people."

Tabitha smiled. "You know how glad I am for that. You know how good it is to see you come back to life again."

Michal grasped her hand. "Thank God for the road. And thank God it is almost over."

"Yes. Almost."

It seemed the most natural thing to drift into prayer rather than talk out loud and wait for the service to begin. The three of them bowed their heads. Even as the sanctuary filled up the hush was preserved. Families sat quietly in their pews, even those with young children, waiting, smiling at others, closing their eyes to pray, reading from their Bibles.

Then Pastor Raphael—Father Raphael to the bikers—walked to the front of the room dressed in a white robe. He was carrying an acoustic guitar and was followed by two other young men who were also carrying guitars.

One of the guitars was a 12 string. Raphael was tall and deeply tanned by the desert. Facing them, he opened in a prayer that was a mixture of Spanish and English. A screen slid slowly from the ceiling and Powerpoint beamed words onto its surface. The people stood and began to sing in Spanish and clap. Milwaukee and Michal and Tabitha stood with them and, not knowing any of the songs that morning, whether they were in English or Spanish, watched and smiled or closed their eyes and took it all in.

Michal was fascinated at how the men's fingers flew over the guitar strings during the fast tunes, tunes that made her want to dance, something she had never done. She decided she must at least clap her hands together in rhythm with the swift and furious playing and thought of how Fat Poppa Daddy would laugh to see her being so not Amish. Tabitha began to clap too. Milwaukee stood with his eyes closed and Michal thought, *He is in another world with God.*

When Raphael preached, he spoke in English at the quiet places, but when he got excited, his arms moving rapidly in the air, the sun from the windows and a large skylight on his face and hands, he always broke into rapid fire Spanish while people shouted and clapped and called out *amen*. It was no different, in that way, than some of the worship Michal had been part of in Savannah and Natchez and New Orleans. When Pastor Raphael was done persons lined up for prayer and stood or knelt as he placed his hands on their heads or shoulders. The men who had been playing guitar with him during worship returned to the front and helped, taking men and women and young people aside and praying for God to bless them.

"I need some of that," Milwaukee said and walked to the front. Michal and Tabitha joined him, patiently waiting in line. It was Raphael's eyes that fell on the three of them first and he said something in Spanish. When their faces remained blank he smiled. "The Anglos God has sent us all the way from Pennsylvania. Shot and Shoulder called me about you. Am I right?"

Milwaukee nodded and smiled in return. "Except we are not Anglos, pastor. Our background is Amish. We speak in Pennsylvania Dutch and German."

"Ah. So the Alemans Christ has sent us. How can I bless you?"

Milwaukee glanced at Michal and Tabitha. "We can't put it into words. But—we need protection, we need guidance."

"You are heading back home?"

"Not yet."

"So. Something is still undone. Something." He looked at them carefully. "Even the Pennsylvania women are tall. Would you kneel for me? Or not so much for me—for Jesus."

As she knelt, Michal immediately felt the warmth of his hand on the top of her head. She was not wearing a do rag. Her black hair was gathered up in a crown braid.

Raphael's voice was soft, the words Spanish. He seemed to be making no demands of God. It was as if he were talking gently about his concerns for a friend with another friend who might be able to do something about the problem. Briefly, Michal opened one eye to see whose head Raphael's other hand was on. It was Tabitha's.

The praying became like a dream. Everything within her felt at rest and the verse kept flowing through her mind: *Thou wilt keep him in perfect peace whose mind is stayed on thee because he trusteth in thee.* Nightmares of the night before, nightmares she had not mentioned to Milwaukee or her sister over breakfast in Vidal, dissolved along with the pricks of fear they had spawned. She felt full of God's light and knew the truth of the words of Jesus when he said those that believed in him would have streams of living water flowing out of them. It was as if she had become a fountain of brightness.

Then they were in the sunshine of the gravel and sand parking lot and Pastor Raphael was saying, "I would ask you to stay to lunch with our church, there is plenty of food for all, enchiladas from the Big Marias to eternity. But I sense not only from you, but from the Lord, that there is something important you must do today. Now that Jesus has spoken to each of you here, well, I should not persuade you or detain you. Go and do his will. Only—" He grasped their hands one after another. "Take care and come back to us again for that meal."

A slender woman, dark and sparkling with enormous amounts of life in her eyes and smile, walked up to them holding an infant. *"Usted no puede convencer a que se quede?"*

Raphael shook his head. "It is not my place to coax them to stay, Christina. God has something for them to do. I have only asked them to return one day and break bread with us."

She put out a small brown hand to Michal. "We do mean that. Shot and Shoulder had a great deal to say about the three of you. I prayed with them over the phone. How we would love to see more of you and talk about the Lord."

Christina shook Tabitha's hand and Milwaukee's as well. She caught Milwaukee looking longingly at the tables set up on the church patio under an overhang. Platters and bowls of food had been laid out and people were picking up paper plates and laughing with one another while children played tag and chased each other around the church building.

"It's tempting." Christina nodded. "A growing boy never gets enough food when he's on the road."

Milwaukee smiled and looked down. Raphael clapped him on the shoulder.

"A week from now, two weeks from now, you will still be hungry," he said. "Come back to us then. Christina will phone the church families and we will have a special fiesta in your honor—and not only in your honor, but in honor of all of you."

"We have done nothing to deserve any great honor," Milwaukee replied, "but I know I would look forward to the food just the same."

"The Lord decides who is worthy of honor. And then

he tells me and my wife." Raphael laughed. "Go. Do what *Jesus Cristo* commands. *Adios. Vaya con Dios.*"

Raphael and Christina walked back to their people and tables thick with food of every color imaginable— blue, purple, green, yellow, orange, red. Tabitha watched them while she tugged on her helmet.

"The same colors as the gang, but the people are so different," she said.

"What are you talking about?" Michal asked as she climbed onto the gleaming crimson Harley.

"The gang Nick is hanging with. They are the same as this mission here—Anglos, Hispanic, African-American. Only these people deal with life and Nick's people, they take it away."

"What do you call this gang?" asked Milwaukee, pulling on a pair of black leather gloves.

"*Los Muertos.* The Dead."

They all heard the buzzing from the phone. Michal had placed it in a chest pocket of the denim jacket she was wearing. She ignored it and turned the key in the bike's ignition. Several teenagers looked up from their food as the burst of sound cut through the hot afternoon air.

"Aren't you going to see who it is?" asked Tabitha.

Michal adjusted her helmet and placed on her mirrored sunglasses. "I know who it is."

Tabitha's face, bright from the glory of the prayer time, suddenly darkened as if from a sharp change in the weather. "How often has he texted?"

"There were twelve or thirteen messages when I turned the phone back on this morning."

"You didn't tell me."

"There's nothing to tell. They're all the same. Until they start to get worse."

"How worse?"

"He starts threatening you."

Tabitha put on her blue aviator sunglasses. "The gang will be all over the highways looking for us. Let's get going and get this done before one of them spots us."

Milwaukee started The Big Easy. "How will we recognize them?"

"Even in this weather they are in black head to foot. If they are Anglos or African-Americans the jackets will say The Dead on the back and have a skull with a stake driven through it. If they are Latinos they have the same skull, but use *Los Muertos* for the gang name instead."

"Sounds like they couldn't make up their minds whether to go with one language or the other."

"Nick told me they had a war over it. I mean, a real war. Members from Juarez and El Paso fought it out on the streets. A dozen of them killed each other before they agreed to use English or Spanish. Whatever people liked. One faction split off and used a completely different name and started a new gang."

Milwaukee began to walk his bike forward. "What name?"

"The Destroyer."

Milwaukee blew out a lungful of air. "Such a nice neighborhood you've been hanging out in."

Once they got on their way it did not take them long. It was little more than a half hour before they turned west onto the I-10 and passed through Blythe. In under an hour they reached Joshua Tree National Park. Soon after Tabitha indicated they should take highway 111 at Indio and they followed it through Palm Desert and Cathedral City to Palm Springs. Michal was stunned by the number of trees and the vast stretches of green grass and man-made lakes on either side of the highway. "What is all this?" she called back to Tabitha.

"Golf courses for the rich and famous."

"It hardly counts for desert around here."

"Oh, it's all a mirage. There's desert, sister. Inside the heart and out." She pointed. "That road will take us to Gold's Gym and the storage center."

They showed their IDs at the gate of the center and Tabitha pulled out her slip of paper proving she had rented a unit. She checked out on the computer, but they would only let her and Michal in. Milwaukee waited while the sisters rode through the gate. They had to make several trips. There were four large suitcases. Milwaukee strapped three of them onto the back of his Harley with bungee cords and tied the last one on behind Tabitha while the guards watched from their booth. Then they headed out of Palm Springs as fast as they could go without attracting attention from the police or anyone else.

"What's our destination?" shouted Milwaukee.

"I don't know!" Tabitha shouted back. "I've never been west of Palm Springs! Get back on the interstate and I'll tell you when it feels right!"

"Feels right?"

"God's walking me through this!"

Every time bikers came toward them on the 111 or the I-10 Michal could feel Tabitha's body and arms tense. She realized her own fingers were getting stiff and sore from doing the same thing on the grips of the handlebars. California highway patrol cars only added to the stress she felt. One squad car tailed them for more than five minutes and Michal was certain they were going to get pulled over because of the luggage piled on to the back of the bikes. She could see the police opening one of the cases and finding the heroin. *Lord, get us through this, please. And tell my sister where to get rid of this stuff as soon as possible. In the name of Jesus. Really.*

The patrol car suddenly flashed its lights and sent Michal's heart leaping into her throat, did a fast and noisy U-turn, and streaked back east toward Palm Springs and Indio with its siren howling.

Thank you, Lord. I hope no one is badly hurt back there. And next time perhaps you could do it less dramatically.

They hadn't traveled 20 miles from Palm Springs before Tabitha tapped Michal on the shoulder.

"Cabazon," Tabitha said into Michal's ear. "Get off here and go past the dinosaur statues into the desert. Aim for that casino or whatever it is."

"You want me to head for that tall building?"

"No, I don't want you to end up in its parking lot. Just go into the desert and get behind some hills or dunes."

"This is what God is saying?" asked Michal.

"No, this is what I'm saying. But I'm pretty sure God told me. Don't you want to get rid of this stuff?"

"Yes, I want to get rid of this stuff. I just don't want to do in front of the whole Casino Morongo or whatever the sign back there called it."

"We won't. I'm just using it for a marker."

Milwaukee turned off the interstate behind them and shouted, "Do we know what we're doing?"

"No!" Michal and Tabitha shouted back at the same time.

Michal found a wide track behind the huge figure of a Tyrannosaurus Rex and followed it toward a gully.

"If the cops think we're trying to find a place to camp they'll be right on us!" yelled Milwaukee.

"Trust God!" Tabitha yelled back. "Okay! I'll tell them that too!"

The sky was reddening in the west toward LA as the sun dropped into the ocean. Moving slowly Michal maneuvered her Harley behind a small hill littered with gray rocks. Milwaukee followed. There was no one on the other side of the mound and the desert was growing dark rapidly.

"Cut your engine," Tabitha told her sister.

The silence was not complete. They could hear the sounds of traffic from Cabazon and the freeway. The growing blackness was not complete either—the casino shone like a tall fire ahead of them. But Tabitha smiled as she took off her helmet and felt a breeze from the direction of LA and the Pacific on her face.

"This is it," she said. "Can I pray before we do anything?"

"Of course you can pray," Michal responded. "Let's just get it over with quickly."

"Okay, sis, okay. But we didn't go through all this to rush things now. It's like some Old Testament story and we're sacrificing this enemy plunder to the Lord God of Israel."

Michal couldn't stop herself from uttering a short

laugh. She glanced at Milwaukee. "Skinhead here was always a good Bible student."

Tabitha was untying the suitcase that had been placed behind her. "Can you get the other three, Milwaukee?"

"I can."

"They weigh a ton."

They set the four suitcases on the rock and gravel. Tabitha knelt in front of them facing east. She prayed out loud.

"Not in any child's veins. Not in any schoolboy's body. Not in any young girl's blood. Scatter it, Lord, to the four winds and the seven seas and seven continents. Scatter it as you scatter all your enemies and all the works of darkness. May Jesus reign over all and in all and through all. In your name we pray. Amen."

"Amen," said Milwaukee and Michal, who had remained standing, looking at the ceremony as something of Tabitha's own offering before the Lord and not wanting to intrude.

"Milwaukee?" asked Tabitha getting up. "Do you have a knife in your saddlebags? A good one?"

"Yes. Skid shoved it in there when I wasn't looking."

"Have you ever used it?"

"Not yet."

"Then let's break it in right now."

The sunset was a black and red wash over the desert and over the four cases. Milwaukee pulled a huge blade out of its sheath and stood over them.

"What is that?" asked Michal. "A Bowie knife."

"It looks like you could take on that T Rex with it." Tabitha tried to open the cases. "They're all locked."

Milwaukee squatted beside one. "I'll cut them open."

It did not take long. The big blade was 14 inches and Skid had honed it to razor sharpness. Milwaukee made two vertical slashes and another horizontal one. Tabitha opened the flap he had cut out of the hard top of the first case. There were dozens of large, clear plastic packages inside. Each of the packages was solid with white powder. There were more than thirty.

Milwaukee opened them all. As he did so Tabitha took them and held them up into the breeze. The wind took the powder into the night in clouds of white.

Milwaukee opened the other three suitcases and the dozens of packages each of them held. Tabitha asked her sister to help and Michal knelt beside her, took packages Milwaukee had sliced open, and lifted them underneath the moon and stars. *Take them, Lord,* she prayed silently, *take them away.* Some of the powder fell on her hair and arms and hands, but most simply vanished into the darkness and the sand.

When it came to the final case a strange thing happened. After Milwaukee had slit open the top row of packages the breeze gusted and blew the powder out into the desert before anyone could lift the packages up.

Milwaukee cut the next row and the same thing happened, a huge ball of white powder bursting out of the case and into the night. When he finished with the final row a dust devil roared out of the burning red line to the west, stung their eyes so that they could not see, and lifted all the suitcases up, spun them around and around, then flung them against the rocks. The last of the heroin swirled in a circle for several seconds and then disappeared. They cleared their eyes in time to see the final streaks of white break apart and scatter.

"Thank you, Jesus." Tabitha was awed. They all were. She got to her feet and helped Michal up. "Let's leave our headlights off and just walk our bikes out of here as quietly as we can."

Milwaukee was watching the sky and the stars with the big knife hanging from his hand. "Good idea."

They took their time wheeling their bikes to the streets of Cabazon. Michal and Tabitha worked together. No one was around to notice them. They pulled on their helmets and leathers and were preparing to make their way back to the I-10 when Michal's phone buzzed and did its tune.

"Let me see that," demanded Tabitha in a strong voice.

"All right," Michal replied. "Don't get caught up in some big conversation."

"I don't intend to."

She read Nick's text out loud: I'm serious. You better start talking to me. You think The Dead are going to just let you take off with their heroin? There's at least a hundred bikers hunting southern California for you. Look, we know the bike you're on is red. The staff at the hotel were very helpful about that. We know the Nevada license plate number. We even know you headed into California. You and your sister are way too good looking for male desk clerks to forget overnight. You're also way too good looking to wind up with your throats cut and in a ditch beside the I-10 or I-40. The Dead could even call in the license number to the cops and say the bike is stolen. The highway patrol pick you up and the gang hear about it on their scanners. Then they know exactly where to find you. So stop playing around and text me before this whole thing gets way out of control and I can't talk them out of killing the three of you.

Tabitha thumbed a message back.

"What are you going to tell him?" asked Michal.

"What we did."

"Are you serious?"

"They'll leave us alone. There's nothing to chase us for."

"Except revenge," Milwaukee said.

Tabitha read out her text. We don't have the heroin. We dumped it.

OK? So there's no reason to look for us anymore.

Nick texted back immediately. I don't believe you.

I'm serious. What? You think I'd try and find a buyer for it? I'm not you, Nick. None of us here are you.

Where'd you dump it? If it's still intact I can probably call off the wolves.

Tommy had it in a storage unit next to Gold's Gym in Palm Springs. I took it out and dumped it in the desert by Cabazon.

Nick asked, Where in the desert?

Tabitha replied, Find the T Rex statue. There's a track behind it that heads in the direction of the big casino. Goes into a gully and behind a kind of small hill. You'll find the four cases there.

You telling the truth? Nick demanded.

Yes, I'm telling the truth, Tabitha texted. You'd recognize the suitcases, wouldn't you?

Yeah.

So that's where they are.

Tabitha stopped messaging. "Let's go."

Milwaukee started his bike. "They'll look for us traveling together. You guys take the lead. I'll be a hundred yards behind so I can keep my eyes on you. And—" Milwaukee leaned over with a pocket screwdriver and swiftly removed the Nevada plate from Michal's Harley. He yanked a different one from a saddlebag and screwed it on.

"California!" exclaimed Michal. "Where did you get that?"

"In the ditch near Vidal this morning. There's always license plates in the ditches. If they do call in the Nevada plate it won't matter." He looked at Michal. "You okay?"

"Sort of."

"You ready to ride good, hard, and steady? Maybe half the night?"

"If God rides with me."

Milwaukee began to steer his bike aside so they could go first. "He has to. Or we aren't going to make it."

"Can't we go to the police now, Gideon?"

"They won't understand it, Michal. It's too complicated. And they won't be able to save us. They sure won't be able to save Tabi."

Milwaukee thanked God for LA whose sprawling lights swallowed them up within half an hour of Cabazon. They stayed on the I-10 right through the heart of the busy city and were soon just another two bright specks in the constant flow of headlights. Once he was sure a cluster of six bikers flashing past them and heading east were from The Dead. Each of them had black leather do rags with a staked skull on their fronts. Tabitha hadn't noticed them, but when he described the do rags to her later she nodded grimly. "*Los Muertos*."

They hit Highway Number One and went north, moving with the heavy traffic past Santa Monica and Malibu. Milwaukee constantly glanced over at the Pacific as the white moon set it on fire. It took his breath away, but he didn't get a chance to really stop and stare until they gassed up in Ventura. Then he took a minute while the pump ran to look at the silver sea. Michal and Tabitha gazed at it as they stood beside him.

"Are we going to make it, Gideon?" Michal asked.

He turned from the sea to look at her. The beauty of her eyes and face always surprised him, especially when he saw it under different lighting, in this case under the yellow lights of the gas station. She saw the effect she had on him, but she was not in the mood to kiss or cuddle or ask for a hug. She needed something else from him.

"Yeah," he promised her quietly. "You're going to make it. I'll do everything I have to do to make sure you and your sister make it."

"I said we. The we includes you."

"You're both going to make it."

"I don't like you putting it that way."

He touched her cheek with his hand. "Can you go for another couple of hours?"

"If you can, I can."

"Tabi?"

Tabitha looked at him steadily. "It's life or death, isn't it?"

"Something like that."

She gave him a small smile. "When it's life or death I'm up for it."

They continued on north, the long, wide, white sea and breaking waves on their left, the shining lights of various communities glowing ahead of them or off their right shoulders. Michal and Tabitha still in the lead, the bikes swept past Santa Barbara and Goleta, then took the faster 101 through Santa Maria and Paso Robles where they gassed up again. By that time, they were all exhausted.

"That's it," Milwaukee said. "We push it any further and the highway'll kill us before *Los Muertos* do."

Michal had dark rings under her eyes. "A motel's not a good idea."

"Their bikers will all be south of us for now. But yeah, I think we have to do without showers for a few days. Or weeks."

"We can't run forever."

Milwaukee ran a hand over the blonde beard that had sprouted up on his jaw. "Maybe not forever. But now is a good idea." He looked at the map Michal had spread over her Harley seat under the gas station lights. "They'll comb the interstates for us because that's where we can make the fastest time. So we're going to use the secondary highways for a day or two. Not long because they'll put their bikers on them too

and it'll be easier to see us. But they can't cover all
the interstates and all the secondarys. And for all they
know we headed back for Nevada or Arizona or Utah.
It's too much ground for them to cover well." He put his
finger on the Mission San Miguel Arcangel. "This old
mission is only a few miles ahead. We'll sleep out in the
desert close to its walls. Four hours is all we can give
ourselves to recharge our batteries. Then we'll take this
little road through the Cholame Hills in the morning
and hitch up with the 25. That'll get us to Hollister, just
south of San Jose and San Francisco. When we make
it there we can decide what to do next."

It was another 20 minutes. They went past the mission a bit and then turned off into a field and into some
scraggly brush. Milwaukee hauled out the sleeping
bags and told the sisters to pray, talk, do whatever they
needed to do to lose the adrenaline rush they'd all been
thriving on since Palm Springs.

"Looking at the constellations might help," he suggested. "And there's water bottles in the left saddlebag
if you're thirsty. I'll go a little ways over here to give
you two some privacy."

Michal stood over her bag with her arms folded.
"Don't go too far, Gideon."

"I won't."

He had hardly walked four or five steps before the
cell phone went off. Tabitha had it in her jeans pocket.
The screen lit her face in the dark. She read what it
said to Milwaukee and her sister.

Okay, Tabi. What did you do with the stuff?

She sent a message back. I told you.

We found the suitcases all ripped up. Where's the stuff?

I told you. We dumped it.

Dumped it where?

You see all the plastic bags are cut open. We let the wind take it.

Nick texted, Don't be crazy. What did you put the stuff into and where is it?

Tabitha responded, Take a look around with your flashlights. You'll probably find some powder in the sand or on the rocks or in the scrub. It's gone, I'm telling you. You have no reason to track us anymore. We don't have anything you want.

There was nothing from Nick for several minutes. Then another text came. You crazy, crazy, stupid kid. Six million dollars worth of heroin. You stupid, stupid girl. What is wrong with you? I thought you were smart. How smart is this?

She texted back. It's over, Nick. Leave us alone. We have nothing you want.

His response came swiftly. We want your blood. You think you can just walk away from this and go back to Marietta? We're not some sweet Christian charity that hands out income tax receipts. You'll never see Pennsylvania again, Tabitha. You're dead. You're all dead.

Chapter Twenty-Three

Milwaukee slept for three hours and woke up. Stars still covered the sky. He glanced over and saw that Michal and Tabitha were in their bags and quiet. After a few moments he decided to head down to the mission. Perhaps praying there would clear his head.

It was only a five minute walk. As he made his way over the field bits and pieces of his dreams jabbed at his mind. He was trying to explain to the police that he had been storing four suitcases of heroin and needed protection from a drug cartel. The police asked where the heroin was.

Milwaukee said he and two friends had destroyed it. The police asked to see the suitcases. Milwaukee told them they didn't have the suitcases anymore. Without any hard evidence that Milwaukee's story was true the police began to lose interest. Even when he mentioned a dead DEA agent it didn't matter. Stepping up to the mission door Milwaukee realized again how difficult their story was to explain to anyone—except *Los Muertos* themselves.

A sign said the mission was open from 9 AM to 5

PM. But the door had not been properly locked and Milwaukee was able to get inside. The moon put its white light through the windows. He looked at the statues and icons and what he assumed was an image of Saint Michael the Archangel on the wall at the front. Michael, the one who led the fight of the good angels against the bad angels when there was rebellion in heaven. Michael, the Slayer of the Dragon and the Defender of the Children of Israel. Milwaukee walked quietly across the floor and sat in one of the benches. He stared ahead at the figure of the archangel and at the cross on the altar just below it.

Lord, if you do send an angel to help, it wouldn't hurt if it were Michael. He seems to have experience with this sort of thing.

He sat perfectly still and prayed for ten minutes. Then, concerned about the sisters' safety, he looked one last time at Michael and at the cross and left. The moon was getting lower. His brief time in the mission had started certain thoughts rolling in his head. The cell phone was on a flat stone by Tabitha's sleeping bag. Her face was turned away when he picked it up and walked back across the field to the mission. When he was certain the sisters would not hear him talking and wake up Milwaukee punched in a number.

A voice spoke in his ear. "Nick."

"Hey, Nick," Milwaukee responded. "Still looking for three needles in a very big haystack?"

"Who's this?"

"Milwaukee."

"Milwaukee. I thought you had some good Amish common sense in your head. I thought you could rein Tabitha in. Now you're all dead."

"You haven't caught us, Nick."

"We will."

"I could be calling you from an airport. Our flight to Philly could be leaving in five minutes. Or I could be calling from a train that's almost in Chicago."

"You do that and you take the fight to Pennsylvania. Lucifer will send hitmen all the way to Lancaster County if he has to. Then it gets really nasty."

Milwaukee frowned. "Lucifer?" Nick replied, "That's the head man."

"Great name."

"Yeah. And he acts like his namesake too."

"Is that what you want, Nick?" Milwaukee asked. "Lucifer sending killers into Amish country?"

"Yeah, I want it. You ripped off our gang. If we want to keep any business credibility down here we have to show everyone we can take care of the people who do damage to our assets."

"Even Tabi?" Milwuakee asked.

"Especially Tabi," Nick answered.

"So you want her dead? Cut open? Beautiful Tabi? Gone forever?" Nick did not respond.

"I can offer you a deal," Milwaukee said. "What deal?"

"My life for theirs."

"What?"

"You said you had to make an example of us. Okay. So just make an example of me. Let the girls go back to Pennsylvania and live there for the rest of their lives. Don't bother them again. Me you can do whatever you want with."

Nick was astounded. "Are you crazy? You know what Lucifer will do to you?"

Milwaukee was staring at the mission. "I have an idea."

"No, you don't. Before you go too far with this Jesus Christ thing I can promise you that you'll beg for death and won't get it. You'll scream until he drops your head on a street in Juarez or El Paso or LA."

"He'd do it anyway if he caught us."

"No," Nick said. "He'd just kill you and keep the girls stashed in Mexico. But if it's only you he gets his hands on, if it's only you he can play with, believe me, you will be getting his full attention. What he'll do to you will make the other gangs fear crossing The Dead even more than they do now."

"So," Milwaukee replied, "my deal might interest him?"

"Maybe. Maybe not."

"Sure it will. Does he really want to go over into some northern gang's turf in Pennsylvania and risk starting a biker war? Word will get around he's sent some assassins north to take care of business. Do you really think the gangs up there will believe the shooters are in Penn just to do a hit on two Amish girls?"

Nick hesitated. "We can find you long before you get to Lancaster County."

"No, you can't. We could be anywhere right now—Oregon, Utah, Colorado—or waiting for a connecting flight out of Salt Lake City."

"We have people watching the airports."

"All of them?" challenged Milwaukee.

Nick was quiet. Then he spoke up, "I'll tell him what you're offering. Make sure you're at this number five minutes from now."

The signal went dead. Milwaukee walked back toward Michal and Tabitha. They were still asleep. He watched both their faces a moment and then headed far out into the field again. The cell phone played the Star Spangled Banner.

"Milwaukee," he answered, putting the phone to his ear.

"Okay, Milwaukee," came Nick's voice, "you got your deal. Where and when?"

"Give me 72 hours. Meet me at Cannon Beach in Oregon."

"Cannon Beach? Where's that?"

"Just outside Portland. I saw it on the map."

"So is that where you are? Portland?"

"No," Milwaukee replied. "I'm three days from Portland."

"You don't get 72, you get 48. No cops, no feds, no DEA. You cross us up and Lucifer will risk the biker war just for the pleasure of personally slitting your throats in Marietta."

"I'll be there in two days. Alone. You do your part."

"Yeah," Nick grunted. "We'll do our part. Wednesday morning. Cannon Beach. First light. Make sure you're not late."

"I won't be," Milwaukee promised.

"Adios, Jesus Cristo."

Milwaukee hit the red key. The sun had cut a silver opening in the east and he watched it widen. Then he called several more numbers. One of them was Ghost's.

"Hey," complained Ghost when he finally answered. "Not everyone gets up as early as you guys do to pray."

"Ghost. It's Kee. I'm putting the girls in a B and B in California tonight. You need to meet them there and get them back to Natchez or Marietta or wherever you think they'll be safe."

"Whoa, whoa, whoa. What B and B? Keep them safe from who? What's going on?"

"Tabi had a line on a heroin stash. She took us there and we destroyed it."

"Whose stash? How much was it worth?"

"It was *Los Muertos'* stuff. There was six million dollars worth."

Milwaukee could hear Ghost suck in his breath. "Are you kidding me?"

"Just get them out of that B and B tomorrow and keep them safe."

"And where will you be?" asked Ghost.

"Drawing the gang off," Milwaukee said. "What about the police?"

"The heroin is gone. The gang has the suitcases the stash was in. We have nothing to prove our story. No evidence. Just our word."

Ghost grunted. "Give me the name and number of the B and B. Are you there yet?"

"No, it will take us most of the day." Milwaukee told him the name of the place and the phone number.

"You want me to meet you there tonight?"

"I don't, Ghost," Milwaukee said. "I need the night. To be with Michal and Tabitha. But anytime after the crack of dawn tomorrow would be great."

"Where are you going tomorrow morning, Kee?"

"I'm going where I need to go."

"Why the secrecy? What did you do? Strike a deal with those murderers?"

"Please. Just take care of the sisters. Christ be with you, Ghost."

Milwaukee ended the call. Then he erased all of his texts with Nick as well as the record of his connection to Ghost's number. He kept the phone in his pocket and crossed the field to wake the sisters.

"Where's the cell?" Tabitha asked, checking the grass beside the rock she'd placed the phone on.

"I'll take care of it today," Milwaukee told her. "In case Nick calls. Is that okay?"

Tabitha shrugged. "Yeah, it's okay. I have nothing more to say to him." She turned around in her bag to look at the sunrise. Then she glanced back at Milwaukee. "But lots to say to God."

Milwaukee nodded and smiled at Michal. "How are you doing?"

Michal hugged her knees to her chest. "I know I'm supposed to say okay. All the English say they're okay even when they're not." She smiled a thin smile. "But I'm not okay. I'm scared."

Milwaukee nodded. "I know. I'm sorry. Let's put some distance between ourselves and *Los Muertos*."

"Gideon. Now that the night's over, and they're not right on top of us, why can't we get to an airport and catch a plane to Philadelphia?"

"Let's get a bit farther away. I'm worried they'll put people in the airports in the big cities. We need to get further north. Tomorrow will be a better day to get tickets for a flight east."

"Ja?"

"For sure." Then he changed the subject. "How do you look so good after a hard night and only four hours sleep?"

Michal made a face. "Yeah, I'm certain I look like one of your movie stars."

"Better."

She threw her star spangled do rag at him. "Go away and give us five minutes to get ready."

It took them a couple of hours to make it to Hollister where they wolfed down a breakfast in ten minutes. Then they headed through San Jose and into San Francisco. Milwaukee pointed to their right as they crossed the Golden Gate Bridge, joggers and walkers and cyclists crowding the sidewalks that ran on both sides of the lanes of traffic.

"Are you pointing at the sailboats?" called Michal.

"That's a prison!" called Milwaukee. "I mean, it used to be!"

"The island with the buildings?"

"They call it Alcatraz!"

"A good place for Nick and his friends?" she asked.

"Very good!"

White fog drifted in off the ocean and covered them as they rolled off the bridge. It lasted for more than an hour as they headed up the coast on the 101. Now and then bikes would appear in the mist ahead of them and roar past like a dark blur. If any of them had been *Los Muertos* Milwaukee or the sisters would never have known it. Neither would any of the bikers have realized who the women on the red Harley were or the man on the 2007 Fat Boy.

A gift, thought Michal, *even though I would love to see the ocean.*

It took all afternoon to make it up the coast to the redwoods. Once the fog vanished the Pacific opened up off their left shoulders in blue and white and silver and the sun blazed in a solid blue October sky. Clouds appeared at the approach of the giant trees and brooded over them. Ignoring the gray they often parked their bikes at turnouts to wander among the huge trunks.

At one stop a part of Milwaukee screamed that outlaw bikers were coming down from Portland and Seattle or up from San Francisco. So he used the threat of rain as an excuse to haul out a black tarpaulin and bungee cord it over both bikes without drawing attention. The tarp did not look out of place as clouds thickened and blocked the light. Even with the possibility of *Los Muertos* taking plane flights into Portland or San Francisco, renting Harleys, and scouring the 101 or I-5 for them, Milwaukee was determined not to miss seeing something he had dreamed about since childhood, touching the greatest living things on earth. Especially if they were some of the last natural wonders he would ever look at.

"It is a cathedral, a sanctuary, this forest," Michal exclaimed in awe, holding hands with both Milwaukee and Tabitha while she walked between the two of them. "In my head, a voice says, Run! Run! But another voice says, There is time, stay, stay."

"The voices are in me too," Milwaukee admitted.

"We all have the same heads," laughed Tabitha. "Can you imagine if this were a Hollywood movie? The people being chased would never stop to look at a forest."

"But these are not ordinary trees," murmured Milwaukee. "And ours is not an ordinary story."

"So these trees tell us how incredible the God is who made them," Michal said, squeezing both their hands. "He can take care of us."

"We must do our part," cautioned Milwaukee.

"We are doing our part." Michal smiled at him.

"Doesn't all this grandeur bring you to worship and prayer?"

"It does."

"Then that is to our advantage." She leaned into Milwaukee's arm. "I was frightened this morning. On the road I began to feel better. Now, walking between the trees, I feel fully alive in Christ. I can't explain it."

"Then it was good to do all these stops and take all these risks to see the redwoods?"

"Oh, *ja,* definitely."

Tabitha nodded. "I feel the same way. Perhaps not so much as you do, sis. But when I go over all of it in my mind—what we did with the heroin, the danger we put ourselves in to make sure that junk did not reach the schoolkids in Pennsylvania—I'm not sorry for the risk, I'm not. But I feel guilty about dragging you two into it."

"Don't," responded Michal. "God let you know about the stash. You needed our help to get ahold of it and get rid of it. I couldn't have lived with myself if I didn't do anything to stop Nick from taking that stuff north."

They stopped at an enormous trunk rooted firmly in front of them. Milwaukee leaned both hands against the tree. Then he wrapped his arms around it as far as they could go.

"I haven't covered much distance," he laughed.

"Here." Tabitha went to his left and stretched her arms over the trunk. "Now you're a little bit farther."

"And farther yet." Michal went to his other side and spread her arms.

They returned to the road and eventually reached a village where well-maintained Victorian era houses fascinated the sisters as they came through on the main street.

"Look at the bay windows!" cried Tabitha as they crawled along. "And the balconies and the rooftops are amazing."

"If only it were a better time in our lives," sighed Michal. "If only we could stay awhile in a place like this and not be worried about the evil things men do."

"I have booked us rooms here," Milwaukee said.

The sisters snapped their heads around to look at him from their bike. "What?" they exclaimed at the same time.

"A nice bed and breakfast in a nice Victorian home. It's a good idea. *Los Muertos* will check the parking lots of motels they ride past. They can't find every B and B in every community and look to see if they have Harleys in front or out back."

"You think?" Tabitha kept her eyes on him while Michal turned her attention back to the traffic.

He smiled. "I do think."

When they found the bed and breakfast on a side street it astonished all three of them, even Milwaukee whose mind was beginning to whirl darkly at what was in store for him over the next 24 hours. The windows were bright in the evening mist, the woodwork around the glass was intricate and freshly painted, the curtains hung perfectly and invitingly. There was a hidden place to park their bikes next to a dumpster behind the massive three storey house. After tarping them, they all relaxed even more.

The interiors were immaculate with Victorian sinks and fireplaces and bedspreads. Michal and Tabitha actually squealed when they found their bed had a canopy draped over it. Hugging Milwaukee they told him it took away the sting of what they were facing just to sit at the table in the bay window and play with the tea set as if they were little girls again.

"You couldn't have done a better thing," said Michal, wrapping her arms around him as she had wrapped them around the redwood. "A haven in the middle of the storm. We will sleep like logs."

"And have a hot breakfast," added Tabitha, hugging Milwaukee from behind.

"And hot baths."

"I am happy to be so popular," Milwaukee laughed. "But what about supper? Do either of the Troyer sisters want a hot meal?"

"Yes!" they said loudly together. "It is raining out now."

The sisters turned their heads toward the large bay window. And then looked at each other. Nodding, they turned back to Milwaukee and gave him the sharp Troyer smile with the dark slanted eyebrows.

"We could eat in," Michal said.

"You could get us a pizza or something," added Tabitha.

"We're really too cozy in this nice room you got us," purred Michal, "to go anywhere."

Milwaukee grinned. "How can I say no to a roomful of American beauty?" He put up the collar of his leather jacket. "I'll be right back."

He returned in half an hour with a big bag of Chinese food. The dishes steamed as he set them out on the small table in the window. They ate off of Styrofoam plates, the sisters sitting cross-legged on the bed, Milwaukee stretching his legs out in front of him on the floor. After the meal they decided to walk up and down a few blocks in the rain and look at the houses, thoughts of *Los Muertos* getting pushed farther and farther to the backs of their minds. When they made it back to the bed and breakfast, soaked, Michal won scissors cuts paper two out of three times against Tabitha and drew the first bath.

Milwaukee went to his room and had a long shower. He liked the look of his beard and chose not to take the razor to it. His knock on the sisters' door was answered by Michal. Her hair was loose and black and wet and she wore a royal blue terrycloth robe that had been hanging in the closet next to a white one. Grim images of *Los Muertos* bikers that were trying to edge closer to the center of his thinking were completely displaced when he saw the blue robe and the blue eyes and the long, shining hair. She couldn't miss his intense look.

"I'm all wet," she protested. "Lancaster. The movie date."

"Excuse me?"

"It was raining and you sat on my jacket. You had three AM hair and I fooled around with the top of your head."

Michal laughed deeply from the bottom of her stomach. "Okay. But I'm still wet."

"I like you wet." He pulled her toward him and she did not push away. "Where's Tabi?"

"Just got in the bath."

"Great news. Does she like long baths?"

"I don't think she's had one in months. She'll soak till dawn."

Milwaukee smiled. "Despite our hazardous circumstances, things keep getting better and better."

She returned his smile. "Do they?"

They looked at each other and heard the rain pick up, gusting against the windows.

"Sea breeze," Milwaukee said, not breaking his gaze. Michal didn't break hers either. "What do you mean?"

"I mean a breeze off the sea is pushing the rain against the glass."

"Oh."

Milwaukee ran her hair through his fingers. "I like this stuff. This crowning glory stuff."

She put her fingers on the hand that was playing with her hair. "I think God meant you to."

"We've been on this road a long time now, Michal. It'll be five months soon. Almost half a year."

"I know."

"I'm so glad we did it. I'm so glad your father asked. I thank God you said yes."

"I feel the same way."

He began to stroke the side of her face. "What an incredible beauty you are. Eyes that are gemstones. Hair a night of stars. Lips like red sky. Skin soft as air."

She felt the blood move into her face and the warmth. *I thought I was over that kind of stuff,* she thought, unconsciously putting a hand to her throat.

"And what a heart you have. What a love for God and the world he died to save. A strong mind. Strong arms. Courage. Compassion."

She put her fingers to his lips. "Oh, stop, Gideon Milwaukee Bachman. A girl can only take in so much at a time."

"It's all true. It's not flattery."

"In your mind it's true anyway."

"No." He shook his head. His face had such earnestness in it she bit her lip and thought she might cry. "No," he repeated, "it's true for anybody who takes the time to get to know you. Like I did over thousands of miles of highway. It's as true as the ocean across the street. Or the rain falling on the roof. It's as true as the Son of God."

She smiled at the light that flamed in his eyes, a light she knew was only for her. "Gideon, I—"

But she never finished her sentence. His lips came over hers and they felt like fire. Her whole body felt like fire. As if a match had ignited a forest and the light and heat from the blaze had leaped immediately into the sky.

His arms were around the blue terrycloth robe, his arms were around her. He held her more and more tightly as the kiss burned more and more deeply. Her mind began to turn around and around and she no longer knew if her feet were on the floor of the room or if he had lifted her in the air. She lost her breath and her sense of time and place. She lost herself. When the kiss ended he placed her gently on a soft couch, the kind woman in hooped dresses perched on in 1861. Now she wanted to sleep, just sleep, and never lose the feeling of heaven on earth she had experienced in his arms.

Her eyes were closed. "Was that The Kiss?"

"Yes. That was The Kiss."

"Do you mean it?"

"What do you think?"

She smiled a slow, easy smile, her eyes still shut. "I think you want to marry me and kiss me goodnight for the rest of your life. I think you love me, Gideon Milwaukee Bachman."

"You've nailed it." She heard the door open. "Sweet dreams, my beautiful woman."

"Sweet dreams, my beautiful man."

"I love you, Michal."

The door closed.

Milwaukee did not sleep. Instead, he read from her father's small black Bible. Then he wrote a letter on stationery he found in a drawer, placed it in an envelope with the remaining travelers checks, put Michal's name on the envelope, and arranged the Bible and envelope and cell phone by his pillow. He kept two hundred dollars for gas and bottled water in his wallet and that was all. Then he lay on his back on the floor with his hands behind his head and thought about the stars gleaming in the sky above the rain and prayed.

At four he left. The rain was softer and quieter now. He pulled the tarp off The Big Easy, bound it more tightly to the red Harley, then wheeled his bike four long blocks before twisting the key. There was no traffic. He headed north toward Oregon.

He kept to the 101 all the way to Portland. It took him most of the day. The highway tossed and turned like the sea. He had to keep his speed down. The rain and wind grew in ferocity. The Pacific boiled white at the foot of the cliffs the road was perched on. He kept wondering if he would miss a turn and end up falling hundreds of feet onto the rocks and sand and waves. Then he made up his mind that was not going to happen. If he wasn't at Cannon Beach in the morning the sisters would be killed. So he prayed and the bike roared steadily north and the Oregon coast roared back in its own wild and powerful way.

The weather broke as he neared the beach. High

rock formations loomed out of the sand and a sharp red sea. The tide was high, but receding. A few couples walked the edge of sand with the hoods of their rain jackets up. A man threw a Frisbee for his dog who yelped in excitement as he chased it through the air.

Milwaukee parked his Harley under some trees and sat on the seat a while, watching the red become maroon and the maroon become black. He opened a bottle of water and gulped it down. When there was enough beach he walked to the huge towers of rock and placed his hands on them. Then he went to the sea and splashed the salt water against his face.

Most of the night he paced and prayed over an empty beach. He might have slept leaning against the rock columns, he wasn't sure. Finally he lied down. Stretched out under the thickening stars, with wet sand against his hair, he closed his eyes several times. But mostly he looked at the flashing constellations and a moon that was now three-quarters full.

At 3:30 he heard the sound of bikes. Two Harleys rumbled onto the sand with their headlights stabbing into the dark and spotted him right away. Then they zig-zagged back and forth checking the beach, circling around the rock towers, going far to the left and far to the right. After five minutes of this one bike went away and the other stayed put, its light on Milwaukee, blinding him. He sat down.

A loud noise made him try to look past the headlight beam. He counted twelve or fifteen motorcycles streaming onto the beach. Several came very close to where he was sitting. Men got off the bikes and walked toward him.

He recognized Nick's voice. "Yeah. That's him."

Nick stood over him. "Why weren't you answering your cell phone?"

"I didn't bring it with me. I left it behind."

"Well. You're here. That's what matters." He suddenly kicked Milwaukee in the ribs. The pain made Milwaukee gasp and bend over. Then Nick kicked him again. "Don't mind me, Amish boy. Just trying to bust some ribs. This was what you wanted, right? To be an Easter Jesus?" He kicked him a third time and stepped back.

Milwaukee's head was in the sand as he tried to get his breath. A slender figure appeared out of the headlight beams. The person had no hair and no eyebrows. He didn't even seem to have lips. His eyes were so narrow they were almost not there.

He looks like a needle.

"So you're the German kid. You're the hero." The voice was thin, almost inaudible.

Milwaukee tried to respond, but it hurt too much to try and get enough air inside to give himself a voice.

"Hey. You're not going to fold on me this fast. The fun's just beginning."

The man knotted his hand in Milwaukee's thick hair and pulled him to his feet. The fresh pain jerked Milwaukee's mouth open, but he did not have the breath to make a sound.

"Nothing to say? I'll help you find your vocal cords."

Milwaukee saw a glint of something made of metal. It struck high in his shoulder. The agony made him yelp. It was not much and the man laughed.

"I think we can do better than that."

He punched Milwaukee in the stomach and Milwaukee's body jack-knifed. The man pulled him up straight by his hair and slugged him in the stomach again. Milwaukee groaned. He hit Milwaukee a third time.

Milwaukee groaned louder and the man let him collapse on the sand. "There we are."

The small hand wound itself in Milwaukee's hair once again, yanking him slowly to his feet, his mouth hanging open.

"You know, we have a saying. We only reserve it for special people like yourself. People who are our enemies and who are going to die for their misdeeds. *Dia de los Muertos.* The Day of the Dead. We tell them it is their special day." He put his face close to Milwaukee's. "So let me be the first to congratulate you on your special day. Do you see that cooler behind me?"

Milwaukee noticed a large chest on the beach nearby.

"Yes? Well, that is for you. Not all of you. Just your head. Packed in ice. To keep it beautiful until we drop it on a street in southern California. Did you think it was for cans of Pepsi?"

He smacked a smooth rock into Milwaukee's face and let him drop again, blood running into his mouth.

"But the Day of the Dead is only beginning, *amigo.* It goes on a long time. It is something people talk about for years afterward. That is why we do it right. That is why we take our time."

He hauled Milwaukee to his feet by the hair. "Do you know who I am?"

Milwaukee whispered a name.

"Very good. Lucifer. The Light Bearer. Good, good, good." Again he brought his face close. "It will not be quick. It will not be easy. It will not be clean. But I like it that way. Understand? I like it that way. Because that is who I am. That is what I am."

Milwaukee saw the knife come out again. As moonlight glanced off its blade a sound suddenly swelled in the early morning air. Lucifer hesitated and listened. Then he smiled.

"Do you hear that? More *Los Muertos*. More of my men. No one wants to miss the show. Isn't it something to be the feature attraction for once in your life? You can thank me for that."

The blade went in and out of Milwaukee's leg. Milwaukee shouted as a shock went through his body. He fell. The roaring sound grew louder and louder. He could feel the beach vibrating against his cheek.

Now even Lucifer was surprised by the sheer volume of the engines.

He turned his head, then he turned his whole body to face the land. The knife was still in his hand when the first Harleys burst out of the trees and headed straight for him at top speed.

Chapter Twenty-Four

❧

Lucifer began to run.

Dozens of headlight beams stabbed through the blackness, sharp white lines that lit up the *Los Muertos* bikers, the rock pillars, the beach, and the bald-headed figure racing toward the water's edge. Milwaukee could barely keep his eyes open, but he began to count the bikes that surrounded *Los Muertos* and sped back and forth over the firm sand: six, thirteen, twenty-three, thirty-nine, fifty-four. He watched Lucifer stagger through waves slapping against his waist and chest as three bikes moved in on him. One biker's jacket had the Hells Angels winged skull. But the other two were the barbed wire cross of Heavens Gate.

Lucifer collapsed in deep water and the sea rushed over him. The tide was surging toward shore. The three bikers planted their Harleys in the sand and waded into the waves to fish him out. Milwaukee watched them struggle in the foam and reach under the water with their hands. Finally they dragged Lucifer free of the ocean's grip and hauled him farther up on the beach. One of the Heavens Gate bikers started pumping Lucifer's chest and doing CPR in the light of the headlight beams while the other two squatted beside him. Then someone put a hand gently under his head.

"His eyelids are fluttering. He's alive. He's breathing."

"Get some light over here."

"There's blood all over the sand. His pulse is lousy. He's not gonna make it."

Milwaukee suddenly heard a voice he recognized. "Don't tell me he's not gonna make it. The kid's got an overload of guts. He's gonna pull through and we're gonna make sure he pulls through. Do you get it?"

"Skid," he whispered.

"He's calling for you, man."

"Skid," Milwaukee said again.

Skid's face appeared. "I'm here, Milwaukee. You gotta hang in. Okay? You gotta hang in."

"The girls. The sisters."

"Ghost's got 'em. They're cool. They're safe."

Milwaukee tried to get saliva in his mouth. "How— how did you—?"

"Ghost called me in. You should've done it yourself."

Milwaukee felt like laughing. "Gentle Skid—meek and mild—thought you'd start—a war—"

"I did anyway. Sometimes you need a war, Amish boy."

"This reminds me—of the Carolinas—only now— I'm the one on my back—"

"Yeah. Yeah."

"Ought to call your club—the Good Samaritans—"

"Hey, watch it, dude. You're gonna ruin my hard-as-rocks reputation among the Angels."

Milwaukee tried to smile. "Pretty funny—you being like a Bible story—"

"Okay, that's enough, kid. You should be saving your breath and keeping your strength in."

"Why? I feel myself—going—"

Skid growled. "Shut up with that talk."

"I can't stay—it's like the old corny black and whites—you know—I leave a message—you give the message to Michal—"

"Shut up, I said!"

"It is chick flick stuff—but do it anyway, Skid—tell her anyway—"

Milwaukee heard Skid yell for someone with the biker name Sutures and he heard a man shout back that Sutures was coming. He didn't have it in him to say anything else to Skid. He felt himself going to sleep and thought he saw Jesus coming toward him with a drink of water in a clay cup.

"I can't do anything for him, Skid, he's too far gone and we're too far from an emergency ward."

"No. You do it. You do what you need to do to stabilize him. Just like you did for the boys in Iraq."

"I can't."

"I am not going back down that road and tell those sisters the guy is dead. I'm not doing it. It's not going to happen. You try something, Sutures, anything, but the boy lives."

"Then you'd better help."

Milwaukee heard Skid grunt. "I'll do whatever you want me to do."

"Do Hells Angels pray?"

Skid was silent a long time before he answered. "Not much."

"Well, you'd better try it, Skid. Because that's about all we've got."

Skid shouted. "Heavens Gate! I need some of you Heavens Gate riders over here! Now!"

"I'm going to give him some pain killer. And all right, I'll rig up a battlefield transfusion. But it's not going to work."

"Shut up, Sutures. Quit tellin' me what you can't do and just do it. Rig it."

"I'll rig it. You pray it."

The last thing Milwaukee felt was a huge hand resting on his head. The last thing he heard was the strange sound of Skid reciting the Lord's Prayer and then saying, "Jesus, why would you listen to me? You know what I am. But I'm asking—don't do this—don't take him. We need him more than you. Those two girls need him more than you. Look, what do you want from me? What kind of bargain do you want me to strike with you? Go ahead. Name anything. I won't renege. I never renege. Everybody wants something. Name your price."

In the black of sleep Milwaukee saw Michal sitting on a rock in the forest and crying her heart out. He tried to reason with her, but she wouldn't listen.

"Don't talk to me about what I should or shouldn't feel, Gideon Bachman!" she snapped. "You can't kiss a girl like that and then take off into the night. This isn't Hollywood. I wake up in the morning and you're gone. You leave me some sappy note and that's supposed to be good enough? Well, it isn't good enough."

"I did my best."

Her blue eyes ignited. "You did not do your best. Don't you say that. Your best would have been staying alive and marrying me and holding our son in your arms and kissing our daughter goodnight. What good is your death to me?"

"I had to do it."

"You did not have to do it. You could have fought back. You could have run. You could have put us on a plane."

"None of that would have worked. They would still have come after you and Tabi." He reached out with his arms. "Come on."

Michal threw up her hands. "Get away from me! Don't touch me!" She jumped to her feet and stalked into the woods.

"Michal!"

"Get out of here, Gideon Bachman. I am not interested in a corpse. Dead men don't do anything for me."

"What do you want?"

Tears were streaking from her eyes. "I want you to want to live. I want you to come back to life. I want a resurrection. Do you understand? Don't come around unless you've made up your mind to come back to me. Do that and we can talk. Do that and I'll let you take me in your arms. But if you're not interested in life I'm not interested in you."

Milwaukee blinked open his eyes. A young woman's face was bent over his, but it was not Michal's. He tried to sit up.

"Where am I?"

The woman's eyes widened. "Please. Lay back down. You're in a private emergency clinic. I'll get the doctor. And your friends."

Michal and Tabitha were the first ones to rush into the room. Michal looked just like she had in Milwaukee's dream, right down to the tears on her cheeks. Except now she was smiling.

"Gideon! Gideon! Thank God!"

She threw her arms around him and kissed him on the mouth. "Wow," he said. "I should die and come back to life every day."

She laughed as she continued to cry. "You and your talk. You think you are Lazarus?"

"What happened?"

Tabitha kissed him on both cheeks. "Sweet boy. You were hurt. You lost blood. You went into shock. Skid's biker doctor was able to turn things around. Now you are in a clinic in Portland run by friends of Ghost."

"Was the biker doctor someone named Sutures?"

Michal nodded. "You remember a lot. Yes, that was him."

A tall thin doctor in a white shirt and dark pants came briskly into the room. "You're awake. Wonderful." He brought out his stethoscope. "Let me check a few things."

He listened to Milwaukee's chest and heart, took his pulse, and peeled back his eyelids. Turned to the nurse and asked her to do his blood pressure and temperature. Then put his hands on his hips.

"You're doing fine. You have cuts in your shoulder and thigh from a switchblade. Your ribs are pretty badly bruised, but none were fractured. The police have been and they took your friends' statements. They'll be back to take yours. But you're doing well. A couple more days and you're out of here if you remain rock steady."

He left and the nurse took Milwaukee's temperature in the ear and then wrapped a blood pressure cuff around his upper arm. Michal and Tabitha stepped aside while she worked, but once she was finished they returned to Milwaukee and each of them held one of his hands tightly and kissed it.

"Hey, hey." Skid came up beside Milwaukee's bed and mussed his mop of sun-blonded hair. "You don't look any the worse for wear. We'll have you riding again in no time."

Milwaukee turned his face to him while Michal took one of Milwaukee's hands in both of hers and held it to her lips. "Skid, I remember the bikes coming in and fanning out over the beach. Some were your crew. Some were Heavens Gate."

Skid pulled up a chair. "The Angels were from the Portland club. The Gates rode up from Frisco."

"What about you?"

"Ghost and I met in Baton Rouge and flew out together. Then he took a local flight into Eureka while I got a bike and organized things here."

"But I never told anyone where I was going."

"You told *Los Muertos*. Nick texted you twice on the cell you left behind with the girls. He mentioned Cannon Beach both times."

"So Ghost picked up Michal and Tabitha?"

"Yeah, he did. Talked Redwood Harley in Eureka into renting him a Sportster so he could fetch the girls from the B and B. Between you and me, I think he's going to buy the hog. He says it needs to be fine-tuned in order to reach its potential."

"What's this?" Ghost walked in. "Hey, Kee, praise God. You make prayer real in my life. This is great." He leaned over and kissed Milwaukee on the forehead. "How are you feeling?"

"Hey. Tired. My left arm and leg are sore. And oh, man, my ribs ache. Other than that, I want to get up and go."

They laughed. Ghost put a hand on Skid's shoulder. "This guy get around to telling you about his conversion?"

Skid shook his head. "Don't go gettin' ahead of God, Ghost. I ain't one of your converts. At least not yet. I struck a deal, that's all."

"What deal?" Milwaukee asked.

"Look. I told God and Jesus that if he put the life back in you I'd go to Bubba Win's church for a year. Help out. Listen to his sermons. But never sing. That's all. I didn't ask the Red Sea to part."

Milwaukee stared. "A Hells Angel in church?" Skid grunted. "I don't renege."

"Your boys'll have a good laugh over that."

Skid narrowed his eyes. "Anyone laughs I'll kick the heads off their necks."

"You actually believe God answered your prayer?"

"Yeah. I do. You were pretty far gone. Sutures couldn't believe that you held in there." Skid shrugged. "God did his part. I'll do mine."

"That's the truth." A young man in jeans and jean jacket came through the doorway. "I've seen your kind of face on the battlefield. Even from just a single bullet or a little chunk of shrapnel. Never could pull those boys back. I went through the motions with you, but Skid had to talk me into making the effort to begin with. We were just too far from an emergency ward or a well set-up clinic. But then old Hells Angel Skid started to praying and the rest is history."

Milwaukee lifted his hand free of Tabitha for the

young man to take. "I guess you're Sutures. Thank you for your effort. You saved my life."

Sutures took Milwaukee's hand in a hard, dry grip. "The credit belongs to Skid there. But I appreciate the thanks just the same."

Milwaukee looked at the faces around the bed. "It's still not clear to me. The doctor said the police were here and that they'll be back. What on earth did you tell them?"

Ghost lifted his hands. "We didn't get into every-thing and make it too complicated. We told them *Los Muertos* had it in for you. That the Angels were sworn to protect you. That the Gates tried to keep the peace."

"And that was enough?"

"They saw it as a small scale biker spat. But you got knifed so they'll ask if you want to press charges. Otherwise it'll blow over."

"What are *Los Muertos* saying?" Milwaukee asked.

"Nothing," Ghost told him.

"What's Lucifer saying?"

"Not much. At least not here. He's dead."

Milwaukee stared at Ghost. "I saw a Gates biker doing CPR on him."

Ghost nodded. "Members of The Dead vouched for that. They also told the cops no one had held him under or forced him into the water. They said he ran there on his own and fell into the waves and drowned."

"Is that really what happened?"

"Yeah. That's really what happened. He hit his head on a rock hard piece of driftwood when he went under. That's why he never came up for air."

Milwaukee sank his head back on the pillow. "So what do I tell the police officers?"

"The truth. Lucifer stabbed you. Lucifer is dead. End of story."

"What about the heroin stash in Palm Springs? What about Tommy?"

Ghost shrugged. "Look, brother, tell them if you want. But you have no proof the heroin ever existed or that you destroyed it. You'll never be able to implicate *Los Muertos*. The Dead'll just haul out their lawyers and say you're lying. Same with this Tommy that Tabi talks about. Was he DEA? Was he rogue? Who knows? But you can't prove who killed him or if he really was law enforcement. Do we even have a body? To the cops it's another dead end."

Milwaukee moaned. "I knew all along the whole thing would only look like a crazy mixed up mess to anyone else. That's why I never went to the police for help in the first place."

"So, bro, you have to pray about it and then ask yourself—should you be dragging Lucifer's whole gang into the assault he laid on you? I know they were his crew, but he did the dirty work last night, not them."

"I've got nothing to say about *Los Muertos* so long as they leave me and the Troyer sisters alone."

Skid coughed. "No problem there. We had a little talk before Sutures phoned in the fatality. They don't want a whole scale war with the Angels. I mean, we had them dead to rights on that beach. I told them a war could easily be avoided so long as they stuck to their turf and their business.

"Anyone harms a hair on your head or Tabi's or Michal's, well, all bets are off and I call out the bloodhounds and assassins." Skid coughed again. "You won't be seeing them in Pennsylvania. Or anywhere you decide to ride and pitch your tent."

"Have they gone back to San Francisco?"

"They'll be allowed to leave once you make your statement and don't point fingers. Luc stabbed you. Luc had an accidental drowning. Luc was doing his own thing. Done."

Milwaukee blew out a mouthful of air. "I hope they come by soon. I want what the English call closure on this."

Ghost agreed. "Good idea. I'll give them a call." He pulled a cell from his pocket and walked from the room into the hall.

Skid got to his feet as well. "I'll drop by to check on you tonight. You probably could use some free time with the blue-eyed girls."

Tabitha gave Milwaukee a kiss on the top of his head. "Not this blue-eyed girl. I'll see you in the waiting room, sis. Take your time."

"What are you going to do?" asked Michal.

"There's a small chapel. I'll spend some God time in there. So if I'm not in the waiting room watching CNN I'll be praying there."

"Okay. Thanks."

"No problem." She stopped in the doorway and looked back. "Thank you for working so hard to save my life, Amish boy."

"Anytime, Amish girl."

Michal sat on the edge of the bed and kissed Milwuakee on the lips for a long time. Then she smoothed back his hair. "You missed breakfast at the Victorian house."

"Was it good?"

"Well, it should have been good. It would have been good if you hadn't pulled your Hollywood I'm-off-to-die act."

"I never called it that."

"I don't care. That's what it was. I couldn't eat a thing. The poor host thought she'd done something wrong with her muffins and crepes."

Milwaukee closed his eyes. "Sorry. Didn't know what else to do. The police plan was no good because we didn't have any evidence. The airplane plan was no good because I knew they'd follow us to Marietta."

"So getting yourself killed was the better plan?"

"I had to do the right thing."

Michal's eyes flared up. "The right thing? Giving me a dead husband was the right thing?"

"You know, we had a conversation like this before I came back to consciousness," Milwaukee told her.

"Did we?"

"You can be just as German in my dream state as you are in real life." Michal lifted an eyebrow. "Oh?"

"Which is all right. You are as perfect in real life as you are in dream life. So I can live with it."

"I am glad to hear it. Since I have no intention of letting you out of my sight again." She played with his beard. "When was the last time you shaved?"

"I don't know? Vegas? Mesquite?"

"I think I have lived a lifetime in the last two or three days, Gideon. Now I would like to start a new life. Can we do that?"

"What do you want to do?" he asked. "Where do you want to go?"

"Well, myself, personally, I am not finished with the road yet. I would like to see Washington and Idaho and

Montana. We did not even get to the Grand Canyon or Santa Fe or the King Ranch in Texas."

"The King Ranch? What's that?"

She pinched his nose. "And you want to be a farrier. It is one of the most famous ranches in the world. All their horses are sorrels. Can you imagine watching hundreds of sorrels running together, their coats gleaming, their tails and manes flying? So yes, I want to see that and, well, I would like to dress cowboy for once—have a hat, and boots, and sit in a saddle, not just in a buggy."

Milwaukee looked at her in surprise. "Are you serious? You never mentioned this dream of yours before."

"So it seems childish to me."

"Why? Thousands of American women do what you are talking about."

She wrinkled her face. "Not many Pennsylvania women."

"You are not in Pennsylvania. Michal, you'd look terrific in that sort of get up. I'd buy a camera just to take photographs of you riding a Texas pony."

"You would not."

"Of course I would. You'd look stunning. I'd fall in love with you."

"I thought you already were in love with me."

He grabbed her hand and kissed it. "So I'd fall in love all over again. I would like that."

She was about to punch him in the shoulder and remembered the wound. "Oh, you crazy man. Now I can't even give you the whacks you deserve because you had to play hero at Cannon Beach."

"Texas here we come."

She shook her head. "Tabitha has had enough. She

wants to go home. Our wild, rebellious *Rumspringa* teenager wants to bake Shoofly pie and lay out loaves of homemade bread to cool by the window. She wants an ordinary Amish boy to court her in an ordinary Amish way. I want the horse, she wants the buggy."

"I didn't ask about Nick."

Michal rolled her eyes. "Oh, Nick, Nick. She talks about saving Nick. Ghost told me he was with the others they rounded up from *Los Muertos*. He wouldn't even talk to Ghost or Skid. But they picked up from some of the others that he's pushing to take Lucifer's place and be the next Lord of The Dead. Can you imagine? And Tabi says to me, 'I think he still likes me, I think I can get him to change his ways'."

"No way."

"She said it. I took her chin in my fingers and I shook it. 'Crazy girl,' I almost shouted. 'You have ridden thousands of miles with him and all he wanted to do in the end was give heroin to ten year olds. And you think you can change him? What will you do that you haven't already done? This is God's department. Let him figure out the next step. You go home'. So—she is going home, thank goodness. But she does not want to ride anymore. I think her last idea was to take Amtrak. From Portland to Philadelphia. It would not be possible for me to let her go alone. I would travel with her."

"And me?"

"And you? Well, you could come with us. Or you could wait here with the bikes."

"Wait for what?"

She pretended she was going to hit his shoulder. "Wait for me. What do you think?"

Milwaukee stared up at the ceiling. "If it has to be,

it has to be. I wish we could head south as soon as I'm out of here."

"I'm sorry."

"Don't be sorry. I will come along on the train ride. Skid or Ghost can arrange for someone to keep the bikes."

Her eyes gleamed. "Yes?"

"Yes. Do you think I could go a day without getting lost in those dreamy blue eyes? I've had you pretty much to myself since May. Old habits die hard."

"Is that what you've been doing all this time? Getting lost?"

"Lost and found."

She leaned over and kissed him. "I get lost in your eyes too. You look tired. Take a nap. I will come by this evening with the others."

"I don't have my watch. What time is it?"

"Just after three. Will you sleep?"

He yawned. "I think I will. You are in my dreams anyway. I won't miss a thing."

"Oh, so tell me all about it tonight. I love you."

"I love you too."

Michal did not find Tabitha in the clinic chapel or in the waiting room. Glancing out the glass doors she saw her seated on a bench in the sunshine, orange leaves blowing past her feet over the emerald green grass. Her bare head was resting on the back of the bench, her eyes were shut, and the sun was bright upon her skin.

"Hey," Michal said, sitting beside her.

"Hey," Tabitha responded, not moving or opening her eyes. "How's our hero doing?"

"Well, he's still our hero. He wants to travel with us

on the train to make sure we get to Lancaster County safe and sound."

"Mmm. I've been thinking that over. I don't think it's really what I want to do."

Michal paused a moment. "Well, what do you want to do then?"

"I didn't have any desire to go back on the road because it reminded me of Nick and the drug dealing and *Los Muertos*. But I don't want that to be my only memories of traveling across America. I need some new experiences. Clean and pure and strong."

"All right. That makes sense."

"I know the weather is just going to get colder and colder up here. But I'd still like to go through a bunch of places and wind up, I don't know, in Montana or the Dakotas."

Michal frowned. "What? And spend the winter there?"

"No, no." Tabitha laughed and opened her eyes, turning her head to look at her sister. "I'm not that brave. Pennsylvania's cold enough for me."

"Then what do we do in Montana?"

"I will ask papa to meet me there. In one of the cities. I will ask him to come by train. Then I can travel back with him and you two can be off about your business."

Michal ran her hand over her sister's head. The hair was thickening. "Are you sure this is what you want to do?"

"Spend another couple of weeks tooling around on the Harley with you at the wheel? Absolutely. It'll rinse out my mind."

A police car pulled up at the curb. Three officers,

one in plainclothes, got out and walked through the front doors of the clinic.

"Milwaukee?" asked Tabitha.

Michal nodded. "I'm afraid they're going to wake him up. But he wanted to get it over with."

"Oh, look. We've got company. How wonderful."

Tabitha's voice dripped with sarcasm. Michal followed her look and saw Nick standing on the sidewalk by the squad car. Hands in his pockets he came toward them.

"Hey," Nick greeted them. The sisters did not respond. "How's Milwaukee doing?"

"Pretty good," replied Tabitha coolly. "No thanks to you and *Los Muertos*."

Nick spread his hands. "He's an old Lancaster County dude. I didn't want anything to happen to him. Tried to talk him out of making a deal with the devil. He wouldn't listen."

"He wouldn't listen because he knew if he didn't do something your crew was going to kill all three of us."

"We're not woman killers. Luc might have kept the pair of you stashed away, but he wouldn't have killed you."

"Stashed away? What does that mean? I think I'd rather die than be locked up in a drug lord's basement."

Michal caught Nick's eye. "What do you want, Nick? Why'd you come here?"

"To say hello's not a good enough reason?"

Michal waited.

"Okay," Nick said. "Look, my crew's nervous about what Milwaukee's going to say to the cops."

"You mean you're worried he might bring up all the

death threats? The six million dollars worth of heroin? The plans to deal to schoolkids in Pennsylvania?"

"Maybe."

"Why shouldn't he?"

Nick's gentleness vanished in an instant.

"Tabi was with me the whole time," he snarled. "Whether I was dealing in Florida or New Orleans. Or wherever. You could even say she was my partner. Milwaukee talks about me, I talk about her."

"I never dealt drugs!" Tabitha flared.

"You knew what I was doing. Why didn't you go to the cops? Why didn't you tell me to stop using drug money to put gas in the tank and food in your stomach? You were a dealer as much as I was, Tabitha Amish Troyer. Take off your halo."

Tabitha jumped to her feet. "I went on the road with you to get you away from dealing drugs in Lancaster County. I stayed on the road with you because I hoped I could get you to stop dealing drugs completely."

Nick sniggered. "Tell it to the judge."

Tabitha struck him with her fist and knocked him backward. She was going to strike him a second time, but he pinned her arms to her side and thrust his face into hers. "Does this mean the honeymoon's over, Tabi girl?"

"You're despicable!" she spat.

"That's a big word. Does it include people who come along for the ride and then look the other way and pretend they're innocent?"

"I wanted to help you!"

"Oh, you did, you did."

Michal was on her feet. "Let go of her, Nick. Let go of her and get out of here."

"Why? What's big sister going to do? Sic her crippled boyfriend on me?"

"Why not sic Skid and his Angels? Why not Ghost and his preachers? Why not the cops who just walked into the clinic?"

Nick shot a glance at the front doors and dropped his hands. Tabitha turned and ran across the lawn behind a cluster of tall bushes. Nick watched her go and a look of regret passed swiftly over his face and was gone.

Michal kept her steel blue eyes locked on him.

"For your information," she said in a low voice, "Milwaukee has no intention of telling the police anything except that it was Lucifer who stabbed him. He is not pressing charges against any member of your gang. He is not bringing up the heroin. Tell them that and tell them to go away, far away. And, if you dare, tell them we will be praying for their souls for the rest of their lives."

Nick stared at her face a few moments. Then he walked back to the sidewalk and headed along the street. Michal watched him leave before going to Tabitha. Her sister had her head down and was sobbing into her hands.

"Tabi, Tabi," Michal soothed, "it's okay, he's gone, he's gone for good, shh, shh."

Tabitha threw herself into her sister's arms. "He may be gone for good, but I'm not. I have a bad heart and a bad soul. He's right. I'm nothing more than a wicked, wicked excuse for a human being."

"That's not true. Stop. You're beautiful."

"Oh, sure, I'm beautiful," Tabitha moaned. "I could have turned him in when he was still dealing in Pennsylvania."

"You wanted to save him," Michal reminded her. "Well, it didn't work, did it?"

The police came out of the clinic. The uniformed officers went straight to the car, but the plainclothesman lingered by the clinic doors, watching the two sisters. He waited until he had caught Michal's eye, nodded, then came toward them.

Showing them his badge, he said, "I'm Lt. Brewster. Are you two Michal and Tabitha Troyer?"

Tabitha looked up, her eyes swollen, but said nothing. She continued to hold on to her sister.

"Yes," Michal replied. "This is Tabitha. I'm Michal."

"I'm sorry if this is a bad time, but Gideon Bachman described the pair of you and wanted me to have a chat if I saw you in the clinic or on the grounds."

Michal nodded. "All right."

"Gideon told us everything. Not just about the assault at the beach. All about the heroin and *Los Muertos*. That Tabitha was traveling with Nick Ferley and trying to get him to go clean. About this Tommy who might have been a DEA agent who'd been flipped and how he made sure she knew where the heroin was hidden. That he was shot. That Tabitha took you and Gideon to the storage center to pull the heroin. How you dumped it out in the desert. How *Los Muertos* came after you for revenge."

He paused. "Officers Bishop and Henkle thought his tale was a bit of a stretch. After all, he couldn't give us a single piece of hard evidence that it was true— no heroin, not even one of the plastic wraps the heroin was wrapped in or one of the suitcases. Nothing he said would stand up in court. Not even if Tabitha testified. It would just be her word against Nick's."

Michal examined his face. "But you believe Gideon." Brewster nodded. "I do."

"Are you—are you going to charge my sister?"

"With what? Trying to convert a person to Christianity? This isn't Iran."

"Will you make her testify?"

Brewster shook his head. "I told you. Her testimony wouldn't hold any water in court. The *Los Muertos* attorneys would tear her to pieces on the stand. I wouldn't do that to a 16 year old girl. I wouldn't do it to anyone."

"So then—we're free to go?" asked Michal.

"As soon as Gideon is back on his feet the three of you can get out of Dodge. One piece of advice." Michal and Tabitha watched Brewster's face turn to rock. "It's great you kept the heroin from getting out on the street. But don't ever pull a stunt like that again. Putting away the hardcore dealers is the job of the FBI and DEA and special police and narcotics units. The money in illicit drugs is unbelievable and the persons involved are ruthless. Both of you should be dead. All three of you should be dead. Never again. I have daughters of my own. Look me in the eye and promise me— never again."

His gray eyes were like stone. Michal and Tabitha nodded and looked away after a few moments, unable to hold his gaze.

"God bless you," he said and left.

He got into the patrol car. It waited, pulled into an opening in traffic, and sped away. The sisters were trembling. They made their way back to the bench and sat down, holding each other's hands.

"I feel awful," whispered Tabitha. "I can't even talk."

It felt to Michal as if the blood had drained from her face. "I guess he made what we were caught up in hit home. We were among killers and we survived because God protected us. That's the only reason we're sitting here and still breathing. How would Ghost and Skid put it? God had our backs."

"*No weapon formed against thee shall prosper,*" quoted Tabitha, still speaking in a whisper.

Michal was looking up at perfectly white seagulls soaring and swooping in the blue afternoon sky. "Yes. Something like that."

Chapter Twenty-Five

Day 153

I don't have words to describe the land in western Montana.

Everything just sprawls and takes up as much room as it possibly can. The spiciness of the air and the deep blue of the autumn sky makes you thank God you're alive. And the mountains! There is a ruggedness and a rawness to them at this latitude that makes me feel I'm at the beginning of time.

Looking up at them, hiking up into them, I feel so lonely, yet I never feel alone. The Creator and Redeemer is all around me. It reminds me of a verse I love from a modern translation of the Bible that Ghost had lying around his place. It was done up in biker leather and silver studs. Psalm 27 and verse one: "Light, space, zest, that's God!"

We have been on the road most of October and tomorrow we say goodbye to my sister. Papa is meeting us at the Amtrak station in Whitefish, not far from Glacier National Park in Montana. The three of us have been camping and hiking in this wilderness park for a week. It has done amazing things for all of us. Not just the awesome scenery. Our times sitting around the fire have made a big difference too: cooking ordinary food that tastes extraordinary, reading God's Word together, praying, listening to one another, listening to the breeze in the spruce trees, hearing the coyotes yip and yowl, falling asleep with the light of the flames skipping happily over our faces. Now all of our clothes are full of wood smoke. But who cares? It smells wonderful on your skin when you are far from cities and towns and freeways. It suits the wild places we spend our time in right now. Really, these days have been some of the best days of the whole journey.

I am so grateful Gideon and I have shared them with Tabitha. The hours and weeks of sunrise and sunset and stars have been so healing for her. The Bible says, "The mountains shall bring peace to the people." That is so true, so very true. We praise the Lord for his goodness to us.

"What time are we meeting papa tomorrow, Michal?"

"About eleven, sis. Just before lunch."

"Do you think he will be excited to see me?"

"Does mama sound excited that you are coming home when you talk with her on the phone?"

"Yes, oh, yes."

"Papa will be the same way, Tabi. Maybe even a little more."

"So why a little more?"

"Because you are his baby girl. And you have been lost."

"Well, you may not be the baby, Michal, but you too are much loved, and you too have been lost."

They were tidying their campsite after a breakfast that had also been a lunch. It was after one in the afternoon and the air had finally warmed up a bit as the sun struck their tent and bikes and the smoke curling up from the firepit. The dishes were drying on the brown picnic table. As they brushed their teeth and spat in the bushes far from their site Milwaukee came along the gravel road with his new binoculars in his hand. He still had a slight limp, but Michal never asked about it because Milwaukee preferred to act as if both legs were fine.

"I am sure I saw a grizzly," he announced cheerfully. Michal stared at him. "Oh, you did not."

"I believe I did. It had a hump, long claws, and that dish shape to the snout."

"How close were you?"

He shrugged. "Two hundred yards?"

"And you are smiling?"

His smile became a huge grin. "I love this place. I love the animals we see. If only I could spot another elk. And a lion—I'd love to put my eyes on a mountain lion."

Michal put her hands on her hips. "Crazy man. What else do you hope to get a look at? A meat-eating dinosaur?"

"I had something slightly more gentle in mind." He lifted the binoculars and looked at her. "Though she is still a meat eater."

Michal bared her teeth. "Does that frighten you?"

"If you started gnawing on my arm it would."

"Well, I am full now. You won't have anything to worry about until supper time."

"Where's Tabi?" Milwaukee asked.

"She was just here. We were cleaning our teeth. I think she was going to find a sunny stump and read the Bible a bit."

Milwaukee glanced around them. "No one else is camping even though the weather is stellar."

"Stellar?"

"Like the stars."

"You and your English. I think the campground will fill up this weekend if the weather holds."

"And by that time we will be gone."

"But gone where?"

Milwaukee put his arm around her shoulders and she put hers around his waist. "Wherever God tells you."

She lifted his hand to her lips and kissed it. "Tells me? What about you?"

"I'm not thinking this week. Just relaxing."

"So maybe I am not thinking either."

"You are always thinking."

Michal nodded with her head. "There she is. That's a picture."

Tabitha, a coating of glossy black hair growing back over her head, sat on a fallen tree, her father's small Bible open, light glinting off her earring with the cross. Quietly, Milwaukee slipped an SLR digital camera from a black case slung over one shoulder. He put it to his eye, focused, and the shutter clicked softly, too softly for Tabitha to hear. Michal leaned against his shoulder, the one that had not been hurt, to look at the picture displayed.

"That's good," she whispered, "but take another. And zoom in closer."

Milwaukee took four more.

"Okay." Michal tugged on his arm. "Let's move on. If she finds out we're taking photographs of her she'll go ballistic—as the English say."

"Suddenly she is all Amish."

"Not suddenly. She's been 'all Amish' all along. Right from the day she rode out of Marietta on the Ironhead. She just covers well."

"Still uses the cell phone," Milwaukee argued.

"Only to talk to mother. And the reception's poor in the mountains so she doesn't use it much unless we go into Whitefish or Kalispell. No, Techno Tabi's days are numbered."

In the evening they made a final fire that Tabitha started with her Zippo lighter. She sat in front of Michal who wrapped her arms around her. Milwaukee, as usual, lay on his back with his hands under his head, even though it made his left shoulder throb.

"There are a few clouds up there," he said. "We could get a dusting tonight. You two might want to think about crawling into the tent when it's time for sleep."

"Not on my last night," replied Tabitha. "Even if we get half a foot."

"Brave words," teased Milwaukee. "We shall see."

A cutting edge came into Tabitha's voice. "I am not going into that tent if we get ten feet of snow."

"Shh. God's listening."

"So I want him to hear."

Michal laughed. "Enough you too. You carry on like

a brother and sister. I am trying to focus on the night talk. Twice I've heard Great Horned Owls up here."

The snow came, but it landed on the peaks, covering the gray rock in white. As they broke camp, Tabitha kept looking up at the glittering slopes, brilliant in the sharp sun. Michal thought her sister was going to cry. They took their time getting to the train depot. It would be the last time Tabitha would ride a motorcycle in her life.

They waited at the station with suddenly little to say to one another.

Tabitha was no longer with them. She had already placed her head and heart in Pennsylvania. The train from the east was late. She paced and kept glancing at the large clock on the wall. When it finally arrived Michal knew Tabitha wished she had not cut her hair or pierced her lips, afraid her father would be upset or even repulsed. She had removed the rings, but could not do anything about her hair. Yet she remained rooted to the spot and watched with as much excitement as anxiety once people began to come off the train. Many stepped onto the platform over the next few minutes, but not her father.

Suddenly he was there, a tall slender figure in Amish black, pausing in the train's doorway to look over the faces turned toward him. Michal watched his eyes sweep the platform once and begin again. Then he saw Tabitha. Hair or no hair, he knew his youngest daughter. His face lit up as if sunshine had fallen upon it. Still, he did not move, but tears were running down his cheeks. Finally he came toward her and opened his arms. Tabitha ran and hugged him and he lifted her off the ground as if she were weightless. All around them people were greeting one another and laughing and shouting. But Michal still heard the Pennsylvania Dutch, heard her father telling Tabitha how much he loved her, how much he and her mother and brothers had missed her and prayed for her, how lovely she looked, heard his weeping, and felt the wet heat on her own cheeks.

Ah, thank God, thank God.

Holding on to each other her father and Tabitha made their way to Michal and swept her into their embrace of love and joy and praise.

Milwaukee was not spared. Even though he offered his hand for Mr. Troyer's handshake, the father would not take it, but released both his children so that he might hug Milwaukee tightly with both arms. Then he kissed Milwaukee on the cheek, his eyes still streaming.

"You have honored God," Mr. Troyer told him in a choked voice, "and you have treated my daughters with honor as well."

Expecting something like this, Milwaukee had planned a response that he had practiced again and again in front of startled squirrels, patient dark-eyed deer, and raucous Whiskey Jacks. "Mr. Troyer, thank you, but I have only done what anyone would have done—"

He did not get past his first sentence. Mr. Troyer held him at arm's length and said, "You have not done what anyone would have done. Few people would have done this. Traveled so many miles, borne so much heat and storm, so much wind and desert, so much danger. Do you think I do not know how far you went for my children? Do you think I only know a few superficial details? Perhaps you thought Michal and Tabitha would not tell me. But I know, young man, I know."

Milwaukee looked at the sisters in surprise. He opened his mouth to say something to them. Mr. Troyer put his hands on both sides of Milwaukee's face. He was not finished.

"They would be dead, but for you."

"No—"

"You offered your life in place of theirs. You told no one where you would be so they could not stop you from doing what you felt you must do. Were it not for a few mistaken calls from Nick Ferley you would have died alone with no one to help. My children would have come home to me, but to your mother and father you would never have come. I owe to you and to God the lives of my daughters. Do you think I will forget? Do you think I will ever forget?"

The man's emotion was so strong and his eyes and voice so fierce Milwaukee stopped protesting and simply stood and took it in. People swirled around them, many of them staring at the man in odd Amish clothes, so far from home, holding on to the young man with long hair and beard in a biker jacket and chaps. Milwaukee scarcely noticed them. His eyes never moved from the father's face.

"On the train I read a book of prayers," Mr. Troyer continued. "In one passage the writer quoted a poem. It made me think of my joy that I was going so far to bring those my wife bore me so close. *Home is the sailor, home from the sea, and the hunter, home from the hill.* I know I cannot convince you and my first born to return to Marietta today. In God's time it will become clear to you. But, for now, it is enough I have my

Tabitha, my sailor of America's roadways and seas, it is enough she is coming home with me. Thank you, Mr. Bachman. I call you Mr. Bachman because although you left us a boy, I see you now as a man. God's man."

Now came the handshake as steady and firm as rock. "*Danke, mein Herr.* Thank you. Thank you."

"Mr. Troyer, you're welcome." Milwaukee hesitated and then blurted, "I love them, Mr. Troyer, I love them both. But Michal I love so much I don't think I can live if I don't make her my wife."

Mr. Troyer beamed. "Such a good desire. I thank God. Did you think I would say no? No to you? If it is my daughter's will you have my blessing and the blessing of her mother. Yes, this we talked about before I boarded the train."

Milwaukee turned to Michal awkwardly. "I—I don't know how to tell you how much I love you."

She smiled and put a hand on his arm. "As if you have not told me a thousand times in a thousand different ways. Of course I know. And I hope you know how much you mean to me, Gideon Bachman."

"I think I do."

"You think you do? Well, once we are alone, I shall try to be more convincing."

Suddenly realizing her father had listened to her say that her face turned a furious red. But her father only nodded and smoothed back her hair from her cheek.

"Am I right in doing some thinking of my own?" he asked. "Am I right in thinking you love this man and wish to marry him?"

"Oh, yes, father, yes. With all my heart."

"Then it is so. The bishop and leadership know the story of this long road the two of you have been on.

Last night they came by and added their blessing and approval to the match. It is done."

"Father." They embraced each other again and she buried her face in his shoulder. "Thank you, thank you, father. It took me so long to tell him what I should have told him half a year ago."

He patted her on the back. "I know, my dear. But that is your way. Thank God you always get to where you need to be even if you can take a very long time." He looked up at Milwaukee. "I ask only this. No matter where else you roam please come home and marry my daughter in Marietta. Before her family and all her people. Even if you are still *Rumspringa*. Even if the wedding is not Amish. Come home to marry my Michal."

Milwaukee nodded. "We will come to you, Mr. Troyer—to you and your wife, to your family and mine, your people and our people, no matter where we must travel from or how far. I promise." He glanced at Michal. "We promise."

She smiled. "Yes, papa. We promise."

"Then everything is settled." Mr. Troyer pulled a white handkerchief from the pocket of his black overcoat and wiped his face before blowing his nose. "It is two hours to the train that takes us east. Show me these mountains of yours."

Michal linked her arm through his. "Surely you saw them from the window of the train's passenger car, papa."

"No, hardly at all. The shade was down so I slept."

They walked him up and down the streets of Whitefish, the mountains with their ski runs surrounding him, the snow catching fire under the noon sun. He could not go a block without stopping and gawking.

People parked their cars and rushed in and out of the shops without a glance at the peaks, but always throwing a look at the man in Amish black who stood gazing at the sky with his mouth partly open. Tabitha giggled and hugged her father's arm.

"Papa, you are just like a tourist, gaping at everything."

"There is plenty to gape at. Why is everyone in this town in such a hurry? Why don't they stop a moment and look and see what the Lord has made?"

"Most of them have seen it a thousand times, father."

"Seeing it one thousand and one times does not make it any less a miracle."

He eventually went into some of the shops himself. At a store that sold local pottery he bought coffee mugs for the boys and for his wife and himself. In another he purchased heavy gloves made from elk hide dyed a deep black and lined with lamb's wool. A third store found him picking up bags of homemade candy to share at the next church supper. Then he decided to go back to the pottery shop and get a large bowl of reddish brown to place the candy in at the supper.

"What will you do with the bowl once the candy is all gone?" asked Michal. "Put it on the shelf?"

"Ho," he snorted, "what a waste of money that would be. No, I simply buy more candy and sweets and cinnamon rolls and fill the bowl up at the next church supper."

In one store window were hand-dyed scarves of various colors and fabrics. Mr. Troyer looked them over and asked Tabitha, "Would you like one of these, my dear? It is entirely up to you."

Tabitha nodded. "I think they are beautiful, father."

"Does one of them strike your fancy?"

She scrutinized the scarves that hung from polished wooden pegs.

Then she pointed. "That color is handsome."

It was a rich, deep blue. Her father nodded his approval. "It is both lovely and plain. And it suits your eyes. Wait here."

He stepped into the shop. A moment later a woman sales clerk was taking the long blue scarf out of the window. He returned to the sidewalk without a bag, holding the scarf in his hands.

"Do you wish to place it in your purse?" he asked.

"I will put it on now, papa."

"There is no need. We are days away from Marietta."

"I would like to just the same."

He smiled. "Very well, my child. May I?"

"Of course, papa."

She bent her head. He folded the scarf carefully so that it was the right size and then wrapped it over her, tying a gentle knot at the throat, and kissing her on the cheek.

"My autumn beauty," he said. "Now the young men of the church will be greatly agitated."

"Oh, papa."

"I only speak the truth." He turned to Michal and Milwaukee. "I do not exaggerate, do I? I do not flatter. What do you think of our lady in the blue scarf?"

Michal smiled. The blue in the cotton scarf seemed to add a richness to the hue in Tabitha's eyes. "Stunning."

Tabitha reddened under her dark tan. "Stop it, sis." The father waited.

Milwaukee cleared his throat. "I must not be accused of being disloyal to my fiancée. But—" He winked at Tabitha. "If Michal is one constellation, you are another. Everything about you shines."

Tabitha rolled her eyes and looked away, an embarrassed smile on her face. "Oh, you are all driving me crazy. Any more compliments and I'm going to take the scarf off and shave my head again."

Milwaukee persuaded everyone to sit down for a lunch of soup and Reuben sandwiches at a small deli. He knew Mr. Troyer loved a good Reuben. Milwaukee had ordered one earlier in the week and had seen for himself that they overflowed with corned beef and sauerkraut and hot mustard. He was sure the sandwiches would be a big hit. He was rewarded with a grunt and nod from Mr. Troyer every time he bit into his, chewing slowly and carefully so as, he told them, not to miss any hidden flavor.

"It is worth coming all this way to get my daughter," Mr. Troyer announced, wiping mouth and beard with a paper napkin, "but God throws mountains and Reubens and family into the bargain. Such a deal from such a Savior. Who can do life better than him—eh?"

They took their time getting back to the Amtrak depot. Milwaukee carried Mr. Troyer's parcels for him so he could wrap his arms around his daughters as he walked. Many times Milwaukee wanted to set the parcels down and reach for his camera and take a picture whether they liked it or not. But his SLR was locked in one of the saddlebags. So he concentrated on holding the image of the three of them in his imagination so that one day he might sit down and try and sketch it out on a large piece of white paper.

They passed the Harleys that were standing in the parking lot at the station. Tabitha ran her hand over the chili pepper red Sportster and half-smiled. Her father watched, his face peaceful.

"I do like them, papa," she said, almost sheepishly.

"Of course. The motorbike has been your horse and carriage for half a year and taken good care of you. I thank God for that." He nodded, absently running his fingers through his dark beard. "Our Lord works in mysterious ways and uses unusual objects or events to bring his people to himself. I say nothing against the machine that he has worked miracles with in both my daughters' lives." He jerked his chin at the train that sat waiting for them. "A machine brought me to Tabitha and the same machine will carry her home with me."

Milwaukee put his hand to his pocket. "Sir, I have the rest of the travelers checks. We won't be needing them anymore."

Mr. Troyer stared at him. "So you no longer need food or shelter?"

"Well, of course, but I will be working with your brother in Natchez or with the Harley dealership in New Orleans and the reason we were given this money was to find Tabitha—"

Mr. Troyer folded his large hand over Milwaukee's and the checks. "This too has been discussed. It is the Lord's. Use it as you have need."

"But, sir—"

Mr. Troyer's eyes and grip were strong. "It is the Lord's. Take care of my daughter. Bless her."

Milwaukee paused and nodded. "I will."

People were boarding. Mr. Troyer hugged Michal a final time. Tabitha hung onto her sister for several minutes. They kissed each other and Tabitha pulled away. Both Tabitha and her father embraced Milwaukee and then Mr. Troyer guided his daughter onto the train. He paused at the doorway.

"Spring," he said. "Spring is a good time for weddings."

"But papa," Michal replied, "the Amish like to have those kinds of things in November or December when the farming season is quiet. Not during spring planting."

He shrugged. "So many exceptions have been made for you two. The Amish can make another. *Auf Wiedersehen.* Our prayers are unending, you know that."

Tabitha could not smile. "I owe both of you my life. So I will not say goodbye. Come to us soon. You know I love you, you know I love you both."

In a few minutes the train had pulled out of the Amtrak station and was gone.

They walked slowly back to their bikes. Michal was biting her lip and fighting back her feelings. Milwaukee gently placed a hand on her shoulder.

"Hey."

She hesitated, then found her voice. "Hey."

"You ready for more of the road?"

"Yes."

"So then let's go."

"But—go where?"

Milwaukee put on his mirrored sunglasses. "We have a bike to return to Shot and Shoulder in Vegas for starters."

"I'll miss that bike."

"I know. But I've missed your arms around me more." She laughed a bit. "Okay."

"Then we have a meal waiting for us in the Big Maria Mountains. Enchiladas from here to eternity, Pastor Raphael said. Are you up for that?"

"I'm up for it."

"Then it's on to New Orleans to hear Skid give his testimony."

Michal finally smiled. "I still can't believe we got a text from Ghost saying that. What's going on with Skid and God? And what's Ghost doing hanging out in New Orleans?"

Milwaukee patted The Big Easy. "Only one way to find out, sister."

They got on their Harleys, twisted the keys, and the double roars burst through the depot. Michal slipped on her glasses and half-helmet and gloves. Milwaukee began to turn his bike toward the exit. Michal came up beside him.

"So what's the verse for the day, Gideon?"

"Funny you should ask," Milwaukee replied. "I read something from the Old Testament this morning: *And the Lord answered me, and said, Write the vision, and make it plain upon tables, that he may run that readeth it.*"

"And what does that mean?"

"Well, I'm not sure. But I think we both have a vision of the future. Maybe we need to write them down and share them. Maybe you need to put the visions in that journal of yours. One thing I do know though—we can run, these bikes can run, so let's take our visions and run with them."

"Is that the plan?"

"It's God's plan." He grinned. "Mine is to get us

down to Missoula and onto the I-90 east. Then hook up with the I-15 south to Vegas."

"God's plan sounds good. So does yours."

"And what plan do you have, Michal Troyer?"

She revved her Sportster. "My plan is to love you both. Are you ready?"

"Yeah." He gave her the thumbs up. "You're looking good, Roadburn."

She returned the thumbs up. "You are too, Chrome. God bless you, Almost-Husband."

He laughed. "God bless you back a hundredfold, Almost-Wife."

They made their way out of Whitefish and onto highway 93. The sun blazed over their shoulders and autumn leaves poured across the asphalt.

Side by side they raced south for Missoula, Las Vegas, New Orleans, and America, and the beginning of a life together that six months before they had never dreamed could happen or be so perfect or so right or so full of the love of Christ.

* * * * *

"I'm sorry, Kate."

She gave an adamant shake of her head. "No. I won't have you
feeling sorry for me. You never did when we were younger, so
don't start now. I can't look at you and see pity in your eyes, Jess.
Nothing good can come of that."

The set of her jaw and the frown on her face said Kate was
annoyed. He'd hit a hot button for sure. Though she sped up, her
long legs were no match for him. He put a hand on her arm.

"Kate, empathy is not pity."

"Is that what your father had? Empathy?"

"My father?"

"Your father used to pity me, until you and I became friends.
That's when his pity turned to hate. Why do you suppose he hated
me so much?"

Jess's head jerked back at the words. "My father didn't hate
you. He thought being poor was contagious." Saying the words out
loud for the first time was uncomfortable. Admitting to the obvious
flaw in Jacob McNally made Jess feel complicit for not calling him
out years ago.

"Are you serious?" Kate said and kept walking. Her pace
picked up again, as though she were running from something.

"Sadly, yes. My grandfather was a dirt-poor farmer. Dad scraped his way through college and then on to medical school."

Kate released a frustrated breath. "Shouldn't that have made him compassionate?"

"It made him afraid. Afraid that he was one bank deposit away from his past."

"That's terrible, but it sure explains a lot."

As he stared at her, an ominous tightness filled his chest. "What do you mean?" he murmured.

"Your father warned me away from you."

Jess froze, eyes fixed on Kate while people streamed around them. "My father did what?"

"We're blocking traffic." She took his arm and pulled him to a secluded spot near a fire exit. "Your father told me I wasn't good enough for you, and that I should back off."

He could only continue to stare, unable to complete a sentence as he worked to process her words. It was one thing for him and his dad to disagree, but he was stunned and disappointed that his father had reached out to Kate.

Kate kicked at a stone on the ground with the tip of her boot. "I can't believe we're talking about this now. Here."

"Is that why you left?" He asked the question that had haunted him for ten years.

"I was always going to leave. I told you that. You didn't listen. Your father's disapproval… Maybe it helped me to justify walking away."

"He was wrong, Kate." The words burst from his lips as their impact barreled straight into his gut. Could he have prevented Kate from leaving? Did it matter anymore?

She stared at him, eyes round.

"You know that, right?" he persisted.

"I'm not sure what I know, Jess."

Don't miss
The Cowgirl's Sacrifice *by Tina Radcliffe,*
available August 2021 wherever
Love Inspired books and ebooks are sold.

LoveInspired.com

LIEXP0721

Love Harlequin romance?

DISCOVER.

Be the first to find out about promotions, news and exclusive content!

Facebook.com/HarlequinBooks

Twitter.com/HarlequinBooks

Instagram.com/HarlequinBooks

Pinterest.com/HarlequinBooks

YouTube.com/HarlequinBooks

ReaderService.com

EXPLORE.

Sign up for the Harlequin e-newsletter and download a free book from any series at **TryHarlequin.com**

CONNECT.

Join our Harlequin community to share your thoughts and connect with other romance readers! **Facebook.com/groups/HarlequinConnection**

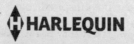

HSOCIAL2021

HARLEQUIN

Heartfelt or thrilling, passionate or uplifting—Harlequin is more than just happily-ever-after.

With twelve different series to choose from and new books available every month, you are sure to find stories that will move you, uplift you, inspire and delight you.

SIGN UP FOR THE HARLEQUIN NEWSLETTER
Be the first to hear about great new reads and exciting offers!

Harlequin.com/newsletters

Get 4 FREE REWARDS!

We'll send you 2 FREE Books plus 2 FREE Mystery Gifts.

Love Inspired books feature uplifting stories where faith helps guide you through life's challenges and discover the promise of a new beginning.

FREE Value Over $20